Praise for
Across the Blue

‖‖‖‖ ‖‖‖‖‖‖‖ ‖‖‖ ‖‖‖‖‖‖
D0193924

"Carrie Turansky's latest novel swept me back a hundred years into the elegant world of a wealthy British family named Grayson and the dangerous mission of an aviator intent on crossing the English Channel with his flying machine. Once again, I savored Carrie's beautiful description of England, and as a writer and daughter of a commercial pilot, I thoroughly enjoyed learning about both aviation and journalism in 1909. With its compelling mystery and romance, *Across the Blue* was a pure delight to read!"

—MELANIE DOBSON, award-winning author of *Catching the Wind* and *Shadows of Ladenbrooke Manor*

"*Across the Blue* provides a fascinating insight into the early days of aviation whilst also delving into questions of identity. Readers of sweet romance will enjoy the blossoming relationship between a young man of questionable birth and the young lady of privilege, whose dreams surge beyond societal expectation. Carrie masterfully weaves issues of faith and vivid descriptions into this story of hope and determination, with exciting scenes destined to make your pulse soar!"

—CAROLYN MILLER, author of Regency Brides: A Legacy of Grace series

"With all the elegance and intrigue of Downton Abbey, *Across the Blue* is an exciting tale that features the race to be the first to fly across the English Channel. I admired the spunk in heroine Isabella Grayson and her dream to become a journalist. She's the perfect match for the determined James Drake, a hero that lives on even after you close the book. This story is one of Carrie Turansky's finest!"

—MICHELLE GRIEP, award-winning historical romance author of *12 Days at Bleakly Manor*

Praise for
Shine Like the Dawn

"*Shine Like the Dawn* is a shining gem of a story. Intrigue, secrets, and dangerous conflicts make the plot riveting until the very end."

—JODY HEDLUND, author of *Luther and Katharina,* ECPA
Book of the Year

"Reading a Carrie Turansky novel is the next best thing to taking a trip to England. This hope-infused story is as lovely as the cover!"

—LAURA FRANTZ, author of *A Moonbow Night*

"Turansky's latest English historical romance, rich in mystery and intrigue is uplifting and highly recommended."

—CATHY GOHLKE, Christy–award winning author of *Secrets
She Kept* and *Saving Amelie*

"With her trademark heart and attention to historical detail, Carrie Turansky paints a picture of loss, inner torment, and—ultimately—healing. A moving, life-impacting, engrossing story."

—KIM VOGEL SAWYER, best-selling author of *Guide Me Home*

ACROSS
the BLUE

ACROSS
the BLUE

A NOVEL

CARRIE TURANSKY

MULTNOMAH

ACROSS THE BLUE

All Scripture quotations and paraphrases, unless otherwise indicated, are taken from the King James Version. Scripture quotations marked (NIV) are taken from the Holy Bible, New International Version®, NIV®. Copyright © 1973, 1978, 1984 by Biblica Inc.® Used by permission. All rights reserved worldwide.

The characters and events in this book are fictional, and any resemblance to actual persons or events is coincidental.

Trade Paperback ISBN 978-1-60142-942-1
eBook ISBN 978-1-60142-943-8

Cover design and photography by Kristopher K. Orr

Published in the United States by Multnomah, an imprint of the Crown Publishing Group, a division of Penguin Random House LLC, New York.

MULTNOMAH® and its mountain colophon are registered trademarks of Penguin Random House LLC.

Library of Congress Cataloging-in-Publication Data
Names: Turansky, Carrie, author.
Title: Across the blue : a novel / Carrie Turansky.
Description: First edition. | Colorado Springs : Multnomah, 2018.
Identifiers: LCCN 2017038153| ISBN 9781601429421 (softcover) | ISBN 9781601429438 (electronic)
Subjects: LCSH: Man-woman relationships—Fiction. | Women journalists—Fiction. | Air pilots—Fiction. | BISAC: FICTION / Christian / Historical. | FICTION / Christian / Romance. | FICTION / Romance / Historical. | GSAFD: Christian fiction. | Love stories.
Classification: LCC PS3620.U7457 A65 2018 | DDC 813/.6—dc23
LC record available at https://lccn.loc.gov/2017038153

Printed in the United States of America
2018—First Edition

10 9 8 7 6 5 4 3 2 1

This book is dedicated to my grandchildren:
Hudson, Hayden, Hanalei, Sahlor, and Everett.
May you always fly high and follow your dreams!

For great is your love, higher than the heavens;
    your faithfulness reaches to the skies.
Be exalted, O God, above the heavens,
    and let your glory be over all the earth.

—PSALM 108:4–5, NIV

One

Isabella Grayson's shoes sank into the plush red carpet of Broadlands' south hall, and she released a soft sigh. What luxury! Her parents strolled ahead of her with their new estate agent, Mr. Fielding, and her sister, Sylvia, walked beside her.

Bella slipped her arm through Sylvia's and leaned closer. "My stars, have you ever seen anything like this?"

Sylvia's blue eyes darted from the large paintings hanging on the wall to the six white sculptures evenly spaced down the hallway. "It looks like a palace or an art gallery."

"Exactly." Bella exchanged a smile with Sylvia, and they continued through the hall together.

Bella had visited many lovely homes in London after her presentation at court and the rounds of balls and dinner parties during her first two seasons, but she'd never seen a more lavish home than Broadlands, her family's new country estate.

Her father, Charles Grayson, had purchased it practically sight unseen when he heard it was for sale a few weeks ago. His solicitor had handled most of the details, and this was the first time he and the family were touring their new home.

He puffed out his chest and surveyed the hall with a critical eye. "If this doesn't impress those London toffs, I don't know what will." Her father turned to the butler. "Pierson, has Sir Richard taken away everything he wants?"

The butler's lips pulled down at the corners. "Yes sir. The last of the family's furnishings were removed two days ago."

"Very good." He turned to Bella's mother. "Well, Madelyn, what do you think?"

"It's beautiful, Charles, but it makes my head swim just thinking about managing all of this."

"Don't worry. We'll hire enough staff to take care of everything."

Her mother's unsettled gaze traveled down the long hall. "I can't imagine what we'll do with all this space."

"We'll entertain!" Bella's father boomed. "Shooting parties, dinner parties, house parties." He lifted his eyes to the painted ceiling. "We'll invite all the right people to Broadlands and make all the connections I need."

"Now, Charles, we've come to the country so you can get more rest and take care of your health."

Bella's father huffed and waved off his wife's words.

Bella's shoulders tensed as she watched her parents. Her father owned three prestigious London newspapers, the *Daily Mail*, the *Evening Standard*, and the *London Herald*, but his rise to fame on Fleet Street and his drive to gain a fortune had taken a toll on his health and strained his relationships with his family.

Bella hoped moving to Broadlands would motivate him to change his ways and balance work and rest. But her father had a different goal in mind. He wanted to bridge the gap between old money and new, and close the distance between himself and those who had inherited rank, titles, and respected family names.

Mr. Fielding pushed open a set of large double doors. "This is the drawing room." He smiled and extended his hand. "Broadlands is a remarkable example of mid-Victorian architecture. The house is built of white magnesian limestone quarried right here on the estate in the 1860s. It was decorated and furnished by Lapworth Brothers of London."

Her father strode into the drawing room, looking like a proud king surveying his new kingdom. The butler pulled the chain attached to the chandelier, and the gas flames flickered to life.

Bella's breath caught as she lifted her gaze to the glittering lights and painted ceiling. They were stunning and certain to impress the guests her father planned to entertain. She lowered her gaze and looked around the drawing room. Coral patterned silk covered the walls, and heavy gold-and-coral drapes hung around the four tall windows. On her right, an elaborately carved white marble mantelpiece surrounded the fireplace with a gilded mirror above.

The furniture the previous owners had left behind looked as though it had been made for the room—overstuffed chairs and couches in matching shades of coral and gold, a grand piano, and several tables and display cases.

Sylvia's face glowed as she looked around the drawing room. "If we pushed back the furniture and rolled up the carpets, this room would be large enough for a ball."

Bella smiled, her heart warming as she watched her sister. Sylvia had recently turned eighteen and would take part in the London season for the first time that spring. No doubt her beauty, charm, and caring disposition would make her shine among the other debutantes. In a few weeks, she would probably have a line of suitors eager to win her hand. But their parents had a firm list of qualifications, and they would only give their consent to a young man from a wealthy, respected family who was in line to inherit a title and an estate.

Memories of Bella's past two seasons rose in her mind, dampening her spirits. She had suffered through a series of ill-fated introductions and unpleasant pursuits by young men who had nothing more in mind than marrying her for her future inheritance. It had been painful and embarrassing, and she didn't want to repeat it this year.

If she ever married, it would be for love, to a man who cared more about her than her fortune.

Mr. Fielding motioned toward the doors on the outer wall. "These open onto the south terrace and lawns, with a view to the fountain garden and the sunken gardens beyond." He pushed open the doors and stood aside for the family to pass through.

Bella stepped outside and pulled in a deep breath of cool, fresh air. The February morning was clear and bright with only a slight breeze that teased her nose and carried the scent of tilled earth and cedar trees.

The gardens were neatly trimmed, but mostly brown while they waited

out their winter's rest. She crossed her arms against the chill and was glad she'd
left her coat on for the tour of the house.

A low buzzing came from beyond the trees, and she turned and scanned
the field across the road. The persistent noise grew louder, but she couldn't see
its source.

"What is that racket?" Her father frowned.

Mr. Fielding lifted his hand to shade his eyes and looked across the road.
"I'm sorry, sir. I have no idea."

No sooner had those words left his mouth than an airplane swooped over
the tree line and flew across the field toward them.

Bella's mouth fell open, and she lifted her hands to her heart. "It's a flying
machine!"

Sylvia gasped and clutched Bella's arm.

"By George, it is!" Her father glanced over his shoulder at the family, his
grin spreading wide. "Look at that! Just like the one we saw in France!"

Bella's mother hurried to his side. "But it looks different from Mr. Wright's
flying machine."

Last August the family had been on holiday near Le Mans when they
heard Wilbur Wright planned to demonstrate his Wright Flyer at a racetrack
not far from the city. They joined journalists, aviation enthusiasts, local dignitaries, and townsfolk to watch the American aviator fly his airplane for the
first time in Europe. After waiting several hours, they'd finally watched him
take off with ease. He circled the field several times before he landed with a
precision and skill that outshined every other aviator in Europe. The crowd
went wild and rushed onto the field to congratulate him and take a closer look
at his amazing flying machine. It was a thrilling memory she would never
forget.

"Who is that aviator?" Her father pointed across the field. "And what is he
doing flying at Broadlands?"

The airplane's wing dipped, and the pilot circled back toward the trees.

"I don't know, sir. But I'll certainly look into it. He shouldn't be flying over
Broadlands without your permission."

Bella was about to protest and tell Mr. Fielding her father was an avid supporter of aviation, but the airplane's engine sputtered and cut out. The flying

machine tilted to the left, and the nose dipped toward earth. Bella gasped and lifted her hand to cover her mouth.

The airplane descended at an alarming rate and landed hard, sending a shower of brown grass and leaves into the air as it bumped across the field with its left wingtip dragging along the ground.

Before the plane came to a stop, her father hustled down the terrace steps and jogged toward the road.

"Charles, be careful!" Mother called.

Bella pulled away from Sylvia and hurried after him.

"Bella, come back!" Her mother's words reached her ears, but she didn't stop. What if the pilot was hurt? She couldn't stand at a distance when he might be injured and need assistance.

The gray-haired agent passed Bella and soon caught up with her father. She grabbed up her skirt and ran across the road and into the field after the men.

They approached the plane from the back, and as they came closer, the pilot ripped off his flat cap and slapped it on his leg.

"Are you all right?" her father called, making his way around to the front of the airplane. Bella and Mr. Fielding followed close behind.

The pilot lifted his head and scowled at her father. "I'm fine, but my airplane isn't."

Bella released a shaky breath, thankful he was not injured.

He grumbled under his breath as he climbed down and stalked toward the wing. Ignoring them, he squatted to examine the crumpled wingtip buried in the dirt.

"This is disastrous." He lowered his goggles and dropped them around his neck.

A jolt of surprise traveled through Bella. He was not middle-aged like Wilbur Wright. Instead, he looked as though he was in his early twenties, close to her age. She studied his face for a moment, noting his unique amber eyes and strong jaw. She had the distinct impression she'd seen him somewhere before, though she couldn't recall where.

The pilot ran his hand through his dark-blond, wavy hair, then brushed the dirt away from the wingtip and tugged on one of the support wires. Shaking his head, he rose and limped a few steps toward the body of the plane.

Bella's heart clenched, and she reached out her hand. "You're limping . . . Are you sure you're not hurt?"

He glanced her way, and some unreadable emotion flickered in his eyes. "It's an old injury. I'm all right." But his gruff voice made his frustration clear.

The sound of horses' hooves traveled across the field, and Bella looked up. A large farm wagon pulled by a team of two came through the trees and rolled toward them.

"Who is that?" Her father looked at Mr. Fielding and then nodded toward the wagon.

"I'm sorry, sir. I've never seen him before."

Her father sent Fielding a pointed look. "There seems to be a lot happening here at Broadlands that you know nothing about."

Fielding's face turned ruddy. He stepped toward the pilot and cleared his throat. "Who gave you permission to conduct your flying machine experiments at Broadlands?"

The pilot turned his glare on Fielding. "You own the air over this field?"

"No, Mr. Grayson is the owner of Broadlands, and this is his private estate."

The pilot huffed. "Well, he doesn't own the sky above it, and I certainly didn't intend to land in his field."

"Whether you intended to or not, you've crashed your flying machine on his property. It's much too dangerous to be conducting your experiments so close to Mr. Grayson's home."

"I had control of my plane even after the engine died. I wouldn't have crashed into his house. I would think that's quite obvious."

Bella could hardly hold back her smile. The aviator was not only handsome, but he was also quite clever and able to hold his own against the stuffy agent.

Fielding narrowed his eyes. "There is no need to be impertinent, young man."

The pilot's eyes flashed. "I'm not being impertinent. I'm simply stating the facts."

Fielding looked ready to argue that point, but her father lifted his hand.

"I'll handle this, Mr. Fielding." Bella's father stepped forward. "I'm Charles Grayson, the new owner of Broadlands."

The pilot shot Bella a quick look, then met her father's gaze. "James Drake, the owner of this Steed IV." He nodded toward his downed flying machine.

The wagon rolled to a stop a short distance away. An older man wearing a long rumpled overcoat and red necktie climbed down. A breeze sent his long white hair flowing back from his angular face. He looked at least seventy, but he moved with the agility of a much younger man. Two lads, who looked about twelve or thirteen and who were dressed in simple country clothes, climbed down after him.

"James, are you hurt?" The older man strode around the plane toward them.

James's expression eased. "No, but the wing is damaged and I'm afraid the wheel supports are bent."

"But you're all right?"

"Yes. I'm fine."

The older man approached Mr. Grayson. "Good morning, sir. I'm Professor Thaddeus Pierpont Steed, and you are?"

"Mr. Charles Grayson of Broadlands." Her father glanced toward the house.

"Ah, I see." The professor smiled. "And you've met my protégé, Mr. James Drake?"

"Yes, we've met."

"Good. We're pleased to make your acquaintance." He smiled at Bella. "And this young lady?"

"My daughter, Isabella."

She smiled at the professor.

He nodded to her, then shifted his gaze to Mr. Fielding. "And you, sir?"

"Fielding is my name. I'm Mr. Grayson's estate manager, and as I was saying to that young man, Broadlands is a private estate. No one should be flying so close to the house."

The professor lifted his index finger. "Ah, that is a very good point." He shifted his gaze to the flying machine. "And as you can see, Mr. Drake had turned away from the house and was headed back toward Mrs. Shelby's farm. That's where we have our workshop and are conducting our experiments."

Mr. Fielding cocked his head. "Mrs. Martha Shelby?"

"Yes sir. She is a very kind friend who has allowed us to use her farm as our base of operations. Her large open fields are ideal for takeoff and landing."

Mr. Fielding leaned toward her father and lowered his voice. "Mrs. Shelby is one of your tenant farmers, sir. She's a widow and manages Green Meadow Farm with the help of her son."

Her father nodded. "I see."

A thrill raced through Bella. They were conducting their experiments right here at Broadlands. Perhaps she'd see Mr. Drake flying again soon.

The professor studied her father for a moment, and then his dark eyes lit up. "Are you *the* Mr. Charles Grayson, the owner of the *Daily Mail*?"

Her father straightened and puffed out his chest. "That's right. I own the *London Herald,* the *Evening Standard,* and the *Daily Mail.*"

The professor took hold of her father's hand and pumped it heartily. "Well, sir, we are certainly very happy to meet you."

Her father smiled, looking pleased the professor was aware of his reputation. "I'm very interested in aviation. I often say it's the next great frontier and worthy of government and private support."

"We couldn't agree more, could we, James?" The professor beamed a smile at James and lifted his white eyebrows, looking as though he was trying to send a message to the young pilot. James gave a brief nod but returned a questioning look.

Her father cocked his head. "I suppose you've heard about the prize offered by the *Daily Mail* to the first aviator who flies across the English Channel?"

"We have, and I believe we're very close to perfecting our design and setting the date for our first attempt." The professor clamped his hand on the young pilot's shoulder. "I have every confidence James will be the winner of that prize."

James straightened, and a smile tugged up the corners of his mouth, making him even more handsome.

"That's wonderful!" Bella looked at her father. "Wouldn't it be amazing to see an Englishman fly across first and beat the French?"

"It certainly would. I can't wait to silence all those naysayers who insisted it could never be done and mocked us for offering that prize."

Bella stifled a smile, recalling her father's outrage when a rival newspaper posted an editorial saying it would make as much sense to offer one thousand pounds for the first flight to the moon.

"A successful flight across the Channel might finally make those government officials wake up," her father continued, "and get them moving forward with a commitment to support aviation."

Professor Steed gave a firm nod. "Convincing the government of the value of aviation is a very worthy goal and the best way to ensure Britain's defense in the future."

"I couldn't agree more." Her father's eyes shone as his gaze traveled over the airplane. "How soon will you be able to repair your machine and continue your test flights?"

"It shouldn't take too long to rebuild the wing and straighten the wheel supports." The professor scanned the plane once more. "With any luck, James should be back in the air in two or three days."

"Unless we continue having issues with the engine." James shot a perturbed glance at the propeller and engine behind it.

"Yes, we can't risk a Channel crossing until we solve that puzzle, as well." The professor's brow creased, and he slipped his hands into his coat pockets.

Bella's gaze shifted from Professor Steed to James. Surely he wouldn't attempt another flight until they were certain the engine was working properly. "Flying with an unreliable engine sounds like it would be terribly dangerous."

James studied her, and his amber eyes seemed to search past her words to the emotion behind them. Her cheeks warmed at his intense gaze, and she glanced away.

Her father stepped toward the professor. "We have a few men at the *Daily Mail* who are very skilled and mechanically minded. They keep our presses working around the clock. Perhaps one of them could come down from London, take a look at your engine, and see if there's anything he could do to help."

James and the professor exchanged a quick glance, but it was impossible to tell what they thought of the idea.

"That's kind of you to offer," the professor said, "but we wouldn't want to inconvenience any of your employees."

"I'm sure one of them wouldn't object to a day in the country and a chance to take a closer look at a flying machine." Her father shifted his gaze from James to the professor. "Well, gentlemen, what do you say?"

The two exchanged another look, and James gave a slight nod.

Professor Steed's smile returned. "Very well. We'd welcome a consultation with one of your men from London. He could come to our workshop and take a look at the engine there."

"Good." Her father nodded and shifted his gaze back to the airplane. "I'd be interested to learn more about your work, myself. If you're agreeable, I'll come with him."

Bella's heart leaped. How exciting! If her father was going to visit their workshop, perhaps she could go along.

"Of course." The professor's smile spread wider. "We'd be happy to show you our workshop and discuss the modifications we've made to the design of our airplane."

"Excellent! I'll send a message to our London office today."

The professor extended his hand. "Thank you, Mr. Grayson. You're most generous."

Her father shook his hand. "There's nothing I'd love more than seeing a British pilot cross the Channel first and take home that prize."

"That would be outstanding." The professor beamed. "So, you'll let us know when to expect you and your man from London?"

"I'll make the arrangements as soon as possible and send you a message."

"Very good. Anytime would be fine with us," the professor added.

Her father stretched out his hand toward James. The young pilot took hold and shook hands, but his expression remained guarded. The professor glanced toward the wagon and motioned his two young helpers forward.

Bella shot a glance at James and then her father. She had to say something now or she would miss her chance. "I'd like to visit your workshop, as well."

James cocked his eyebrows. "You would?"

"Yes, I'm very interested in airplanes."

"Nonsense, Bella!" Her father waved away her words. "Visiting an aviation workshop is not something for a young lady. And even if it were, you shouldn't be inviting yourself along."

Bella's face heated. She wanted to argue her point, but challenging her father in front of these men they barely knew would only lead to more embarrassment.

"The young lady would be most welcome." The professor looked her way, genuine kindness shining in his eyes. "Mrs. Martha Shelby is a regular visitor to our workshop."

Her father's eyebrows dipped, and he shot Bella a quick glance. "We'll discuss this later. It's time we returned to the house." He turned toward James and the professor. "Thank you, gentlemen. I'll look forward to seeing you soon. Good day." He nodded to Mr. Fielding, and the two men started back across the field.

Bella followed her father, but after a few steps she slowed and looked over her shoulder. The two young lads lifted the broken wing from the dirt, while James and the professor pushed the airplane toward the wagon.

James glanced her way with a nod and half smile.

Her heart lifted, and she sent a smile back.

"Bella, come along," her father called.

Her gaze connected with James's once more, and then she turned and set off across the field. It might not be ladylike, and her father might not approve, but there had to be some way she could visit their workshop at Green Meadow Farm and see James Drake and his airplane again.

James pushed open the heavy wooden door and strode into the workshop. He tugged off his cap and gloves and tossed them on the workbench, then shrugged out of his jacket.

How could he have forgotten Charles Grayson was the owner of the *Daily Mail*—the very same man who was offering the prize to the first pilot who would fly across the English Channel? And what a prize—one thousand pounds! But it wasn't just the prize money that mattered. The prestige that would come from winning might help them secure a government contract to build airplanes for the British military. But he'd never win the prize or Charles

Grayson's favor by crashing his airplane near Grayson's house or arguing with his estate agent.

"Blast!" When would he learn to control his temper and stay on an even keel?

Professor Steed followed him across the workshop, then slipped off his overcoat and hung it on a hook on the wall. "There's no need to continue stewing."

"I can't believe I didn't recognize Charles Grayson or connect his name to the *Daily Mail*. He probably thinks I'm an idiot, and that conclusion would not be too far off base."

"James, you know that's not true. You must stop berating yourself for making mistakes."

"How can I, when I seem to go from one catastrophe to the next?" James opened the door to the woodstove and tossed in a few chunks of firewood. The heat of the flames warmed his cold, stiff fingers and eased some of his frustration. "Why can't we solve our design problems and keep our plane in the air?"

"This time it was not our design. It was a faulty engine."

James acknowledged the professor with a slight nod. "We've got to find out why the engine failed and how to prevent it next time." He closed the door on the woodstove and tried to shake off his gloomy feelings.

The professor placed his hand on James's shoulder. "We must not be discouraged. Think how far we've come in just a few months."

He tried to focus on the positive steps they'd made, but there were still so many obstacles to overcome before they could attempt the Channel crossing.

"Your takeoff was seamless today, and you were in the air for almost fifteen minutes."

That was true, but he wasn't thinking as much about his last flight as he was about his embarrassing encounter with Charles Grayson and his daughter Isabella.

Her image rose in his mind, replacing his view of the workshop. He'd seen her somewhere before—he was sure of it. Who could forget a woman like that, with her haunting blue eyes and fetching smile? The large straw hat she'd worn today had shaded her face, but it couldn't hide her creamy complexion or her teardrop pearl earrings that contrasted so nicely with her chestnut-brown hair.

She was lovely but definitely out of reach for someone like him—the illegitimate son of a young woman who had died in a suspicious and tragic manner. He clamped his jaw and tried to banish those thoughts. He might not know the full story about his mother's death or the identity of his father, but that didn't mean he couldn't make something of himself and put his shameful past behind him.

Professor Steed held out his hands to warm them by the woodstove. "Remember, James, every great scientist and inventor must make many attempts before he finally succeeds. Each attempt should not be seen as a failure, but an opportunity to learn something new. We must press on and find the answers we're seeking."

James nodded, but he struggled to silence the inner voice that told him he was not worthy and would never accomplish anything significant. "I certainly didn't make a good impression on Mr. Grayson."

The professor took a cup from the shelf. "I wouldn't worry. The conversation ended well." Confidence glowed in the professor's dark-brown eyes as he filled the cup with hot water from the steaming kettle. "I'm sure he'll be impressed when he sees our airplanes and we explain what we've learned and how we've modified them."

James blew out a breath. The professor was probably right. The encounter had ended on a positive note. "Do you think his man from London can help us find a way to keep the engine running?"

"I hope so, but the most important thing is to strengthen our relationship with Mr. Grayson. He is a man with great influence."

James nodded, then scanned the converted milking shed. What would a wealthy, powerful man like Mr. Charles Grayson think of their humble workshop?

Most of the long shed was filled with neat stacks of equipment, airplane parts, and tools. A workbench was attached to the wall on his far right. Two beds, a round table with four chairs, and small kitchen area filled the end of the shed to his left. The wall behind the kitchen was lined with shelves of canned goods, pots and pans, and dishes, although Martha Shelby insisted on cooking most of their meals for them.

The professor owned a home in London, where James had grown up, but they had stayed at the workshop since their return from France last September. Seeing Wilbur Wright demonstrate his Wright Flyer had inspired them to continue their experiments and test flights in earnest. The announcement of the Channel-crossing prize two months later spurred them on, and they decided to stay at Green Meadow and work through the cold winter months. Wilbur Wright might have declined to attempt the Channel crossing, but they'd heard there were other pilots who were preparing to try for the prize. If James was going to beat them, they'd have to keep working at a steady pace.

James focused on the partially built second plane to his right, and new determination coursed through him. Now was the time for men to break free from the bounds of earth and fly unhindered. And he was resolved to rise in the ranks of those brave aviators who would find the answers and make powered flight safe and accessible to anyone who wanted to learn.

He'd never forget the thrill of his first flight. With the cool air rushing past his face and the vibration of the engine buzzing through him, he'd felt more alive than ever before.

The shed door slid open and Martha Shelby stepped into the workshop, carrying a large tray with two plates covered by cloth napkins. "How was the flight?" Her rosy cheeks creased with a warm smile as her blue eyes darted from James to the professor. She wore a red striped apron over her simple blue dress, and her silver hair was tied back and covered by a blue head scarf.

"Excellent!" The professor looked her way. "Though I'm afraid James had a bit of a rough landing when the engine died."

"Oh no! The engine died again?" She quickly scanned James. "Are you all right?"

"Yes, I'm fine."

"Where did you land?"

"In the field across the road from the manor house."

Her eyebrows rose as she set the tray on the table. "I'm sure that must have caused a stir."

James gave a resigned nod. "You could say that."

"Not to worry." Professor Steed crossed toward Martha. "We met Mr. Grayson, the new master of Broadlands, his daughter, and their agent."

She grimaced. "Mr. Fielding?"

The professor nodded. "That's the man. He was not very pleasant, but Mr. Grayson and his daughter seem to be aviation enthusiasts."

"Is the airplane all right? I saw you tow it back with the wagon."

"There are some minor damages."

She lifted her gaze to the professor, her eyes lighting up. "I'm sure it's nothing you can't fix."

The professor stared at her for a moment, then cleared his throat. "Yes . . . well, we will get right to that . . . but first I do believe I smell something delicious."

Martha glanced down at the tray. "It's just some steak and kidney pie and oat bread."

The professor lifted his index finger. "I would never say *just* when describing any dish you prepared."

Martha's cheeks bloomed pink. She lifted the plates from the tray and set them on the table.

James crossed to the table and took a seat. Steam rose from the plates, carrying a savory scent and making his mouth water. "This looks delicious."

The professor pulled out his chair, but he remained standing. "Thank you, Martha. It's just what we need on a cold day like this."

James glanced at Martha. "Why don't you bring out a plate and join us?"

She stepped back. "No, I've plenty of work to do in the house. You two go ahead and eat your meal."

"We'd enjoy your company," the professor added.

She laughed softly. "I don't know about that. After two bites, I expect you and James will be deep into a discussion about what changes you want to make to your airplane."

The professor returned her smile. "I suppose you're right, but still, we'd be glad to share a meal with you."

She studied him for a moment, and then her expression softened with a smile. "I'll be roasting a chicken for dinner tonight. Why don't you come to the house at seven?"

The professor's eyes widened for a second. Then he looked down and brushed his hand across the sleeve of his jacket. "I didn't mean to invite myself to dinner."

James tried not to smile, but it was hard to hold it back. Martha obviously had a growing affection for the professor, but he seemed unaware of it, or at least he pretended to be. "That's kind of you to invite us, Martha," James added. "We'd enjoy having dinner with you, wouldn't we, Professor?"

The older man blinked a few times, then nodded. "Why yes, of course. That sounds splendid."

Martha's eyes brightened. "Seven o'clock, then?"

"Yes. We'll be there."

"All right. I'll see you then." She turned and sashayed out the door, carrying her tray.

James grinned as he watched her go. After the door slid shut, he looked across the table at the professor. "I believe Martha is sweet on you."

"Bah! That's nonsense. We've known each other since we were children."

"All the more reason for her to have special feelings for an old friend."

The professor sat in the chair opposite James and sent him a stern look. "Let's pray."

James smirked and lowered his head.

The professor clasped his hands. "Dear heavenly Father, we thank You for this meal and for the hands that have prepared it. Thank You for protecting James today, and we ask You to watch over us as we continue our experiments and test flights. You know how long we have labored and how much we've set our hearts on reaching our goal. We ask for Your grace and favor in the eyes of those who will help us toward a successful flight across the Channel. We thank You for all You have done for us and all You will do. In Jesus's name, amen."

The professor's sincere prayer touched James in a way he hadn't expected. He pulled in a slow deep breath and let it out. The professor was right. James could've been injured or killed today and his plane could've been destroyed, but he'd landed safely with only minor damages that could be repaired in a few days. Mr. Grayson could've been angry and insisted they leave Green Meadow. Instead, he'd asked to visit their workshop and wanted to bring along a man who might help them resolve their engine trouble.

It looked like the professor's prayer was already being answered. Maybe it was time James focused on the grace he had already received rather than his present troubles or the stain of his past.

Two

Bella followed her father and Mr. Fielding back toward the house and up the terrace steps, but her thoughts remained on James Drake and his amazing flying machine. How thrilling it must be to break away from earth's gravity and soar through the air like a bird. He must have great courage and skill to design an airplane and plan to fly it all the way across the English Channel to France. She couldn't help admiring a man with that kind of dream.

They entered through the drawing room and walked into the south hall before entering the central hall.

Mr. Fielding slowed and turned to her father. "Shall we continue the tour of the house, sir?"

Her father pulled his gold watch from his vest pocket and checked the time. "Not today, Mr. Fielding. I need to catch the two o'clock train back to London, and I want to have a meal before I leave."

"Very good, sir. Let me know if you have any questions or concerns. I hope you'll soon feel at home at Broadlands."

Her father glanced away, looking distracted. "I'm sure we will."

"If you don't require anything else, sir, I'll return to my duties."

"That's all I need now. I'll speak to you after I return from town."

"Very good, sir." Mr. Fielding nodded to her father and started toward the front door.

Her father scanned the central hall, then looked at Bella. "Where is your mother?" His expectant frown made it clear he thought she should know.

Pierson, the butler, stepped out from the shadows. "I believe Mrs. Grayson is in the morning room with Mrs. Latimer, sir."

Her father raised his eyebrows, obviously surprised to find the butler hovering nearby. "Very well." He set off through the central hall.

"Excuse me, sir. The morning room is this way." Pierson motioned to the right.

Her father huffed and changed directions to follow the butler.

Bella walked behind them, but she took her time, soaking in the beauty of the house. Overhead, a breathtakingly high vaulted ceiling with upper story windows spread soft light around the central hall. Two white marble sculptures, one on each side of the huge fireplace, drew her attention. One was a young woman seated with a dog on her lap, and the other was a young man reading a book. She would enjoy looking at them more closely in the days to come.

A large painting featuring three women in flowing white dresses hung above the staircase landing. Two had dark-brown hair and eyes, but the third, who looked to be the youngest, had wavy golden-blond hair and soft golden eyes. All three were remarkably beautiful. They looked as though they might be sisters, or perhaps cousins. Were they relatives of Sir Richard? If so, why hadn't he taken the painting with him when he sold Broadlands and moved to London?

Her gaze traveled up the elaborately carved staircase to the three large tapestries decorating the wall, and on to the open upper gallery. It was all so magnificent, a palatial manor house steeped in family history . . . but it wasn't their family's history. All these beautiful furnishings had belonged to Sir Richard. Her father had bought them with the house, hoping to impress others and make it look as though he had inherited Broadlands from his distinguished family, but nothing could be further from the truth.

Bella sighed and shook her head. Moving up in society was not easy, and she wasn't sure owning this beautiful home would accomplish what her father hoped.

Pierson opened the door to the morning room, and Bella and her father entered. Her mother and Sylvia were seated by the fireplace. Their new housekeeper, Mrs. Latimer, sat across from them.

Mother looked up. "Oh, Charles, thank goodness you've come. Mrs. Latimer wants to discuss hiring additional staff. She says we need at least three footmen and four more housemaids, a hall boy, and two additional kitchen maids."

Impatience creased her father's forehead. "Hire as many servants as you need, Madelyn."

"But, Charles, I don't feel comfortable making those decisions on my own. I've never run a house this size."

"It can't be that difficult." He shifted his unhappy gaze to the housekeeper. "I'd like luncheon served as soon as possible. I have to leave in time to catch the two o'clock train to London."

"Yes sir." The housekeeper rose and hurried out of the room.

Her father turned away from them. "I have to put some paperwork together before I leave for the train. Have Pierson let me know when luncheon is ready. I'll be in the library."

"But, Charles, what about the staff?" Mother's voice rose and wavered. "How many shall we hire?"

"I'm sure Pierson and Mrs. Latimer can advise you." He strode out the door without waiting for her mother's reply.

Bella's mother lifted a trembling hand to her forehead. "Oh dear, I'm afraid I feel one of my headaches coming on."

Sylvia reached for their mother's arm. "Perhaps you should go upstairs and lie down."

"Yes, I believe I should."

Sylvia sent Bella a worried glance, then looked back at their mother. "Did you bring your medicine?" She often suffered from severe headaches that left her feeling weak and sick for days at a time. If she took her medication as soon as one started, it seemed to lessen the impact.

"Yes, it's in one of my cases, but I'm not sure which one."

"Don't worry. I'll find it." Sylvia stood.

"Thank you, Sylvia." Their mother rose from the settee looking pale and a bit dazed. Sylvia slipped her arm around Mother's shoulders.

Concern for her mother pushed Bella into action. She crossed the room and pressed the servant's bell. "I'll ask Mrs. Latimer to send up a cloth and basin of cool water. That should help."

Sylvia sent Bella a grateful glance, then focused on her mother. "I'll go up with you."

Her mother gave a slight nod, then winced and lifted her hand to her forehead again. "Today has been so taxing. First the train ride from town, then trying to take in everything about the house, that flying machine crashing across the way, and now all this talk of hiring staff."

Bella had enjoyed traveling to Kent and seeing their lovely new home. Their unexpected meeting with James Drake and Professor Steed had been exciting, the highlight of the day for her, but she and her mother were quite different.

The housekeeper walked into the room again, and her eyebrows rose as she watched Sylvia help her mother walk toward the door.

"I'm sorry, Mrs. Latimer. I'm not feeling well. I'm going upstairs to rest."

"Of course, ma'am. We can discuss hiring more staff another time."

Her mother slowed and looked over her shoulder. "Bella, would you take care of it for me?"

Bella pulled in a quick breath. "You want me to decide how many servants to hire?"

"Yes, you're so sensible and organized. I'm sure you can make sense out of Mrs. Latimer's list." She grimaced and leaned on Sylvia. "I just can't deal with it right now, not with my head pounding the way it is."

Bella crossed the room and met her mother by the door. She lowered her voice. "I'm sure it could wait until you're feeling well."

Her mother closed her eyes. "Please, Bella. Just do as I asked. I don't want to upset your father or make Mrs. Latimer's job more difficult. Whatever you decide will be fine."

Bella swallowed. "All right."

Her mother leaned on Sylvia again and they walked out the door. Bella turned to Mrs. Latimer. "Is there a maid who could take up a pitcher of cool water and a cloth for Mrs. Grayson?"

"Yes miss. I'll send Bessie."

"Thank you. When you return, we can discuss the new staff positions."

"Very good, miss." The housekeeper nodded to Bella and hurried out of the room again.

Bella sighed as she watched the housekeeper go, her thoughts churning. They might have moved to Kent and taken up residence in a large country house, but it seemed their roles had not changed. Her father was still focused on running the *Daily Mail,* dashing to and from his office on Fleet Street, and taking little time to care for himself or his family. Her mother would continue to struggle with her health and have some good days and some bad. Kind-hearted Sylvia would be her mother's caregiver and companion and perhaps have to put some of her hopes for the season on hold if her mother's health didn't improve.

And Bella would be expected to fill her mother's shoes as mistress of Broadlands when her mother wasn't well. It would be her duty to see that everything ran smoothly for the family and staff until her mother could re-sume that role.

The temptation to feel resentful tugged at her heart, but she resisted its pull. It wasn't her mother's fault. She didn't choose to have poor health and push her duties off on Bella. And there was a positive side to taking over her mother's role—it was good preparation for the day she would oversee her own home. Whether she married or not, running her home, perhaps even Broad-lands, would definitely be part of her future.

Still, she had a hard time rising above the wave of disappointment that flooded through her. When would she be free to pursue her own hopes for the future?

For years she had been scribbling in notebooks and dreaming of becoming a journalist, just as her father had been at the beginning of his career. Nothing sounded more exciting than reporting the latest events and writing articles that would inform the public about the important issues of the day and stir them to action. New inventions and information were reshaping the world, and she longed to be one of those writing about them, just like her father.

But her father was not in favor of it. He might have a few women on his staff and a women's column in one of his newspapers, but that was not the life he wanted for his daughter. Her mother was in agreement, making it clear to Bella that she needed to be practical, prepare for marriage, and encourage the young men who had shown interest in her.

But Bella's heart pulled her in a different direction.

Just because she was a woman, that didn't mean there was only one path she could follow. Of course she hoped to marry someday and have a family, but couldn't she also write for one of her father's newspapers? What if she wanted a different life from the one her parents or society prescribed for her?

Mrs. Latimer returned. "I've sent Bessie upstairs to see to Mrs. Grayson."

"Thank you." Bella set aside her thoughts about her future and focused on the housekeeper.

Mrs. Latimer took a small notebook and pencil from her skirt pocket and looked expectantly at Bella. "Shall we discuss the staff needs now?"

Bella gave a resigned nod. "Yes. Please sit down."

The housekeeper took a seat.

Bella's heart sank a few more degrees as Mrs. Latimer opened her notebook and began reading her list. She forced herself to focus and listen, but her heart was far from the task at hand.

⚜

After dinner, James juggled a stack of plates, cups, and silverware as he pushed open the door leading into Martha's kitchen. "I'm sorry I forgot to bring these back earlier."

Martha turned away and brushed her hand over her cheek.

James followed her across the kitchen. It was odd that she hadn't greeted him as she usually did. "Martha, are you all right?"

She kept her back to him. "I'm fine."

She didn't sound fine, but he had no idea what could be wrong. They'd just left her not more than ten minutes earlier after sharing a delicious meal and what he thought had been a pleasant conversation. Had he upset her by something he'd said or done? He hoped that wasn't the case, but he'd spent most of his growing-up years with the professor and almost no time with his mother. That often left him feeling like he didn't understand women.

But he'd grown very fond of Martha in the last few months. Her kind invitation to come to Green Meadow to test and develop their airplanes had won her a special place in his heart. And that kindness pushed him to try to help her now. He set the dishes on the counter. "I hope I haven't done or said something to upset you."

She grabbed the dish towel off the counter and began drying a bread pan. "No, it's not you. I'm just being a silly old woman, that's all."

The sadness in her voice tugged at his spirit. "Don't say that."

"It's true. I'm just as foolish now as I was when I was eighteen."

He studied her, trying to make sense of her words. "I'm sorry, Martha. I don't understand."

"That makes two of us." She looked up at him with moist, glimmering eyes, her cheeks flushed.

He'd never seen her so close to tears before. "Tell me what it is."

She pressed her lips together and looked down for a few moments. Finally, she set the pan and the dish towel on the counter and turned back to him. "I suppose you'd understand if you knew the rest of the story." She lowered herself into a chair on the opposite side of the kitchen table and motioned for him to take a seat. "Thaddeus and I grew up living only a few miles apart—he in the village and me right here on this farm."

James nodded slowly. The professor had mentioned having known Martha since they were children, but James hadn't heard the particulars.

"He was a good friend of my older brother, Harry, and I was close to his sister, Anna."

James stilled at the mention of Anna. She was the one who had taken him in after his mother died and cared for him from the time he was four months old until shortly before he turned six. Then the professor had stepped in after Anna's death.

Though James had only been in Anna's care for a few years, he would never forget her warm hugs and tender words. She was the only mother he'd ever known, and he would always be grateful for what she'd done.

Martha released a soft sigh. "We went to school together, and I always admired Thaddeus. He was so smart, and he had that creative spark that set him apart from all the other boys. I knew he would do great things one day."

James nodded in agreement. Thaddeus Steed was an intelligent, humble man who'd had an impressive career as a physicist, inventor, and university professor. He'd become secretary of the British Science Association several years ago and won the Spellman Award, a prestigious research grant for his early aviation experiments. After crashing a series of model gliders, he lost the backing of the association and returned to his position at the university, but he never gave up on the idea of powered flight.

"Thaddeus and I used to enjoy walks through the countryside with Harry and Anna—picnics, bird watching, collecting wildflowers. We became quite close." Martha's expression softened, and her eyes took on a faraway look. "When he was preparing to go away to university, I thought he might ask me to wait for him, but he didn't. His parents moved to London. He stayed in touch with Harry, but he never wrote to me. In fact, I didn't see him for more than forty years."

James blinked. "That's a long time."

"Yes, it is. We went our separate ways." She sighed and shook her head. "He focused on his teaching and experiments, and I stayed here on the farm. Albert came to work for my father a year after Thaddeus left. He proposed to me a few months later, but I waited another year before I accepted. I think in the back of my mind I was waiting to see if Thaddeus would come back."

Surprise rippled through James. He thought Martha's interest in the professor was something that had developed after she became a widow and they'd reconnected. He didn't know she'd cared for him all those years.

"Anna said I should've told Thaddeus how I felt before he left for university, but I was young and afraid. Or maybe I was too proud. Whatever the reason, I finally decided to accept Albert's proposal. We were married for forty-four years. He was a good man, a fine husband and father . . . but I never forgot Thaddeus."

James studied Martha, touched by the traces of sentiment and regret in her eyes.

"When Albert died, Thaddeus came to the funeral with my brother, Harry. I was surprised to see him and even more surprised to hear he'd never married." She shook her head. "It's sad that he never found someone to love him and care for him. But he said he had you and his work, and that was enough for him."

James leaned back in his chair and pondered Martha's comments. The professor seemed content, but was he sorry he'd never married? He'd poured his energy into his students, his experiments, and caring for James. But did he ever feel lonely and wish he had a wife and companion to share his life, especially now that he was growing older?

Martha shifted in her seat. "When he accepted my invitation to come back to Kent and work on his airplanes at Green Meadow, I thought things might be different, that we would reconnect in a special way. But he's still just as focused on his work as he's ever been. All he wants is to see you fly across the Channel. He has no time for or thought of me."

She waved away her words with an embarrassed chuckle. "You see, I told you I was a foolish old woman." She clicked her tongue and shook her head. "I ought not to be thinking about things that happened decades ago."

James looked across at Martha. "Maybe it's not so much what happened years ago, but it's seeing those hopes rise again and being uncertain about the future."

She looked into his eyes. "Even if you're not his son by birth, you take after him in so many ways."

James reached across the table and laid his hand over hers. "You're a kind and caring woman, Martha. The professor might have a brilliant scientific mind, but I'm afraid he's not always attuned to matters of the heart."

Martha tipped her head and looked ready to reply when the back door opened and the professor stepped in. "Ah, James, here you are." His gaze darted to Martha and back to James. "I wondered what had happened to you."

Martha flashed James a warning glance, then stood to face the professor. "James was just listening to an old woman rattle on about things that don't matter."

The professor's mouth tipped up at the corners. "I can see why he might enjoy your company more than mine."

"There's nothing wrong with your company." Martha pushed in her chair. "Now you two had better go on out to the workshop. I've got to feed Miss Tibby and get back to my knitting."

At the mention of her name, Martha's tiger-striped cat stirred from her spot on the kitchen hearth and padded over to weave around Martha's legs.

Martha picked up Miss Tibby and cradled the fluffy creature in her arms.

"You're hungry, aren't you, my dear?" The cat purred and rubbed her head on Martha's cheek.

James's chest tightened as he observed the affection between Martha and her cat. Martha was a good woman. She deserved to be happy and have someone other than her cat to comfort her. "Good night, Martha."

The professor bid her good night as well. She nodded but didn't look his way.

James stepped out on the back porch, feeling unsettled by his conversation with Martha. Should he speak to the professor and tell him what Martha had said?

The professor followed him out and closed the door. He glanced over his shoulder with a frown. "Martha seems to be in a strange mood tonight."

James walked down the steps, debating his reply. He'd hinted before that Martha had feelings for the professor, but each time the professor shut him down with a scowl and change of subject.

If he spoke up again, would he make the professor so uncomfortable he'd want to leave Green Meadow? Finding another location like this, with a spacious workshop and proximity to the coast and open fields, would be difficult if not impossible. Martha didn't charge them, and they had no money to lease another location.

He shook his head. He couldn't risk it. He would keep Martha's conversation to himself for now. That was best for everyone. But he had a hard time brushing off the guilty weight of his decision.

⁂

Bella scanned the selection of breakfast items on the dining room buffet, and her stomach contracted in anticipation.

Pierson stepped forward and lifted the lid on one of the silver serving dishes. "Would you care for sausages, miss?"

"Yes, thank you." Succulent steam rose and tickled Bella's nose. She helped herself to a plump sausage and a poached egg.

Sylvia took a plate and joined her at the buffet. "This certainly looks much nicer than the breakfasts Mrs. Hastings prepares in London."

"Yes, it does." Bella smiled at her sister, scooped a spoonful of baked beans onto her plate, then added a grilled tomato, some mushrooms, and a slice of toast. She crossed the dining room to join her father at the table. "Good morning, Father."

He lowered his copy of the *Daily Mail* an inch. "Morning, Bella. Sylvia."

"Anything interesting in the news today?" Bella took a seat on her father's right and placed her napkin on her lap.

"The suffragettes are making fools of themselves with their protests." Her father shook out the paper and glared at her over the top. "And there's more nonsense from the Liberal Party, defending their foreign relations policies. It's enough to make a man choke on his breakfast. Why can't they understand Germany's goal is to dominate Europe?"

Sylvia sent Bella a quick glance as she took a seat on her father's left. He had a short fuse when it came to discussing relations with Germany. Sylvia usually handled it by quietly ignoring his comments, but Bella couldn't resist challenging him.

"They probably think Germany would never attack England because the kaiser is Queen Victoria's grandson."

"Ha! I don't think his ties to his grandmother can compare to his desire to conquer his neighbors and extend his control across the continent." Her father narrowed his eyes. "Mark my words, after the kaiser has conquered his neighbors, he'll set his eyes on Britain."

A bite of toast stuck in Bella's throat. She reached for her tea and took a sip. She didn't like to think ill feelings between Germany and her neighbors would actually lead to war. But her father was probably right. Germany's military and industrial strength, along with the kaiser's determination to gain more power, put England in a dangerous position. It didn't matter that the kaiser was related to the previous monarch, or that most people didn't want to believe he would attack his grandmother's homeland.

Her father had visited Germany the previous year and witnessed their hostile attitude toward other countries. His reports had convinced Bella that Germany could become a dangerous enemy. And her father wasn't hesitant to share his opinion with anyone who would listen. He had written several editorials to the point, and Bella had helped him polish them.

"It irks me to no end that so many people continue to ignore Germany's malicious intentions."

Bella took another sip of tea and gave her father a moment to calm down before she spoke. "If you're finished with that section of the newspaper, I'd like to read it."

He lowered his eyebrows, but he handed Bella the section. He seemed to think it was fine for him to read the newspaper at the breakfast table, but he didn't like to see Bella doing the same.

She ignored his frown and scanned the headlines on the front page: *"Women Demand the Vote at Hyde Park Rally" . . . "Death Duty Bill Debated in Parliament" . . . "The Committee on Foreign Relations Meets with the Prime Minister."* Her gaze dropped to the article in the lower left corner: *"French Aviators Prepare for Channel Crossing."*

Bella's breath caught in her throat. "Father, did you see this?" She held up the paper and pointed to the article.

He squinted. "What does it say?"

She read him the headline and quickly scanned the first paragraph. "At least three French aviators have arrived in Calais and are preparing to attempt a flight across the English Channel."

His eyes flashed. "Let me see that!"

She handed him the newspaper. His eyebrows drew down in a V, and his face flushed as he pulled it closer and read the rest. "Who is this Louis Blériot? I've never heard of him or Count Charles de Lambert." He folded the paper and smacked it on the table. "We can't let the French win!"

"No, we mustn't." Bella's thoughts shifted to James Drake and his flying machine. Could he be ready in time? Would he be able to solve his engine trouble and make his flight before one of the French aviators beat him to it and won the prize? She looked up and met her father's gaze. "When do you plan to visit James Drake and Professor Steed at their workshop?"

"One of our pressroom mechanics is coming down from London this afternoon. I sent a message to Professor Steed to expect us around two."

"I'd like to go along." Bella tried to sound nonchalant, but she gripped her napkin under the table.

Her father's frown returned. "Bella, I've already told you what I think about that."

"But Professor Steed said it would be all right."

"Only because you put him in an awkward position by asking to come." Her father shook his head. "I'd rather you stay here and help your mother and Sylvia."

"But you took me to see Wilbur Wright fly in France, and there were hundreds of women in the stands. There's nothing unladylike about watching aviators fly their airplanes."

He huffed. "Watching a public demonstration is not the same as visiting an aviator's workshop."

"You're going to be there with me. I don't see how it could be inappropriate if we're together."

"You would be the only woman in a man's domain."

Bella bit her lip, praying for an idea. "I know! Sylvia could come along. Then I wouldn't be the only woman."

Her sister looked up and met her gaze. "You want me to go?"

Bella smiled. "Yes! I'm sure you'd find it fascinating. The professor and Mr. Drake are working on their flying machine at one of our tenant farms, right here at Broadlands."

Sylvia's face lit up. "I did enjoy seeing Mr. Wright fly at Le Mans." Both girls turned to their father and sent him imploring looks, but he continued to frown.

Bella smoothed her napkin on her lap. There had to be some way to convince him. An idea popped into her mind and she turned his way. "You've often said aviation is an important issue, especially if Germany continues to threaten our peace and security. Don't you think we ought to learn as much as we can about aviation's potential?"

He drummed his fingers on the dining room table.

"If I went with you, I could collect information to help you with your next editorial. Perhaps that would persuade the government to see the advantages airplanes could give our military and convince them to expand their support."

He closed his eyes and rubbed his forehead for a few seconds.

"I'm sure it will be all right, Father." Bella gentled her voice. "Please let us go with you."

He sighed and lowered his hand. "Very well. You may go, but you must conduct yourselves like proper young ladies. And for heaven's sake, Bella, don't ask too many questions."

"I won't. Thank you, Father." She beamed a smile at Sylvia, and her sister returned the same.

She had won her father over and opened the door to helping him with his next editorial. That was two victories, and she hadn't even finished breakfast yet.

James lay down on his back and scooted under the body of the Steed IV, positioning himself beneath the airplane's engine. He lifted the wrench and loosened the first bolt. The cold from the wooden floor seeped through his shirt, chilling his back and neck. The day was clear, but the temperature outside hovered around forty-five. It was warmer inside near the woodstove, but at this end of the shed it was quite chilly.

The professor rolled the hand crank hoist closer. Lifting the heavy engine out of the airplane would be almost impossible without it. "Let me know when you're ready."

"All right." James set his jaw and tugged on the next stubborn bolt. A few minutes later he had loosened them all. Both men attached the hooks, and the professor cranked the handle. The chain grew taut as the engine slowly rose out of the airplane. With a few careful movements, Professor Steed rotated the hoist and swung the engine onto the workbench with a loud *thunk*.

James rolled over and began collecting the screws and bolts. The sound of a motorcar engine reached him, then tires crunching on the gravel outside. He scooted a few inches to the left so he could look up through the chassis of the airplane and see the professor. "Are we expecting someone?"

Professor Steed shifted his gaze toward the window and his eyebrows rose. "Ah yes. It must be Mr. Grayson and his man from London."

Alarm shot through James. "Why didn't you tell me they were coming?" He glanced at his greasy hands and the stains on his shirtsleeve and released a disgusted breath. The old shirt and patched trousers were comfortable to wear while working on the airplane, but this was not how he wanted to look when he greeted Mr. Grayson.

"Sorry, I forgot to mention it." The professor pushed the hoist aside. "I received his note this morning while you were in the house returning the breakfast dishes. I guess I got busy working and it slipped my mind."

James shimmied out from under the airplane, stood up, and brushed his hand down his trousers, but it didn't help.

A knock sounded at the workshop door. The professor sprang forward and pulled the door to the side. "Welcome, please come in."

Mr. Grayson and a short balding man stepped inside, followed by Grayson's daughter and another young woman. Her hair was lighter than Isabella's, but her features were similar.

Heat rushed up James's neck and into his face. Not only was he going to embarrass himself in front of the owner of the *Daily Mail,* but his two daughters would also see him dressed like a scruffy field hand.

James shoved aside those thoughts, straightened his shoulders, and faced Mr. Grayson. "Good afternoon, sir." He nodded to the other man and the young ladies, then grabbed a rag and tried to wipe the grease from his hands.

Mr. Grayson motioned to the man at his side. "This is Mr. Finch from London. He keeps our presses running at the *Daily Mail.* And this is my younger daughter, Sylvia."

She smiled and nodded to them. "I'm pleased to meet you."

Mr. Grayson's expression dimmed a bit. "And I'm sure you remember my elder daughter, Bella."

"Yes, of course." James found her watching him with a small smile. Was she pleased to see him again, or was she amused by his untidy appearance? He looked away, hoping it was the former and not the latter.

Mr. Finch's nose twitched and his eyes darted around the workshop. "Mr. Grayson said you'd like me to take a look at the engine of your flying machine."

"Yes." The professor motioned toward the workbench. "We have an eight cylinder in-line engine that produces up to fifty horsepower."

Mr. Finch nodded. "What kinds of problems are you having?"

"It seems to be working well on the ground, but then dies at the most inconvenient times. As you can imagine that is not helpful when you're several hundred feet in the air." Professor Steed continued explaining their engine trouble while he walked toward the workbench with Mr. Grayson and Mr. Finch.

James was about to follow, but it seemed rude to leave the women standing by the door. Perhaps he'd give them a brief tour and then rejoin the professor and the others.

Bella glanced around the workshop and then met his gaze. "I see you have an airplane outside, as well as the one in here."

"Yes. This is the Steed IV, the one I flew yesterday." He motioned toward the window. "The one outside is our earlier design. We're using a different engine now, and we've modified the length and width of the chassis. We also use wing warping with this one."

Bella's eyes lit up. "Oh, like the Wright brothers' airplane."

He lifted his brows. "You've heard of wing warping?"

"Yes. It gives the pilot better control and the ability to turn and take the airplane in a circle."

"That's right. How did you know that?"

"My father has been a member of the Aero Club for a few years. His interest stirred mine. He receives their weekly newspaper, *Flight,* and I've been reading it since we saw Wilbur Wright fly at Le Mans last August."

That must be where he'd seen her! He smiled as the memory came into focus. She'd worn a broad white hat and white linen jacket and skirt. He'd spotted her seated in the stands while they'd all waited for Wilbur Wright to bring out his Wright Flyer and set it up for takeoff. Then he'd seen her again when she'd rushed across the field with the crowd to greet Wright after his landing.

James and the professor had followed the throng, but only a few people had been allowed close enough to speak to the famous aviator, and fewer still were allowed to touch his Wright Flyer. Bella and her father had been welcomed into that inner circle, while he and the professor had been kept at a distance.

She returned his smile. "We were on holiday in France with our parents when we heard Wilbur Wright was going to give his demonstration. It was quite a stroke of luck that we were staying close enough to attend."

James glanced at Bella's sister. "Are you a fan of aviation as well, Miss Grayson?"

Sylvia sent him a shy smile. "Well, it is terribly exciting to see flying machines in the air, but I don't know as much about them as Bella."

Bella's gaze traveled over the Steed IV. "Could you tell us more about your airplane?"

James glanced at the men clustered around the workbench, examining the engine. They didn't seem to mind he'd stayed behind, so he nodded to Bella. "I'd be happy to."

He led Bella and Sylvia closer to the Steed IV and reached out to touch the wingtip. "The framework is made of spruce because it's strong and lightweight. It's also straight-grained and not prone to splitting. We cover the framework with varnished fabric, finely woven linen, then cover it with cellulose varnish called *dope* to make it airtight, strong, and taut."

He moved to the front of the plane, and Bella and Sylvia followed. "The propeller is carved from a solid block of walnut." He ran his hand down the smooth surface, admiring the fine craftsmanship. They'd searched for weeks to find a competent wood-carver to fashion it.

Bella looked up at him. "What's the purpose of the blades in the front?"

"The propeller slices through the air and lifts the airplane forward. Think of the propeller as a spinning wing, and like a wing, it produces lift, but in a forward direction. We call that *thrust*."

Bella nodded, her inquisitive gaze traveling over the airplane once more.

"We want to cut down on drag and be as lightweight as possible," James continued, "so we use very little metal in our design, aside from the engine and wires."

Bella touched a guide wire with her gloved finger. "How fast do you fly?"

"I've gone up to thirty-five miles an hour, but I think when we solve our trouble with the engine, I might be able to fly faster."

She studied the airplane. "The Wright Flyer has a double-wing design, but yours has a single wing. Why is that?"

James grinned. "I'll ask you a question. Are birds bi-winged or mono-winged?"

She returned his smile. "Mono-winged, of course."

"And that's why we've chosen a mono-winged design." He motioned toward the singular set of wings. "We spent hours observing birds in flight, and then we applied those observations to our design."

"So you've taken your cues from the birds?" A glint of amusement lit her eyes.

"Yes, we have." His gaze traced the wings, remembering all the changes they'd made to them. "It's actually a matter of wing loading, which is simply the weight carried by each square foot of wing surface. This new design gives us better structural integrity."

She nodded. "I see what you mean."

He and the professor usually worked in solitude, with only occasional visits from Martha. He'd had few opportunities to discuss their designs with others. Bella's interest and intelligent questions made him want to tell her more. "Overall, there are three principles we seek to balance: thrust, lift, and control."

"Yes, I've read most aviators have focused on thrust and lift, but control seems to be the key issue now. Would you agree?"

"Bella!" Mr. Grayson called, a warning in his voice.

She spun around. "Yes, Father?"

"I'm sure you don't want to wear out Mr. Drake with your questions."

Her cheeks flushed, and she sent James an apologetic look. "I'm sorry, I don't mean to monopolize your time."

"No apology necessary. I enjoyed our conversation. It's not often I meet someone who has such a keen interest in aviation."

She sent him an appreciative smile.

"Mr. Drake, come and join us." Mr. Grayson motioned James toward the workbench. "We'd like your opinion about the changes Mr. Finch is suggesting."

"Of course." James turned to Bella. "Excuse me."

She nodded, her cheeks still flushed. "Thank you for showing us your airplane."

"It was my pleasure." He crossed the workshop and joined the men, making an effort to shift his focus to Mr. Finch while the man explained his ideas.

James rubbed his chin, his awareness of Bella breaking through his thoughts and causing him to glance her way.

She stood with her sister, still studying his airplane. The view of her profile highlighted her slightly upturned nose, softly rounded cheeks, and full lips.

He swallowed and forced himself to look away. Bella Grayson was charming, attractive, and intelligent, but he could not afford a distraction, not when he was so close to accomplishing his goal, and not when his life and future depended on him giving total focus to his work.

Bella replayed her conversation with James as she watched him join the men at the workbench. His knowledge of aviation was impressive, and his manners and winsome personality equally so. They certainly seemed a sharp contrast to his unkempt appearance, but she supposed building his own airplane required a hands-on approach. His rumpled clothes and stained hands didn't dim her opinion of him. In fact, it made her admire him for his dedication to his work.

She smiled as she remembered the way his expression had brightened when they discussed the changes he'd made to his latest design. He seemed pleased to answer her questions, rather than irritated, as her father suggested he would be.

Sylvia leaned toward her. "He's certainly handsome in a rustic sort of way, isn't he?"

Bella lowered her voice to match Sylvia's. "Yes, rustic, intelligent, and handsome. That's quite a combination."

They exchanged smiles.

The door to the workshop slid open and an older woman stepped through carrying a large tray with a teapot, cups, and a plate covered with a cloth napkin. She was tall and thin, and she wore a simple brown dress, with her silver hair pulled back in a bun at the base of her neck.

She greeted Bella and Sylvia with a warm smile. "Good day to you. I'm Martha Shelby."

Bella met her at the door, then closed it after her. "I'm Isabella Grayson, and this is my sister, Sylvia."

"Ah, the new family at Broadlands. Welcome! Welcome to Green Meadow." She placed the tray on the table. "I saw you drive up, and I prepared some tea." She lifted the napkin, revealing a plate of sweet tea biscuits and releasing the spicy scent of cinnamon into the air.

Bella walked with her to the table. "Thank you. That's very kind."

Martha glanced toward the men at the workbench. "They seem caught up in conversation. Perhaps I'll serve you ladies first, and the men can join us when they're ready."

Bella and Sylvia sat at the round wooden table, and Martha poured the tea into pretty white china cups. Bella glanced around the workshop. Cooking supplies and canned food lined the shelves behind the sink, and a few bowls and pans were stacked on the wooden counter. To her right were two neatly made, narrow beds. Evidently James and Professor Steed slept at the workshop, at least part of the time.

Sylvia took a sip of her tea and looked up at Martha. "How long have you lived at Green Meadow?"

"All my life. My father was a tenant farmer for Sir Richard and his father before him. My husband, Albert, and I took over the tenancy in seventy-two. He passed away three years ago. Now my son, Ethan, and some farmhands help me carry on. It's been a good life."

"It sounds like your family has quite a history here."

Martha chuckled. "We love this old place. There have been lean years and years of plenty. You never know with farming. But Sir Richard was a fine land-lord, and we're grateful Mr. Grayson is allowing us to continue on."

Bella took a biscuit from the plate. She liked Martha Shelby and appreci-ated her warm welcome. Martha looked nothing like the well-dressed women in London society, but kindness radiated from her eyes, and the pleasant lines that creased her face looked like they had come from years of smiling and time spent in the sunshine. She seemed to have strength and dignity that set her apart from so many other women Bella had met.

"Ah, Martha, you've brought tea." Professor Steed crossed the workshop toward them.

"Yes. I thought you and your guests might like a bit of refreshment." She looked up at the professor with a warm smile and glowing eyes.

Bella's father, Mr. Finch, and James approached the table. There were only four chairs, and the professor insisted her father and Mr. Finch should take the two open seats. He and James each pulled up a crate.

Martha took a step back. She'd brought enough cups for her to join them, but lacking a seat, she looked uncertain.

James motioned toward the crate he'd just pulled over. "Martha, why don't you sit here?"

"No, that's all right. You enjoy your guests." She took a step toward the door, then glanced back at Bella and Sylvia. "I hope you'll come and visit me sometime."

"Thank you." Bella smiled. "I'd like that very much." Her gaze followed Martha as she walked out the door. There was something special about Martha Shelby. Bella definitely wanted to follow up on her invitation.

"So, Mr. Finch, do you have any final thoughts about the engine?" Her father crunched on a biscuit, and crumbs dropped onto his waistcoat.

Mr. Finch's gaze flicked back to the workbench. "Well, as I said before, if you refashion those pistons and adjust the timing, you'll have a more dependable machine."

Bella's father leaned forward, his gaze intense. "Will that make the engine reliable enough for a flight across the Channel?"

"I wouldn't risk that until you've had several successful test flights at different speeds and altitudes."

Professor Steed nodded. "I agree. I don't want James to attempt a Channel crossing until he's been able to stay in the air for at least an hour, no matter how high he's flying or what the wind and weather conditions might be."

A shiver traveled down Bella's back. The thought of flying the twenty-two miles across the rough Channel waters sounded daunting, even for someone who seemed as brave as James Drake.

Her father took a second biscuit. "How quickly can those changes be made to the engine?"

The professor rubbed his chin. "I think it will take at least a week or two. We'll have to take it to London to have the pistons refashioned. Then we'll have to reinstall it and take the airplane up for a few test flights to see how it performs."

Her father narrowed his eyes. "You'll have to work quickly if you're going to beat the French."

The professor's snowy eyebrows rose. "Have you received word from France? Is someone ready to attempt a flight?"

"There was an article in the paper today that said three Frenchmen are making preparations." Bella's father's gaze flickered over his daughters. "What were their names, Bella?"

"Louis Blériot, Count de Lambert, and Hubert Latham."

James and the professor exchanged worried glances.

"I have no idea how close they are to making an attempt, but we've no time to waste," her father continued. "Do you need financial backing to make those repairs and carry out the rest of your test flights? If so, I'd like to pledge my support."

James straightened. "That's very generous, sir."

The professor leaned forward. "I'm not sure what it will cost to make those changes to the engine—perhaps somewhere in the neighborhood of fifty pounds?"

Her father nodded. "I can take care of it. What else do you need?"

The professor glanced around the workshop, then back at her father. "We are running low on supplies for making some of the structural repairs. Twenty or thirty more should cover those expenses."

Her father lifted his hand. "I don't need to know the total today. I'm headed back to London tomorrow, but I'll return to Broadlands on Friday. Why don't you join us for dinner that evening? Say, seven o'clock? We can discuss it then."

Professor Steed beamed. "Thank you, sir. We'd be most happy to come to dinner on Friday."

"Good. Just let me know what's needed. I'll write a bank draft that night." Bella's father rose from his chair. "Now mind you, these funds are coming from me personally, not the *Daily Mail*. It wouldn't be fair for the newspaper to support one particular aviator over the others, but I don't see any reason why I can't lend a hand myself."

"We appreciate it very much!" The professor stood and shook hands with her father and Mr. Finch.

James rose and did the same.

Bella's father turned to her and Sylvia. "It's time for us to go."

Bella stood and faced James. "Thank you for allowing us to visit your workshop. It's wonderful to see all you've accomplished. I'm sure you're going to make a successful flight across the Channel very soon."

He seemed to stand taller as he took in her compliments. "I appreciate your confidence in me. I'll look forward to seeing you Friday."

Her smile spread wider, and she nodded to him. Then she and Sylvia followed their father and Mr. Finch out of the workshop. Their chauffeur hurried around and opened the motorcar's doors for them. Bella settled into her seat, then glanced toward the workshop. James and Professor Steed stood in the open doorway.

The chauffeur started the motorcar, and as it rolled forward, Bella leaned toward the open window. James smiled and lifted his hand. She returned a wave just before they rounded the curve. James disappeared from sight, but his image stayed in her mind as they traveled home.

Three

Bella picked up her notebook and fountain pen and headed for the library in search of her father. She'd spent the last hour in her room poring over Octave Chanute's book, *Progress in Flying Machines*. Much had changed in the fifteen years since it was published, but she'd noted several facts that her father might be able to include in an editorial in support of aviation.

Entering the library, she found him seated in a large overstuffed chair by the fireplace. He held an open newspaper and rested his feet on a footstool near the fire. Her mother and Sylvia sat across from him, each with a book open on her lap.

"Father, have you started your editorial yet?"

He lowered the newspaper and sent her a slight frown. "No, not yet."

"I thought you said you were going to work on it this evening."

"I planned to, but it's been a busy day. I just want to relax and read the paper."

Bella's thoughts skipped ahead. "But you're leaving for London in the morning."

"That's right. I am." His stiff reply made his irritation obvious.

She tightened her hold on her notebook. If she didn't get him moving, he wouldn't write another editorial until he returned from London on Friday. That was too long to wait. Advances in aviation were being made every day, but most of them seemed to be happening in France or the United States. The British government needed to put their support behind pilots like James Drake, or Britain would be left behind.

"I think you'd be very interested in Octave Chanute's research." Bella took a seat in the chair next to his. "I'd like to show you the notes I've taken from his book."

Her father's eyebrows dipped. "Who is Octave Chanute?"

ACROSS *the* BLUE 41

"He's a brilliant American civil engineer who has collected all kinds of information about aviation from men like Otto Lilienthal and—"

"Otto Lilienthal? That name sounds German."

Bella tipped her head, acknowledging the fact. "I believe Lilienthal was German, but he passed away, so he's not a threat to Britain."

Her father huffed and shook out his newspaper.

"Octave Chanute has been corresponding with men from many countries, documenting their research and reporting their test flights and airplane designs." She held out her notebook, showing him her notes.

Her mother sent her a troubled look. "Honestly, Bella, I don't understand your fascination with flying machines."

"They're going to change the world, Mother. Why shouldn't I be interested in them?"

"Because you are a young lady."

"I don't see why that should make a difference. Father is interested in aviation. So am I."

Her mother snapped her book closed. "Your father has many interests, and they're all quite masculine, as they should be."

"You'd understand my interest if you had come with us today." Bella fixed her gaze on her mother. "Mr. Drake explained how his airplane works and how they observed birds to make adjustments to their design. It was all so very interesting."

Her mother gave her head a slight shake. "I wish you would show half as much enthusiasm for feminine pursuits as you do for aviation or for pestering your father about his editorials." Her mother's voice rose. "How do you expect to find a husband if you spend all your time poring over research books, writing in your journal, and dreaming about flying machines?"

Bella stilled, stung by her mother's words and tone.

Sylvia sent her a sympathetic look, but she didn't speak up in Bella's defense.

Bella straightened her shoulders. "I am interested in journalism and aviation, but that doesn't mean I'm not interested in feminine pursuits. I want to marry one day."

"I should hope so!" Her mother set her book on the side table. "You'd be much wiser to focus on preparing for the season and encouraging some of the fine young men who have shown an interest in you."

Bella suppressed a groan. "Not one of those *fine young men* is more interesting than a bowl of pea soup."

"Don't be ridiculous. Miles Hamilton comes from an excellent family. He will make a very suitable husband for some lucky young lady." She sent Bella a pointed look. "And there is nothing wrong with Roger Trentworth." When Bella didn't answer, her mother continued. "They might not be your romantic ideals, but they would give you security and a position in society."

Bella crossed her arms protectively across her middle. "Well, I'm not interested in either one of them."

"Oh, Bella! How can you say such a thing?"

"I can say it because it's the truth."

"But you're going into your third season and you haven't had one proposal. If you don't find a husband this year, it may be too late."

"Mother, I'm only twenty years old!"

"Most young women your age are already married or at least engaged."

"Well, I'm not *most* young women. I'm your elder daughter, and I'd think you'd want me to be happy and have a loving marriage."

Mother lifted her trembling hand to her forehead. "This conversation is making my head throb."

Bella pulled in a deep breath. "I'm sorry. I don't mean to upset you. But I don't think it's kind or fair to encourage a man unless there's a possibility I would marry him, and I could never marry Roger or Miles."

Mother sighed and rubbed her forehead.

Bella leaned toward her father and lowered her voice. "I'm sure it wouldn't take more than thirty minutes to write that editorial if we worked on it together."

"Bella, that's enough." He sent a worried glance at her mother, then glared at Bella. "Put your notes away. I'm not going to write an editorial tonight, and you need to stop badgering me about it."

"But that article we read this morning made it sound as though one of those French pilots would fly across the Channel any day. Don't you want to state your opinion about the importance of aviation before that happens?"

"The French pilots are only making preparations. It could be weeks or months before they're ready to attempt a flight. And there's no guarantee they'll be successful." Father lifted the newspaper again. "If they want to qualify for the prize, they have to give the *Daily Mail* twenty-four hours' notice so we can cover the story. That means we'll be the first to know when someone is actually ready to fly."

Bella sank back in the chair. What if one of those French pilots did succeed? What would happen to James Drake then? If only there was some way she could help him and assure he would be the first.

An idea struck, and she sat up straighter. Perhaps there was a way she could bring James and the professor's efforts to light and make people understand the importance of their experiments. Her idea began to form into a plan, and she smiled. Her father might not be ready to write an editorial in support of aviation, but she wouldn't let that stop her from making her opinion known.

◦◦◦

A knock sounded at Bella's door. She froze, then quickly slid her papers under the blotter on her desk. She couldn't let anyone find out what she was writing, at least not yet. "Who is it?"

"It's me, Sylvia."

Bella released a breath and relaxed her shoulders. Her sister wouldn't say anything to her parents even if she discovered her secret. "Come in."

Sylvia slipped in and quietly closed the door behind her.

Guilt tugged at Bella's heart. "Is Mother all right?"

"Her medication finally took effect. She's asleep now." Sylvia sat on the end of the bed. "I think she'll be fine in the morning."

"I hope so. I know I try her patience, but I have a hard time backing down once she starts pressing me to encourage suitors."

Sympathy shone in Sylvia's eyes. "She just wants you to marry well and have your future settled. You can't blame her for that."

"No, but I hope there's more than a suitable marriage in my future."

Sylvia studied her for a moment. "What do you want, Bella?"

Bella walked across the room and sat on the bed next to Sylvia, while ideas danced through her mind. Her dreams might not be realistic, but she couldn't help wishing they might come true. She focused on Sylvia again. "I want a front-row seat, next to Father, to see all that's happening in the world, and then I want to write about it for one of his newspapers." She grinned. "Doesn't that sound grand?"

Sylvia nodded and her gaze warmed. "Your dreams are certainly different from mine. All I want is a quiet life with a man who loves me, a home in the country, and a family to cherish. That would be more than enough for me."

Bella blew out a breath and lay back on the bed. Why were her desires so different from her sister's? Why couldn't she be satisfied with the plans her parents had made for her—courtship with a suitable man who would strengthen their position in society, then marriage, a home, and children?

If she followed that path, what would happen to her dream of writing for the newspaper? Surely if her father would give her a chance, she could prove she was just as clever and talented as those men on his staff. But beyond that dream was another hope. If she became a successful journalist, perhaps her father would finally see her for who she really was, a unique person with talents, skills, and desires, someone worthy of his love and affection.

Would becoming a journalist help her win her father's approval—or would she have to give up her dreams and agree to a courtship with one of the young men her parents had suggested? Was that the only way she could gain a place in his heart?

Just the thought of marrying a man simply to raise her family's social standing made her feel ill. She swallowed and shook her head. Never! She couldn't agree to a lifeless marriage and years of dutiful submission to a man who didn't love her.

Sylvia lay beside her and turned her way. "Are you certain you couldn't be happy with a marriage proposal from Roger Trentworth or Miles Hamilton? I'm sure with just a little encouragement they'd both propose, and then you'd have your pick."

Bella shook her head. "I'd rather be single for the rest of my life than marry either of them."

"But Roger's family is very wealthy. He'll probably have more money than Father one day."

"Money doesn't ensure a happy marriage." She thought of her parents' distant relationship, and a shiver traveled down her back. If that was what she had to look forward to, then she wasn't sure she wanted to marry anyone at all, especially not someone as self-absorbed and haughty as Roger Trentworth.

Thoughts of her parents' marriage increased her uneasy feelings. They'd seemed much closer years ago, before her father had become a newspaper tycoon. But as the years passed, they'd grown further apart. Now they shared little true affection and only seemed to tolerate each other. Bella didn't want a marriage like that.

"What about Miles? He seems like a nice fellow, and one day he'll inherit his father's title and be Earl of Dorchester with an estate even more grand than Broadlands."

"Miles and I have nothing in common. I don't think he's read one book since he left school. All he talks about is hunting, fishing, and shooting. Can you imagine me married to someone like that?"

"But you'd have a comfortable life, a home in London, and an estate only a few miles from here."

"If you have such high regard for Miles, why don't you marry him?"

Sylvia blinked. "Why, I hardly know him, and he hasn't shown the least bit of interest in me."

"That's only because you haven't been presented yet. As soon as you're out in society, I'm sure Miles and a whole troop of men will beat a path to our door."

Sylvia's cheeks flushed. "You really think so?"

"Of course. You're beautiful and charming and more than ready to make every bachelor in London sit up and take notice. Just you wait, you'll see."

Sylvia pulled Bella in for a hug. "You're such a dear sister. I don't know what I'd do without you."

"I'm the one who'd be lost without you." She tightened her hold on Sylvia. "Thank you for listening to all my complaints and not scolding me about Roger and Miles."

"Of course I won't scold you. I understand. You want to marry for love, and you're willing to wait for the right young man." Sylvia scooted back and smiled at Bella. "Perhaps you'll meet someone new this season. Then you won't have to consider Miles or Roger."

James Drake's image rose in Bella's mind, and a smile lifted the corners of her mouth. Maybe she would . . . Maybe she already had.

⸻

James and Professor Steed stepped down from the train at London's Charing Cross Station. Steam hissed from the train as they made their way through the crowd toward the baggage car.

The professor tugged on his gloves. "Perhaps it would be best if we split up to take care of our business."

"What do you suggest?"

"Why don't I transport the engine to Chapman's Tool Shop, while you go to the house and collect the items on our list."

"All right." James signaled a porter who had a cart and gave him the ticket to claim the crate containing the engine. It took two porters and some help from James to transfer the heavy engine onto the cart. Then they made their way through the station and out to the street.

The professor hailed a driver with a wagon for hire, and they loaded the crate into the back of the wagon.

The professor shook his head. "I should've let Hannah know we were coming." Hannah Hamlin, their cook-housekeeper, stayed in their London home and kept an eye on everything for them while they were away. She had worked for the professor for twenty-five years and was more like a family member than a servant.

"We'll only be in town for a few hours. I'm sure she won't mind a surprise visit."

"I suppose you're right. Still, give her my apologies for not sending word."

"I will." James took the list from his coat pocket. "Is there anything else you want me to pick up at the house?"

The professor leaned closer and scanned the list. "No, just be sure to collect the post as well."

James nodded and tucked the paper away.

The professor climbed up into the front seat of the wagon next to the driver, then looked down at James. "I'll meet you back at the house after I finish at Chapman's. Then we'll have some lunch and see if we can take the three o'clock train back to Kent."

"All right. I'll see you there." James touched his hat brim and watched the wagon roll off down the street. It was only a fifteen-minute walk to their house on Maiden Lane, so he lifted his collar against the wind and set off, his thoughts focused on his list and what he needed to accomplish.

When he reached the house, he pushed open the front door and stepped inside. Hannah was hard of hearing, though she never liked to admit it, so he raised his voice and called, "Hannah, it's James!" His greeting rang out through the house, and he slammed the door for good measure.

Their housekeeper bustled into the front hall, her hand over her heart. "Goodness' sakes, you nearly gave me a heart attack, bursting into the house like that." A white cap covered her hair, and she wore a white apron over her simple gray dress.

James grinned, then leaned down and kissed her pink cheek. "How are you, Hannah?"

"I'm fit as a fiddle. Why didn't you tell me you were coming? I would've baked you a pudding." She looked past his shoulder. "Where is the professor?"

"He's taking our engine to Chapman's to be repaired, but he'll be here soon."

James took off his hat and shrugged out of his jacket, then hung them on the carved oak hat tree by the door. "We're hoping to have some lunch before we take the train back to Kent this afternoon."

She placed her hands on her hips. "You were, were you?"

"Yes, if it's not too much trouble."

"It will be a whole load of trouble." She shook her finger at him, but her eyes glowed with a teasing light. "But don't you worry. I'll find something for you. We can't send you back to the country hungry."

James smiled, glad to see Hannah in fine spirits. "I'm going to collect some items we need to take back with us."

"I hope you don't plan to raid my kitchen stores. I haven't been to see the grocer for almost a week."

"No, just some tools and supplies." He started to turn away. "Oh, I'm also looking for some blankets and flannel sheets. It's much colder in Kent than we expected."

"You'll be wanting the single size, and those are in that big black trunk in the attic." Her brow creased. "I hope you're not wanting me to go all the way up there." Hannah's knees had given her trouble the last few years, and she struggled with the stairs.

"No, I'll go up. Just make us a fine lunch, and I'll take care of the rest."

Her cheeks creased with her smile. "You're a good boy."

James groaned. "Hannah, I'm twenty-four. I'm not a boy."

"You'll always be a boy to me." She reached up and patted his cheek, then turned and bustled back toward the kitchen.

James chuckled as he climbed the stairs. He walked past his bedroom, the professor's room, and the guest room. At the end of the upper hallway, he opened the door to the attic stairs. A dry, dusty scent floated down, reminding him he hadn't climbed these stairs in a long time.

When he was a boy, he used to love rummaging through the trunks and boxes the professor had stored under the eaves. On quiet afternoons he'd spent hours poring over the old magazines and books, trying on the professor's discarded clothes, and pretending he was a great inventor like Professor Steed.

James smiled at the memories as he reached the top of the stairs and scanned the cluttered attic. Old furniture, trunks, and boxes were stacked in a haphazard manner across the rough wooden floor. A few cobwebs hung from the exposed rafters. Obviously, Hannah hadn't come up here for quite a while.

He made his way toward the large black trunk and lifted the lid. Inside, he found folded stacks of bedding. He squatted and sorted through the pile, pulling out two sets of flannel sheets. Digging deeper, he searched for blankets, but he didn't see what he needed.

He closed the trunk and glanced around. Where could Hannah have put the extra blankets? He lifted the flaps on a few boxes, but none seemed to contain bedding. He contemplated stripping the blankets from his bed, but they were larger than he needed and would be bulky to carry back to Kent.

Pushing aside the boxes, James made his way to a tall wardrobe in the corner and pulled open the double doors. The scent of cedar and mothballs drifted out. Old coats and suits hung on one side and open shelves stuffed with papers and small boxes filled the other. He was about to close the doors when a fabric-covered hatbox on top of the wardrobe caught his attention. It looked decidedly feminine compared to the other items in the attic.

He reached up and took down the hatbox, then blew off a fine layer of dust that covered the top. He lifted the lid.

The hairs on the back of his neck prickled.

Several sets of baby clothes, tiny shoes, and a yellow crocheted baby blanket lay inside the box. Were they his?

He pushed aside the blanket and looked underneath. In the bottom of the box he found a little blue coat and matching hat, and a silver baby rattle.

Nestled between the coat and hat was a slim ivory envelope. His name was written on the front. His breath caught in his throat. He reached for the envelope and carefully opened it. Inside, he found a sheet of ivory stationery. He pulled it out and unfolded it.

Dear James,

You are so precious to me. From the first moment I looked into your eyes, I knew we shared a bond that could never be broken. Whatever you've been told about the circumstances of your birth or about me, the most important thing to remember is that I love you dearly, and I refused to give you up.

Your father, my family, and most of my friends have turned against me because I chose to bring you safely into this world and raise you as my own. I don't know what the future holds for us, but I will do everything in my power to make sure it is bright and full of hope for you.

Anna was very kind to take me in and care for me when no one else would. She loves you almost as much as I do, and she has promised to watch over you if anything should happen to me. My hope is that we'll have our own peaceful home one day where we'll be safe and where I can watch you grow up. But if that's not to be, then please remember that I loved you with all my heart. Be wise and strong, my dear boy! Give your heart and life to God and His service. Make your mama proud by living a life of integrity and honor, a life so very different from mine.

All my love,
Your Mama

James stared at the words, trying to make sense of them. Why had she written, "if anything should happen to me"? And why had she said she "loved" him—past tense? Did she sense she wouldn't live long enough to see him grow up? Was she simply being practical, mentioning Anna's commitment to care for him if needed? Was his mother ill when she wrote that letter, or did she believe she was in danger?

An even more dreadful thought struck and shook him to the core. Was she feeling so desperate that she planned to end her life?

He pulled back and shook his head. That couldn't be true.

"James?" Hannah called from the bottom of the attic stairs. "Would you rather have chicken soup, or I could warm up some beef stew?"

James stuffed the letter back in the envelope with an unsteady hand, and as he did, he saw a photograph. He plucked it out and stared at the young woman.

"James, are you up there?"

He blinked and replayed Hannah's words. "Yes, I'm here." He shifted his eyes away from the photo. "Make whichever you'd like. Both sound fine."

"Chicken soup it is, then." The door at the bottom of the stairs closed.

James stepped closer to the window where there was more light. He'd never seen a photograph of his mother before. She was very young and pretty with wavy light hair and large expressive eyes. The shapes of her nose and eyes were remarkably like his. Her expression reflected innocence and expectation, as though there was not a cloud on the horizon of her future.

He turned it over. *Laura Markingham, May 1883* was written in the corner. He stared at the name. He'd always thought her name was Drake, like his. Could Drake have been his father's name? He studied the date and realized the photograph must have been taken a year and a half before he was born, eighteen months before her world turned upside down and the future she had hoped for disappeared.

He gazed at her image once more and his chest tightened. What had happened to her? The professor said she'd died after a fall off a cliff near the ocean. But James had always sensed there was more to the story than what he'd been told. Why had she fallen? Was it an accident? Had she been pushed . . . or had she jumped?

He shook his head again, rejecting that final thought. If she loved him as much as she said in the letter, then she would never have ended her life and left him in the care of others, no matter how kind.

Urgent questions rushed through his mind, and he clenched his hands. Who was his father, and why had he turned his back on them? Bile rose in his throat as he thought of the nameless, faceless man who had shirked his responsibility and abandoned James and his mother in their time of need.

It wasn't right. His father should have taken care of them no matter what the circumstances were. How could he be so hard-hearted? Didn't he even care that he had a son?

He'd tried to avoid these questions for years, pushing them down each time they rose to the surface. But now, holding his mother's photograph, the questions blazed to life, like a fire had been ignited in him.

For too long, the brief story he'd been told about his mother had shadowed his thoughts and left him feeling ashamed and unworthy. There had to be more, some explanation for what had happened to her.

It was time he found out the truth.

***

James walked into the kitchen a few minutes later, following the scent of Hannah's chicken soup simmering on the stove.

She stirred the pot and looked over her shoulder. "Did you find everything you needed?"

James arched an eyebrow. "Yes, and more than I expected."

"What do you mean?"

He'd pushed his questions down for so long it was hard to bring them up now, but he couldn't ignore them any longer. "What do you know about my mother?"

Her eyes widened, and she swung back toward the stove. "Very little."

James moved to her side. "But you've worked for the professor since before I was born. Surely you knew her or heard something about her."

She shook her head. "I mind my own business. I don't go prying into other people's affairs."

"Hannah." That was about as far from the truth as could be, and they both knew it.

"If you have questions about your mother, you'll have to ask the professor."

James reached into his pocket and took out the photograph. "This is my mother, isn't it?"

Her eyes widened, and the spoon she'd been holding clattered to the floor. "Mercy sakes! Where did you get that?"

"I found it in a hatbox in the attic, along with a letter she'd written that was addressed to me."

"Oh dear." Hannah snatched up the spoon and dropped it into the soapy water in the sink.

"Hannah, please tell me what you know about her."

She pressed her lips together and shook her head. "The professor wouldn't want me to speak of it."

"I'm a grown man. I have a right to know the details about my birth and my parents."

She wiped her hands on a dish towel, still looking uncertain. Finally, she released a deep sigh and motioned toward the table. "I suppose it's time. You best sit down. It's not a happy tale."

He took a seat on a stool at the end of the worktable, and she pulled up a second stool next to him.

"I only met your mother once. You were about two months old at the time. She and Anna came to visit the professor. She didn't speak to me about you or her circumstances. All I know is what Anna told me later." She bit her lip and glanced toward the kitchen door. "I asked the professor about it a few times, but he never wanted to discuss it."

That sounded like the professor. He always seemed to avoid difficult topics by scowling and changing the subject rather than explaining. "Why won't he talk about it?"

Hannah gave a slight shrug. "I suppose that's his way of shielding you, but as you said, you're a man now. It's time you knew the rest of the story."

"It's past time." He laid the letter and photograph on the worktable.

Hannah shifted on her stool and placed her hands in her lap. "I'll tell you what I know, but you'll have to ask the professor to tell the rest."

James nodded, his gaze riveted on Hannah.

"The professor's sister, Anna, was a nurserymaid and then a housemaid working for your mother's family from the time Laura was born until she turned sixteen. Then Anna left service to marry Peter, but he died two years later, leaving her a young widow." Hannah looked at him expectantly, as though that part of the story should mean something to him.

He nodded. "Go on."

"After Peter died, Anna knew she had to find a way to provide for herself. She was thinking of going back into service, but then your mother paid her a visit and told her she was expecting a baby. Her parents were upset and wanted to send her away to Ireland to have the baby in secret and give it up for adoption, but she wanted to keep the baby. Anna had always been fond of Laura, and when she asked if she could stay and rent a room, Anna agreed. Laura had enough money to support them both for a time."

James's throat grew tight as he thought of Anna's kindness toward his mother. She had stood in the gap and helped her when everyone else turned away, and then she'd faithfully cared for him after his mother's death.

"I think Anna would've taken Laura in even if she hadn't had any money. But as it was, Anna cared for Laura and helped her when the time came for you to be born. She said they were so pleased when you arrived." Hannah's expression warmed into a teary-eyed smile. "She said you were perfect, a beautiful baby boy.

"But, sadly, it wasn't to last. When you were four months old, Laura's money was almost gone. She decided to write to your father and ask for help."

James stiffened. "My father? Do you know who he is?"

"No, Anna never told me his name."

"My mother said he refused to help her when she told him she was going to have a baby."

"Yes, that's what Anna said. He knew about . . . her condition, but he didn't offer to marry her or give her any money."

James's irritation flared, and he clenched his jaw. "So did he finally step up and do the right thing after I was born?"

"I don't know," Hannah said softly. "Anna never said, but it wasn't long after that when she told us about the accident."

James's stomach clenched. "What did she say?"

Hannah looked away and fiddled with the edge of her apron. "Laura fell off a cliff at Saint Margaret's Bay." She looked at him then, with a sorrowful dread in her eyes. "You were with her."

A shock jolted through him. "What?"

Hannah clasped her hands. "She must have been holding you when she fell."

He stared at her for a moment, trying to understand how it could've happened. "But if the fall killed my mother, how did I survive?"

Hannah shook her head. "Her body must have cushioned you, or the good Lord just decided it wasn't your time."

James sat back as painful questions tumbled through his mind. Could she have slipped or tripped and then fallen? Or had someone pushed her over the edge, hoping she and James would both topple to their deaths? But who would do that?

The front door opened, jarring him back to the moment.

"James? Hannah?" the professor called as he came closer.

James shoved the photo into his pocket. "Don't say anything to him."

"But he's the only one who—"

"Please, Hannah, let me handle it."

Before she could answer, the professor strode through the kitchen doorway. "Ah, here you are." He sniffed the air. "Is that chicken soup I smell?"

Hannah rose from her stool. "How did you guess?" Her voice sounded higher than usual, and she turned away from him.

"It's one of my favorites. You know that." He grinned and plunked a package on the worktable. "This is for you."

She turned and eyed the package. "What is it?"

"I stopped at Maxwell's and brought some of that Irish breakfast tea you like."

"Well, now, that's a nice surprise." She studied him a moment. "It's not Christmas or my birthday. Why are you bringing me a gift?"

"It's not a gift. It's just some tea."

She cocked her head and placed her hands on her hips.

"I simply wanted you to know we appreciate the way you've stayed on and taken care of the house while we've been away." He slipped off his jacket. "It's been longer than usual this time."

"Yes, almost six months now."

"That's true, but we're making great progress. It won't be long until James will be making his flight across the Channel."

Hannah's smile returned, and she lifted her hand to her heart. "Oh my. I can hardly imagine it."

"You won't have to imagine it. Very soon his flight will go down in history as an astonishing accomplishment. Our reputation as prize-winning airplane designers will open new doors for us. We'll start our own company and be set for the future."

A longing stirred in James's heart. Could he win that prize and the recognition that would go with it? If he did, would he finally be able to feel proud of his reputation rather than ashamed of his past?

If he did win, his name and photograph would be in every newspaper in England and on the continent. Reporters would clamor for interviews. They'd want to know about his education, his training . . . and his family background.

His stomach plunged. What would he say to those questions? How would he explain who he was and where he was from?

Another thought jolted through him and stole his breath. Would his father read those stories and realize their connection? Would he seek James out? And if he did, would James finally meet the man who had abandoned his mother and never cared enough to reach out to him in the last twenty-four years?

Four

B ella looked in the mirror and checked her reflection, while their maid, Bessie, placed a jeweled comb in Bella's upswept hair. Bella wore one of her favorite gowns, light blue with beading around the neckline and a silky sash across the waist. The color highlighted her ivory complexion and was a near perfect match with the color of her eyes.

Bessie's gaze connected with Bella's in the mirror. "How is that, miss?"

"Perfect. Thank you, Bessie."

The maid smiled and nodded to her. "Will there be anything else?"

"No, that's all for now. Thank you."

"Very good, miss." Bessie bobbed a quick curtsy and left the room.

As soon as the bedroom door closed, Sylvia slid into the chair next to Bella's dressing table. "I wish Mother would let me wear my hair up." She fingered a golden curl on her shoulder.

"Your hair is beautiful, up or down. I wouldn't waste a moment worrying about it."

"That's kind of you to say, but I think it would look much more elegant worn up like yours."

Bella smiled. "Only three more months until your presentation, and then you'll wear it up all the time."

Sylvia pushed her hair over her shoulder, then leaned closer and smiled. "What do you think of Mark Clifton?"

Their father had surprised them by bringing the young man home with him when he'd returned from London.

"I hardly know what to think of him. We barely had time to say hello before the gong rang and it was time to come up and dress for dinner."

"Father certainly seems enthusiastic."

A niggle of unease made Bella's stomach contract. Her father had puffed up like a peacock when he introduced Mark Clifton to her. Her mother seemed equally impressed, her hands fluttering and her voice sounding almost like a song when she introduced Bella and Sylvia.

"I wonder why you never met him during the season?" Sylvia ran her hand over her pink gown.

"Father said his home is in Scotland. Perhaps that's why." Bella clipped on her earrings and checked her reflection. "I suppose we'll learn more about him at dinner."

Sylvia's eyes danced. "That should be interesting with Professor Steed and your aviator also coming tonight."

Warmth flooded in Bella's cheeks. "He's not *my* aviator."

Sylvia grinned. "Really? You've hardly spoken about anything else since we came back from visiting his workshop."

"Don't be silly. I've talked about other things."

"A few, but you've said, 'Don't you think James Drake is brave to want to be the first to fly across the Channel?' Or something like it at least half a dozen times."

Bella adjusted her necklace and tried not to smile. "I do admire him. I can't deny that."

The bedroom door opened, and their mother walked in. "What can't you deny?"

Bella shot Sylvia a warning look, then turned toward her mother. "That I'm looking forward to dinner tonight."

Sylvia grinned. "So am I."

Her mother nodded, looking pleased and surprisingly vibrant this evening in her deep purple gown with silver trim. "Are you ready to go down?"

"Yes, we're ready." Bella rose.

"Before we go, I want to have a word with you, Bella." Her mother crossed the room toward her. "I'd like you to pay special attention to Mr. Clifton this evening."

Bella lifted her gaze to meet her mother's. "Special attention?"

"Yes, he's from a very prestigious family, and one day he'll inherit his father's title and estate in Scotland."

Bella cringed inside, but she maintained a neutral expression. "And that's important because . . ."

Her mother lifted her eyes to the ceiling. "Really, Bella. He's a potential suitor, a wonderful prospect, and I don't want you to throw away this opportunity."

"I'll be polite and speak to him, but I can't promise more than that."

"That is not enough." Her mother's firm tone and steady look made her point clear. "I want you to promise you'll be attentive and encouraging."

Heat rushed into Bella's face. "Shouldn't I at least be allowed a few minutes with the man to see if there are any points of compatibility before I have to throw myself at him?"

"Bella! I'm not saying you should throw yourself at him. I'm simply asking you to open your mind to the possibility." Her mother lifted her hand to her forehead and softened her tone. "Your father has gone out of his way to bring Mr. Clifton to Broadlands, and I don't think it's too much to ask that you be considerate and willing to make an effort."

A pang of guilt hit Bella's heart. She didn't want to upset her mother or make her ill. Her parents were trying to help her find a suitable husband. It wasn't their fault that every introduction had led to a disappointing end.

She released a sigh. "Very well, I'll be considerate."

"And you'll make an effort," her mother added.

Bella gave a slight nod, but she would not give up her independence too quickly, even if Mark Clifton was a promising suitor. James Drake was also coming to dinner, and she didn't want anything to diminish the possibility of their friendship.

The butler greeted James and the professor at the front door of Broadlands, ushered them inside, and took their coats. His mouth drew down at the corners when he saw how they were dressed. "If you'll follow me, sirs."

"Thank you." The professor smiled, apparently unaware of the butler's disapproval.

James straightened his necktie and walked behind the butler and Professor Steed into the large central hall. He tried not to stare, but Broadlands was filled with impressive paintings, elaborate sculptures, and furniture that looked like it had been imported from all over the world. A fire crackled in the large fireplace on the right, and a slight scent of wood smoke and lemon oil hung in the air.

The Graysons' beautiful home reflected their wealth and position in society. The difference between James and the professor's simple home in London and the impressive interior at Broadlands couldn't be greater. He told himself it didn't matter—that he could rise to the challenge and feel comfortable associating with the Graysons. Then reality came rushing in and squelched those thoughts.

He would never be on equal footing with the Graysons, no matter how many times he flew across the Channel or how many aviation prizes he won.

Charles Grayson and another man stood at the base of the wide oak staircase. Both men turned toward James and the professor as they approached. They wore well-tailored dinner jackets and impeccable white shirts and ties.

James's neck heated. He and the professor were dressed in business suits, the best they had with them in Kent, but their clothing was definitely not up to par with that of Mr. Grayson and his guest.

Mr. Grayson stepped forward. "Good evening, Professor Steed, Mr. Drake. It's good to see you again."

"Thank you. We're delighted to be here." The professor shook hands with Mr. Grayson and James did the same.

Mr. Grayson motioned toward the other man. "May I introduce Mr. Mark Clifton from the Isle of Mull?"

Clifton smiled as he shook hands with James and the professor. "Our family's estate is on Mull, but I've spent so little time there lately, I feel almost guilty being introduced that way." He had a slight accent, but James couldn't place it.

"I spend most of my time in France now," Clifton continued. "But I try to travel home to Scotland a few times a year to see my father and sisters."

That would explain the accent. Before James could give it any more thought, he heard women's voices in the gallery above. He glanced up just as Bella and Sylvia came into view at the top of the stairs. A middle-aged woman walked behind them, whom he assumed was their mother.

Each woman was dressed in a stylish evening gown, but his gaze was drawn to Bella. She wore a fetching light-blue gown of shimmering fabric that flowed around her figure in the most appealing manner. Tendrils of her chestnut-brown hair curled around her lovely face. A jeweled comb was tucked into her hair on the side, and her diamond necklace and matching earrings sparkled in the candlelight.

Bella's gaze connected with his, and she offered him a warm smile.

His heartbeat picked up speed, and he returned her smile.

When Bella reached the bottom of the stairs, Mark Clifton stepped forward and offered her his arm. "My, you look lovely tonight, Isabella."

Her cheeks flushed, and her gaze darted to James and then back to Clifton. "Thank you."

James's shoulders tensed. Was Clifton an old family friend? Was that why he stepped forward and greeted her like that? Bella had seemed a bit surprised, but her parents had smiled their approval.

The butler approached Mrs. Grayson. "Dinner is served, ma'am."

Mrs. Grayson nodded to him, then turned to the professor. "Come, Professor Steed, let's lead the way."

The professor smiled and extended his arm to Mrs. Grayson. Mr. Grayson motioned for Clifton and Bella to follow them. Mr. Grayson took Sylvia's arm and glanced over his shoulder at James. "I'm sorry the numbers aren't even tonight, but I'll seat you between my daughters. That should give you an opportunity for conversation."

James nodded, but he still felt like the odd man out as he followed everyone else into the dining room. He blew out a breath and shook his head. What did that matter? The point of the evening was to secure Charles Grayson's financial backing. Once they had that, it wouldn't take long to finish the repairs to their airplane and make the final test flights. Then he would be on his way to crossing the Channel, winning the prize, and securing his future.

Ten minutes later, they'd finished the first course, and two footmen and the butler stepped forward to remove their plates. Mr. Grayson and the professor had carried most of the conversation so far. James had done his best not to slurp his soup or draw attention to himself. He glanced to the left at Bella as one of the footmen placed the next course in front of her.

She smiled at James. "So how are the repairs coming along for your airplane?"

"Very well. We finished rebuilding the wing and straightened the struts.

Now we're just waiting to bring the refurbished engine back from London. Once we install it, we'll be ready to resume our flights."

"That's wonderful. I'm eager to see you fly again."

Warmth filled his chest. "I'm eager to be back in the air."

Mr. Grayson motioned toward the end of the table. "Mr. Clifton is also interested in powered flight, aren't you, sir?"

Clifton gave a confident nod. "Yes, indeed. My cousin is the inventor of the Antoinette engine. I raced his powerboat in the Monaco Regatta, and we took home the winner's cup in 1905 and '06. He has moved on to designing airplanes, and he has asked me to fly them for him."

James straightened. "So you're an aviator now?"

"Yes. My cousin, Pierre, and I hold the record for the first night flight across the English Channel in a balloon, and we want to be the first to fly across in an airplane as well."

"Piloting a powered aircraft is quite different from flying a balloon or racing a boat."

"I'm sure it is. But it can't be too difficult to learn. It all depends on the machine you're flying, and my cousin is determined to design the best."

James could barely keep the skepticism out of his voice. "So you're not involved in the design process?"

"No, that's Pierre's area of expertise, but I'll do the flying."

"If you're not involved in the design process, how can you expect to control the airplane?"

Clifton arched one eyebrow. "I didn't design the powerboat or the balloon, and I had no trouble winning with either of them. I don't see why an airplane should be any different."

"I'm sure you'll find piloting an airplane is not like anything you've attempted in the past."

"Perhaps, but I'm sure it won't be difficult for me to master. And I only have to fly a little over twenty miles to win the prize. That hardly seems like a challenge at all."

Heat surged up James's neck and into his face. "It's twenty-two miles from Dover to Calais, and you'll have to fly over rough seas with dangerous wind currents."

Clifton sent him a pointed glance. "As I said, I've already crossed in a balloon, so I'm well aware of the winds."

The professor shot James a warning glance, then shifted his gaze to Clifton. "That's very interesting to hear you're an aviator. We're also preparing for the Channel crossing."

Clifton nodded. "Mr. Grayson told me I would be dining with some of my competitors tonight."

"Well, I'd rather you think of us as fellow adventurers, members of a brotherhood of pioneer aviators," the professor added.

Clifton grinned. "Yes, that's the spirit. We're all in this together." He shifted his gaze to James. "But that doesn't mean I won't do everything in my power to be the first across and win that prize. I'm looking forward to adding that trophy to my collection."

James clenched his jaw. Was there no end to the man's arrogance? Flying was dangerous at any time, but attempting to cross the Channel would mean looking death in the face and pressing on in spite of fear and unexpected challenges.

"Mr. Clifton, my husband said you'd recently traveled to Africa." Mrs. Grayson's practiced smile couldn't hide her attempt to steer the conversation in a calmer direction. "I'm sure we'd all love to hear about your experiences there."

"Of course, I'd be glad to tell you about my travels. I've been to Africa three times, but most recently I headed up a four-month expedition to Abyssinia. We returned to France last July."

Sylvia looked across the table at Clifton. "Abyssinia? My goodness, I don't even know where that is."

"It's in north Africa, just east of Anglo-Egyptian Sudan. It's also known as Ethiopia, but I've always liked the sound of the historical name, Abyssinia."

"I agree." Sylvia smiled. "It sounds very exotic."

Clifton nodded. "Abyssinia is a land of mystery."

"And what was the purpose of your expedition?"

"Our team was collecting specimens for the French National Museum of Natural History. My mother is French, you see, and I've spent almost as much time in France with my friends and family there as I have in Scotland and England."

Bella looked across at Clifton. "Your cousin, the one who designed the Antoinette engine, is he French?"

"Yes, he is the son of Vicomte de Maleyssie. He lives at his family's estate, Château de Maillebois, near Chartres. The vicomte is my mother's brother."

Bella smiled, looking impressed.

James stifled a groan. So, his mother was from a titled French family and his father owned an estate in Scotland. No wonder he could travel around Europe, race powerboats, fly in balloons, and trek through Africa on a scientific expedition.

Bella leaned forward, her eyes shining. "How wonderful to have a dual heritage with family in France and Britain. I think that must give you a greater understanding of world events."

"I believe you're right. I consider my heritage a privilege." Clifton shifted his gaze to James. "Have you spent time on the continent, Mr. Drake?" His arched eyebrows and tone of voice carried a challenge.

James straightened in his chair. "Yes, the professor and I have traveled to France and Belgium. In fact we were at Le Mans last summer to see Wilbur Wright give his flight demonstration."

Clifton cocked his head. "Is that so? My cousin Pierre and I were there as well."

Mr. Grayson chuckled. "Think of that. We were all there to see Wilbur Wright, but there was such a large crowd we didn't even see each other."

"On the contrary." James shifted his gaze to Bella. "I remember seeing Miss Grayson."

Surprise then pleasure lit her eyes. "Really?"

"Yes. You were seated in the stands, and you were wearing a large white hat and white linen suit."

Her cheeks flushed and she smiled. "My, you do have an excellent memory."

"It would be hard to forget someone so lovely." The words slipped out before he thought better of them. But when they were said, he wasn't sorry at all.

Clifton cleared his throat. "Isabella, I'd like to hear more about your interests."

She turned back to Clifton. "Well, I enjoy traveling with my parents. We've spent time in the Lake District, the Peak District, and the Highlands, and we've also visited France, Switzerland, Italy, Denmark, and the Netherlands."

Clifton nodded, looking pleased by her reply. "And how do you occupy your time here in the country? Do you ride?"

She hesitated. "I do, though it's not my favorite activity."

"And what would be your favorite?"

"Well . . . I enjoy reading and writing, especially about important events, new inventions, and the people who are changing our world."

"My, it sounds like you have an interest in world affairs and journalism, like your father."

Before Bella could reply, her mother spoke. "Bella admires her father and shares some of his interests, but I'm sure when she marries and has her own home and family to manage, she'll realize those were only passing fancies."

Pink splotches bloomed on Bella's cheeks, and she lowered her gaze to her plate.

James leaned forward. "I think it's admirable for women to expand their interests, then use them in ways that benefit others."

Mrs. Grayson's eyes widened. "Surely you're not suggesting women should neglect their duties to home and family and join the workforce with men?"

"No, I'm simply saying women ought to be encouraged to explore and develop their skills and talents. Some could be combined with managing a home and family, and others could be used during a season when they have fewer demands at home."

Clifton chuckled. "It sounds like you're a supporter of the suffragettes."

James glanced at the professor and read the caution in his eyes. They'd had some lively discussions about women's efforts to gain the vote and come to different conclusions. But he wouldn't back down from Clifton's challenging question or withdraw his support from Bella.

"I don't agree with some of the radical methods the suffragettes are using to draw attention to their cause, but I do think women should have the right to vote, and I hope they'll win it very soon."

Bella beamed him a smile. "I couldn't agree more."

His chest expanded, and he returned a smile.

Bella checked her watch as she walked through the central hall toward the dining room the following Monday. Her mother had asked them to come down early for breakfast so they would be done in time to take the nine-thirty train into London. That afternoon Sylvia had her final fittings for her presentation gown and dresses for the season, and their father had business to attend to at the *Daily Mail.*

The rest of the family were already seated at the dining room table when Bella walked in, but their plates were still full, so it didn't look as though she was too late.

"Good morning," Bella called as she crossed toward the buffet.

Her mother returned her greeting, and Sylvia sent her an encouraging smile, but her father said nothing from behind his newspaper.

Bella took a plate and served herself some eggs and toast. Pierson poured her tea as she approached the table.

She looked over her father's shoulder at the newspaper as she passed, and her heartbeat quickened. He was reading the first section of the *Daily Mail,* but it didn't look as though he'd come to the editorial page yet.

Had they received her letter? Had they published it?

Bella settled in her chair. "Anything interesting in the news?"

"Trouble is brewing," Father grumbled from behind the newspaper.

"What sort of trouble?" Bella placed her napkin on her lap.

"Those suffragettes at Holloway Jail are staging a hunger strike."

Sylvia looked up. "Why? What do they hope to accomplish?"

Bella had read about the suffragettes' protest in yesterday's newspaper. The women had marched through London on Saturday, carrying signs and shouting, "Votes for women." But when some of them picked up stones and threw them through store windows, police arrested the leaders and took them to jail.

"I believe they want to be recognized as political prisoners." Her father lowered the paper. "They're trying to force the home secretary to release them early on medical grounds, but that's not going to happen."

"Why do you say that?"

"Gladstone doesn't want them to become martyrs. He's going to force-feed them."

Her mother gasped. "Charles, that's dreadful, and definitely not a topic to discuss with our daughters."

"But it's an important issue, Mother," Bella said. "We ought to be informed."

Her father's expression firmed, and he turned the page. "Your mother is right. Their radical tactics are foolish and shameful. Damaging property is no way to change peoples' minds. It just goes to show how emotional and unreasonable some women can be."

Heat flooded Bella's cheeks, but she didn't want to begin the day by arguing with her father. She swallowed her reply and focused on eating her breakfast.

Her mother looked across at Sylvia. "Please remember to bring those fabric samples. I want to return them to the dressmaker."

Before Sylvia could answer, her father cut her off. "By George! Listen to this!" He spread out the paper on the table and read aloud. "'Dear Sir, I am writing to encourage all those who are concerned about the security and prosperity of our nation to rise up and demand that our government support the experimentation and advancement of aviation.'"

Bella's heart soared. They had published her letter!

Her father's expression grew animated. "Can you believe it? Finally, someone is speaking up for aviation!"

Bella's smile spread wider.

Her father dropped his gaze and continued reading. "'For too long the British government has denied assistance to those brilliant scientists and fearless aviators who are designing flying machines. This has hindered their progress and prevented them from gaining the advantage over aviators in other countries. France, the United States, and Germany have all made great strides forward with private, government, and military support, and as a result, they have passed Britain and left us shamefaced and years behind in the development of powered flight.

"'How will we respond if an aviator from another country is the first to fly across the English Channel? What will that mean for our defense and national security? How will we protect our country and prevent attacks from the continent if we allow other nations to rule the sky?

"'Now is the time for all those who are loyal to the Crown and concerned for our nation's future to demand that the government give its full support to the advancement of aviation. That is the only way to protect our empire in the precarious days ahead.'" Her father slapped his hand on the table. "Now that's the way to get the government's attention!"

Bella leaned forward. "Do you think they'll listen?"

He tapped the newspaper. "A well-written letter to the editor can have a powerful impact."

A thrill raced through Bella. "So you think it's well written?"

"Yes. The man has obviously done his research and presented his case in a logical manner. It has just the right tone—firm, but practical and reasonable."

Bella swallowed and summoned her courage. "What if it wasn't written by a man?"

Her father turned toward her. "What do you mean?"

She pulled in a deep breath and looked her father in the eye. "I wrote that letter."

Her father's mouth dropped open, and her mother's fork clattered on her plate.

"Bella!" Her mother's voice trembled. "You sent a letter to the editor of the *Daily Mail*?"

"Yes, I knew it was an important issue, and Father seemed too busy to write about it, so I decided to do it myself."

Her mother lifted her hand to her heart. "You didn't sign your name, did you?"

Her father shifted his glare back to the paper. "No, it's signed, 'A Loyal and Concerned Citizen.'" He shook his head. "What were you thinking, Bella?"

"I was thinking someone ought to speak up and make people understand the importance of aviation."

"But you're my daughter. It's not ethical for you to write an anonymous letter to the editor, no matter how important the topic."

"But I'm not the owner of the newspaper; you are." Bella looked from her mother to her father. "I'll be twenty-one soon. That's certainly old enough to express my own opinion about the matter."

Her father folded the newspaper. "You should have spoken to me before you sent it."

"Would you have allowed it?"

He huffed, making his answer clear. "That's not the point. I'm trying to protect your reputation and my integrity."

Bella sighed. "I don't see how my writing a letter to the editor calls your integrity into question."

"That is the point! You don't fully understand the implications."

A stormy reply rose in her throat, but she refused to give in to her temper and strengthen her father's argument. "We've discussed the importance of aviation for months, ever since we watched Wright fly at Le Mans. You've explained what could happen if our government doesn't recognize the work of men like James Drake and Professor Steed."

His glare softened a few degrees, and Bella's hopes rose.

She reached across and laid her hand over his. "You said the letter is well written. Give me a chance, Father. Let me write an article for the paper."

"No!" Father pulled his hand out from under hers. "That's out of the question. I will not have my daughter's reputation tainted by association with Fleet Street."

"I wouldn't have to write from the office of the *Daily Mail*. I could write from home and send in my articles."

"What? Now you think I would allow you to write more than one article?"

"Yes!" Ideas burst into her mind, and energy surged through her. "I could write a series about the race to be the first to fly across the Channel! I'm sure people would be thrilled to read about the pilots and learn more about their airplanes and preparations. A series like that would inform and inspire people, and it might push government officials to finally do what they should."

The last of Father's scowl faded, and his eyes sparked with interest. "I like the idea, though I'm not sure you're the one to carry it out."

"Charles!" Her mother's high-pitched warning echoed around the dining room.

"Please, Father! Let me try. If you give me this opportunity, I promise you won't be disappointed."

"Oh, Bella." Her mother's face had gone pale, and she lifted her hand to her forehead. "You know it's not proper for a young unmarried woman to write for a newspaper. It would tarnish your reputation and damage your prospects."

Bella bit her lip. She'd almost won over her father. She couldn't let her mother's disapproval steal this chance. The memory of a story she'd read flashed into her mind. "Father, you've had women write for your newspapers in the past."

He shook his head. "We have a women's column, but Frances Harrison writes about society events, fashion, and women's news. I don't employ female reporters."

"What about Sarah Wilson? She's from a well-respected family, and she was a foreign correspondent for the *Daily Mail*."

"That was during the Boer War. She was already in South Africa with her husband, who was the aide-de-camp to Lieutenant General Robert Baden-Powell, the commander at Mafeking. Your situation is completely different."

Bella sank lower in her chair. Why couldn't her parents see how important this was to her? Why wouldn't they give her a chance to follow her dream?

Pierson stepped up next to her father. "I'm sorry to interrupt, sir, but if you are going to take the nine-thirty train to London, you'll need to leave soon."

"Goodness, he's right. Come along, girls." Her mother rose from the table. "We have to collect our coats and hats."

Bella pushed back her chair and stood. "Please, Father. I think a series like that would raise the circulation of the *Daily Mail*."

"We'll discuss this later." But he leaned toward her and lowered his voice. "Preferably not when your mother is present."

Bella's heart lifted. She gave him a quick kiss on the cheek, then hurried from the room.

Five

J ames slid the razor down the side of his face and studied his image in the mirror on the workshop wall. The slope of his nose and the shape of his eyes were strong reminders of his mother's features. He carried her photograph with him every day now and looked at it each evening before he went to bed. He glanced in the mirror again. Had he inherited his strong chin and high forehead from his father?

He clenched his jaw and glanced over his shoulder at the professor. He had considered asking him about his parents several times, but he hadn't broached the subject yet.

He could do it now. But how would he start? What would he say? He didn't want the professor to think he was ungrateful for everything he'd done for him. No one could ever take the professor's place in his life. Still, he couldn't help wondering about the circumstances surrounding his birth and his mother's death. Without the full story, he felt like a part of him was missing, as if he would never really fit in, never belong anywhere or to anyone.

"We should leave in about ten minutes." The professor drank the last of his breakfast tea and dunked his cup in the pan of soapy water on the counter.

"I'm almost ready." James pushed aside his questions and rinsed the shaving soap from his blade.

A knock sounded at the door. The professor looked up and called, "Come in."

The door slid to the side, and John, one of the young lads from the neighboring farm, strode in. "Good morning, Professor. Have you read the *Daily Mail*?" He held up the folded newspaper.

"Not yet." The professor rinsed his cup and set it aside.

"My father said you'd want to see it." John hustled over and handed the newspaper to him.

"Thank you, John." The professor opened it and studied the headlines.

"Look at the editorial page. That's the part you'll want to read."

The professor laid the paper on the table and flipped through the first section. James wiped the last of the shaving soap from his chin. He dried his hands on a towel, then joined the professor and John at the table.

"There!" John pointed to the middle of the page. "It sounds like they're writing about you and your flying machines."

The professor squinted, then looked up. "Where are my glasses?"

"I'm not sure. I'll read it." James leaned over the paper. " 'Dear Sir, I am writing to encourage all those who are concerned about the security and prosperity of our nation to rise up and demand that our government support the experimentation and advancement of aviation.' " He smiled at the professor. "Well, it's about time."

"Go on, what else does it say?"

James dropped his gaze and read the next few paragraphs aloud. When he came to the section that said, "How will we respond if an aviator from another country is the first to fly across the English Channel?" he stopped and stared at the newspaper.

Up until now he thought the writer was speaking in general terms about aviation. But it was clear he was focusing on the race across the Channel. It almost sounded as if he knew about their efforts.

The professor touched his arm. "Is that all?"

"No, there's more." James continued reading. " 'What will that mean for our defense and national security? How will we protect our country and prevent attacks from the continent if we allow other nations to rule the sky?

" 'Now is the time for all those who are loyal to the Crown and concerned for our nation's future to demand that the government give its full support to the advancement of aviation. That is the only way to protect our empire in the precarious days ahead.' "

James lifted his gaze to meet the professor's.

"That's brilliant! Who is the author?"

James checked. " 'A Loyal and Concerned Citizen.' "

"Hmm, it would be helpful if it were written by someone prominent, but whomever he is, he sounds intelligent, informed, and persuasive."

"Yes, very persuasive." There were only a few people who knew about their airplanes and test flights, but he couldn't imagine any of them writing an anonymous letter like this. Did the writer know other pilots working toward the same goal?

"The tide is turning, my boy! Soon we'll have supporters begging to back our projects and join our efforts. Then you'll fly across the Channel and launch us into a prosperous future." The professor looked his way with an expectant expression.

James wanted to agree, but doubts tugged at his conscience. Did he have what it would take to fulfill their dream? What if he failed? What would become of them then?

John looked from the professor to James. "I wish I could stay and help you today, but I have to go to school."

The professor laid a hand on the boy's shoulder. "Education is a gift, John. Be a diligent student, and learn all you can. And don't worry. You won't be missing anything. James and I are off to London today."

John's eyes widened. "Is the engine ready?"

The professor nodded. "We're meeting with our machinist to go over the modifications this afternoon. We hope to return to Kent this evening or tomorrow. Then we'll prepare our airplane for our next test flight."

"That's great!" John's smile spread wide. "I'll stop by after school tomorrow. And I can come on Saturday too, if you need me."

"Of course we need you!" The professor slung his arm around John's shoulder. "Come whenever you can, but first be sure to finish your schoolwork and chores at home."

John nodded. "I will."

"Good lad. We'll see you tomorrow or Saturday, and I promise we'll find something interesting for you to do."

"You can count on me!" John started toward the door, then turned and lifted his hand before he stepped outside.

Affection glowed in the professor's eyes as he watched John go. "He reminds me of you when you were young."

James smiled, remembering how he'd helped the professor with countless projects and experiments. They'd built bicycles, kites, and gliders for years before they began designing airplanes. "Was I as eager as John when I was his age?"

"Yes, even more so." The professor shifted his gaze from the door and pulled his watch from his pocket. "We'll have to hurry if we're going to make our train to London."

James straightened, focusing on the plan for the day. "I just need to grab my hat and coat; then I'll be ready." He and the professor would pick up the engine first. After that they planned to stop by the house and check on Hannah. It would be a full day of travel and business in town. Would he take this opportunity to speak to the professor about the circumstances of his birth, his mother's death, and his father's desertion?

He fingered the photograph in his pocket and swallowed hard. Was he ready to hear those answers?

The crowd surged around Bella and her family as they stepped down from the train at Charing Cross Station in London. They set off across the platform, and Bella hurried to keep up with her father. She had been forming a plan all the way from Kent, and it was time to put it into action.

"Father, may I go with you today?"

He slowed and looked her way. "To the *Daily Mail*?"

"Yes. I'd much rather spend the afternoon there than at the dressmaker's."

Her mother's brow creased. "Your sister went with you when you prepared for your first season. Don't you think you ought to support her now?"

"I've gone with Sylvia every time she visited the dressmaker, the milliner, and the shoemaker. I even went along to order the invitations for her ball." Bella turned to Sylvia. "You wouldn't mind if I went with Father today, would you?"

"Not at all." Sylvia offered her an understanding smile. "It's just a final fitting to check the hems. I'm sure it won't take too long. We should be back before teatime."

They followed their father out of the station and onto the busy street. He stepped out of the crowd and motioned the family to gather around. He cleared his throat and cocked one eyebrow. "I think Bella would enjoy a visit to the *Daily Mail*. What do you say, Madelyn?"

Her mother's wary expression eased and was replaced by what looked almost like a smile. "I suppose you're right, Charles. Yes, of course, Bella may go with you."

Bella blinked and stared at her mother. Why was she releasing her with so little protest? Had she finally accepted the idea that Bella wanted to become a journalist?

"All right, then. I'll summon you a cab." Her father lifted his hand, and a driver pulled forward. Mother and Sylvia climbed into the cab, and they gave the driver directions to the dressmaker. As soon as they were off, her father turned back to Bella. Before he could speak, someone called his name. Bella turned and scanned the street.

Professor Steed lifted his hand and waved, then wove through the crowd toward them. James Drake walked beside him.

Bella's heart lifted. What a happy coincidence.

James nodded and sent her a warm smile, which she returned.

The professor lifted his hat. "Good day to you, Mr. Grayson, Miss Grayson."

Her father greeted them both and shook hands with the men. "It's good to see you. What brings you to London?"

"The airplane engine has been repaired. We're here to retrieve it." The professor's eyes shone. "And we have you to thank for it. Because of your generous support, the work was done quickly by the best machinist in town."

Her father rocked back on his heels, apparently pleased with the praise. "Well, I'm very glad to hear it." He glanced down the street and then back at Professor Steed. "We're headed to the offices of the *Daily Mail*. I'm giving a bit of a tour today. Perhaps you'd like to join us?"

Bella glanced at her father. A tour? She thought he was going by the office to check in with Mr. Elmwood, the editor.

"That's a very kind invitation. It would certainly be interesting to see how the *Daily Mail* is published, but I must retrieve the engine." The professor nodded to James. "Why don't you go along with Mr. Grayson? I can take care of matters at the machine shop and see that the engine is crated and delivered to the station."

Bella could hardly hold back her hopeful smile. Would James agree?

James glanced at Bella and then her father. "I would like to see how the newspaper comes together." He turned to the professor. "If you're sure you don't need me to go with you."

"Please, go with the Graysons. Take the tour. Enjoy the day."

James grinned. "All right. I'll see you back at the house later."

"Excellent! I should be there no later than three." The professor set off down the street.

James turned and met Bella's gaze. They exchanged a smile, and her heart fluttered. What a delightful surprise. Not only was she going to visit the *Daily Mail,* she was going there in the company of a man she greatly admired.

⚜

Ten minutes later, James climbed out of the cab in front of the offices of the *Daily Mail,* then turned and offered his hand to help Bella.

She thanked him as she took his hand and stepped onto the pavement. Today she wore a royal-blue walking suit that flattered her slim figure, and a yellow straw hat decorated with a large blue-and-yellow-striped bow at the side. Her pearl-drop earrings swayed as she turned her head and sent him a smile.

"Follow me." Mr. Grayson motioned toward the double-glass front doors and set off at a brisk pace.

James barely had time to look up and scan the impressive, four-story building before he and Bella followed Mr. Grayson into the large cool lobby with its marble floors and dark paneled walls.

A man in a neat black uniform adorned with gold braid looked up from behind the reception desk, then quickly stepped out to greet them. "Good morning, Mr. Grayson."

"Morning, Wilson." Mr. Grayson barely slowed as he marched past the desk and on toward the lift. He pushed the button, and the lift door slid open.

"We'll start at my office on the top floor." Mr. Grayson tapped the button for the fourth floor and stood back.

James had ridden in a lift a few times before, but it was still a bit unsettling to feel the floor rise beneath his feet. It was nothing like flying in an airplane where he could look out, see his surroundings, and judge the altitude. When the door opened, they stepped out into a quiet office corridor. Mr. Grayson walked down the hallway and opened the second door on the right.

A young man looked up from behind his desk in the small outer office and rose to his feet. "Good morning, Mr. Grayson."

"Morning, Stanford. This is Mr. James Drake and my daughter, Miss Isabella Grayson."

Stanford nodded to them, then held out a stack of folders. "Mr. Larson left these papers for you, and Mr. Clifton is waiting in your office."

James blinked. Mark Clifton? What was he doing here? He darted a glance at Bella, and from the surprised look she gave her father, it appeared she was not expecting to see him, either.

"I'll take those papers." Mr. Grayson held out his hand for the files, and Stanford passed them to him. Mr. Grayson opened the door to his inner office and motioned Bella and James to enter ahead of him.

Mark Clifton rose from his chair and greeted Mr. Grayson with an outstretched hand. "Good day, sir. I'm sorry I was a bit early."

"Don't apologize. I'm glad you're here. We can start the tour without delay."

"Hello, Isabella." Clifton leaned toward her, kissed her on one cheek and then on the other.

James clenched his jaw and bit back his irritation. That might be the way the French greeted each other, but this was London, not Paris, and Clifton should not take advantage of the custom.

Clifton shifted his gaze to James with a slight lift of his chin. "Hello, Drake. I didn't expect to see you here today."

James straightened. "Yes, I'm sure you didn't."

"Not that I'm displeased, not at all. It gives me another opportunity to get to know my competitor. And as they say, understanding the competition is the first step toward winning the battle."

Bella's questioning gaze shifted from Clifton to James.

Another round of irritation shot through James, heating his neck and face, but for Bella's sake he swallowed the reply rising in his throat.

Her father seemed oblivious and motioned toward the door. "Shall we start the tour?"

"Yes. I'm eager to see it all." But Bella's tone suggested she sensed the tension between James and Clifton.

"We'll go to Horace Elmwood's office first. He's our senior editor. We've worked together since we started publishing *Comic Cuts* in the nineties."

James had read *Comic Cuts* when he was younger. It was an amusing, inexpensive newspaper filled with human-interest stories. It had a higher moral tone than the penny dreadfuls, and it was famous for running unusual contests to try to boost circulation.

Mr. Grayson opened the next door on the left, and a young man greeted them and showed them into the editor's office.

"Morning, Horace." Mr. Grayson introduced them to Mr. Elmwood.

The editor set aside his cigar and rose from his chair. He was a rotund man with thinning gray hair and a rather large red nose. He shook hands with the men and nodded to Bella. "So, what brings you all to the *Daily Mail*?"

"Father is giving us the grand tour." Bella's warm smile made it clear she was pleased with her father's plan.

Amusement lit the editor's eyes. "I'm surprised your father hasn't shown you around before now."

"As I'm sure you know, my father is a very busy man. But I'm pleased he's making time for us today."

Elmwood grinned, obviously enjoying Bella's gracious reply and charming smile. "Well, Charles, I believe it's past time you showed your daughter and her friends how you made your fortune, or I should say *our* fortunes."

"Yes, very clever, Horace. That's just what I intend to do. They'll see it all, from the newsroom to the loading dock." Mr. Grayson motioned toward the window. "But before we go, you might like to take a look at the view. Mine isn't nearly as nice."

"You don't spend as much time in your office as I do in mine." Elmwood lowered himself into his chair.

"True, but I hope you appreciate that I gave you the nicest office with the best view."

Elmwood gave a grudging nod, but humor lit his eyes. "I suppose that helps make up for all the time and energy I pour into this newspaper."

Mr. Grayson chuckled. "It should."

Mr. Grayson and Elmwood continued their good-natured banter while Bella, James, and Clifton walked over to the window.

Bella gazed out at the London skyline. "Is that the spire of Saint Bride's?"

"I believe so." James shifted his gaze to the street below.

"Look at the crowd where Ludgate Circus meets Fleet Street." Bella continued to gaze out the window.

"It is quite a sight," Clifton added. "And it's nice to share it with such a charming companion."

Bella's cheeks flushed, and a smile tucked in the corners of her mouth.

James stifled a groan. Did Clifton always use flattery to try to impress women? Was Bella actually swayed by it?

Mr. Grayson joined them at the window and pointed out a few sights. Then he motioned toward the door. "Off we go. Our next stop is the newsroom."

James, Bella, and Clifton followed Mr. Grayson out into the hallway. They took the stairs down to the next floor and entered the large newsroom. Four rows of desks filled the long open space. Typewriters clacked away, and cigarette smoke hung heavy in the air. Several men sat hunched over notepads, scribbling away, while others stood in small groups, smoking and discussing the latest news.

Mr. Grayson introduced them to a few reporters and three staff editors, and Bella looked as though she was soaking up every bit of information her father offered.

As they walked down the last aisle, Mr. Grayson pointed to the doors on the right. "Those are our meeting rooms where the editors gather to plan their sections each morning. And that is our telegraph room. We're connected with the international wire service to receive news and information from around the world."

Clifton turned to Mr. Grayson. "How quickly can a story reach you?"

"If news breaks on the continent, we'll hear about it in a matter of hours, sometimes even minutes."

"That's amazing, isn't it?" Bella glanced up at James.

"It certainly is." James and Bella peeked through the window into the telegraph room where four men were seated at desks, recording the incoming information.

"Let's head down to the next floor." Mr. Grayson motioned toward the stairs at the end of the room.

Clifton moved into place next to Bella as they approached the stairs. "You've really never seen all of this before?"

"No, I've been to my father's office, and we stopped in to see the new presses last year, but I've never visited the newsroom or met any of the reporters or editors."

Clifton nodded, and James pondered her reply. It did seem odd that Mr. Grayson hadn't shown Bella the inner workings of the newspaper before today, especially when she seemed so interested in everything they'd seen.

Mr. Grayson pushed open the door, and they walked into the next room. Several large machines lined the wall on their right. Men sat in front of each machine, fingering what looked like a keyboard of some sort.

James stepped closer to Mr. Grayson. "What are they doing?"

"These men take the articles written by the reporters and set the type, line by line, for each page."

"That sounds like a tedious job," Clifton remarked.

"Actually, these Linotype machines are great time-saving devices. The men used to set each individual letter, but this method is four times faster."

"My goodness." Bella motioned to the nearest man seated at one of the machines. "Can you imagine setting the entire newspaper letter by letter? That would be exhausting."

They followed her father toward one of the large machines to take a closer look. One of the typesetters stopped and showed them the process. Bella asked him several questions, which he seemed happy to answer.

Then Mr. Grayson led them across the hall to the advertising, sales, and circulation departments, where at least twenty men and a few women worked at desks crowded into a large square room. It was quieter than the newsroom, and James wondered if it might be because of the presence of the ladies.

Clifton asked about the circulation, and Mr. Grayson proudly told them they'd sold 523,000 copies the previous week, which set a new record for the *Daily Mail*.

They took the stairs again and walked down to the main floor.

Mr. Grayson stopped at a heavy metal door, looked through the glass window, then turned back to them. "The presses are running, so it will be quite loud beyond this door. We won't be able to ask questions, and you must be sure to stay close to me. We don't want to upset the pressmen or put anyone in danger. Do you understand?"

They all nodded. Bella and James exchanged smiles, and they followed Mr. Grayson and Clifton through the doorway.

The clamor coming from the presses was surprisingly loud. Six huge presses, at least ten feet high, stood like giants around the cavernous pressroom. Large rolls of newsprint were attached at the end of each machine. The paper wove in and through the presses, and was printed on both sides. Then, it shot through to another area where it was collated. Finally, it fanned out on a conveyer belt as a complete, folded newspaper.

"That's amazing!" James called above the din.

Bella nodded her agreement, her sparkling eyes reflecting her delight.

Mr. Grayson motioned for them to follow him through the pressroom and out the doorway on the far side. "This is our warehouse and loading dock." He pointed toward the large open area where stacks of newspapers were bundled and ready to be loaded on carts and wagons.

"We plan to purchase new motorized trucks later this year. That should help our papers reach the delivery points much more quickly."

Clifton nodded. "That's an excellent idea. You don't want to let the competing newspapers beat you to that improvement."

"Precisely! The *Daily Mail* must be the most up-to-date and efficient operation in London." Mr. Grayson motioned them to follow him, and they walked back through the pressroom and out into the lobby.

"Well, what do you think?" Mr. Grayson's gaze darted from Clifton to James, looking as though he anticipated their positive comments.

"It's marvelous!" Bella's gaze swept the lobby and rose to the floors above. "Thank you, Father. I had no idea it took so many people to publish the *Daily Mail*." Bella glanced to the left, past the reception desk. "What's inside that office over there?"

"Oh, that's just the file room and our research library." Mr. Grayson dismissed it with a sweep of his hand. "We keep copies of our past newspapers, and we have all kinds of reference materials in there for the reporters. It really ought to be up on the same floor as the newsroom, but we didn't have space for it there."

Bella nodded, her gaze lingering on the one area they had not toured.

James narrowed his gaze as an idea formed in his mind. "May we take a look?"

"Yes, of course, if you're interested." Mr. Grayson motioned in that direction, as if dismissing them to view the room on their own.

Before they could step away, Clifton looked at his watch. "I'm sorry, but I must take my leave. My cousin is arriving from France today, and I'm meeting his train at Victoria Station at one o'clock."

"That's too bad," Mr. Grayson said. "I was hoping you'd be able to join us for luncheon."

"I would've enjoyed that." Clifton shifted his gaze to Bella. "But I'm afraid it will have to be another time."

"That cousin you're meeting," Mr. Grayson added, "is he the one who invented the Antoinette engine?"

"Yes, Pierre Levasseur. We'll be working on our airplane and taking our test flights only a few miles from Broadlands, near Dover." Clifton sent James a smug look. "I believe you're flying in that area, as well."

"That's right. We're at Green Meadow Farm on the Broadlands estate."

Mr. Grayson nodded. "Anywhere near Dover is a good location to prepare for your flight across the Channel." He shifted his focus to James. "What about you, Mr. Drake? Can you stay and join us for luncheon?"

James wished he could, especially since it would give him more time with Bella without Clifton seated between them, but he couldn't accept today. "I'm sorry. The professor is expecting me to meet him at our house. We plan to return to Kent this afternoon, if possible."

Clifton stepped closer to Bella. "Perhaps you'd like to join me and my cousin this evening for dinner?"

James tensed. Surely Clifton knew a young unmarried woman could not meet a man for dinner without a family member or chaperone present. It wasn't even proper for him to ask.

As if Clifton had read James's mind, he added, "Of course your family is welcome to dine with us."

She hesitated and sent her father a questioning look, but James couldn't tell if she was pleased by the prospect or simply surprised.

"That's a splendid idea." Mr. Grayson rose up on his toes. "I'd like to meet this cousin of yours and hear more about his engines and his plans for the flight across the Channel."

Bella's smile returned. "I'd be pleased to meet him as well. Thank you, Mr. Clifton."

James's stomach dropped. It seemed Bella and her father were both eager to have dinner with Clifton and his French cousin. Would they shift their support to Clifton and Levasseur for the race across the Channel?

Clifton suggested the time and place to meet, and Mr. Grayson agreed. James watched Clifton go, relieved he was on his way, but he didn't like the thought that Bella and her family would be back in Clifton's company that evening.

"I suppose I should be going as well." James turned to Mr. Grayson. "Thank you. I enjoyed the tour. The *Daily Mail* is an impressive operation. It's obvious your leadership is responsible for making it such an influential and successful publication."

Mr. Grayson shook his hand. "Thank you, Mr. Drake."

Bella glanced at James. "Shall we take a look at that last room before you go?"

"All right."

Mr. Grayson checked his watch. "I have to prepare for a meeting. Take a quick look at the research library, then meet me up in my office. Good day to you, Mr. Drake." Bella's father turned away and headed for the lift.

Bella lifted her gaze to meet James's. "I'm sorry you won't be able to join us for lunch or dinner tonight. I'm sure there's much you could discuss with Mr.

Clifton and his cousin." Her sincere expression and kind words soothed away his frustration.

"I would like to meet Pierre Levasseur, but my deepest regret is not being able to spend the evening with you."

She smiled, then ducked her chin. "Mr. Drake—"

"Please, I hope you'll consider me a friend and call me James."

She looked up and met his gaze. "All right, and you may call me Bella."

His heartbeat kicked up a notch. "Bella it is." He nodded to her, happy she seemed as pleased with the prospect as he was.

They crossed the lobby and looked through the window into the research library. Rows of cabinets filled one side, while bookshelves and flat open shelves lined the other. Newspapers hung from wooden dowels on a long rack to the left, and a rectangular table with four chairs took up the center of the room.

"Would you like to go in?" Bella asked.

"Yes, I would." James opened the door, and Bella passed through first. He left the door open and followed her in.

James crossed to the bookshelves and scanned the titles. Atlases, census records, directories, and a few copies of *Burke's Peerage and Baronetage* were lined up on the shelves. All the titled families in Great Britain and those who owned ancestral estates were listed in those books, along with a brief history of each family.

Would his mother's family be listed there? Now that he knew her last name was Markingham, not Drake, he might be able to learn more about her if he dared to look. And what about his father? He supposed his last name was probably Drake. Would he be listed there as well?

"Find something interesting?" Bella's soft voice was very near.

James pulled in a quick breath. "No, not really."

She sent him a quizzical look, and he could feel the heat radiating into his face. For a split second he considered telling her the questions running through his mind, but he quickly dismissed that thought. What would she think of him if she knew about his parents and his past?

Bella tipped her head, reading the titles of the books on the shelf. "Think of all the stories you could find here." She smiled. "I could get lost in a room like this."

"Yes, I'm sure there are many untold stories in the pages of those books."

She gave a satisfied sigh and looked his way again. "Well, I don't want to keep you. I know you and Professor Steed must be eager to return to Kent."

He knew he should go, but he found himself torn. "I enjoyed the tour and our conversation."

She pressed her lips together and dipped her chin, but that didn't hide her smile. "I've enjoyed it as well."

"I hope you'll visit our workshop again. You'd be welcome anytime."

She looked up. "Thank you. I'd like that."

"We'll have the engine remounted in a day or two, and then I'll be flying again."

Her smile spread wider. "I definitely don't want to miss that."

His spirits soared. "All right, then. I'll see you soon." He tipped his hat to her and strode out of the room, his mood brighter than it had been in a long while.

Six

Bella's feet felt so light, she practically floated through the front door of her family's London home in Belgravia. James had invited her back to Green Meadow to watch him fly, and she couldn't wait to follow up on his invitation as soon as they returned to Broadlands. Not only would it be thrilling to see him take his airplane up again; it would give her more firsthand information for her article.

Surely her father's decision to give her a tour of the *Daily Mail* meant he was taking her interest in becoming a journalist seriously. Now all she needed to do was pen her first story and convince her father and Mr. Elmwood to publish it.

"Oh, good. You're finally home." Sylvia hurried down the stairs and met Bella in the entrance hall. "Wait until you see the lovely hats Mother and I bought today."

"I thought you were going to the dressmaker's." Bella pulled off her gloves and unpinned her hat.

"We did go there first, but on our way home we saw a new millinery shop on Strathmore Street and decided to stop in and look for hats to go with some of my new dresses."

Father followed Bella through the entrance hall. He removed his coat and hat and handed them to Bradford, their London butler, then turned toward Sylvia. "Where is your mother?"

"I think she's in the drawing room."

He glanced at the butler and lifted one eyebrow.

Bradford nodded. "She just called for tea, sir."

"Very good." Father strode off toward the drawing room.

"Come upstairs, and I'll show you the new hats."

Bella glanced toward the drawing room and back at her sister. "I need to speak to Mother and Father first."

"You sound very serious. Is everything all right?"

"Yes, but say a prayer for me. I'm going to press my case and try to convince them to let me write those aviation articles for the *Daily Mail*."

"Oh that's wonderful!" Sylvia squeezed Bella's hand. "You have the talent to be an award-winning journalist. I'm sure of it."

"Thank you." Bella pulled Sylvia close for a hug. "I can always count on you to boost my spirits."

Sylvia stepped back. "Come up as soon as you're done. I want to hear what they say." She sent Bella an encouraging smile, then trotted up the stairs.

Bella pulled in a deep breath. *Lord, please help my parents have open minds. And please give me a chance to prove I can write articles that will make them proud.* She straightened her shoulders and walked toward the drawing room.

When she entered, she found her father standing by the fireplace and her mother seated in a chair to his left. They seemed to be in the middle of an intense conversation, but they fell silent as she walked toward them.

Her mother sent her father a quick glance, then motioned to the chair opposite hers. "Sit down, Bella. Your father and I have something we want to discuss with you."

A shiver of anticipation traveled down Bella's arms as she settled into the chair. What were they going to say? Whatever it was, she should probably listen to them first before she brought up the idea of writing articles again.

"Did you enjoy your time at the *Daily Mail*?" Mother's tone seemed to suggest there was something more behind her question.

"Yes, it was very interesting. The place practically hums with energy. I can see why Father is so drawn to newspaper publishing."

"And you had a pleasant time with your . . . companion?" Mother smiled and lifted her eyebrows.

Understanding flashed through Bella, and heat filled her cheeks. So, her mother had known Mark Clifton was going to meet her father at his office. That must be why she'd agreed Bella could go along. Her parents had hoped it would give her another opportunity to get to know him.

Well, two could play this game. Bella met her mother's gaze. "I was surprised and pleased to see them both."

"Both?" Her mother blinked and looked at her father.

He cleared his throat. "Yes, we met James Drake at the station, after we sent you off with Sylvia, and I invited him to come along."

Her mother shifted in her chair. "Well, I suppose you had to include him."

"Yes, I did. If he's the first to fly across the Channel, he may very well become a national hero. I don't want to offend someone like that."

"No, of course not." She fixed her gaze on Bella's father and gave a slight nod, as though urging him to continue.

He lowered his chin and sent Bella a serious look. "Your mother and I are concerned about you, Bella. You'll be twenty-one in a few months, and it's time for you to think seriously about getting married and settling down in your own home."

Bella's stomach tensed. This was not the direction she wanted to take the conversation, but if she argued with them, they would never agree to let her write anything except thank-you notes for wedding gifts.

She pulled in a slow, deep breath and carefully formulated her words. "I understand your concern, truly I do. But I don't think I need to rush into marriage simply because I'll be turning twenty-one."

"It would hardly be rushing. This will be your third season." Mother lifted her hand to her forehead. "And if you don't find a husband this year . . ."

Bella swallowed hard. She didn't want to upset her parents or frustrate their plans for her, but she couldn't imagine marrying any of the men she'd met in London the previous two seasons. She had little in common with any of them, and she suspected if she wasn't going to receive a large inheritance, they would not be the least bit interested in her. What was she supposed to do? She couldn't just snap her fingers and make an interesting, worthy man step forward and propose.

Her mother leaned forward. "You must promise you'll make the most of this season and encourage suitable men like Mark Clifton."

Bella shifted her gaze away as her thoughts tugged her in one direction and then another. She had enjoyed her conversations with Mark Clifton. He was charming, and he seemed genuinely interested in her. He came from a prominent family, and he was adventurous and attentive. She'd been pleased with his invitation to dinner this evening. But was that enough to recommend him as her future husband? What about his character and reputation? Would he be a loyal husband and kind father? Would he love her and care about her hopes and dreams?

She wouldn't really know unless she spent more time with him. An idea rose in her mind, and it sent a tremor through her. Did she dare suggest it to her parents? They seemed insistent that she find a husband, and she might be able to use their hopes to her advantage.

She looked at her parents again. "I understand what you're saying, and if I promise to encourage suitors this season, will you agree to let me write that series of articles about aviation for the *Daily Mail*?"

Her mother gasped. "No! Absolutely not! That would make you a magnet for gossip and ruin your chances of making a good match."

Her father lifted his hand. "Now, Madelyn, let's not be too hasty." He narrowed his eyes and studied Bella. "There may be some merit to the idea."

Bella sat up straighter, hope rising in her heart.

"Merit?" Her mother's face flushed. "Charles, if you allow our daughter to join the staff at the *Daily Mail,* no respectable man will want to call on her, let alone propose marriage!"

Her father's brow knit, and he shifted his gaze from Bella to her mother. "I didn't say I wanted her to join the staff. I'm simply thinking about those articles." He rubbed his chin, and his expression relaxed. "Perhaps we can come up with a compromise."

"A compromise?" Her mother's tone made it clear she was not in favor of the idea.

"If your mother and I agree to let you write the articles, you would have to write them under a pseudonym and keep your authorship a secret."

Mother's mouth dropped open. "Charles!"

Joy burst in Bella's heart. "You're saying I can write them?"

"Yes, you may," her father continued in a serious tone, "*but* only if you'll promise to encourage your suitors this season *and* accept a marriage proposal from a man we approve of by December thirty-first."

Bella bit her lip. For years, she'd longed for the opportunity to write articles that would capture people's imagination and promote progress and changes for the better. And now her dream was within reach—if she would agree to her father's conditions.

Could she tie herself to those promises?

Once she made the decision, there would be no going back. If she said yes, that would mean fully taking part in the season with the goal of finding a husband and securing a proposal before the end of the year.

Mark Clifton seemed interested, and her parents obviously thought he would be a good match. But he wasn't the only prospect. With her family's wealth and connections, she and Sylvia would be introduced to many other young men when the season got underway.

James Drake's image rose in her mind, stirring her heart. Of all the men she'd met, he was the most intriguing. She admired him for so many reasons, and today, when they toured the *Daily Mail,* she thought she'd sensed a special connection with him. Had he sensed it too?

Doubt rose in her mind, stealing away her hope. She was probably just imagining the connection because she wished he would find her as unique and interesting as she found him. If he were interested in her, would her parents approve of him? She knew less about his background and family than she knew about Mark Clifton's.

"Well, Bella, what do you say?"

"Charles, I don't think this is a good idea." Her mother rose from her chair. "How can you consider allowing Bella to write for the *Daily Mail* when—"

"That's enough, Madelyn! I've made up my mind." Her father shifted his serious gaze to Bella. "Will you agree to encourage suitors and accept a proposal this year in exchange for the opportunity to submit your articles?"

Bella clenched her hands, still debating her reply.

"And you must remember," he continued, "I can't guarantee their publication. Horace Elmwood will decide if they're well written and if they fit the style and editorial direction of the paper."

Bella's heartbeat pounded in her ears. What if she did her best and the articles were not accepted? What if she put herself in this difficult position for nothing? And what if she did all that she could to attract a husband, but she still didn't receive a proposal? Would her parents extend the deadline or release her from the promise?

Either way, achieving her dream was worth the risk.

She stood and faced her parents. "All right, I agree to your conditions. I'll encourage suitors this season and put my best effort into writing those articles."

A gruff smile lifted the corners of her father's mouth. "That's a wise decision, Bella. I'm sure it will all work out for the best."

Bella darted a glance at her mother. Her face was pale, and a worried frown creased her forehead, but Bella wouldn't let that discourage her. Her father had agreed she could submit her articles to the *Daily Mail,* and now nothing would stop her from becoming a real journalist.

⁕

James rested his chin in his hand and stirred his spoon through the thick beef stew. Flames leaped and crackled in the kitchen fireplace of the professor's London home, but it did little to lift James's mood.

Across town, Bella was having dinner with Mark Clifton and his French cousin. The thought made the few bites of stew he'd eaten feel like sour lumps in his stomach. Clifton was probably entertaining her with more stories about his world travels and prize-winning escapades. Could they all be true, or did he inflate those tales to try to impress Bella?

A sinking feeling washed over James. Clifton probably had won all those races and led that expedition to Abyssinia. At this very moment, he and his engine-designing cousin were probably persuading Mr. Grayson to give his full support to their aviation efforts. Clifton was a charmer, a smooth talker, and incredibly well bred, and there was no doubt he could be very persuasive.

James blew out a deep breath and tried to shake off those gloomy thoughts.

"What's wrong, James?" Hannah tipped her head and sent him a concerned look. "Don't you like the stew?"

"Oh, there's nothing wrong with the stew. I'm just not very hungry tonight."

The professor lifted his eyebrows. "Not hungry? Are you feeling unwell?"

"No, I'm fine." James shifted in the chair and tried to come up with an explanation. "I thought we'd be back in Kent tonight."

The professor took a slice of bread from the serving platter. "With the weather turning so cold and stormy, I thought you wouldn't mind staying in London one night and sleeping in a warm, comfortable bed."

"I don't mind. But Mr. Grayson invited me to have lunch with them, and I turned him down because I thought we were in a hurry to get back to Green Meadow."

"Ah . . . I see." The professor and Hannah exchanged a look.

She sent James a tender smile. "I'm sorry you missed your chance to spend more time with that nice young lady."

James sent the professor a heated look. He must have told Hannah about Bella, because James hadn't said a word about her.

"There's no need to scowl at me like that. I simply mentioned that you seemed to enjoy the time you've spent with Miss Grayson." The professor lifted his eyebrows. "That's true, isn't it?"

"Yes, but there was no need to say anything to Hannah. I don't have much of a chance."

Hannah sent him a cautious glance. "Why would you say that?"

James huffed. "Her father owns three newspapers and has an estate that rivals those owned by royalty. I doubt he'd allow someone like me to call on his daughter."

"I don't see why not." The professor scooped up his next spoonful of stew. "You're an up-and-coming aviator and the protégé of the finest airplane designer in England."

"Very funny."

The professor met his gaze. "I am trying to lighten your mood, but I'm not making light of your situation. You're a fine young man, James, with excellent prospects. There's no reason why you shouldn't develop your friendship with Isabella Grayson and see what the Lord has in mind."

James shook his head. How could the professor say that? It wasn't only his lack of income that threw a shadow over his future. It was the stain of his past. His illegitimate birth, his mother's mysterious death, and his father's abandonment built an impossibly high wall between him and any hope of a future with Bella.

James rose and snatched his bowl off the table. "A wealthy, powerful man like Charles Grayson would never consider me a suitable match for his daughter."

"You're always too hard on yourself." The professor's tone was dismissive, as though James's concerns meant nothing.

James swung around, heat pulsing into his face. "Think about it! I know next to nothing about my parents, except they were not married, and my father didn't even care enough to support my mother after she became pregnant and was forced out by her parents."

The professor's spoon stilled halfway to his mouth. He stared at James, pain glittering in his eyes.

Regret washed over James for his harsh tone, but those were the facts and it was time they faced them.

"Who told you that?" The professor slid a glance at Hannah.

"I found this in the attic when we were here last week." He pulled his mother's photograph from his pocket and held it out to the professor. "It was in a hatbox with my baby clothes and a letter she addressed to me."

The professor stared at the photo, then slowly reached out and took it from James's hand.

James swallowed hard. "Hannah told me some of the story, but she said you'd have to tell me the rest."

The professor shifted his painful gaze to Hannah.

She lifted her hands. "I'm sorry. But he's older now and he wanted to know about his family."

"We are his family!" The professor's voice shook.

James returned to the table and sat across from the professor. "That's true. You'll always be my family, but I want to know about my parents and what happened between them before my mother's death."

Lines deepened around the professor's eyes and across his forehead.

James leaned forward. "You've given me so much, my very life, and I'm truly grateful. No one can ever take your place. But I need to know the truth about my mother and father."

The professor blew out a slow, shaky breath. "I knew we'd have this conversation someday, but I certainly didn't expect it would be tonight."

James clasped his hands under the table and waited. He respected the professor, loved him like a father, but he would not back down this time. For years, questions about his past had lingered in his mind, and not knowing the answers had carved a hole in his very being. It was time he heard the rest of the story. Every shameful secret needed to be brought into the light if he was ever going to feel whole. "Please tell me what you know."

The professor released a weary sigh. "What did your mother say in the letter?"

James opened his wallet, carefully unfolded the sheet of stationery, and held it out to the professor.

He adjusted his spectacles and slowly scanned the page. When he finished, he looked up at James. "I knew about the box. Anna's friend gave it to me after Anna passed, but I didn't know it contained the letter or photograph."

James gave a slight nod, relieved that the professor had not purposely kept those from him.

"Your mother, Laura, was a lovely young woman, the youngest daughter of a wealthy nobleman, and just eighteen years old when you were born. She had two older sisters. I believe their names were Judith and Maryann. My sister, Anna, worked for the family as a nurserymaid and then a housemaid for a few years while the girls were growing up. Anna was always fond of Laura, and when Laura's family cast her out and she needed help, she turned to Anna."

James sat back and bit the inside of his cheek. It still stung thinking about his mother's family turning their backs on her at a time like that.

"I'm sure you remember Anna was a very loving soul. She took Laura into her home and cared for her and for you."

James nodded. He'd learned most of those facts from Hannah, but the information about his grandfather and aunts was new. "What happened to my mother?"

The professor glanced at Hannah and looked as though he were trying to discern how much she'd told James.

She bit her lip and looked away.

"Your mother died when she fell from a cliff at Saint Margaret's Bay. You were only four months old at the time. Anna contacted Laura's father and told him about the accident and that you were in her care, but he never replied to her letter."

James clenched his jaw. He'd known his father had deserted him, but he hadn't realized his grandfather had also shunned him when he was only an infant.

"So Anna continued caring for you, loving you, and giving you a fine start in life." The professor sent him a weak smile. "And when she left us, I took on that role and raised you as my own son." His voice choked off. He blinked a few times and looked away.

James's throat tightened. "I'm grateful for all you've done. I couldn't have asked for a finer upbringing."

The professor's expression eased. "I did my best for you then, and I hope to continue that for many more years."

James nodded. "What do you know about my father?"

The professor's mouth firmed. "Only that he must be a very hard-hearted man to ignore your mother's pleas for help. I still don't know how he could shirk his responsibility, not just once, but twice!"

James frowned. "What do you mean?"

"Anna told me Laura was in contact with him a few days before her death. He knew her situation, where she was staying, and how they were running low on funds, but he refused to help her."

"Do you know his name?"

"I assume his last name is Drake, like yours, but I'm not certain."

"No first name or address?"

The professor shook his head. "Anna knew those details, but she never told me. And since he seemed unwilling to acknowledge you or offer his support, I saw no reason to try to find him."

James gave a slow nod, taking in the professor's explanation and trying to push away the hurt that went with it. There was one important topic the professor had skipped over. James lifted his gaze and met the professor's. "What else can you tell me about my mother's death?"

The professor hesitated. "The police said it was an accident. It had been raining that day. She went out for a walk, and the ground was slippery. She probably stepped too close to the edge and lost her footing."

"And you believe that?"

"I have no reason not to."

"But in the letter she seemed to know she might not live to see me grow up. It sounded as though she was fearful of something happening to her."

The professor lowered his gaze and studied the letter again. "I suppose you could read it that way."

"Do you think her family or . . . my father might have wanted to harm her?"

The professor straightened. "That's a dreadful thought."

"What other explanation could there be . . . except . . ." James couldn't put words to that possibility.

Tears shimmered in Hannah's eyes, and she shook her head. "Surely she wouldn't take her own life, not with you in her arms, not when she loved you as much as she did."

The professor's eyes flashed. And it was clear he hadn't wanted James to know his mother had been holding him when she fell.

"It's all right. Hannah told me that part as well."

"I'm sure that was not your mother's intention." His voice was firm. "She and Anna visited us only a few days before the accident. She was hopeful about the future and obviously smitten with you."

"But you said they were running low on funds."

"Yes, I offered them a place in my home if they needed it. Laura was grateful, and Anna was agreeable as well. We were still talking about that possibility at the time of the accident."

James mulled over everything the professor had told him, but the question remained—was his mother's death a tragic accident as the professor and Hannah believed, or had someone tried to kill him and his mother by pushing them off that cliff?

***

Bella took the next book from her stack, opened it, and scanned the table of contents. It looked like there might be some helpful information about French aviation in the third chapter. She flipped to that section, began reading, and jotted down a few notes.

The outline of her first article was almost complete. She planned to include a brief history of aviation, give a firsthand account of Wilbur Wright's demonstration at Le Mans, and then tell how that event had sparked the rapid development of airplane designs on the continent and in Britain. She hoped to inform and inspire readers but also leave them wanting to know more. Most of all she hoped her father would be pleased with her ideas.

Sylvia peeked through the library doorway and smiled when she spotted Bella. "Are you still working on your article?"

"The outline, yes." Bella looked up, but she didn't lay aside her pen.

"You've been at it since after breakfast. Don't you think it's time for a break?"

"I want to gather all the information I can here. Then I'll know what I need to find when we return to London."

"You're going to get a crick in your neck if you're not careful."

Bella lifted a hand and massaged her shoulder. "I'll be all right. I have to finish the outline so I can show Father when he comes home tomorrow night."

Sylvia looked over Bella's shoulder. "My goodness, you have pages and pages of notes. Surely that's enough."

"Remember, I have to impress Mr. Elmwood, the editor of the *Daily Mail,* as well as Father."

"Oh, I'm sure they'll both love your articles." Sylvia smiled and held up a folded note. "I have something that may tempt you to set it all aside for a while."

"What's that?"

"Martha Shelby invited the 'ladies of the house' to come to Green Meadow for tea this afternoon." She passed Bella the note.

Bella's thoughts skipped ahead as she read the invitation. A visit with Martha might give her a chance to see James as well. And she might learn something new she could include in her article.

"If we're free she'd like us to come at four." Sylvia glanced at the desk where Bella had spread out her papers and books. "Please say you'll come with me. You can always finish this later."

"What about Mother?"

Sylvia sighed. "She has a headache, but she said she wouldn't mind if we went without her."

Bella glanced back at her notes. She'd looked through every book in the Broadlands library that mentioned aviation, and she'd scanned several issues of *Flight*. Her father had saved every issue since the first one had rolled off the press.

Bella lifted her gaze to Sylvia. "You're right. It's time to take a break, and a visit to Martha Shelby is exactly what we need."

"Wonderful! Why don't I order the governess cart, and we can drive over around three thirty?"

"That sounds perfect." Bella rose from her chair.

"I'll go up and tell Mother." Sylvia started for the door, but she stopped and looked over her shoulder with a teasing grin. "I wonder if we'll see that handsome aviator of yours."

Bella started to protest, but she'd already admitted she admired James Drake. There was no use pretending it wasn't true. She returned Sylvia's smile. "I hope we do."

"So do I!" her sister said, then hurried out the door.

An hour later, they drove through the estate and up the winding road toward Green Meadow Farm. As Bella guided the horse past the long stone workshop, she looked for James, but the doors were closed and no one was in sight.

Disappointment tugged at her heart. She pushed it away and drove on. Pulling back on the reins, she parked the governess cart by Martha's front gate, then climbed down and tied the horse to the gatepost.

Sylvia climbed down and joined Bella. "Isn't this the sweetest little cottage? Look at the way the ivy climbs the front wall."

Bella's gaze traveled over Martha's thatched roof and the tidy front and side gardens. "Yes, it's lovely." A moss-covered stone wall encircled the house, and smoke rose from the brick chimney, giving the air a pleasant, welcoming scent.

Bella picked up the bouquet of flowers they'd brought with them, and they walked up the path toward Martha's front door.

Her sister glanced back at the workshop, the teasing light in her eyes again. "It looks like your aviator must be hard at work inside today."

"You must promise to stop calling him that," Bella replied in a hushed tone.

"If you insist."

"I do, especially while we visit Mrs. Shelby."

"All right. If you say so." But Sylvia's smile left Bella wondering if she would keep her word.

Bella knocked on the front door. A few seconds later the door opened and Martha looked out at them with a warm smile. "Well, here you are! I'm so pleased you could come."

"Thank you. We're grateful for your invitation."

Martha looked past Bella's shoulder. "Your mother is not with you?"

"No, she sends her regrets. She's not feeling well."

"I'm sorry to hear that."

"It's just a headache," Sylvia said. "She's plagued by them, but we hope it won't last too long."

Bella grimaced, certain her mother would not want Sylvia mentioning the specifics of her illness.

Martha pulled the door open wider. "Please come inside, sit by the fire, and warm yourselves. I'll put on the tea."

Bella offered her the bouquet. "We brought you these flowers."

"Oh my, they're lovely. You don't often see flowers like these in the winter."

"They're from our greenhouse," Sylvia added. "Our gardeners grow flowers year round, and we can pick a bouquet whenever we'd like."

Martha's eyes glowed as she accepted the colorful bouquet. "Thank you. I'll put them in water and fetch our tea." She walked off toward her kitchen.

Bella and Sylvia settled in two comfortable chairs near the fireplace in Martha's sitting room. Bella glanced around, noting a tall bookshelf on the right side of the stone fireplace. On the left was an inviting window seat with several embroidered cushions. It looked like the perfect spot for reading. Small pots of African violets were lined up on the windowsill next to the front door, and a braided rug covered the center of the room's wooden floor.

It was a cozy, comfortable home, and as Bella looked around, she felt as though she'd been here before. Then she realized it reminded her of their old house in London on Hanford Street. They'd only lived there for a few years when she was young, but Bella could still picture each room. Her father didn't own any newspapers then, and he hadn't yet gained his fortune. He'd worked as a reporter and spent many evenings reading books aloud to her and Sylvia, and enjoying time with the family. Her mother had been surrounded by friends, and her health had been better. Those were simpler, happier times, or at least they seemed so as Bella looked back on them.

Martha returned with a tea tray and set it on the low table in front of Bella and Sylvia. She poured tea from a steaming pot and offered them small egg sandwiches and scones with strawberry jam and clotted cream.

Bella bit into a scone and savored the sweet, buttery treat. "These are wonderful. The jam tastes so fresh."

Martha smiled. "Thank you. That's my mother's recipe. The berries were grown right here on our farm."

"They're delicious." Sylvia scooped another spoonful of jam onto her scone.

Martha's gaze traveled from Bella to Sylvia. "So, I hope you're feeling settled at Broadlands."

"We're beginning to feel at home," Bella said, as she added a sandwich to her plate.

Sylvia took a sip of her tea. "Broadlands is certainly much grander than any of our other homes."

"Is that so?"

"Yes, we lived in London year round until we came to Broadlands," Sylvia continued. "Our home there is spacious and in a fine neighborhood, but nothing like Broadlands."

Bella didn't think her parents would be pleased with Sylvia's comments. It was time to steer the conversation in a different direction. She glanced at the lace curtains hanging on the front windows, the family photographs on the wall, and the comfortable furniture. "You have a lovely home."

"Oh, it's a fine old place, just right for me." Martha stirred sugar into her tea. "I was worried when I heard Sir Richard was selling Broadlands. I thought the new owner might not want an old woman like me farming his land. I'm pleased your father agreed to let me stay on."

"Our estate agent advised Father to retain the tenants, and he is happy to see things carry on as they did with Sir Richard."

"That's good of him. He seems like a fine man. Tell me more about your father."

Bella thought for a moment before answering. "My father is a newspaper publisher and the owner of the *Daily Mail,* the *Evening Standard,* and the *London Herald.* He doesn't spend too much time working with the staff at the *Standard* or *Herald,* but he's very much involved in the production of the *Daily Mail.* That keeps him quite busy. We hope our move to Broadlands will give him more time to rest and focus on his health as well as enjoy country life."

Martha sipped her tea. "There's no finer country estate than Broadlands. Fresh air, clean water, and nourishing food from his own land. That should be good for his health."

Bella nodded and placed her teacup in the saucer. Would country life make a difference for her father? He hadn't slowed his pace since the move. If anything, he'd spent more time away from home, traveling back and forth to London to take care of business there.

"And your mother?"

"She is a great support to my father, and she's a talented artist, though she doesn't paint as often as she used to."

Sylvia brushed a crumb from the napkin in her lap. "Her headaches have grown worse over the years, and they prevent her from doing many things she used to do."

Bella sent her sister a warning glance, but Sylvia caught it too late. Her sister's cheeks turned pink, and she looked down and took another bite of her scone.

"And what about you, Bella? Do you paint like your mother?"

"No, I didn't inherit my mother's artistic talent, nor do I play the piano or sing like Sylvia."

"I'm sure you have your own talents."

"Oh, she does." Sylvia's eager smile returned. "Bella is a very talented writer. I'm sure she'll become a world-famous journalist one day."

Heat flooded Bella's face. "Sylvia."

"It's true! There's no need to be modest."

Martha didn't seem shocked by Sylvia's comments. Instead, she sent Bella a warm smile. "How did you become interested in journalism?"

"When I was younger, my father used to read the newspaper aloud to me. I attended school for a few years. After that we had a governess who oversaw our education. But I learned more about history and world events from discussions with Father. I suppose that's why I have a passion for journalism."

Bella stopped and pressed her lips together. She wished she could tell Martha about the articles she planned to write. Even though she couldn't share the specifics, it might be all right to say a bit more. "I do hope to write for a newspaper one day."

Martha studied Bella with an understanding gaze. "A hope can become a reality if we work hard to do our part and then trust the Lord to do the rest."

Martha's words stirred Bella's heart. "I do pray about it sometimes and try to trust the Lord."

"That's a good start."

Bella leaned back. "But I'm afraid my faith is not as strong as it should be."

"I wouldn't worry about that, my dear. Jesus said if you have faith as small as a mustard seed, you can move mountains and nothing will be impossible for you."

A sweet yearning flooded through Bella. Could that be true? Was faith the key to seeing her hopes become a reality? She'd always believed in God, but she often went days without praying or thinking of Him. Had she ever seriously prayed about her hopes of becoming a journalist? Regret pricked her heart when she realized she hadn't. That wasn't the kind of faith that would move mountains or make her hopes a reality.

"Why don't you come with me to Saint Matthew's on Sunday? Reverend Jackson's messages are practical and encouraging. And worshipping with friends and neighbors always gives my faith a boost."

Bella pondered Martha's invitation. With her father's busy schedule and her mother's poor health, they hadn't attended church services since they'd arrived at Broadlands. But that was no excuse for Bella to stay away. She looked up and met Martha's gaze. "Thank you. I'd like to attend services with you."

"So would I," Sylvia added. "It sounds like a wonderful way to meet our neighbors and make new friends."

"I'm sure it will be." Martha's eyes shone. "The church is at the center of village life. Our Sunday service starts at eleven. I'll be watching for you both, and your parents too, if they're able to come."

"I'll let them know about your invitation." Bella wasn't sure if her parents would attend, but she planned to go if she could.

Martha shifted her gaze to Sylvia. "I understand you'll be going to London for your first season soon."

Sylvia's face glowed. "Yes. We're just waiting to hear the date for my presentation to the King. My ball is scheduled for May twenty-fifth."

"That sounds very exciting."

Sylvia nodded. "I'm so glad Bella has already been through two seasons, so she can tell me what to expect."

"That should be helpful," Martha added with a smile.

Bella shifted in her chair. Yes, two seasons and no proposals. It was time to change the subject again. "I was wondering, how did Professor Steed and Mr. Drake come to set up their workshop here at Green Meadow?"

Martha smiled and dipped her head. "Oh, Professor Steed and I have been friends since we were children. His family lived in East Langdon, and he and my brother, Harry, were good friends. His sister, Anna, and I met at school, and we became as close as sisters." A touch of sadness shadowed her eyes. "Anna has been gone for several years, but Harry stayed in touch with Thaddeus. And last summer, Harry told me Thaddeus was looking for a place to work on his airplanes. Harry thought Green Meadow would be the perfect spot, so he urged me to write to Thaddeus and invite him to come."

Bella nodded, pleased to hear about the long-standing connection between Martha and Professor Steed.

"Thaddeus and James had just returned from seeing Mr. Wright fly his airplane in France when he received my letter. They came for a visit and liked what they saw here. It only took them a few weeks to convert the old milking shed into a fine workshop, and they've been carrying on their experiments and test flights ever since." Her gazed shifted toward the window. "It's a real thrill to see James take off and soar over my fields."

"I've only seen him fly once, but it was amazing." Bella followed Martha's gaze. "Are they out in the workshop today?"

"Yes, I believe they're putting the engine back in the airplane. If the weather stays clear and it's not too windy, Thaddeus said they might try another test flight tomorrow."

A loud bang sounded in the kitchen, and Bella nearly dropped her cup.

"Martha! Come quick! We need your help!" James appeared at the sitting room doorway, his face pale and his eyes wide.

Martha rose from her chair. "What happened?"

James's gaze darted to Bella and back to Martha. "It's the professor. He cut his hand. Do you have a medical kit? We need something to stop the bleeding."

"It's upstairs. I'll get it." She hurried out of the room.

Bella stood. "What can I do to help?"

Sylvia darted a frightened glance at Bella, but she stayed frozen in her chair.

"Come with me." James walked back into the kitchen and Bella followed. The professor leaned against the far counter, his jaw tight, and a dirty rag clutched around his hand.

"Martha's coming." James hustled across the room and laid his hand on the professor's shoulder. "You better sit down."

"I don't want to get blood on her tablecloth."

James shook his head. "She won't mind."

"Here." Bella grabbed a clean kitchen towel from the shelf. "We can put this under your hand."

James took the professor's arm and guided him toward the kitchen table. Bella pulled out the chair, spread out the towel, and moved the vase of flowers to the side counter.

"Thank you," the professor managed between tight lips. "I can't believe I made such a foolish mistake. I always tell James to be careful; then I'm the one to slice my hand with a knife."

Martha hurried into the kitchen, carrying a small metal box. "What happened, Thaddeus?"

"I was trimming the fabric on the wing, and the knife slipped."

She set the box on the table, glanced at the dirty rag wrapped around the professor's hand, and pursed her lips. "Goodness, is that all you could find?" She darted a glance at Bella. "Bring me that pitcher of water by the sink. James, grab another towel from the shelf."

Bella carried the pitcher of water to the table.

Martha unwrapped the professor's hand, and blood oozed from the cut. "I'm sure it's painful, but I don't think you'll need stitches if we can slow the bleeding and bind it tight."

"I hope you're right." The professor leaned closer and looked at his hand. "I think it's longer than it is deep."

"I need to wipe away the blood, so I can get a better look and be sure." Martha dipped the corner of the towel in the pitcher, then gently dabbed at the red stain.

James stepped closer to Bella. "You're not squeamish around blood?"

"No, I've bandaged quite a few cuts and scrapes for my sister."

He nodded, and his gaze shifted back to Martha. She worked quickly but was cautious and caring. She obviously didn't want to cause him any more pain, but she was determined to make sure the wound was clean.

The professor looked up at Martha. "It appears you've done this before."

"When you have a farm and men working with equipment, there are bound to be accidents. I've been binding wounds like this since I was a girl."

"I'm grateful, Martha." His voice softened and carried a touch of tenderness.

She paused and met the professor's gaze. Some undefined emotion passed between them. It lasted only a moment, and then Martha looked away and nodded to Bella. "Pour a little water over the cut. We want to be sure it's clean before we bandage it up."

Bella lifted the pitcher and dribbled water over the professor's hand, washing away more blood.

Martha took a small bottle from her kit and twisted off the cap. "This will sting." She dripped some iodine across his hand.

The professor clenched his teeth and pulled in a sharp breath, but he held still while Martha continued her ministrations.

Finally, she wound a clean bandage around his thumb and then wrapped it around his hand several times before tying it off with a neat knot. "Now, you must rest your hand and not use it today."

"But we need to—"

"Please, don't argue with me, Thaddeus." Martha returned the small bottle to her kit. "If you want that cut to heal properly, you must take care of yourself." She closed the lid on the box. "It would be best if you stayed in the house this afternoon where it's warm. You can put your feet up and read a book."

The professor scowled. "I can't do that. We have to prepare for our test flight tomorrow."

"I can finish what's needed." James rested his hand on the professor's shoulder. "Why don't you stay here and do as Martha says?"

"There's no need to waste the day simply because I have a little cut on my hand."

Martha crossed her arms. "It's not little, and it won't be a waste if you rest and make sure the bleeding stops."

The professor released a heavy sigh. "All right. I'll stay in for a few hours, but only until after dinner. Then I want to go out and make sure we're ready for tomorrow."

Martha scooted the rocking chair closer to the fire. "Sit here. I'll get a cushion to make you more comfortable."

"There's no need to fuss."

"There is a need. And I have guests to see to. So please sit down and do as I ask."

"All right." The professor lowered himself into the rocking chair, and Martha bustled off to retrieve the cushion. He rocked back in the chair with a sigh that seemed to suggest he was relieved and secretly liked to be on the receiving end of Martha's attention.

Bella stepped into the professor's line of vision. "I'm sorry about your hand. I hope it heals quickly."

"Thank you, Miss Grayson, for your kind words and assistance."

"It was no trouble at all."

"I'm sorry I interrupted your visit with Martha."

Bella smiled. "Don't worry. We've had a very pleasant visit."

Martha returned, and Sylvia appeared at the kitchen doorway. She bit her lip as she watched Martha adjust the cushion for the professor. "I'm sorry I was no help."

Martha looked up. "It's all right. We took care of him."

Sylvia sent an embarrassed glance around the group. "I'm afraid I usually faint at the sight of blood."

James pressed his lips together and looked away, but Bella caught his eye. They exchanged an understanding smile.

"There's no need to apologize, my dear." Martha slipped her arm around Sylvia's shoulder and guided her back toward the sitting room. "Not everyone is cut out for a nursing role, and you may find as you grow older it will become easier for you to bandage a wound."

Bella watched them leave, then shifted her gaze to James. "I hope the professor's injury doesn't set back your test flights."

"No, I'm sure it won't." He hesitated, then said, "We hope to fly tomorrow. Would you like to come watch?"

"What time?"

"We'll wait for the temperature to warm up, and we have to be sure the winds are calm. I think we should be ready around one."

"All right." Bella smiled. "I'll look forward to it."

"So will I," he said, a hint of mischief in his eyes.

She turned away and walked toward the sitting room, her heart dancing with the hope of seeing James fly again.

Seven

James grabbed hold of the wheel on top of the control stick with both hands and settled his feet on the pedals of the Steed IV. It was time to see if the changes they'd made to the engine would help him stay in the air more than fifteen minutes.

"Remember what I said." The professor looked around the propeller and made eye contact with James. "Don't take any unnecessary risks. If you have any trouble, circle around and come back this way. I'd rather you take a short, safe flight than stay up too long and crash in a field somewhere out of sight."

James grinned. "So would I."

The professor shook his head but smiled as well, then lifted his hand and saluted James. "Godspeed, my boy!" He spun the propeller once, twice, and with the third spin the engine roared to life. The professor hustled across the field to watch from a safe distance.

The engine's vibrations shook the plane and sent a surge of energy through James. He lifted his hand and waved to Bella, Sylvia, and Martha. They stood at the side of the field with Martha's son, Ethan, and two field hands who had helped them roll the airplane into position for takeoff.

Bella sent him a bright smile and returned his wave. She tucked her arm through Sylvia's, and Martha walked over and joined the professor. It was quite a send-off, with more observers than he'd had for any other test flight. He hoped he wouldn't disappoint them.

He adjusted the throttle, the engine revved higher, and the airplane rolled down the field, picking up speed as it bumped along. He clenched his jaw, urging the airplane forward and up. He had to lift off before he reached the end of the field where the ground dipped lower and a hedgerow kept the sheep out of his path.

With only a few yards to spare, the airplane rose into the air and soared over the hedgerow and pasture. The cold wind whipped around him, tugging at his cap and the scarf he'd tucked around his neck and into his coat. Thankfully, his goggles kept most of the cold wind out of his eyes.

He climbed above the trees and fields and flew south for a few minutes, then started into his first turn over the road leading to Broadlands. He and the professor had mapped out the route in case he needed to bring the plane down before he could make it back to Green Meadow. They wanted to be sure the professor could find James and there was a path for the wagon if needed.

Bella's stately home came into view with its impressive parkland and outbuildings.

Without warning, the engine sputtered. James's stomach clenched and he held on tight, fighting the urge to jerk the stick and tighten his turn. That could be disastrous. Every movement had to be smooth and calculated or he could throw off the plane's balance and end up crashing into the woods or field, or worse yet, into Bella's beautiful home.

The sound of the engine evened out, resuming its normal roar, and James blew out the breath he had been holding. Using his feet, he adjusted the rear rudder, then carefully pulled back on the stick and changed the warping of the wings to take him higher.

Why had the engine misfired? He cocked his head and listened, but he didn't hear anything unusual now. He checked the airspeed indicator and oil pressure gauge. Everything looked normal. Those were his only instruments. He had to control the airplane by feeling how it responded to the air currents and make adjustments as they were needed.

Flying the Steed IV was an exhilarating, fearsome test of his focus and courage. There was no room for panic or reckless actions. If he gave into fear and made foolish choices, he could crash and lose months of work in a few seconds—and maybe even lose his life.

James pulled in a deep breath to steady his nerves. He flew on past the stables and estate offices at Broadlands and then over a winding stream. He took another turn and headed back toward Martha's fields. The engine hummed along at a steady pace now, reassuring him the changes to the engine had been helpful.

He leaned to the left and looked out at the amazing view. The countryside

spread out below him in a brown-and-green flowing carpet. Fields were inter-
spersed with wooded areas. Sheep dotted some of the pastures, and up ahead
he could see the village of East Langdon, with its homes, shops, and church
steeple rising in the center. To the right in the distance was the faint blue line
of the Strait of Dover and the cliffs above Saint Margaret's Bay.

The memory of what had happened there struck him again, and a wave of
urgency flowed through him. He had to find out how his mother had died that
day. He was tempted to take the plane in that direction and see the cliffs and
beach from his present altitude, but if he left the flight path and then had
trouble, how would the professor find him?

He shook his head and abandoned the idea. This was not the time to get
caught up in the past. He needed to stay on course and focus on the goals for
today's flight—test the engine, increase his flight time, and hone his skills.

He roared over Martha's cottage, the barn, and the workshop. His friends
on the ground shouted and waved their hats and arms in the air. Bella's cheerful
smile and vigorous waves made his chest expand. Knowing she was there,
watching and cheering, was a huge encouragement.

He glanced at his watch and a thrill raced through him. He'd been flying
for eighteen minutes! His spirits soared as he flew higher. If he followed the
same circular path at about the same speed, it would take him thirty-six minutes. That would be more than enough to please the professor and impress
Bella.

A gust of wind caught him by surprise. The airplane tilted and dipped,
and his stomach plunged with it. He gripped the wheel atop the stick and
forced himself to make slow, smooth adjustments to his wings and ailerons.

The airplane leveled out, and he blew out a ragged breath. He had better
keep his mind on the task at hand. Flying took quick thinking, nerves of steel,
and a steady hand, or he would end up in a ditch with broken dreams.

The wind died down, and he eased into the next turn, following the same
route he'd flown on the first circuit. When he passed over Bella's house a second
time, he took a more careful look. The broad lawns surrounding the house
were starting to turn green, reminding him spring was fast approaching. The
design of the fountain garden to the west of the house was more evident from
the air. He imagined the garden would overflow with flowers in a few months.

Would he walk there with Bella when the spring sunshine warmed the air and flowers and trees bloomed again?

A loud clunk came from the engine, and the plane jerked.

James's heart clenched. *Please, Lord, not again!*

The engine coughed and sputtered a few more times. He eased back on the stick, gliding lower and slowly turning toward the open field—the same one he had crashed in last month!

The roar of the engine evened out again, but it was running at a lower speed, and he almost felt as if he were limping along. He leaned forward, straining to see Green Meadow. Finally the silo and barn came into view, and beyond them, Martha's cottage and their workshop.

James aimed for the field they had cleared, his muscles taut as he made each adjustment to his controls. Bringing the airplane in for a landing was the most difficult skill he needed to master. If he came in too steep or too fast, he would crash, but if he misjudged his speed and was too slow, he could drop into the hedgerow or roll the plane.

With a white-knuckle grip, he adjusted the wings, slowing the plane and bringing it lower and lower. His front two wheels touched the ground, sending a jolt through him. The rear wheel followed, and he breathed a prayer of thanks as he rolled down the bumpy landing path toward his waiting friends.

He glanced at his watch, then gave a shout. Thirty-seven minutes! That was a new record and more than double the time of his last flight!

The professor, Martha, and Bella ran toward the airplane even before it came to a stop. The others followed.

"Well done, my boy! Well done!" The professor beamed a broad smile.

James turned off the engine and the propeller slowed its spinning. He lifted his goggles. Grinning and breathless, he climbed down and walked around the wing toward his friends. He'd not only set a new record; he'd maneuvered his way through two serious engine misfires and landed without a mishap. That was something to celebrate.

The professor slapped him on the back. "That was spectacular! What a flight! Your landing was spot on!"

"Thank you." He basked in the professor's happy approval for a second, then focused on Bella. "Well, what did you think?"

Her blue eyes glowed, and her cheeks took on a rosy hue. "It was amazing! I can't believe the way you controlled the airplane and made such smooth turns."

Martha reached for his arm and gave it a squeeze. "We're so proud of you, James. What an achievement!"

"How was the engine?" The professor leaned toward him. "Did it give you any trouble?"

James hated to put a damper on everyone's joy, but he had no choice. "Something is still not quite right."

The professor's bushy white eyebrows rose. "What do you mean?"

"The engine sputtered a few times."

"*Sputtered?*" The professor shifted his worried glance to the front of the airplane.

"It might be the timing. I'm not sure, but it only lasted a second or two. Then the engine ran smoothly, except near the end it made a loud clunking sound. After that it didn't seem to have as much power."

The professor rubbed his chin. "Do you think it could be a clog in the fuel line?"

James considered it and shook his head. "It's more likely an issue with the pistons or some other malfunction in the engine."

The professor clasped his shoulder. "Well, I'm glad you made it back safely. We'll run some more tests and find the answers before we take it up again." He ran his hand over the edge of the wing. "I'm so pleased you were able to stay up as long as you did. Surely we're on our way to even greater things."

James nodded and loosened the scarf around his neck.

The professor lifted his finger. "With our success today, I believe I'm ready to accept the invitation from the Aero Club."

James stepped back. "What invitation?"

The professor sent him a sheepish look. "They asked me to be one of the guest speakers for their spring lecture series."

"Why didn't you tell me?"

"I only received their letter a few days ago, and I wasn't sure if I would accept."

"Why wouldn't you? That's a great honor to be invited to speak."

"I didn't want to go unless I had something significant to report." He scanned the Steed IV with a proud gaze, then focused on James. "We've overcome many obstacles and refined our design. Today's successful flight proves we're ready to share our findings with the world."

Bella stepped closer to James. "When will the lectures be given?"

"It's always the third week of April."

"We should be in London by then." But her hopeful smile quickly faded. "I suppose you must be a member of the Aero Club to attend, and I don't imagine ladies are allowed."

"On the contrary." The professor turned to Bella. "One of the founders, Vera Butler, believed the Aero Club should be open equally to ladies and gentlemen, and we've followed that rule since it began in 1901."

"Really? I had no idea."

"Of course, membership is subject to election, and every candidate must have a sponsor who is already a member," the professor added.

Bella sighed. "So much for that idea."

James touched her arm. "You don't need to be a member to attend. The lectures are open to the public."

"Oh, that's wonderful!" Bella's eyes glowed. "Did you hear that, Sylvia?"

The young woman nodded, looking pleased. "It sounds like it would be a great opportunity for you to learn more about aviation for your . . ." Sylvia's voice trailed off, her cheeks flushed pink, and she looked away.

James sent Bella a questioning glance.

Bella quickly slipped her arm through Sylvia's and smiled. "I'll look forward to attending those lectures, especially yours, Professor Steed. I'm sure you'll be an outstanding speaker with your years of experience."

He chuckled. "Well, that is a fine compliment."

James turned to Bella. "We'll let you know the date and time as soon as it's confirmed."

"Thank you. I'll give you our London address. We'll be spending most of our time in town this spring and summer."

"I'm coming out." Sylvia beamed. "We've already started accepting invitations to attend all kinds of social events, and my ball is set for the twenty-fifth of May."

A wave of uneasiness traveled through James. The London social season was often called a marriage market for a very good reason. Young, upper-class women spent mid-April to late-July being paraded from one event to the next in hopes of meeting the right man and receiving a marriage proposal.

Was that the goal Mr. and Mrs. Grayson had for their daughters? No doubt wealthy, well-bred men like Mark Clifton would be eager to spend time with attractive young women like Bella and Sylvia at those events.

How could he compete with that?

He blew out a breath and tried to clear away those thoughts. He had a race to prepare for and a future to build. He couldn't let his attraction to Bella pull him off course.

But when he glanced her way, she sent him a warm smile, and the truth hit his heart. He wasn't just attracted to Bella. He truly cared for her. She was a unique woman with an inquisitive mind and a cheerful, determined spirit. He could imagine them teaming up to build a bright future together. But the question remained—how could he win her love and convince her family he was worthy of her?

Bella walked down London's Fleet Street with her portfolio under one arm and her father by her side. For the last two weeks, she'd worked diligently, finishing her research and then writing and rewriting her article several times. She'd also outlined four more articles with the hope her father and Mr. Elmwood would agree to let her continue writing the series.

Finally, the day had arrived for her to show her first article to Mr. Elmwood. He would either accept it and launch her journalism career, or reject it and dash her hopes and dreams.

Bella pulled in a calming breath. She must not allow her father or Mr. Elmwood to see her churning emotions. That would only make them more inclined to say women were not equipped for the serious work of journalism, and then her article would be rejected for sure. She couldn't let that happen, not after all the time and effort she'd poured into it, to say nothing of how long she'd been waiting for this door to open.

That thought pricked her conscience, reminding her she hadn't prayed about her meeting today. She walked on, and a silent prayer rose from her heart.

Father, thank You for guiding me in my research and writing. I've given it my best effort, and now I'm asking You to go before me and do what only You can do. Prepare me for the answer, whatever it may be, and help me accept it with a gracious spirit . . . but please let Mr. Elmwood say yes!

Since her conversation with Martha at Green Meadow, she had attended Sunday services at Saint Matthew's twice. She'd found the people friendly and the messages uplifting and surprisingly practical. She left church each week resolved to bring her faith into her daily life. That desire had sparked a renewed commitment to prayer, and Bella found it was a lifeline.

Today would be a test of her fledgling faith. And she was determined to have courage and rise above her fear with the Lord's help.

She glanced over at her father, thankful he was with her, but she wished he had given her a few words of encouragement on the way to town.

Last Friday after dinner, she had decided it was time to show him her article.

The scene rose in her mind now, and the memory of their conversation sent a tremor down her arms.

Bella had walked into the library after her mother and Sylvia had gone up to bed. Her father was sitting in his favorite chair by the fireplace with his feet up on a stool and a newspaper open on his lap.

"I finished my article, Father." Bella held it out to him, forcing her hand to remain steady. "I'd like your opinion."

He lowered his newspaper, glanced up at her, then took the two pages from her hand. Bella pressed her lips together, waiting in agony while he read the first page and then the second.

"Is it . . . all right?" She wished she could make her voice sound more confident, but that was impossible. His opinion meant so much to her, and she longed to hear him praise her efforts.

He gave a grudging nod. "The opening gives enough information to capture the attention of the readers, but not too many facts to overwhelm them." He glanced at the article again. "The writing is clear and concise, and the account of Wilbur Wright's demonstration at Le Mans establishes the writer as someone who has firsthand information about the subject."

Bella rose up on her toes, barely able to hold back her smile. "So, do you think it's ready to show Mr. Elmwood?"

"The ending could be stronger. You might want to rework that section and give it more punch."

Bella nodded, although she wasn't exactly sure what he meant by "more punch" or how she should change the ending.

Her father handed back the pages. "I'm going to London on Monday. I'll show it to Horace and see what he says."

Bella straightened her shoulders. "I'd like to go with you."

"I don't think that's wise, Bella."

"But I'd like to hear his response, and if he suggests changes, I could discuss those with him and make sure I understand what he wants done to improve it."

Her father sat back in his chair. "What if he criticizes your writing and turns it down flat? Are you sure you want to be there if that's his answer?"

Bella steeled herself and lifted her chin. "Yes. If the article is not acceptable, I'd like to know why. And if he does accept it, I want to present my ideas for the series."

"So you haven't given up on that idea?"

"No, I have four more articles outlined."

He rubbed his forehead for a few seconds, then looked up at her. "All right. You may go with me, but remember I made no promise of publication."

"I understand."

"I'll present the article to Horace, but he'll decide if it will be published or not. And either way, you must keep your promise about the season."

"I will." Bella gave a firm nod, though her stomach tightened at the thought.

A policeman blew his whistle across the street, and Bella snapped back to the moment. They were only a few yards from their destination. She'd done everything she could to prepare for this meeting. It was time to remember Martha's advice—trust the Lord and wait for Him to do His part.

Her father pulled open the front door of the offices of the *Daily Mail,* and Bella preceded him into the lobby. They walked past the young man at the reception desk and headed directly toward the lift. After a quick ride to the top floor, they entered Horace Elmwood's office and the young clerk announced them to the editor.

"Good morning, Horace." Her father stepped forward and shook hands with the editor.

Mr. Elmwood greeted him, then shifted his gaze to Bella. "It's a pleasure to see you again, Miss Grayson."

"Thank you. I'm happy to see you as well." She smiled and nodded to him, while her stomach did a nervous dance.

"We've come on business today." Her father motioned for her to speak. "Go ahead, Bella."

She blinked, searching for a way to begin. She'd thought her father would at least explain why they'd come. But it seemed it was up to her. "As you know, my father has a great interest in promoting the advancement of aviation. That's one reason he suggested the *Daily Mail* offer a prize to the first pilot to fly across the English Channel."

Mr. Elmwood folded his hands over his protruding midsection. "He received a lot of criticism when it was first announced, but I think those detractors are going to be put in their place very soon."

"I agree," Bella continued, "and I believe a series of articles, highlighting the progress of aviation and featuring the men who are preparing for that race across the Channel is just what's needed to encourage support for aviation and raise the circulation of the *Daily Mail.*"

The editor narrowed his eyes. "That's an interesting idea."

Bella suppressed her smile in an effort to be businesslike. "Yes, it's very interesting. I've done some research and written an article that could be used as the first in a series of five or more."

The editor's busy eyebrows rose. "*You've* written an article?"

"Yes, I have it right here with me." She opened her portfolio, took out the pages, and handed them to Mr. Elmwood.

"Is this your idea, Charles?" The editor scowled at her father.

"No, Bella has a mind of her own."

Mr. Elmwood shifted his serious gaze to Bella. "We are not in the habit of publishing articles written by freelance reporters, especially women."

Bella remained silent, hoping her writing skills would speak for her.

"Just take a look, and give her your honest opinion." Her father motioned toward the article in Mr. Elmwood's hand.

Mr. Elmwood pushed his spectacles up his large nose and lowered his gaze to the papers. His forehead creased, and he grunted when he reached the bottom of the first page.

Bella sent her father a quick glance, trying to gauge what that grunt meant, but he was focused on Mr. Elmwood.

The editor read the second page, then looked up. "You say you wrote this . . ." He sent her father a sideways glance. "Not your father?"

Bella's cheeks warmed. "Yes sir. My father and I have discussed the issues for months, but I am the author."

Mr. Elmwood laid the papers on the desk and leaned back in his chair. "So you want to write for the *Daily Mail,* and not just one article but a whole series."

"Yes sir. I do." Bella swallowed and took two more sheets of paper from her portfolio. "Here's an outline of the other articles I have in mind for the series." She handed them to him. "I thought if we featured the individual English aviators first, and then grouped the French aviators, that would draw the most attention to the stories."

The editor rubbed his chin. "From what I hear, the French pilots are miles ahead of the English. We should tell their stories first, in case one of them actually does make that flight and wins the prize. If we don't, our series could end up being old news."

Bella's stomach did a somersault. Was he actually saying he wanted to publish the series? She pressed her lips together, trying to squelch her glee. This was no time to let her emotions overflow. If she wanted to be taken seriously, she had to conduct herself with restraint and decorum.

"Yes, that's a good point. We could feature the French pilots first, although I witnessed one British pilot make a thirty-seven-minute flight not long ago."

"Really? Who was that?"

"His name is James Drake. He and Professor Thaddeus Steed are working on their airplanes at one of the tenant farms at Broadlands."

"I see." Mr. Elmwood's gaze shifted toward the windows.

Her father stepped closer to the editor's desk. "So what's the verdict, Horace? Do you think Bella's article is strong enough to be published in the *Daily Mail*?"

"Well, it needs some editing, but the framework is there and the idea is unique." Mr. Elmwood drummed his fingers on his desk. "But there is one problem."

Bella held her breath, her gaze darting from Mr. Elmwood to her father and back.

"I'm not sure the public will believe a female is a reliable source of information on a topic like this."

Bella's stomach sank, and she clasped her hands. She couldn't let this chance slip away just because she was a woman. "My parents would prefer I write under a pseudonym. I thought perhaps I could use I. J. Wilmington." She'd chosen Wilmington because it was her mother's maiden name, and the I. J. would be a silent nod to her first and middle names, Isabella Jane.

The editor looked at her father again. "I suppose you're in favor of this since you brought her here today."

"I believe the idea has merit."

"I agree with you on that point."

"And you know how much I want to see us win the race across the Channel," her father continued, "but you must decide if Bella's writing skills are equal to the task."

Mr. Elmwood picked up the article and scanned her writing once more.

Bella held still and tried not to nervously tap her foot.

Finally, he looked up at Bella. "I like your style, Miss Grayson, and I don't just mean your writing style. You've got gumption." A smile tugged up one corner of his mouth. "I'll print this first article in the Sunday edition."

Bella felt like her heart would burst. "Thank you!"

The editor lifted his hand. "I'm not saying we'll publish the full series, but

I'm willing to look at the next article after we see what kind of response we receive from this first one. Are you agreeable to that?"

"Yes sir."

"Good. Can you write the next article featuring one of the French aviators and get it to me in one week?"

She pulled in a sharp breath. How could she do that? Her thoughts flashed back to the Aero Club weekly journal editions she'd read. Those would be helpful. She could also visit the library and look through the research room downstairs, but it would be a challenge.

Her father looked her way and cocked his eyebrow. "Perhaps we ought to take a trip to Calais and see if we can track down a few of those French aviators."

"Oh, Father, that would be wonderful!" His eyebrows rose, and she quickly toned down her voice. "I'm sure that would add depth to the story."

She shifted her gaze back to Mr. Elmwood. "I appreciate this opportunity. I'll start working on it today, and I promise I'll give it every effort."

"Very good. I'll look forward to reading it as soon as you're finished, but it must be on my desk no later than next Wednesday morning."

"Yes sir. You can count on me."

Father thanked Mr. Elmwood, and they shook hands. Bella bid him good day and sashayed out of the office. She was on her way to becoming a real, published journalist. Nothing would stop her now.

Thank You, Lord!

James leaned his bicycle against the pillar of the covered entrance at Broadlands and walked toward the front door. His hands were clammy in spite of the cold, and his stomach felt as though he'd swallowed a flapping fish.

What was he doing here? Did he really think he could just waltz up to the front door of Broadlands, ask to see Bella, and be invited inside?

He closed his eyes. *Lord, I'm trying to follow the professor's advice and see where You want to take my friendship with Bella. If this is a bad idea, I'd like to find out now, before I make a complete fool of myself.*

He puffed out a breath, straightened his shoulders, and lifted the heavy knocker on the door. He'd never know if he didn't try.

A few seconds later, a footman he didn't recognize opened the door. "May I help you, sir?"

"Good afternoon. My name is James Drake, and I'd like to speak to Miss Isabella Grayson."

"Is she expecting you, sir?"

"No, but I think she'll want to see me." He forced confidence into his voice.

The footman lifted one eyebrow. "Right this way, sir." He ushered him through the entrance hall and into the larger central hall.

James breathed out a sigh of relief. At least he'd made it in the door.

He glanced around the hall. It certainly looked different in the daylight than it had in the evening on his previous visit. Dark wooden beams arched overhead in the vaulted ceiling that rose three stories high. A huge, white marble mantelpiece carved with elaborate battle scenes surrounded the fireplace.

"If you'll wait here, sir, I'll see if Miss Grayson is receiving visitors."

James thanked the footman and watched him climb the main staircase. As the footman passed the landing, James's attention was drawn to the large painting hanging above the stairs. He hadn't noticed it on his first visit. He supposed the hall had been darker that night, and he'd focused on greeting Mr. Grayson and Mark Clifton when he'd entered this room.

James studied the three young women featured in the painting. The tallest was a handsome brunette with high cheekbones, a long nose, and dark-brown eyes. She stood in the back with her hand resting on the shoulder of the second young woman, who was seated in a wicker chair. Her face was rounder, but her hair and eyes were as dark as the first. A third woman sat on the grass in front of them. She had enchanting hazel eyes and looked like she was the youngest of the three. Her honey-gold hair was all pulled to one side and curled over her shoulder.

His breath caught as he scanned her face and hair again. He squeezed his eyes shut, then opened them and stared at the young woman.

It couldn't be his mother, could it?

He reached into his pocket for her photograph, but he'd changed his clothes before he left Green Meadow, and he hadn't transferred the photograph to this jacket. He studied the painting again. That woman had to be his mother or someone very closely related to her. Could the other two be her sisters, Judith and Maryann?

But an even stranger question flooded his mind. If it was his mother, why was a painting of her and her sisters hanging at Broadlands?

❦

Bella folded her nightgown into her suitcase and reached for her journal and pen. She and her father would be leaving for France early in the morning. The thought brought a smile to her lips. She could hardly believe how quickly the trip had come together, and she was even more surprised by her father's efforts to make it possible.

After their meeting with Mr. Elmwood at the *Daily Mail,* her father had sent a telegram to a contact at a newspaper in Calais. A reply arrived less than two hours later, giving them leads on locating two of the three French aviators who were preparing to attempt flights across the Channel.

If all went as she hoped, they would find those men, conduct their interviews, and return home the day after tomorrow. That would give her time to write her next article and turn it in to Mr. Elmwood before the deadline.

Bessie walked into the room. "Your black shoes are clean and ready to go, miss." The maid slipped them into a cloth drawstring bag and tucked it in the side of Bella's suitcase.

"Thank you, Bessie. That's all I need. I can do the rest."

"Are you sure, miss? I'd be glad to help."

"We're only going to be gone for two days, so I won't need much more than what we've packed." She folded the skirt of her navy-blue walking suit into the case and added a pair of stockings.

A knock sounded at Bella's bedroom door. She looked up and called, "Come in."

The door opened and Neal, the new footmen, stood in the hallway. "There's a gentleman here to see you, Miss Grayson."

"A gentleman?" She glanced at the clock. It was almost four thirty, and she wasn't expecting anyone to call.

"Yes, a Mr. James Drake."

"Oh." She lifted her hand to her hair and glanced in the mirror. "Please tell him I'll be down in a moment."

"Very good, miss." Neal pulled the door closed, and his footsteps faded down the corridor.

Bella hurried to the dressing table. "Bessie, can you help me with my hair?"

"Of course, miss."

Bella sat on the bench, and Bessie made quick work of tucking in a few strands of hair that had come loose. "How is that, miss?"

Bella sighed. "I look a bit worse for wear, but it will have to do. I don't want to keep him waiting too long."

Bessie smiled. "I'm sure he'll be pleased to see you no matter how long he has to wait."

Bella's cheeks flushed at Bessie's comment, but she did not reply. She hurried across the upper hall and then slowed when she reached the top of the stairs. Her heart was pounding, but there was no need to appear overeager.

James looked up at her as she descended the stairs.

She sent him a warm smile as she passed the landing. "Hello, James."

"I hope you don't mind me stopping by." His smile seemed a bit hesitant, and his gaze drifted past her shoulder.

She reached the bottom of the stairs. "Not at all. You're always welcome at Broadlands."

"Thank you." He looked up the stairs again. "That's a remarkable painting. Do you know who those women are?"

It seemed odd that he'd ask about the painting before he'd even told her the reason for his visit. She shifted her gaze to the portrait of the three women. They were lovely, and she supposed they would attract any man's attention.

"No, I'm sorry, I don't. I've wondered about that myself."

He looked her way again with a lift of his eyebrows.

"They might be sisters since they look so much alike."

James nodded. "Yes, there is a family resemblance."

"I thought they might be related to Sir Richard, but he left the painting here when he sold Broadlands, so it seems unlikely."

"Maybe he's not *sentimental* about his family." James's cool tone surprised Bella.

"Perhaps the painting is too large for his new home."

James gave a brief nod, but her explanation didn't erase the line between his eyebrows.

"Why do you ask?"

A muscle in his jaw flickered, and he turned away. "No reason. I was just curious."

She sensed there was more behind his questions, but she didn't want to ask him to explain and make him uncomfortable. "What brings you to Broadlands today?"

"We've tested the engine, and I believe we've solved the problem for the present. I'll be flying again tomorrow." His expression eased into a boyish, crooked smile. "I was hoping you might like to come and watch."

Pleasing warmth spread through her. "I'd like that very much, but my Father and I are going to France tomorrow."

"France?" He sent her a curious look. "For business or pleasure?"

"Oh . . . a little of both." She glanced away, trying to shake off a small wave of guilt for not explaining the purpose of her trip.

"How long will you be gone?"

"Just two or three days." She looked back and forced a smile, hoping he wouldn't ask her any more about it.

The line appeared between his eyebrows again as he waited for her to speak.

Heat rose in her face. She wasn't lying to him. She just wasn't telling him the whole truth. She couldn't.

"Well, I hope you have a pleasant trip."

"Thank you. I'm sure we will."

He glanced at the painting once more and then back at Bella. "I suppose I should be going."

"Would you like to have some tea first? I should've offered that right away."

He shook his head. "Thank you, but I should get back. I don't want to leave the professor on his own for too long."

"How is his hand? I hope it's healing."

"It's much better."

"Good. I'm glad to hear it. Please give him my greetings, Martha too."

"I will." He reached up and touched his cap. "I'll say goodbye, then." He turned and walked toward the entrance hall.

Her heart squeezed, and she bit her lip. He'd come all this way to invite her to watch him fly, and she'd turned him down with hardly any explanation or encouragement. She couldn't end his visit with those stiff, formal words between them.

"James, wait!" She hurried after him.

He turned, a slightly wary look in his eyes.

"Thank you for coming and for inviting me to watch you fly. I truly appreciate it."

He nodded, his expression easing a bit.

"I loved watching your last flight, and I'll look forward to seeing you again as soon as we're home from France." Goodness, she sounded almost breathless.

His expression warmed into a true smile. "I'll look forward to that as well."

"I hope you'll come again."

His eyes glowed as he nodded to her. "I will. Goodbye, Bella."

"Goodbye, James."

James walked out the front door of Broadlands, his steps light as he replayed Bella's parting words. It wasn't so much what she'd said as the way she'd said it and the silent message he read in her eyes. Their connection was growing stronger, and though there was still much that separated them, a deeper friendship at least seemed like a possibility. His spirits rose as he contemplated that hope.

If he was the first to fly across the Channel, surely her father would be impressed, and more likely to allow him to court her. Was that the key to winning Mr. Grayson's favor and Bella's hand?

He rolled his bicycle down the gravel path and hopped on. He'd only peddled a few yards when the bike jerked and he had to jump off or he would've fallen face first into the gravel. The bicycle crashed to the ground, and he barely stayed on his feet.

"What in the world?" He scanned the bicycle, glaring when he saw the loose chain. He'd have to get his hands dirty to put it back in place, or take a very long walk back to Green Meadow. With a sigh, he knelt on the damp gravel and tugged on the greasy chain.

"Can I help, sir?"

James looked up as an older man in a brown tweed jacket and cap pushed a wheelbarrow toward him. "Thank you, but I think I can fix it."

"I'd be glad to lend a hand if you need it."

"It's just the chain. It won't take long to put it back in place. No sense in both of us getting our hands dirty."

The old man chuckled. "I'm not afraid of a little dirt—in fact, that's my specialty. I'm one of the gardeners. Harold Jensen is my name."

James lined the chain up and turned the pedal, but the chain slipped off again.

"Are you a guest here at the house, sir?" the gardener asked.

"No, I was just visiting Miss Grayson." The chain finally clicked into place.

Jensen looked toward the house. "They're fine people. I'm grateful they kept me on after Sir Richard sold the estate."

James stood, his curiosity stirring. "You worked for Sir Richard?"

"Yes, I did, for thirty-five years. First as under gardener, then head gardener these last twelve years."

"So you knew him and his family well?"

Jensen gave a slight shrug. "After all those years, you learn a thing or two about the master and his household."

James stepped closer. "May I ask you a question?"

Jensen nodded. "If you like."

"I saw a painting on the landing of the main staircase that pictured three young women. Are you familiar with it?"

"Yes sir. I've seen it many times when I delivered flowers to the house."

"Do you know who those women are?"

"Of course. Those are Sir Richard's daughters."

James straightened. "Is he Sir Richard *Markingham*?"

"Yes sir." Jensen sent him a curious glance.

"And his youngest daughter is Laura Markingham?"

Jensen's brow creased. "That's right, Lady Laura. You knew the family?"

James took a step back. "No, not really. I just thought I recognized Lady Laura."

"She's been gone for many years. How could you recognize her if you didn't know the family?"

James clenched his jaw. He'd said too much. What if the gardener mentioned his questions to Bella or Mr. Grayson? "Never mind. It's not important."

He swung his leg over the bicycle and nodded to the gardener. "Thank you for stopping to help. Good day to you."

He peddled off down the drive, released a shaky breath, and tried to make sense of what he'd learned, but it made his mind spin.

His mother was Laura Markingham. She had been raised right here at Broadlands, her family's estate. She had walked down this road and played in the gardens beyond that hedge.

The memory of all Hannah and the professor had told him came flooding back. Anna, the professor's sister, had worked here at Broadlands as a maid for his mother's family. That was how she'd met his mother and gained her trust.

His mother had turned to Anna in her time of need. Why hadn't her sisters helped her? Where were they now? If he found them, could they help him understand what had happened to his mother?

What about his grandfather Sir Richard Markingham, the Earl of Canningford? Should James try to contact him? That thought made his stomach tense. It seemed the old man didn't care what happened to James. But would Sir Richard know his father's identity? Could he be the key to understanding what had happened between his mother and father?

His gaze traveled across the parkland to the rolling pastures. His mother, her family, and those who had taken him in were all from right here in Kent. Did his father live nearby as well? Did James have the courage to continue his search and face the man who had rejected him?

Eight

Bella looked out the motorcar window at the rain-soaked countryside as they drove down the narrow dirt road a few miles from Calais. Rain pelted the car's roof, and the front wiper barely cleared the windshield before it was drenched again. She leaned closer to her father and lowered her voice. "Do you think the driver knows where he's going?"

Father sat forward and tapped the man on the shoulder. "How much farther?"

The driver shot a quick glance back at them. *"Pas loin, monsieur."* He looked ahead and jerked the wheel, trying to avoid a pothole in the road, but he only ended up splashing them with muddy water.

Father brushed off his coat sleeve and glared at the driver's back.

They'd been on the road for about twenty-five minutes, driving south along the shore and past the small fishing village of Wissant. They continued through the countryside and into the woods, dodging puddles and trying to stay dry. Bella shivered and crossed her arms against the damp, bone-chilling wind.

They rounded the bend, leaving the woods behind, and drove through open fields. Bella squinted and leaned forward. Through the misty rain, a barn and three long, low buildings came into view. One was an open shed and beneath the covering of the roof, two airplanes were visible. "Father, look! That must be it!"

"Oui! Le camp de Comte de Lambert," the driver announced. He turned off the road and drove across the rutted field, finally coming to a stop near the end of the long open shed, where he parked next to two other motorcars.

Three men stood together by the wing of an airplane, under the cover of the roof. They watched the driver as he hopped out and opened the door for Bella and her father.

Bella tingled with excitement. Her first real interview was about to begin!

She and her father hurried through the rain and ducked inside the shed near the three men. Clutching her notebook and pen, she smiled and nodded to them. *"Bonjour, monsieurs."*

The tallest man's expression turned wary. He and the other men returned greetings, speaking French. *"Comment pouvons-nous vous aider?"*

Bella swallowed hard. Why hadn't she paid more attention to her French lessons? Had he said, "How can we help you?" Wasn't that simply a polite way of asking who are you, and what are you doing here?

Her father stepped forward and held out his hand toward the tallest man. "My name is Charles Grayson. I'm the owner of the *Daily Mail* of London. I was hoping we might have a few minutes of your time to ask you some questions."

"Vous ne parlez pas Francais?"

Father's eyebrows dipped. "No, I do not speak French. Do any of you speak English?"

The men sent each other questioning looks, and Bella's stomach tightened. If no one spoke English, how was she going to conduct her interview?

"I am Charles de Lambert." The tallest man reached out and shook her father's hand. De Lambert looked about forty years old with a wiry moustache and piercing blue eyes. "My English is not . . . strong."

Bella smiled. This was progress. "I know a little French. I'm sure we can muddle through together."

A smile tugged up one corner of his mouth. "Your name, *mademoiselle*?"

She held out her hand. "Isabella Grayson."

He took it and gave a slight bow. Looking up he asked, "You also . . . are with the *Daily Mail*?"

She glanced at her father, and he gave his head a slight shake. She looked back at de Lambert. "Not officially."

De Lambert's forehead creased, as though he didn't understand that last word.

She smiled again, hoping to get past that point. "We read about your flight in Paris when you circled the Eiffel Tower."

All three men smiled and nodded. Then one slapped de Lambert on the back and reeled off a string of French that Bella couldn't follow.

"That was quite an accomplishment," she added.

"*Oui.*" De Lambert motioned toward his airplane. "I have a fine flying machine and good friends . . . my right hands."

The two men smiled again, looking pleased de Lambert had praised them, proving they understood more English than they'd first led her to believe.

Another motorcar drove across the field toward the shed and rolled to a stop. Everyone turned and watched as two men climbed out.

Bella pulled in a quick breath. Mark Clifton and his cousin Pierre Levasseur hustled across the grass toward them and ducked into the shed out of the rain.

Mark's gaze connected with hers, reflecting his surprise. "Miss Grayson, Mr. Grayson, what a pleasant surprise."

Pierre greeted de Lambert and his men with handshakes and jovial French greetings. They obviously all knew each other well.

Mark took a moment to speak to de Lambert, and then he turned back to Bella. "So what brings you to de Lambert's camp?"

The French pilot grinned. "They ask questions for the *Daily Mail.*"

Mark's gaze shifted to her father. "You're interviewing the count?"

"We'd like to, but it will be a challenge when I speak little French and he's not confident of his English."

"I'd be happy to translate for you if you'd like."

"Oh, would you?" Bella smiled, relief flowing through her. "That would be so helpful."

"Of course, if Charles is willing." Mark turned to de Lambert and spoke to him in French.

"*Oui, merci.*" De Lambert motioned to several chairs in the back of the shed. "I wish could offer better . . ."

"*Sieges,* seating?" Mark supplied.

"*Oui,* seating."

Bella laughed softly. "I'm sure we'll be comfortable. Thank you."

Mark translated, and he and de Lambert sat down with Bella and her father, while Pierre and the other two Frenchmen conversed near the front of the airplane.

Mark turned to her father. "So, what would you like to ask?"

He nodded to Bella. "Why don't you go ahead?"

She opened her notebook and scanned her list of questions. "How did you first become interested in flying?"

Mark quickly translated the question, and de Lambert rattled off a few sentences. Mark turned back to Bella. "Charles has been interested in flying for many years. He was working on a hydroplane design, but when he saw Wilbur Wright fly last summer at Le Mans, he asked to become his student."

Bella nodded and jotted down a short note. "How many lessons did you have with Mr. Wright?"

Mark relayed the question and listened to de Lambert's answer. "Charles has spent several hours with Wilbur Wright on the ground and in the air. He took his first solo flight after only five hours of instruction." Mark smiled. "He is especially proud to be Mr. Wright's first and favorite European student."

"There are others?"

Mark nodded without asking de Lambert. "Wright has taught three men so far: Paul Tissandier, Captain Paul Lucas-Girardville, and Count de Lambert."

"How do you know that?"

Mark grinned. "As you've heard me say before, understanding your competition is the first step toward winning the battle."

De Lambert laughed. "We are friends, *non*? Not enemies."

"Yes, of course. Competitors can be friends. It simply means they both want to win the prize."

De Lambert sent him a questioning look, and Mark quickly translated. The French pilot smiled and nodded. *"Oui, amis et concurrents."*

Mark nodded. "Yes, friends and competitors."

Bella continued asking questions and filled two pages with notes. Her father occasionally asked for clarification, but he let Bella handle most of the interview.

Finally, she jotted down the answer to her last question and looked up. "Thank you, this has been very helpful. Father, is there anything you'd like to ask?"

He shook his head. "If you have what you need, I'm satisfied."

"Perhaps you could show us your airplane and tell us a bit about it."

De Lambert motioned toward the closer airplane without waiting for Mark to translate. "It's a Wright Flyer, but I make some . . ." He glanced at Mark. *"Changements?"*

Mark nodded. "Changes."

De Lambert walked over to the airplane and pointed out his modifications. The Wright Flyer looked quite different from the Steed IV. It was a bi-wing design with a shorter fuselage, and a rather odd box-shaped device at the tail. Bella made a quick sketch of it, but she wished they'd brought a photographer.

Her father and de Lambert walked a few feet away and attempted a conversation about the wings, while Bella worked on her sketch.

Mark leaned closer. "So what's really going on? Why are you the one asking all the questions?"

Bella's pen stilled. How could she answer him without breaking her word to her parents? "I'm just as interested in aviation as my father."

Mark grinned. "Why do I have the feeling you're avoiding my question?"

"I don't mean to be elusive, but I made a promise, and I want to keep it." She slid her pen into her notebook and closed the flap.

"So you're not going to tell me?"

"That's right."

"Then I suppose I'll have to guess." He narrowed his eyes. "Hmm, I think you must be the true writer behind of all your father's editorials. He lets you do all the hard work, then gives himself the byline."

Bella gave her head a quick shake. "No, that's not it at all."

Mark chuckled. "Then what is it? You're obviously the one taking notes."

She pursed her lips and looked away. It seemed futile to try to hide the truth from him now. He'd most likely see the articles in the *Daily Mail* and know who had written them, even if the byline did say I. J. Wilmington. She turned back to him and whispered. "If I tell you, you must promise to keep it a secret."

He sobered and made an *X* across his heart, then winked at her.

Her cheeks warmed. "I'm writing a series of articles about aviation for the *Daily Mail*—at least I hope it will be a series. The first will be published on Sunday. If it receives a favorable response, the next two articles will feature Count de Lambert and Louis Blériot."

"I see." His eyes crinkled at the corners. "So you're destined to become a famous journalist."

"Well, I am going to write those articles, but I don't know about becoming famous. My parents will only allow me to write if I use a pseudonym."

"And why is that?"

"They think it's not proper for a young, unmarried woman to write for a newspaper, even if her father is the owner."

He grinned. "Well, I think it's fabulous."

She couldn't help her sharp intake of breath. "You do?"

"Yes. Times are changing. Women will have the vote soon, and I see no reason why they shouldn't become journalists, scientists, doctors, or whatever they'd like."

"Well, that's certainly very forward thinking of you."

He chuckled. "Yes, I'm a very modern man."

Her father walked back toward them. "Bella, it's time we thanked these gentlemen and were on our way. I have no idea how long it will take us to reach our next destination in this rain."

"Yes, of course." They hoped to find Louis Blériot and interview him before they went back to their hotel in Calais. She shifted her gaze to Mark. "Thank you for your help. I'm very grateful."

He touched the brim of his hat. "Anytime. I'm glad we happened along."

That comment stirred a question in Bella's mind. "Why did you come here today?"

"De Lambert is changing out his engine and wanted advice from Pierre. I came to see what I could learn about our friend's preparations and how close he is to attempting a crossing."

That was one question she had neglected to ask de Lambert, and it was the most important. She walked back toward the French pilot. "One more question, sir. When do you think you'll be ready to fly across the Channel?"

Mark translated her question. De Lambert narrowed his eyes and stroked his chin, then answered in English. "I will fly across the Channel as soon as I am sure I will not land in the sea."

Bella smiled. "Excellent! Thank you."

They said goodbye, and Bella followed her father back to the car. The driver hopped out and opened the door for them. Her father climbed in, and Bella slid in next to him.

"That went well." Her father settled into the back seat. "What a stroke of luck that Clifton arrived when he did and was able to translate for us."

"Yes. It was a very happy coincidence."

Father cocked one eyebrow. "You two seemed to enjoy your conversation."

Bella suppressed a smile and looked toward the shed. As she did, Mark Clifton raised his hand in farewell. His humor and translation help had been a blessing. And she couldn't help being impressed by his opinion that women should gain the vote and be encouraged to take up careers usually reserved for men.

But an uneasy thought tugged at her conscience. She had broken her promise to her parents by telling Mark she was penning the articles. But on the other hand, their friendship had taken a step forward, which could actually be considered encouraging a potential suitor.

Goodness, was she ready for that?

<hr />

James circled above the far end of the Broadlands estate and set his course for the landing field. He pushed the stick forward, slowing the airplane as he descended over Green Meadow. He had to get this landing right. Bella was back from France, and she would be watching him come in.

The wind picked up and buffeted the airplane. He adjusted the wings, checked his speed, and judged the angle of his descent. A warning shot through him. He was coming in too fast, and he only had seconds to change course or risk a crash.

Gripping the stick, he pulled back, rose up in the air again, and urged the plane higher. Bella and the professor waved as James roared over the barn and workshop with only fifty yards separating him from them.

His heart hammered hard. He pulled in a deep breath and forced himself to focus his attention. He couldn't let the abandoned landing rattle his nerves. He'd made the right choice, the safe choice. Balancing caution with daring was the only way to become a skilled pilot.

He circled around again, and this time he started his descent earlier to give himself more time to slow down. Checking his speed, he gently pushed the stick forward. His stomach clenched as the airplane neared the ground.

The front wheels hit first, sending a jolt through him. He held on tight as his plane rolled across the rough field, finally coming to a stop not far from Bella, Martha, and the professor.

James breathed out a prayer of thanks. He turned off the engine and lifted his goggles. One more successful test flight complete.

The professor hustled across the field toward him. Martha and Bella followed close behind.

"Excellent flight, my boy! Excellent!" The professor reached up to give him a hand.

James grabbed hold and jumped to the ground. "How long was I in the air?"

The professor checked his watch. "Thirty-three minutes."

James nodded and shook off his disappointment. He'd hoped to set a new record today, but that wasn't the only way to judge if his flight had been successful. Each time he took to the air gave him more experience handling the airplane in different situations. And he'd learned some important lessons today.

The professor lowered his bushy white eyebrows. "That was a good decision to pull up and go around again."

James nodded and ran his hand back through his hair. "I was coming in too fast."

"I agree, and I'm glad you realized it in time to pull up."

Martha patted his arm. "Every flight is better than the last. You'll be ready to fly across the Channel any day now."

James sent her a grateful smile, hoping her words were true.

Bella stepped forward, her blue eyes shining. "It was a wonderful flight, but I must confess I was holding my breath when you came in for a landing."

"The first time or the second?"

"Both." Bella's winsome smile and affirming words sent a surge of energy through him. Knowing she was pleased with his efforts boosted his confidence.

Martha stepped back. "I'm going to put the chicken soup on the stove."

She motioned to James and Bella. "Come in and have a bowl when you're ready."

James's empty stomach contracted. "That sounds good. Thank you, Martha."

"I could use your help, Thaddeus." Martha looked up at the professor.

He sent her a surprised glance. "I'm not sure how much help I'd be in the kitchen."

Martha smiled at Bella and James with twinkling eyes. Then she tapped the professor's arm. "Don't worry. I'll give you some easy tasks."

"Such as?"

"You can set the table and slice the bread."

His eyebrows rose, and he seemed to catch on to Martha's efforts to give James and Bella a few moments alone. "Oh yes, I suppose I can try my hand at that if you'll instruct me." Chuckling, he fell in step beside Martha, and they walked back toward her cottage together.

Bella watched them for a moment, a soft smile playing at her lips. "They're very sweet together."

James nodded. "They've been friends since they were children, but they spent many years apart. In fact, they were only reunited last summer."

"Yes, Martha told me," Bella said softly.

James studied Bella's pensive expression. How much more of the story had Martha relayed?

But Bella gave no clue as she reached out and touched the wing of his airplane. "It's a wonderful design. You and Professor Steed should be very proud."

"He's the genius behind the Steed IV. Powered flight has been his dream for years."

"From what he told me, I'd say you've made a great contribution."

"I'm not sure about that."

"Without your input and partnership as pilot, his dream could never become a reality." She turned the full focus of her blue eyes on him. "And I have a feeling this is only the beginning of great things for both of you."

Her words sent a thrill through him. "That's kind of you to say."

A sense of connection seemed to flow between them, strengthening his confidence. Their friendship had reached a new level, and he was not going to miss this opportunity. He took a step toward her. "I'm glad you came today. There's something I'd like to ask you."

She looked up at him. "What is it?"

"We're going to Canterbury to visit the cathedral tomorrow afternoon."

"You won't be making any test flights?"

"No, we don't fly on Sundays."

"Oh yes, of course."

"Martha said she'd pack a lunch and bring it with us. Then we plan to eat on the train." He tensed and looked into her eyes. "Would you like to come with us?"

Her lips parted. "Oh, I've never been to Canterbury. That sounds lovely."

"So, you'll come?"

She smiled, her eyes shining. "I'll have to ask my parents and be sure we don't have other plans, but if they're agreeable, then yes. I'd love to go to Canterbury with you."

He rose up on his toes, feeling like he might just take off without his airplane. "I'm so glad."

Her cheeks turned pink, and she glanced away. "It's kind of you to invite me to come along."

"It was Martha's idea."

She darted a glance his way again, her smile fading.

James pulled in a sharp breath. "No, I don't mean it was her idea to invite you. Martha was the one who suggested the trip to Canterbury, but I thought of asking you to come with us."

"Oh, I see." She pressed her lips together, but it didn't hide her returning smile.

He stifled a groan. He was making a royal mess of this conversation. He mentally scrambled for something else to say. "How was your trip to France?"

She looked down, and her eyebrows dipped slightly. "It went well. The weather was quite rainy, but we were able to see the people we wanted to see."

He waited, thinking she might say more, but she didn't. "How is your family? I hope everyone is well."

"They are, thank you. My sister received word her court presentation will be on the third of May. Now that we know the date, we're moving ahead with our plans for the season. We'll be staying in town from mid-April through the end of July."

James nodded, his spirits sinking. How would he see her if she was staying in London all that time? He pushed away his disappointment and met her gaze. "Are you looking forward to the season?"

"I'm happy for Sylvia, but I've taken part in it the past two years. And, no, I wouldn't say I'm looking forward to it."

"Why not? I'd think it would be the highlight of the year for someone like you."

She tipped her head and sent him a questioning look. "Someone like me?"

He closed his eyes, trying to straighten out his thoughts. "I simply meant you're an intelligent, charming young woman from a prominent family, and you'll probably receive more invitations than you can accept. Isn't that what every young woman hopes for?"

"I'm sure some do, but I have different dreams, and they aren't tied to invitations or the season."

He was about to ask her about those dreams, but Martha called to them. He glanced toward the cottage.

Martha stood in the open doorway. "The soup is ready. Come and have some while it's hot."

He wished their private conversation could continue, but he couldn't ignore Martha's call. At least he could try to extend their time together. "Can you stay and have lunch with us?"

Her smile spread wider. "That sounds perfect."

<hr>

"How can you even think of traipsing around the countryside with a young man we hardly know?" Bella's mother shifted in her chair and looked away from Bella. "This is so unpleasant. Let's not speak of it anymore."

Sylvia sank lower in her chair and kept her eyes trained on the embroidery in her lap.

Bella clutched the sides of her skirt and sent her father a pleading look. He sat across from them in the library. Firelight flickered on his newspaper as he raised it higher, blocking his view of the conversation, but certainly not their voices.

Bella's gaze swung back to her mother. "You said you wanted me to accept invitations and encourage potential suitors."

Her mother's eyes flashed wide. "I was talking about invitations from the respectable young men you'll meet in London during the season, not from some reckless pilot I know nothing about."

"Mother, that's hardly fair. You entertained Mr. Drake here at Broadlands when he and Professor Steed came for dinner, and Father visited him at his workshop at Green Meadow. I don't see how you can say you don't know him."

Mother pursed her lips. "But who is he, really? What is his background? Is his family listed in *Burke's Peerage*?"

Bella closed her eyes and pulled in a deep breath. "I don't believe being listed in *Burke's Peerage* makes someone a worthy suitor or even a valuable friend."

"Honestly, Bella!" Her mother's face flushed pink. "I'm trying to protect your reputation and keep you from ruining your future."

"How could visiting Canterbury Cathedral in the company of three friends ruin my reputation?" Bella's tone grew more insistent with each phrase. "Father, please, make her be reasonable."

He sighed and lowered the newspaper. "Bella, you should listen to your mother."

"But, Father, you like James Drake. You said yourself he may become a national hero if he's the first to fly across the Channel."

"Well, that hasn't happened yet, and there's no guarantee it will." Her father laid the newspaper on his lap. "He and Professor Steed are quite clever, but after meeting those French pilots and Mark Clifton, I'm not convinced Drake will be the first."

"But he's almost ready. His tests flights are consistently longer than thirty minutes. He solved his engine problems, and he's learning more every day."

"That may be true, and I know you consider him a friend. But I don't think you should set your heart on him as a suitor."

Bella lifted her eyes toward the ceiling. "I'm not asking to marry him. I simply want to go to Canterbury for the afternoon."

Her father's expression eased, and Bella's hopes rose. She hurried on, "We'd leave directly from church, and Professor Steed and Mrs. Shelby will be with us the entire time."

Her father lowered his chin and looked at her mother over the top of his glasses. "I suppose we could consider it."

"Oh, Charles!" Mother raised her hand to her forehead. "First you let her write those articles for the newspaper, and now you want to let her go off and spend the day with that pilot."

"She won't be alone with him. Mrs. Shelby is a suitable chaperone, and Professor Steed is a respectable companion. Really, Madelyn, I don't think she's in any danger."

Her mother drew in a long breath. "I don't agree, but apparently no one values my opinion."

Bella sent Sylvia a beseeching look. Her sister returned a sympathetic glance, but then she looked down at her embroidery and remained silent.

"Mother, I understand you want to protect my reputation and make sure I have every opportunity for the future. I appreciate that, and I'm grateful for your love and concern. But I'd like to accept Mr. Drake's invitation and visit the cathedral. I've heard it's an amazing sight with great cultural and spiritual significance."

Her mother's frown faded. She took a handkerchief from her sleeve and dabbed at her nose. "Well, I suppose if your father believes it won't do too much harm, how can I stand in the way?"

"So I may go?"

Her mother gave a reluctant nod. "You may, but you must promise to be home by seven to dress for dinner."

Glee spiraled through Bella's heart, but she kept her smile in check. "Thank you, Mother. I'll make every effort to be home on time." Bella walked out of the library and hurried up the stairs. She would write a note to James and ask one of the servants to deliver it to Green Meadow. And tomorrow morning she would meet him at church and then they'd spend the afternoon exploring Canterbury together.

Nine

James rose to his feet and held the hymnal so Bella could also see the lyrics of the final song. She looked up and sent him a soft smile, then joined in singing the first verse. She wore a burgundy hat today with a small cluster of flowers and a black ribbon around the crown. The color was an attractive contrast to her fair complexion, and it made her brilliant blue eyes stand out.

As he sang the familiar hymn, he recalled the events of the morning.

He and the professor and Martha had waited out in front of the church until Bella arrived. When he'd walked inside with her, several people had turned and watched them, but rather than feeling uncomfortable, he'd been proud to be at her side. They walked up the aisle and slid into the fourth pew from the front with Martha and the professor. His arm touched Bella's as they held the hymnal together, and it sent a rush of energy through him.

His feelings for Bella were deepening every day. When they were apart, she was never far from his thoughts, and when they were together, as they were today, he found her so distracting, it was a challenge to focus on anything else.

But when Reverend Jackson had read Psalm 68 and explained the meaning of those verses in his message, he'd caught James's attention. The words of the psalm ran through his mind again, stirring him and tightening his throat. *"A father of the fatherless. . . . God setteth the solitary in families."*

For so many years, he'd felt ashamed of his background and been determined to hide it from everyone. But the idea that God understood his situation and cared about him in a fatherly way was a surprising revelation. James always thought the circumstances of his birth had created a distance between him and God. But that wasn't true.

As he looked back, he could now see how God had watched over him and set him in a family—first with Anna and then with the professor. His father and grandfather might have cast him off, but God had watched over him, cared for him, and placed him in secure, loving homes.

His father had abandoned him, but that had not escaped God's notice. Instead, God had promised to step in and fill that role in his life . . . if he would let Him.

That invitation to a Father-son relationship with God had a strong magnetic pull, like something elusive he had been searching for his entire life was finally within his grasp. An urgency to accept that invitation and know God as Father flooded through him.

His voice dropped away, and he closed his eyes, letting the song and his thoughts form a silent prayer. God saw his heart and knew his longings and deepest needs. Warmth flowed through him along with assurance that his wordless prayer had been heard and had connected him to God in a new and deeper way.

Gratitude swelled in his heart, and he blinked his stinging eyes. How blessed he was. How thankful. He wouldn't abandon his search to learn more about his mother and earthly father, but he would do it with courage rather than fear and shame. With God's help, he would find out the truth and put his questions to rest, once and for all.

Bella glanced at James as he bowed his head and closed his eyes in the middle of the hymn. Emotion flickered across his face, and his Adam's apple bobbed.

Her heart went out to him, but she shifted her gaze away. She didn't want him to look up and find her watching him. But she was curious to know what had touched him so deeply. Was it the lyrics of the hymn or something Reverend Jackson had said?

Whatever it was, she wouldn't intrude on his private thoughts or question him about it now. If he wanted to tell her later, she would be happy to listen.

The hymn ended and Reverend Jackson asked them to stay standing for the benediction. Bella bowed her head and let the reverend's peaceful words flow around her. When his prayer ended, the organ music began. Some people turned and greeted one another, while others stepped out into the aisle and left the sanctuary.

Martha picked up her purse from the pew and turned to Bella. "That was a lovely service, wasn't it?"

"Yes, Reverend Jackson's messages always give me a lot to think about."

James looked her way. "I thought today's sermon was especially meaningful."

Bella nodded, enjoying the sense of connection that flowed between them.

The professor and Martha led the way down the aisle, and James and Bella followed. They walked through the narthex and shook hands with Reverend Jackson, then stepped out into the sunny churchyard. Martha greeted a few friends and introduced them to Bella. Then they set off through the village and headed for the train station.

Bella walked beside James, enjoying his company and the warmth of the early spring sunshine. "What time does the train leave for Canterbury?"

"Twelve forty." James checked his watch.

"We better step lively." The professor quickened the pace, and a few minutes later they arrived at the station.

Bella offered to pay for her own ticket, but the professor insisted he would take care of it, stepping up to the window to make the purchase.

Bella glanced around, wishing she had time to buy a copy of the *Daily Mail* at the newsstand. For some odd reason, it had not arrived at Broadlands that morning before she left for church. She hoped there hadn't been some catastrophe with the presses that had prevented them from publishing the Sunday edition. Her first article was supposed to be featured today, and she was longing to see it.

A loud whistle sounded, and the train rolled into the station as the professor finished paying at the window. A few passengers stepped down from the train, and the conductor called for everyone to board. The professor opened the door of the third-class car, and Bella, Martha, and James entered the train.

Traveling third class was a change for Bella. Her family always rode in a first-class compartment, but she didn't mind. Glancing around, she didn't really see much difference except the benches were not as well padded.

They settled into their seats, and Bella turned to James. "How long is the trip to Canterbury?"

"It's only twenty miles or so. We should arrive at about one fifteen."

"Shall we have our lunch?" Martha opened her basket and began passing out cloth napkins, meat pies, oranges, and bottles of lemonade.

The professor offered a brief prayer, thanking the Lord for their picnic on the train and asking His blessing on their travels that day. Bella's heart warmed as she listened to his humble prayer and thought of their simple meal. She couldn't remember feeling this happy and content in a very long time.

Bella bit into the meat pie and found the crust was delightfully light and flaky, the filling savory and delicious. "Oh, Martha, this is wonderful."

Martha waved away her words. "It's just a meat pie." But Bella could tell she was pleased by the compliment.

The professor shook his head. "Never say *just* when talking about your cooking!"

Martha's cheeks glowed pink. She took a sip of lemonade and glanced at the professor. "Have you started preparing your lecture for the Aero Club's spring series?"

"I've finished my outline and started filling in the details, but there's still quite a bit to do, and then I'll need to polish my presentation."

"What's the focus of your lecture?" James asked, as he peeled his orange.

"I want to explain the unique design features of the Steed IV. Many aviators have achieved lift and thrust, but control is the key issue now, and I believe we have the answers. I also want to challenge those in attendance to speak up for the advancement of aviation. We must convince the government and military officials that aviation has a role to play in our defense."

James watched the professor with obvious affection. "I'm sure your talk will be the best of the series."

"That's kind of you to say, my boy. I'm hoping it will open more doors for us."

Their conversation continued while they finished their lunch, and soon the conductor announced Canterbury as the next stop. They gathered up their picnic items and passed them back to Martha. As she tucked the cloth napkin over the top of the basket, the train slowed and screeched to a stop. James stepped out first and held the door for Bella, Martha, and the professor.

Bella scanned the station and spotted a small newsstand on the far side of the platform. Would they think it was odd if she bought a copy of the *Daily Mail*? Well, she wasn't going to miss her chance to see her first published article!

"Excuse me just a moment." She turned away from James before he could reply, and she walked to the newsstand. A young boy who looked no more than twelve or thirteen stood at the side of the stand. "Do you have a copy of the Sunday *Daily Mail*?"

"Yes miss." He reached down and lifted one from the shelf, then held it out to Bella.

"How long will you be here today?"

"I usually leave about six thirty."

She nodded and pressed a coin into his hand. "Would you set this copy aside for me? I'll come back and pick it up before you close your stand this evening."

The boy sent her a quizzical look. "All right, miss. If you like."

"Thank you." Bella turned and walked across the platform to rejoin her friends.

James watched her closely. "Everything all right?"

"Yes . . . I was just asking if he had a copy of the *Daily Mail*. We didn't receive ours this morning before I left, and I was hoping to find one to take home."

James glanced at her empty hands. "He didn't have a copy?"

"Oh, he did, but I didn't want to carry it with me. He's going to save one for me, and I'll pick it up before we board the train home." Bella forced a smile, hoping he wouldn't ask her any more about it.

He nodded, though a hint of a question still flickered in his eyes.

"I believe it's only a short walk to the cathedral." The professor motioned to his right, and they set off through town.

Bella enjoyed the bustling atmosphere of Canterbury. Most of the streets were narrow and crowded with interesting shops, tearooms, and other businesses. Some of the buildings were Tudor style and looked as though they'd been built centuries ago. Others were more modern, but all looked neat and well kept.

They crossed a bridge over a small stream and walked up High Street through the center of town, then turned down Mercery Lane.

"Look, there's the Christchurch Gate." Martha pointed toward the end of the lane. "That should take us into the cathedral grounds."

Bella gazed up at the elaborate carvings and statues above the gate as they came closer. A sense of awe flowed through her as she thought of all the pilgrims who had passed through this gate on their way in to visit one of the most famous churches in England.

She'd seen the tall towers of the cathedral as they walked through town, but as they stepped into the open square and she saw the full view, it took her breath away.

"My goodness." Martha lifted her hand to shade her eyes. "It's magnificent."

"That it is." The professor scanned the cathedral with an appreciative smile.

James studied it all with an intense, serious gaze. "How old is it?"

"I'm not sure," the professor added. "Let's ask a guide or see if they offer a pamphlet."

Bella took in the details as they came closer. Towers with tall spires rose on each side of the main entrance, and farther back the huge central tower overshadowed it all. Everything about the building pointed upward and made her lift her eyes toward heaven. She supposed that was what the architects had in mind when they designed the cathedral.

"I've seen some beautiful churches before, but never one like this." James's voice carried a touch of wonder. He and Bella exchanged a smile, and they walked on toward the main entrance.

When they stepped inside, Bella was struck by the vast height and size of the building. Just as the exterior design pointed toward heaven, the interior design had the same effect, drawing her gaze upward, past the pillars, to the colorful stained glass windows and high vaulted ceiling. A hushed reverence seemed to permeate the atmosphere and settled over her like a calming cloak.

She leaned closer to James. "It's amazing, isn't it?"

"Yes, I hardly know what else to say to describe it."

They walked up the center aisle of the nave at a slow pace, taking in the view of the windows, statues, and pillars. Everywhere she looked there were more wonderful details in the carvings and paintings.

Bella stopped before a set of stained glass windows, her gaze traveling over the design. Each circle featured different characters from the Bible. "Who do you think that is on the bottom right?"

James looked up at the window. "I believe it's Noah. See, he's releasing the dove and there's the ark and water below."

"Yes, and that next section must be Jesus at His resurrection." Bella studied the angels around Jesus as He stepped out of the tomb.

"What about the one on the right?" James clasped his hands behind his back and studied the scene. "Who escaped out of a window with the help of a woman?"

Bella pondered that for a moment. "Do you think it's Rahab? Didn't she help the spies escape that way from her house on the wall of Jericho?"

"Perhaps, but there were three spies." James consulted the pamphlet they'd picked up at the door, then looked up with a smile. "It's Michal, helping her husband, David, escape from her father, King Saul."

Bella nodded, though she barely remembered hearing that story once when she was much younger.

They moved on to the next set of windows where the lower central image showed Jesus at His baptism. "There's a dove in that one too." She pointed to the white bird descending over Jesus.

"Yes, there is." James studied it a moment more. "That reminds me of Reverend Jackson's message today."

Bella shifted her gaze to James, not certain of the connection.

"At Jesus's baptism, the voice from heaven said, 'This is my beloved Son, in whom I am well pleased.'" His voice faltered at the end of his sentence.

She looked up at him, surprised by the sheen in his eyes.

He blinked and turned his face away. "Sorry. I suppose I haven't really thought much about that Father-son relationship until today. That part of this morning's message spoke to me, especially when Reverend Jackson read that verse in the Psalms about God being a father to the fatherless."

Bella sensed there was much more behind his comments.

He glanced around and then looked her way again. "You see, I never knew my father. That's been a hard issue for me to face."

Her heart clenched. "Oh, James, I'm sorry. I didn't know."

His brow creased and he looked down. "It's all right. I don't usually talk about it."

"Did your father pass away when you were young?"

"No, he's probably still alive, but I'm not certain. I think his last name is Drake, but I don't know his first name." He met her gaze, a mixture of vulnerability and challenge in his eyes. "He and my mother were not married when I was born."

Bella blinked, and it took her a moment before she could reply. "So, you were raised by your mother?"

"Only for a short time, and then she died in a tragic . . . incident. After that I was taken in by Anna Steed, the professor's sister."

Bella gave a slow nod. She remembered Martha had mentioned having a longtime friendship with Professor Steed and his sister, Anna.

"Anna died from an illness when I was almost six," James continued, "and that's when I came to live with the professor in London."

Bella's heart ached for James. He had endured so many losses at a very young age. Thank goodness the professor had stepped in to provide a home for him. "So Professor Steed is much more than your mentor and partner in airplane design."

"Yes. He raised me, and he's always treated me like a son." His gaze softened. "He inspired my love for science and aviation, and he made sure I had an excellent education. And now he's taken me under his wing and given me the opportunity to fly. I don't know how I'll ever repay him."

Bella sent him a soft smile. "I can see he's proud of you and all you've accomplished. And when you are the first to fly across the Channel, I'm sure that will be more than enough to repay his kindness."

James's expression grew more intense. "We must be first. If we're not, it won't only be my dream that dies, it will be the professor's, as well."

She laid her hand on his arm. "You're staying up longer every time. I'm sure you'll be ready to make that crossing very soon."

"I hope so." His brow creased and his gaze shifted away. "I only wish I knew how close the other pilots are to making an attempt."

She wished she could pass on what she'd learned when she'd interviewed Count de Lambert and Louis Blériot, but that would mean telling him about the articles. She'd already broken her promise to her parents by admitting it to Mark Clifton. She couldn't add to her guilt by telling James as well.

She looked up and forced a smile. "Don't worry. No one has contacted the *Daily Mail* yet, and they must give notice if they want to qualify for the prize."

He nodded, but her words didn't ease his troubled expression. He had more than the flight on his mind, and she supposed it was what he had revealed about his family.

An idea began to take shape in her mind. Perhaps there was a way she could help him. "Have you tried to find your father?"

"No, the professor doesn't like to talk about my parents or the circumstances around my birth. It's only been in the last few weeks that I've learned my mother's full name."

"What is it?"

He hesitated, then met her gaze. "Laura Markingham."

She gasped. "Sir Richard's daughter?"

"Yes. I believe she's the youngest woman in the painting that hangs above the staircase landing at Broadlands."

"Did you know her name when you visited me that day?"

"Yes, but I only have one photograph of her, and I didn't make the connection to Broadlands until I saw the painting. Then, as I was leaving, I spoke to one of the gardeners who used to work for Sir Richard, and he confirmed she is the woman in the painting."

Bella thought for a moment. "My father met Sir Richard, and I've heard a little about his family."

James nodded to her. "Go on."

"His wife, Lady Katrina, passed away a few years ago. Mrs. Latimer, our housekeeper, said one daughter married and moved to America. I believe she was the oldest."

"Judith."

"Yes, that's her name. She said her sister is a widow and lives with relatives in Ireland."

James nodded. "That would be my aunt Maryann." He gave his head a slight shake. "It's hard to believe we're related, since I've never met any of them."

"Perhaps if you contact Sir Richard or your aunts, they might be able to tell you more about your mother . . . and your father."

His mouth firmed into a tight line. "My mother and her parents disagreed about what should happen to me. She left Broadlands to protect me. My grandfather never acknowledged me or offered any help, even after my mother died."

"I'm sorry," Bella said softly.

How could Sir Richard be so cruel? It wasn't James's fault that his parents had not been married when he was born. He was still Sir Richard's grandson, and the man ought to care what had happened to him.

Professor Steed walked back toward them. "We're walking over to see the memorial to Thomas Becket."

James glanced at Bella, and she nodded. "We're coming."

A chill traveled through Bella as she recalled the story about the murdered archbishop, Thomas Becket. He'd been killed right here in the cathedral by four knights loyal to King Henry II after a long-standing dispute between the Crown and the church. But the archbishop's death had a powerful impact on many, including the King who made his own pilgrimage to Canterbury Cathedral, where he donned sackcloth and walked barefoot to show his repentance.

Bella and James followed Martha and the professor across the nave toward a side chapel. A few people had gathered there, but their conversation was hushed and respectful. A single pillar candle sat in the center of the chapel floor. The name *Thomas Becket* was carved into the stone floor nearby.

James leaned down and read the placard aloud. "The candle burns where the Shrine of Saint Thomas of Canterbury stood from 1220 to 1538 when it was destroyed by the order of King Henry VIII."

Bella's gaze rested on James, and her thoughts shifted from the martyred archbishop to what James had told her about his family.

Her throat tightened as she thought of his losses and the questions that lingered in his mind. No one should be left in the dark about the details of his birth and the identity of his parents. It wasn't right.

There had to be some way she could help him find his father. Perhaps if she spoke to some of the older servants at Broadlands, they might remember who had been courting Laura before James was born.

Had James checked the baptismal records at the local church? His father's name might be listed there. She could help him with that part of the search too.

Determination sent energy coursing through her. James should not have to face these haunting questions without the help and support of a friend.

With her family's ownership of Broadlands and their connections in Kent and in London, she could help him discover the truth and perhaps even reconnect with his family. When they met James, they would no doubt be proud of all he had accomplished and all he hoped to do.

She smiled up at him, her decision made. She would partner with him on this quest, and together they would find the answers he was seeking.

Ten

The wind whipped around James as he climbed the path toward the highest point at the White Cliffs of Dover. He pulled his scarf up a bit, trying to protect his ears from the stinging cold. Glancing over his shoulder, he spotted the professor several yards behind. The old man's cheeks were ruddy, and he panted as he made his way up the hill.

James stopped and waited for him. They were both eager to scout out the best areas for takeoff for his flight across the Channel, but the professor's stamina was not what it used to be. James's shoulders tensed as he studied the professor's labored breathing. He'd always seemed invincible, but the last few years had taken a toll on him. He'd turned seventy-two on his last birthday, and though he had no obvious health problems, he wouldn't live forever.

What would James do if he lost the professor?

The thought sent a chill through him, but he tried to push it away. He didn't even want to consider it.

The professor caught up, lifted his hand to shade his eyes, and looked out to sea. "The wind is surprisingly stronger here than it is at Green Meadow."

"Yes, that's going to be a challenge." James watched the clouds scuttle across the sky, obscuring the sun for the moment.

"Do you think this would be a good area for takeoff?" James indicated the open fields to his left.

The professor lifted his chin and searched the landscape. "It's the best we've seen, though I'm not thrilled with the incline. That will create more drag during takeoff." He gave a thoughtful nod. "When we're finished here, let's walk back that way. I'd like to take a closer look."

"Good idea." James gazed out over the ocean again. Waves swirled and heaved in the gray water below. He squinted toward the horizon, searching for the French coastline. On a clear day you could see the slight rise of land around Calais, but on a cloudy day like today, it faded into the sea and sky.

James sunk his hands into his pockets and wiggled his fingers inside his gloves, trying to warm them. "So what do you think? Are we ready?" As he spoke, another cold gust rushed up the cliffs and stung his eyes.

The professor sighed and shook his head. "I'm afraid we'll have to wait until the weather warms and we can count on more clear, calm days."

James gave his head a slight shake. It was already the twenty-third of March. "Do we have time?"

"I think the other pilots will take the same precautions. No one wants to risk their airplane or their life when the weather is this cold and unpredictable."

James strained to scan the horizon again. What was happening over there in Calais? Were the French pilots as cautious as the professor? Would they wait for ideal conditions, or would they attempt a flight before the weather warmed? He clenched his hands. "We can't let them take that prize! Not after all we've put into refining our design, and certainly not after all the nerve-racking test flights I've taken."

"We must have patience, my boy. The Lord knows the desires of our hearts. He has guided us this far. Let's trust Him to take us the rest of the way." The professor watched James, waiting for his reply.

But James grimaced and looked away, wrestling with the idea. How could he wait and trust the Lord when so much was at stake? "How will we know when it's time? What are the most important factors?"

"I'd say the temperature should be at least in the sixties, with the winds from the west, no stronger than seven miles per hour." The professor gazed across the blue-gray Channel. "But the Lord will show us the right day and time. I'm confident of that."

"I wish I could go today . . ." James glared across the Channel. He knew he needed more practice and test flights, especially over the open water.

The professor rested his hand on James's shoulder. "If you went today, you'd probably end up in the drink, with a damaged airplane and broken dreams, and it would take months for us to get back to where we are now."

James tried to push down his frustration, but it bubbled up, and he huffed.

There was too much at stake. He had to be first, for his sake and for the professor's.

⌘

Bella smoothed her hand over the newspaper clipping of her first aviation article published in the *Daily Mail*. Happy warmth spread through her as she read the opening paragraph again.

Mr. Elmwood, the editor, must have been pleased. He'd only made a few changes, breaking some of her longer sentences into two and strengthening some of her verbs. She'd sent him the second article about Count de Lambert, and she was working hard on the third featuring Louis Blériot. Even though Mr. Elmwood had not contacted her, she kept writing, hoping and praying he would continue her series.

A knock sounded at her door, and she looked up. "Yes?"

"It's Mrs. Latimer, miss."

Bella's thoughts quickly shifted to the message she'd sent the housekeeper, requesting a meeting in her room. She didn't want any of the other servants or family members to hear her questions to Mrs. Latimer.

"Come in," Bella called, as she turned in her chair to face the housekeeper.

"You sent for me, miss?" The housekeeper crossed to the middle of the room.

"Yes. Thank you for taking time to talk with me."

"Of course, miss."

Mrs. Latimer had already mentioned a few things about the Markinghams, and Bella hoped the housekeeper might be able to tell her more. "How long have you've worked at Broadlands?"

"Almost thirty years, miss."

"That's quite a long time." Bella sent her an appreciative smile. "What positions have you held?"

"I started as a housemaid, then I was lady's maid for Lady Katrina, and finally I became housekeeper after Lady Katrina passed away."

"I'm sure Sir Richard and Lady Katrina appreciated your faithful service."

"I was pleased to serve them, miss. And I'm happy to continue on as housekeeper for your family."

Bella glanced away, considering what to say next. Then she looked back at Mrs. Latimer. "There is a rather delicate matter that's come to my attention, and I thought you might be able to help me sort it out."

"I'd be glad to help if I can."

"I understand the Markinghams had three daughters."

The housekeeper gave a slight nod. "Yes miss, Ladies Judith, Maryann, and Laura."

"Can you tell me more about the youngest daughter, Lady Laura?"

Some undefined emotion flickered across the housekeeper's face. "What would you like to know?"

"Oh, just your impression of her."

"Well, she was a lovely young woman, very fond of horses and the out of doors, and she was always considerate of the staff." Mrs. Latimer's gray eyes softened. "I'm afraid she passed away when she was only nineteen."

Bella gave a slight nod. "I believe she left home the year before that. Do you know why?"

The housekeeper averted her eyes. "I couldn't say, miss."

She couldn't, or she wouldn't?

Bella waited until the housekeeper looked her way again. "There's not much that happens in a house like this that escapes the notice of the staff."

Mrs. Latimer's expression grew more troubled. "Why are you asking me questions about someone who died more than twenty years ago?"

"Because the reason she left still has an impact on . . . certain people today."

"Who, miss?"

Bella bit her lip. It seemed she would have to be more direct if she was going to convince the housekeeper to give her any more information. She met Mrs. Latimer's gaze. "I know Lady Laura was with child when she left Broadlands."

The housekeeper lifted her hand to her heart. "Who told you that?"

"It's not important. What is important is finding out who is the father of her child."

Mrs. Latimer's face paled. "I wouldn't know, miss."

"But surely you must have seen or heard about a young man who called on Lady Laura?"

The housekeeper shook her head. "I don't remember."

"Please, it's very important."

Mrs. Latimer clasped her hands and looked away, the struggle evident in her troubled expression. Finally, she looked back at Bella. "I suppose now that Sir Richard is gone and I serve your family, I can tell you what I know."

"Yes, please do."

"It was a terribly sad time for the whole Markingham family. They tried to keep Lady Laura's condition a secret, but word got out somehow, and there was no way to stop it from spreading through the village and across the county."

"If people knew Lady Laura was pregnant, then there must have been speculation about the father of the child. Surely someone knew who he was."

Mrs. Latimer shook her head. "Lady Laura wouldn't tell her parents or anyone else, no matter how much they threatened or cajoled. Sir Richard and Lady Katrina were planning to send her away to Ireland to stay with her mother's relatives. They wanted her to leave the baby there to be raised by someone else, but Lady Laura wouldn't agree to their plan."

Bella's heart clenched. How dreadful. Of course she wouldn't want to give up her child.

"Then one night she just up and disappeared," Mrs. Latimer continued. "She didn't leave a note or give a clue about where she was going. They searched for her, but no one could find her."

Bella stared at the housekeeper. She certainly hadn't heard that part of the story from James. Maybe he didn't even know.

"At first everyone thought she and the baby's father had eloped, but a few months later someone saw her, and we learned she'd gone to stay with an old friend who lived near the coast."

"Anna Steed."

Surprise flashed in Mrs. Latimer's eyes. "Yes, that was her name. She used to work at Broadlands as a maid, and she and Lady Laura stayed in touch after she left service. When Laura ran away, she went to Anna's cottage. Anna took her in and cared for her and the baby." The housekeeper released a sad sigh. "She had a little boy, but I don't remember what she named him."

Bella was tempted to supply his name, but that would reveal too much.

"Anna watched over them both until . . ."

Bella leaned forward slightly. "Until?"

Mrs. Latimer crossed her arms. "The accident. It was dreadful. The saddest thing I've ever heard."

Bella swallowed. "What happened?"

"Lady Laura went out for a walk by the cliffs above Saint Margaret's Bay. There had been two solid weeks of rain. She must have gone too close to the edge and the ground gave way. She fell to her death on the rocky beach below." Mrs. Latimer shuddered. "I couldn't believe it. Both of them dead on the same day."

Bella stared at her. "Both?"

"Yes, she was holding the baby boy in her arms when she fell."

Bella gasped. "What? I don't understand. You're saying Lady Laura and her son both died from the fall?"

Mrs. Latimer nodded. "Such a terrible tragedy. Lady Katrina cried for days and days. There was no way to console her."

Bella's mind spun. Who had started such a terrible story? Why would they claim James had died with his mother? Could it have been Sir Richard's attempt to put to rest that painful chapter of his daughter's life and erase every memory of James's existence?

Surely Laura's parents knew the truth. How had they made everyone believe the lie? She supposed a well-placed bribe could have convinced some people to keep quiet and play along. But the thought angered and disgusted her.

Bella focused on Mrs. Latimer again. "Did you attend the funeral?"

"No miss. It was a private graveside service at Saint Matthew's. Only the family attended."

"Is there a tombstone for Lady Laura and her son?"

"I'm not sure, miss. I haven't gone looking for it."

Bella gave a slight nod, storing that thought for later. "After Lady Laura's death, did you ever hear anything about the baby's father?"

The housekeeper sent an uncomfortable glance toward the window.

"If you know anything else, please don't hold back."

The housekeeper gave a slow nod. "A few days after Lady Laura died, a well-dressed young man came to call on Sir Richard. When I passed by the library, I heard them arguing. I shouldn't have listened, but their voices were raised, and I couldn't help hearing."

"What did they say?"

"The young man said he loved Laura and he would've done anything to save her. But Sir Richard shouted at him and told him to get out before he sent for the police."

"Can you describe the man?"

"It was a long time ago, and I only saw him briefly."

"Whatever you remember would be helpful."

The housekeeper nodded. "He was young. I'd say he was in his twenties and quite handsome. He had blond hair and striking blue eyes." She narrowed her gaze as though straining to remember. "I think Sir Richard called him Daniel, but I can't be sure about that."

Bella's heartbeat quickened. Could that man be James's father? It seemed like a strong possibility. But she would need more information to confirm the matter.

"Is there anything else you can tell me about Lady Laura or the man who came to call?"

"That's all I know, miss." She thought a moment more. "But I will say this, after Lady Laura's death, her parents were never the same. Grief broke Lady Katrina's health. She died a short time later. And Sir Richard was so grieved and burdened he could hardly carry on with his duties." Mrs. Latimer shook her head. "All those terrible things weighed him down and made him look as though he'd aged ten years."

"Yes, I'm sure it was difficult for everyone." Bella thanked Mrs. Latimer and released her to return to her duties.

Bella pondered all she'd learned as she watched the housekeeper leave. She could understand Sir Richard's and Lady Katrina's sorrow over the loss of their daughter, but her sympathy toward them didn't match that of the old housekeeper's.

Their plan to send Laura away to Ireland and make her give up her baby had made their daughter believe her only choice was to run away. If they had been more forgiving and supportive, perhaps she would've stayed. Then James would have been born at Broadlands and grown up with the Markinghams, surrounded by wealth and privilege.

But they'd hardened their hearts toward Laura and set in motion the whole tragic series of events, and that made them partially to blame for what had happened. She stilled as another thought struck. Perhaps it wasn't just grief that afflicted Sir Richard and Lady Katrina, but the combination of guilt and regret that made their grief so difficult to bear.

Their decision to try to preserve their reputation had separated them from their daughter and contributed to her death. Then they'd doubled their guilt, trying to blot out the memory of James's illegitimate birth by claiming he had died that day with his mother on the rocky beach of Saint Margaret's Bay.

What a terrible legacy of death and deception.

Rain drummed on the windowpane above the kitchen sink as James lowered the last pan into the soapy water. He scrubbed the inside with a dishcloth, then rinsed it in clean water. Helping Martha with the dinner dishes was the least he could do after the fine meal of roasted chicken and vegetables she had prepared for them.

He glanced at Martha, and one corner of his mouth tugged up in a grin. She looked comfortable, seated by the kitchen fireplace in her favorite chair, reading the Sunday edition of the *Daily Mail,* while the professor paced from the sitting room to the kitchen doorway, practicing his talk for the Aero Club's spring lecture series.

A wave of appreciation flowed through him. There was something special about sharing a quiet evening with Martha and the professor. If only Bella were here, it would be perfect. His spirits deflated a bit with that thought. It had been a week since he'd seen Bella, and each day they were apart he became more aware of how important she was becoming to him and how much he missed her.

What was he going to do about that?

He couldn't very well declare his growing feelings for her until he had more to offer. And he wouldn't really have anything to offer until he made his flight across the Channel and won the prize offered by the *Daily Mail.*

Martha gasped. "My goodness, come and look at this!"

"What is it?" James grabbed a towel and wiped his hands as he crossed the kitchen toward her.

Martha pointed to the headline. "French Pilot Prepares for Flight Across the Channel."

James gripped the back of Martha's chair and leaned over her shoulder. He scanned the first paragraph, and his mind spun as he read on.

"Thaddeus, you'd better come here," Martha called, her voice insistent.

The professor leaned in the kitchen doorway. "What is it?"

James looked up. "There's an article about that French pilot Count de Lambert and his plans to fly across the Channel."

"What!" The professor strode across the kitchen, looked over Martha's other shoulder, and glared at the newspaper.

"'In a rustic camp not far from Wissant, France,'" James read aloud, "'Count de Lambert, a French aristocrat and aviation pioneer, is preparing to make the first flight across the English Channel and take home the one-thousand-pound prize offered by the *Daily Mail*.'"

"Blast!" The professor slapped his leg. "I knew we had competitors, but I didn't think they were ready to challenge us."

"Now, Thaddeus, there's no need to get upset. It doesn't say he's going to make the flight tomorrow or anytime soon; it just says he's making preparations."

The professor huffed. "Charles Grayson and the staff at the *Daily Mail* must think he has a fighting chance, or they wouldn't have sent a reporter all the way to France to interview him."

James straightened. Was that why Bella and her father had gone to France last week? No, that couldn't be it. Charles Grayson owned the newspaper. He didn't write the articles. He glanced at the byline: *I. J. Wilmington*. He'd never heard of the man. Could he be a reporter who'd gone with Bella and Mr. Grayson? Perhaps, but it didn't seem likely.

He leaned down and continued reading about de Lambert's team, his airplane, and his hope to see a French aviator win the prize.

The professor pointed to the final paragraph. "Look, this article is the second in a series about the expansion of aviation and the race to fly across the Channel. The third will be published next Sunday."

James looked up and met the professor's gaze. "How did we miss the first?"

"I suppose it came out the day we made our trip to Canterbury."

James glanced around the kitchen. "Martha, do you still have last Sunday's newspaper?"

"I'm sorry, I only save them for a day or two. Then I use them to start the fire."

The professor sighed and lowered himself into the chair opposite Martha. "I suppose we could look it up the next time we're in London."

When would that be? James shifted his gaze toward the window. Rainy weather had kept him grounded for the last four days, and he was no closer to making his flight to Calais than he had been a week ago. Surely the rain had to let up soon and then he could resume his test flights.

He turned to the professor. "Why don't we try taking off at Dover so I can get a feel for handling the Steed IV over water?"

"No!" The professor gave his head a decisive shake. "I don't think we're ready for that."

"Why not?"

"There are too many risks."

"Taking off and circling around doesn't sound any more dangerous than what we're doing now."

"But you saw the drop-off and felt the strength of the wind. Taking off from Dover and circling over the Channel will be much different from flying at Green Meadow."

"Exactly! That's why I should make some short test flights there and learn how to deal with those differences."

The professor's face had gone ruddy, and he turned toward the fireplace. "When the weather warms and the winds calm, we'll be ready. But until then I say we keep flying inland where I can at least find you if you're forced to crash-land." His voice broke off, and he raised his hand to shield his eyes from James and Martha.

James's throat tightened. He walked over and laid his hand on the professor's shoulder. "You know I always take every precaution."

The professor lowered his hand. "I'm sure you do. But the conditions over the Channel are much more dangerous and unpredictable."

"That may be true, but you've taught me how to weigh the risks and make wise choices."

The professor's troubled gaze rested on James. "It's just hard for me to think of sending you out over the ocean, no matter how confident I am in your skills or how eager I am to test our airplane in those conditions."

"I'll be all right. I promise."

"The young always believe they are invincible."

James faced the professor. "I suppose we do, but that's what makes us brave enough to climb in the cockpit and take our airplanes higher and farther than anyone has ever gone before."

The professor's worried expression eased. "I wish I were younger. I'd take the airplane across myself."

James grinned. "Oh no you don't! I'm intent on winning that prize. We have to show the French who is in charge."

"I suppose you're right. We must have courage, stay the course, and do all we can to prepare."

"So the next time we fly, I suggest we practice our takeoff from Dover."

The professor gave a slow nod. "All right. The next clear day with calm winds let's take the Steed IV out to the cliffs and try a short test flight."

"Yes!" James slapped the professor on the back. "Now that sounds like a plan!"

Eleven

B ella stepped up next to Sylvia and met her sister's gaze in the bedroom mirror.

"I can't wait to wear this dress." Sylvia held her white presentation gown up to her shoulders and beamed a smile at Bella. Yards of satin and lace flowed around Sylvia and pooled on the floor.

Bella released a soft sigh. She had been so full of hope and expectation before her own presentation and first season. She thought she would meet a man she could respect and admire , one who would be supportive of her desire to be a journalist. They would fall in love, and before the season ended, he would propose, and she would happily accept.

Her dreams might not have come true, but she hoped her sister's would be fulfilled. Sylvia deserved to be swept off her feet by a wonderful man who would appreciate and adore her.

Bella focused on her sister again. "You'll look stunning."

Their maid, Bessie, smiled at Sylvia as she placed some folded undergarments in one of the traveling cases.

Sylvia tipped her head, and a dreamy look filled her eyes. "It's hard to imagine my presentation is only a month away. And after that, I'll be attending dinner parties and balls, and I'll meet a whole new set of friends."

"Mother has been filling up our calendar at an amazing rate." A stack of invitations had already arrived, inviting them to at least a dozen social events. More would be delivered as the date for Sylvia's presentation drew closer and they moved to London for the season.

"You know how eager she is for us to make the most of our time in London," Sylvia added, smoothing her hand over the beaded bodice of her gown.

"Yes." An uneasy sensation tightened Bella's stomach. Her first three articles had been published in the *Daily Mail,* and she was working on the fourth about Mark Clifton and his cousin Pierre Levasseur. Soon she would have to start fulfilling her part of the agreement with her parents and encourage the men she would meet in London.

James's image rose in her mind, stirring her heart. Of all her possible suitors, he was the one who had made the deepest impression. She admired his courage and was inspired by his faith. She and James seemed well matched in their interests and personality. But with the questions about his family and the circumstances surrounding his birth, how would she convince her parents to welcome him as a suitor?

If he were the first to fly across the Channel, that might win her father's favor. And if she helped James learn more about his family, and perhaps even reconnect with his father, it might resolve some of the questions about his background and make him more acceptable to her mother.

She blew out a breath and called herself to account. James seemed to enjoy her company, but he hadn't given her any clear indication he hoped for more than that. Was she being foolish to let her thoughts take her down that road? What if friendship was all he ever offered?

Bessie took Sylvia's royal-blue evening dress from the wardrobe. "Did you want me to pack this one, miss?"

Sylvia glanced her way. "Yes, please. And be sure to pack my sapphire necklace and earrings to go with that dress."

"Yes miss."

Sylvia laid her presentation gown across the bed and carefully lifted the ruffled train off the floor. "I'm not sure how I'll ever manage this long train."

Bella set aside her thoughts of James and focused on her sister. "You'll have more time to practice after we arrive in London."

Sylvia's brow creased, and she lifted her hand to her throat. "I'll just die if I fall when I bow before the King and Queen at my presentation, or make some other dreadful mistake."

"It is a bit nerve-racking, but I'm sure you'll do well."

A knock sounded at the bedroom door. "Come in," Sylvia called.

The door opened and Neal, the footman, stood in the hallway with a small silver tray in his hand. He glanced at Bella. "This message was delivered for you, miss. The young lad who brought it is waiting by the back door for your reply."

Questions tumbled through Bella's mind as she crossed to the door and took the note.

Sylvia's gaze followed her. "Who is it from?"

Bella unfolded the note and glanced at the bottom. She looked up with a smile. "It's from James Drake."

"What does he say?"

Bella read the rest and her heartbeat quickened. "He's planning to make some test flights from Dover today, and he's inviting the family to come and watch."

"How exciting!"

"Yes, it sounds marvelous." Bella crossed to Sylvia's desk. "Do you have some note paper?"

"It's in the top drawer on the right. But don't you think you should ask Mother or Father before you give him your answer?"

"I'm sure Father will say yes. He wouldn't want to miss this." At least Bella hoped he wouldn't. She quickly penned her reply, folded the note, and gave it back to Neal.

Bella smiled as she thought of the outing to Dover. It would be thrilling to watch James practice his takeoffs and landings over those high cliffs, but that wasn't the only reason she had accepted his invitation. Being there to observe those test flights would give her a new slant for her fifth article . . . the one she planned to write about James and Professor Steed.

She was a journalist with an assignment, and she was going to Dover to watch James fly, with or without her father.

⁂

James walked around the tail of the airplane and squatted down to check the rudder. Tugging on the wires, he tested the connections to make sure they hadn't come loose on the trip from Green Meadow. Everything looked to be in good working order, but he had to be certain. One disconnected wire or loose bolt could spell disaster for him and his airplane.

He stood, and the salty sea breeze ruffled his hair. The winds were not too strong today, and the sky was mostly clear, with only a few scattered clouds. The deep-blue water of the English Channel rippled and sparkled to the east, and in the distance he could see the faint rise in the French shoreline near Calais.

He continued around the airplane, inspecting the body and the right wing, and then he walked up front. They'd made a few more adjustments to the timing of the engine this morning before they'd towed the airplane to this field above the Cliffs of Dover. James leaned closer and examined the fuel line connection to the engine.

The professor stepped away from Martha, her son, Ethan, and the two young lads who'd helped them bring over the airplane. He crossed the grass to meet James and ran his hand down the smooth face of the wooden propeller. "Does everything seem to be in order?"

James nodded. "Everything I can see."

"Are you ready?"

James frowned, checked his watch, and glanced down the road leading toward Broadlands. Bella's note said she would meet them at the cliffs at two, but it was already fifteen minutes after the hour. "I'd like to wait for the Graysons."

The professor scanned the sky, then checked the road. "We haven't seen fine conditions like this in quite a while. I'm not sure how long they'll last."

"I know, but Bella said she'd come, and I hope she'll bring her father."

There had been no mention of James or the professor in any of the aviation articles in the *Daily Mail*. It didn't make sense. Why would Mr. Grayson send a reporter all the way to France and then ignore the English aviators?

Frustration simmered in his chest, heating his neck. He tugged at the collar of his shirt. He must not let being overlooked by the *Daily Mail* make him lose his focus. There would be more than enough publicity when he made his flight across the Channel.

"We can wait a few minutes more, but if they're not here by two thirty, then we'll need to go ahead without them."

James gave a reluctant nod. The professor was right. Conditions might not be this favorable again for several days or even weeks, and the winds could change at any time. He must not waste this opportunity.

The purr of an engine sounded in the distance, and James turned. Mr. Grayson's sleek black motorcar rolled up the road toward them. Relief pulsed through James.

"Here they are." James strode across the grass to meet the motorcar with the professor at his side.

The uniformed chauffeur hopped out and opened the rear passenger door. Mr. Grayson, Sylvia, and Bella climbed out. Bella smiled at James, and his spirits lifted. Seeing her again felt like taking a cool drink of water after a long hike. He returned her smile, his energy renewed.

The professor stretched out his hand toward her father. "Good afternoon, Mr. Grayson. It's wonderful to see you again."

The men shook hands, and everyone exchanged greetings.

Mr. Grayson shifted his gaze to James. "So, I understand you're going to take your airplane out over the Channel today."

"Yes sir. That's the plan."

"It looks like a fine day. Are you sure you wouldn't like to fly all the way to Calais?"

Before James could answer, the professor shook his head. "Not yet. I want James to have some experience handling the airplane over the water before he makes his Channel crossing."

James nodded. "And we wouldn't want to forfeit the prize money by failing to give the *Daily Mail* twenty-four hours' notice."

"Ah yes, you're right about that. We definitely want our reporters and photographers on hand for that flight. It will be the biggest story of the year, perhaps even the decade. We don't want to miss that."

James chuckled. "Neither do I."

Bella watched him with approval glowing in her eyes. "So your flight today will be an important test and another step toward your goal."

"That's right." James glanced around at those who had come to watch him fly and then at his airplane. He could do this.

Mr. Grayson turned and looked out over the Channel. "You know, I've been thinking. I have some connections with military and government officials. I might be able to make arrangements for them to send a Navy escort ship when you're ready to make your crossing. A ship like that could carry official observers as well as our reporters and photographers, and that way we'd be sure to capture the flight for the *Daily Mail,* and for history."

A thrill raced through James. "That would be fantastic."

"Yes, what an excellent idea!" The professor nodded to Mr. Grayson. "A naval escort would certainly ease my mind."

A wave of wonder flowed through James. He had worked toward this flight for so long, it seemed hard to believe he might actually reach his goal very soon. And there would be a naval escort and a slew of reporters and photographers on hand to make sure the whole world knew what he had accomplished.

"I can't promise they'll agree, but I'll look into it and see what can be arranged." Mr. Grayson narrowed his eyes. "How close are you to making your flight?"

James shot a glance at his airplane and then the Channel beyond. "That's hard to say, perhaps a few days or a few weeks. But today's flight will give us a better idea."

"Very good. Be sure to stay in touch, and I'll let you know what I hear." Mr. Grayson motioned toward the airplane. "I'm eager to see what you can do."

James grinned and nodded to Mr. Grayson. "And I'm eager to show you." He sent Bella one more smile, then strode off toward his airplane.

⌦⌫⌦

Professor Steed spun the Steed IV's propeller, and the engine roared to life. The smell of burning engine oil mixed with the pungent scent of sand and sea blew toward Bella on the salty breeze.

She lifted her eyes to the blue sky. *Please, Lord, watch over James and keep his airplane working properly. Help him stay alert and know how to meet each challenge he'll face. Most of all, please keep him safe, and bring him back to us.*

Professor Steed jogged toward Bella and the others, out of the airplane's path. He turned and lifted his hand. James responded with a quick wave, then focused straight ahead and rumbled off across the open field toward the Channel.

"There he goes!" the professor shouted.

Bella gripped Sylvia's hand, her gaze fastened on James. The airplane picked up speed, rose for a second, and then hit the ground and bounced along for a few yards. A silent plea rose from Bella's heart. *Come on, James! You can do it!*

When he was only about seventy yards from the edge of the cliff, the airplane finally rose into the air.

Bella beamed a smile at Sylvia. "Isn't he amazing?"

"Yes, it's all such a wonder!" Her sister's eyes glowed with a happy light, and they squeezed hands again.

James soared high, straight past the cliffs, but when he flew over the open water, his wings dipped and the plane swayed.

Bella gasped and dropped her sister's hand. She stepped toward the professor. "What's happening? He looks so unsteady."

"He's fighting the wind currents. They're much stronger as they rush up the cliffs, and more unstable over water. He should level out soon." But the professor's brow creased as he watched James battle the rough winds.

An anxious feeling swirled through Bella. It was dangerous flying over the ocean, but she'd seen James fly at Green Meadow many times. Surely he was up to this new challenge. But it wasn't only James's flying skills that would be tested today. His airplane had to perform well in these more challenging conditions, or he would never be able to make his flight across the Channel.

Her interviews with the French pilots, Louis Blériot and Charles de Lambert, rose in her mind. They had both mentioned the challenges they knew they would face flying from France to England. Her father had encouraged Wilbur Wright to make the flight, but Wright had turned him down, saying he did not want to risk losing the only airplane he had with him in Europe.

Did James have the experience needed to make that dangerous crossing? What if, in spite of his best efforts, something happened to him?

Bella swallowed hard and tried to banish that frightening thought. Nothing would happen to James. That was why he took all the test flights, to make sure he and his airplane were ready.

James banked to the left, slowly turning north. Another draft of wind hit him, making his airplane dip and tilt in a crazy pattern.

Bella's stomach plunged, and she could almost feel his struggle to stabilize his airplane and bring it safely around.

Her father strode toward Martha and the professor. "Why is he having so much trouble? Is something wrong with the airplane?"

"The conditions are quite different here. But he'll be all right. You'll see." The professor kept his steady gaze fixed on James. He tried to exude a calm demeanor, but Bella could tell from his tense posture and the lines creasing his forehead that he was concerned.

James finally completed his turn and flew back toward them. As he crossed over the cliffs, the plane suddenly dropped several feet and flew directly toward them.

"Whoa!" The professor ducked.

Bella's hands flew to her mouth, and she hunched her shoulders.

James roared past overhead, not more than forty yards above the ground.

Bella spun around, her gaze riveted on James. He rose higher and started into the next turn that would take him back out over the Channel.

"Ha! Look at that! Amazing flying!" The professor cocked his eyebrows and smiled at her father.

Her father gave a firm nod. "The best I've seen since Wilbur Wright flew at Le Mans."

For the next half hour they watched James circle over the cliffs, fly out to sea, and then return. Each time his flight path seemed a little smoother as he successfully negotiated the changing wind currents. Bella's heart soared with him, her confidence in his skills and her admiration growing by the minute.

The professor glanced at his watch with a proud grin. "He's been up almost fifty-five minutes. That's a new record!"

Joy bubbled up from Bella's heart, and she exchanged smiles with Martha and Sylvia. Not only had James set a new record, but he'd done it over the windy White Cliffs of Dover.

The buzz of the airplane's engine grew louder, announcing James's return. He came in low, his speed dropping as he approached the field and his waiting friends.

Bella clasped her hands in front of her mouth. Holding her breath, she sent off a silent prayer as she did each time she watched him land. *Please, Lord, bring him down safely.*

A gust of wind rushed past, tugging at her hat. A second later it hit James's airplane, causing it to tilt and hit the ground hard. He swerved, then quickly regained control and bumped across the field toward them.

Bella's breath rushed out. She and the others ran across the grass toward the airplane. When it rolled to a stop, James stood and lifted his goggles. His gaze connected with Bella's, and a triumphant smile broke across his face.

She returned a jubilant smile, and her heart felt like it would burst. He had completed another successful flight, under the most challenging conditions.

"You did it, my boy!" The professor rushed past Bella. "You set a new record. What a great flight!"

James grabbed hold of the professor's hand and jumped down. They hugged and slapped each other on the back.

Bella's father stepped forward and pumped James's hand. "Excellent flying! Very impressive!"

"Thank you, sir." He turned to Bella, his eyes shining.

She lifted her hand and touched the silver pin at her neck. "My heart was in my throat the whole time you were in the air, but it was amazing!"

He grinned, and pleasant lines fanned out at the corners of his blue eyes. "It was a whole new experience flying over those cliffs."

"You handled it all so very well."

The professor sent him a proud smile. "Now we have even more to say in our lecture for the Aero Club's spring series."

Bella's eyes misted. It was touching to hear how the professor said *we*. He truly did see himself and James as partners in this adventure. James's success would be his as well. And if James failed . . . She banished that thought, unwilling to even consider the possibility.

Bella's father faced the professor. "I have a question for you."

"Of course. Ask anything you'd like." The professor and her father stepped aside to continue their conversation.

Martha called Sylvia over to help her pour some lemonade for everyone.

This was Bella's chance. She glanced over her shoulder at her father and the professor, then took a step closer to James. "There's something I need to tell you."

James sent her a curious look. "What is it?"

She lowered her voice to a whisper. "I don't want anyone else to hear."

A slow smile tugged up one corner of his mouth. "I like the idea of sharing a secret with you."

Her cheeks warmed, but she sent him a serious look. "I spoke to our housekeeper. She worked for Sir Richard for almost thirty years. I asked her about you and your parents."

His smile melted away. "What did she say?"

Before she could reply, the professor called James and motioned him closer. "Mr. Grayson has connections in Calais, and he thinks he may know a good landing site."

"I'll be right there." James looked back at Bella. "May I come and see you tomorrow?"

"We're leaving for London in the morning. It's time for us to get settled there for the season."

If they were going to keep their conversation private, she would have to meet him away from the house in secret. A thrill raced through her, but she quickly chided herself. This was a serious matter, one that held great importance for James. She should not let romantic notions cloud her thinking. "Can you meet me tonight, after dinner?"

"What time?"

"Nine o'clock." She thought for a moment. "I'll wait for you by the fountain in the garden just past the west lawn."

He looked into her eyes. "Are you sure?"

"Yes. It's quite private. No one will overhear us."

He shifted his uneasy glance from her to her father. "All right. I'll see you tonight." He turned and walked across the grass toward her father and Professor Steed.

Meeting a man alone at night was a risky proposition, but she trusted James. And he needed to know what Mrs. Latimer had told her. That information might help him reconnect with his family and ease the burden he carried.

That was worth the risk . . . He was worth the risk.

Twelve

Moonlight filtered through the trees, lighting James's path as he walked up the hill toward the main gate at Broadlands. The cool night air sent a chill through him, and he lifted the collar of his jacket to warm his neck. He passed under the open stone archway and continued toward the manor house, his heartbeat matching his quick pace.

He mustn't be late. He didn't want to keep Bella waiting.

As he drew near the house, he searched the facade. Lights glowed in the windows of several rooms on the ground floor. He lifted his gaze to the floor above, where gaslight flickered in three windows. Was one of them Bella's bedroom?

He looked away and gave himself a stern warning. He had one goal tonight, one purpose for this moonlight meeting, and he must not let his feelings for Bella make him forget why he'd come.

He had to find out what the old housekeeper knew about his family. Perhaps then he could finally piece together the information about his past and learn what had truly happened to his mother. There might even be a chance he could discover his father's identity, as well.

The crunch of his boots on the gravel seemed a sharp contrast to the quiet chirping of the insects. He stepped onto the grass to soften the sound of his steps.

Did the Graysons have a night watchman? He quickly scanned the grounds, but they looked deserted. He hoped they would stay that way. The last thing he needed was for someone to discover him prowling across the estate at this hour and report him to Mr. Grayson. The only worse prospect would be if he and Bella were discovered together in the garden.

He slipped around the side of the house and started across the west lawn.

The sound of water splashing in the fountain drew him down the path and into the garden.

A light breeze rustled through the trees and carried the scent of early spring flowers. He looked across the flower beds, searching the shadowed corners of the garden near the hedges, but he didn't see Bella. He took out his watch and tilted it toward the moonlight to check the time. Seven minutes past the hour.

Had Bella given up on him and returned to the house? He retraced his steps, stopping at the garden entrance to search the lawn and path to the house.

A door closed, and he scanned the west terrace. A shadowed female figure hurried down the steps and started across the lawn toward the fountain garden. James stepped behind a large bush. He didn't want to make his presence known until he was certain the woman was Bella.

Her steps slowed as she passed through the gateway to the garden. She stopped and looked to the left. When she turned and looked his way, moonlight illuminated her face.

"Bella," he said softly.

Her hand flew to her chest. "James?"

He stepped out of the shadows and onto the gravel path.

She glanced around, then sent him a shy smile. "I'm sorry to keep you waiting. I couldn't get away until my mother and sister went up to bed."

"It's all right. I've only been here a short time."

She motioned toward the stone bench a few feet away. "Would you like to sit down?" Her voice sounded soft and carried a slight tremor.

His chest tightened, and he nodded, trying to take charge of his own feelings. Being alone with Bella was exhilarating and unsettling. Her invitation to meet with him tonight and help him find the answers he was seeking meant so much to him.

She settled on the bench next to him. "Did you have any trouble getting away?"

"No, I told the professor and Martha I was coming to meet you."

Bella's eyes widened. "You did?"

"Yes, they know I want to find out more about my family. And they understand, but they tried to discourage me from seeing you in secret. They said I'd ruin my chances if we got caught."

"Your chances?"

His face flushed. Now he'd done it. He hadn't meant to say that. "To make a good impression on your father and keep his support for our flight."

"Oh yes. Of course." She bit her lip and glanced away.

Had he seen disappointment in her eyes? A thrill raced through him, but he forced himself to focus. "So, what did you learn from the housekeeper?"

"She remembered your mother well, and she knew that Laura was . . . with child when she left Broadlands. Sir Richard and his wife, Lady Katrina, wanted to send her away to Ireland and make her leave you there to be raised by someone else, but she wouldn't agree to their plan. That's why she ran away."

James nodded, grateful his mother had not bent to her parents' wishes. "I heard that part of the story from the professor and Hannah, our housekeeper in London. Did you learn anything else?"

She hesitated and looked down. "She told me when you were only a few months old your mother died when she fell from a cliff at Saint Margaret's Bay."

"Yes, that's true." Still, it made his stomach tighten to hear Bella say it.

"She also said . . . your mother was holding you in her arms when she fell."

He nodded and swallowed. "It's terrible to think of. I suppose I should be grateful I was so young that I don't remember any of it."

"It's a miracle God spared your life."

He leaned back on the bench, letting that thought settle in. He didn't know how far they had fallen. The cliffs at Saint Margaret's Bay were of varying heights. But no matter the height, it was amazing that he had survived.

"But the most surprising thing I learned was that after the accident someone started a rumor that you died that day, along with your mother."

Shock rippled through James. "What?"

"Mrs. Latimer and the rest of the staff were quite convinced it was true."

"Who would've spread a lie like that? Why would they say such a thing?"

"I don't know," she said softly.

The truth suddenly hit him, and he pulled in a sharp breath. "It must've been Sir Richard."

Bella laid her hand over his. "We don't know that."

"Who else could it be? He knew the truth. Anna wrote to him after my mother died. She told him I was alive and well and in her care, but he never answered her letter."

Bella's hand tightened around his. "I'm sorry," she whispered.

"It's not your fault." He shook his head. "But it's terrible to think I have a hard-hearted grandfather who wishes I were dead."

"Oh, James, don't say that."

"It's true. He didn't want to acknowledge me then, and he must feel the same way now. He never tried to find me or provide for me." James clenched his jaw and tried to douse that painful thought. "Did the housekeeper say anything else that might be important?"

"I asked her if she knew who your father was."

He tensed. "What did she say?"

"At first she denied knowing anything about it, but I kept pressing her for an answer. Finally, she told me there was a well-dressed young man who came to see Sir Richard a few days after your mother's death. She overheard them arguing, and the young man said he loved your mother and would've done anything to save her. But that only angered Sir Richard. He shouted at him and threatened to report him to the police if he didn't leave."

"Did the housekeeper recognize the man?"

"No, she didn't know him, but she said Sir Richard called him Daniel."

James stilled. "Daniel Drake?"

"She didn't say his last name, only the first."

James leaned forward and clasped his hands between his knees. "I always thought Drake was my mother's family name, but when I learned she was Laura Markingham, I thought Drake must be my father's name."

"What does the professor say?"

He shook his head. "Anna knew, but she never told him. Martha thinks the professor was trying to protect me, but I wish he would've asked Anna about it before she died."

Bella gazed toward the fountain, then turned back to James. "Your mother must have given you your last name for a reason. It makes sense that she would want you to have a link to your father."

Frustration burned James's throat. Was that the reason? Would he ever know the truth? And if he did discover his father's identity, would it erase the disgrace of his past and give him an honorable reputation . . . one that would give him confidence and hope for the future . . . a future with Bella?

Honor, confidence, and hope seemed like elusive dreams so far out of his reach, and a future with Bella would be impossible if he didn't win that prize and find his father. He set his jaw, picked up a twig from the ground, and broke it between his fingers.

She laid her hand on his arm. "Why don't we do a little detective work when we go to London?"

"Detective work? What do you mean?"

"We could look through the records at the *Daily Mail* and see if Daniel Drake is listed. Mrs. Latimer said he looked to be in his twenties when he came to see Sir Richard, so that gives us an age range. She also said he was well dressed. That could mean he traveled in the same social circles as the Markinghams, so he might be listed in *Burke's Peerage.*"

James straightened. Bella's ideas made sense. There might be a chance they could find his father if they used the resources at the *Daily Mail.* But if they were successful, would he have the courage to contact his father? His grandfather wanted to blot out his memory and pretend he'd never been born. Did his father feel the same way?

Then another thought jolted through James. What if his father believed the story that he had died with his mother that day she fell from the cliff at Saint Margaret's Bay? Could that be why he had never searched for James? How would his father respond if he learned James was alive? Would he be pleased to meet his son and proud of what he had accomplished, especially if he was the first to fly across the English Channel?

"If we speak to the staff at the *Daily Mail,*" Bella continued, "they might give us some more ideas about how to trace your father or other members of your family." She lifted her gaze to meet his. "I'd be glad to go with you and see what we can learn."

Gratefulness flooded him. He had no idea if they would actually find the information they were seeking, but knowing Bella cared enough to help him touched him deeply. "Thank you, Bella."

"I haven't done anything yet."

"Oh, but you have. You spoke to your housekeeper, and you met me here tonight. And now you're offering to use your connections at the *Daily Mail* to help me find my father. I'd say that's quite a bit."

She looked up at him, her eyes reflecting silver moonlight. He was certain he'd never seen anyone so lovely. But it wasn't just her attractive features that drew him toward her. It was also her courage and caring heart, two qualities he deeply admired.

Pulling in a slow deep breath, he reached for her hand. "I'm so glad we met. Your friendship means a lot to me." He wanted to say more, but he couldn't make any promises, not yet.

Her shy smile returned, and he leaned closer. His gaze traveled over her softly rounded cheeks, the gentle curve of her nose, and her full pink lips. She was close enough that he could lean down and kiss her, and from the look in her eyes she would welcome him.

But the impulse pricked his conscience. He lowered his gaze to her hand in his. She trusted him, and though there was nothing he would've liked more than to kiss her sweet lips and show her how much he cared, he would not take advantage of her or that trust. He would wait and pray there would be a day when he could kiss her, not in secret, but freely and openly as an expression of his love for her.

He lifted her hand to his lips and kissed her fingers. "Until London," he whispered, then rose from the bench, drawing her up beside him.

"Yes, until London." Her voice trembled slightly, and her eyes glimmered.

Footsteps sounded on the gravel, and his breath caught in his throat.

"Psst, Bella!" The hushed voice came from the garden gateway.

Bella spun around. "Sylvia?"

"Yes, it's me," she whispered, then took a few steps closer. "I'm sorry, but you must come in before someone sees you."

"But how could they?"

"I heard voices and looked out my bedroom window. I could clearly see you and James. Father and Mother have that same view and could look out at any moment."

James held tight to Bella's hand and stepped into the shadows of the garden hedge, pulling her with him.

Bella glanced back at her sister. "Thank you, Sylvia. I was just telling James good night. I'll be in soon."

"All right, but don't be long."

Sylvia turned and walked toward the house.

"Do you think your parents saw us?"

"No. If they had, one of them would've come instead of Sylvia."

At least that concern was relieved for the moment. "When can I see you in London?"

"I'm not sure. Mother is filling our calendar with all kinds of parties and dinners. But Father promised I could go with him to hear Professor Steed speak at the Aero Club's spring lecture series."

"He asked me to say a few words after he finishes."

"Oh, that's wonderful, James. I'll see if I can arrange to be free after the lecture, and then we can go to the *Daily Mail*."

"Thank you, Bella. I'll be counting the days."

"So will I." She sent him a fleeting smile, then slipped her hand from his and hurried out of the garden.

He watched her go, all the while wishing he could call her back and they could spend another hour together in that moonlit garden.

When he was with Bella, his troubled thoughts calmed, and he felt the most comforting sense of peace and belonging. It was almost as if he'd found what he'd been searching for. For so long he'd told himself he didn't need anyone, that his work and goals for the future were enough to make his life meaningful, but now he knew they would never be enough.

The truth was, he loved Bella Grayson, and she was a treasure worth seeking.

⁓

Bella followed her father into the auditorium at the Phillips Rushmount Centre and started up the center aisle. The program was due to start in about fifteen minutes, and most of the three hundred and fifty seats were already filled. A steady hum of conversation traveled through the crowd, sending tingles up Bella's arms.

She glanced at the program. Professor Steed was the first speaker today, and she couldn't wait to hear what he would say. She'd brought her pen and notebook, and she would be listening for quotes she could use in her next article. No doubt the audience would be impressed when the professor described the unique features of the Steed IV and announced the records James had set with his test flights.

No one else in England had accomplished as much as James Drake. Her research and interviews had confirmed it. His skills matched or exceeded those of the French aviators, and today's lecture would spread that news and build great anticipation for his flight.

She scanned the crowd, searching for James, but it was difficult to see around those who stood in the aisle, engaged in conversation.

Bella rose up on tiptoe, looking for a place to sit. She spotted two empty seats in the second row from the front and pointed them out to her father. He nodded and continued down the aisle, excusing himself around a group of men.

"Miss Grayson," a male voice called.

Bella turned, and Mark Clifton rose from his seat at the end of the row to her right.

She smiled and nodded to him. "Hello, Mr. Clifton." She glanced toward the stage, hoping he would not keep them from claiming those two prime seats.

"Good to see you, Clifton." Her father reached out and shook Mark's hand.

"I'm pleased to see you as well. There are two seats right here. Why don't you join me?" Mark stepped into the aisle and motioned for them to enter his row.

Bella wished she could sit closer to the front, but she didn't want to be rude.

"Thank you." Her father passed Mark and took the third seat, leaving Bella no choice but to take the seat between her father and Mark.

She released a soft sigh, settled into her chair, and then scanned the crowd once more. James had sent her a note this morning, asking her to meet him in the rear of the auditorium after the program. He had cleared his schedule and hoped the two of them could go to the *Daily Mail* that afternoon and look for information about his father.

Bella didn't want to disappoint James, but she wasn't sure how she could convince her father to let her go with him. Perhaps she could say she wanted to speak to Mr. Elmwood about her next article. That was true and it might work, but she didn't want to ask him too soon and risk his refusal. She would wait for the right moment and then use all her powers of daughterly persuasion. She smiled, confidence flowing through her again.

Mark leaned toward her and lowered his voice. "Thank you for that great article in the *Daily Mail*."

"What article was that?" Bella's cheeks warmed, and she took a quick glance at her father. He was engaged in conversation with the man on his right, and it didn't look as though he'd heard Mark's comment.

Mark grinned and sat back. "All right. If you want to pretend we don't know you're the author, I'll go along with it, but that seems rather silly to me."

"It's not silly," she whispered. "The only way my parents will allow me to continue writing for the *Daily Mail* is if I write under a pseudonym."

"Well, phony byline or not, the article was well written."

She could hardly hold back her smile. "Thank you."

"But it would've been better if you'd interviewed me, rather than relying on our past conversations."

"I didn't rely on our conversations. I did my research."

He tipped his head, acknowledging her comment. "Still, if you'd spoken to me in person, you could've reported the facts more clearly."

Bella's brow creased. "What do you mean?"

He lifted his hand. "There's no need to be offended. I simply would've liked the opportunity to talk to you about our airplane and my test flights, as you did with de Lambert and Blériot."

"You're well known for your powerboat and balloon racing, and I found more than enough information to give me background material for the article."

He crossed his arms, his amused grin still in place. "I'm well known, am I?"

Her cheeks warmed again. "Yes, I found several articles about you and your cousin, so there was no need for a personal interview."

"That's a shame. It would've given us a chance to get to know each other in a more . . . personal way." His suggestive tone was unmistakable.

Bella felt a ripple of unease, but before she could reply, the curtain parted and James, Professor Steed, and three other men walked out on the stage. A hush fell over the crowd. She sat forward and leaned to the right to look around the large hat of the woman seated in front of her.

A tall man with silver hair, moustache, and beard stepped up to the podium. "Good afternoon, Ladies and Gentlemen. My name is Alfred Robertson. I am the president of the British Aero Club. It is my privilege to welcome you to the first session of our spring lecture series."

The audience applauded politely.

"It is my honor to introduce our first speaker today, Professor Thaddeus Pierpont Steed. Professor Steed was the recipient of the 1898 Spellman Award for excellence in aerodynamics. He is a past secretary of the British Science Association, and he is considered one of the founders of modern aviation science in Britain."

Mark leaned toward her. "This ought to be interesting. I can't imagine that old man has anything new to say."

Irritation coursed through Bella. "Professor Steed is a remarkable man. He has devoted years of his life to studying powered flight and perfecting his airplane design."

"Perhaps, but he and Drake don't have a chance of being first across the Channel. His design is already outmoded."

Bella's stomach tensed, and she shifted her gaze back to the stage, determined to ignore Mark's comment. How could he make a statement like that? James and Professor Steed had spent countless hours testing and perfecting their airplanes. Mark Clifton's knowledge and skill could never match theirs.

But what if he was right? As she'd gathered information for her articles, she'd noted the differences in the airplane designs. De Lambert's and Mark's were biplanes, while Blériot's and James's were monoplanes. And each team had made many unique modifications to their designs. But James seemed to be the only one who had ventured out over the Channel for test flights. Surely that gave him an edge over the others.

The speaker at the podium finished his introductory remarks and turned to the professor. "Please join me in welcoming Professor Thaddeus Steed."

Bella clapped along with the rest of the audience as Professor Steed walked toward the podium. He looked very distinguished in his neatly pressed black suit. His usually wild white hair was trimmed and combed, and his expression was alert and confident as his gaze traveled over the audience. "Good afternoon, President Robertson and distinguished guests. I'm honored by your invitation and grateful for this opportunity to speak to you today about the advancement of powered flight.

"I'm sure you would all agree this past year has been the turning point in aviation science. We have reached new heights in our accomplishments, but this is only the beginning. The rapid advancement in powered flight will continue and expand as we pour our time, talents, and efforts into the race to fly higher and longer in safer airplanes."

Pride and hopeful expectation rose in Bella's heart. The professor was right. This was only the beginning of great things for aviation. James and the professor were leading the way . . . and she was on hand to capture the moment and tell the world through her articles.

❧

James shifted in his seat and scanned the audience once more, while the professor moved on to the third and final point in his lecture. Bella had to be out there somewhere, but he'd searched each section of the auditorium a few times, and he hadn't found her yet.

Had her father changed his mind and decided not to come, or had her mother insisted she attend some other event today? They planned to go to the *Daily Mail* after the lecture and search for information about his father. She wouldn't let him down, would she? He pushed that discouraging thought away and turned his attention back to the professor as he gave the conclusion to his lecture.

"And now I would like to introduce my partner in research and the brave young man who pilots the Steed IV, Mr. James Drake." The professor looked his way with a proud smile.

James rose and shook hands with the professor, and then he stepped up to the podium. Standing in that position gave him a clear view of the audience.

With one sweeping gaze he spotted Bella about halfway back. She was seated near the center aisle . . . next to Mark Clifton.

The air whooshed out of his lungs like he'd been punched.

Clifton looked up at James with a smug smile.

James dropped his gaze and swallowed. This was no time to lose his focus or his courage. He only had to give a few brief remarks.

Lifting his head, he looked out over the top of the crowd and avoided making eye contact with anyone. "Thank you, Professor Steed. It's an honor to work with you and share this platform today. I want to thank President Robertson and the Aero Club for this opportunity. Your dedication to the advancement of aviation and your support of our efforts have been a great encouragement to us. We look forward to making our flight across the Channel very soon and establishing Britain as the nation leading the way in powered flight."

He told himself not to look at Bella, but it was no use. His gaze sought her out just as Clifton leaned closer and whispered something in her ear.

Heat flashed up James's neck, and the rest of what he'd planned to say vanished from his mind. He pulled his gaze away from Bella and Clifton. *Help me, Lord, or I'm going to embarrass the professor and myself.*

The words he'd practiced flowed back into his mind, and he continued. "Many people have questioned our research methods. And some doubt our design is reliable enough to carry a man through the air and over the ocean, from one country to another. But I tell you it is possible, and very soon you will see it for yourself when I fly from Dover to Calais in the Steed IV.

"Then the world will open up as travel between nations becomes more common, and that will bring new understanding and friendship. I'm convinced the advancement of aviation will play an important role in our search for peace and unity among all people. I look forward to that day, and I count it a privilege to play a small part in this great endeavor. Thank you very much."

Enthusiastic applause filled the auditorium as James walked back to his seat. He might have faltered for a moment, but he'd recovered and finished strong.

Thank You, Father.

As he turned and faced the audience, his gaze shifted to the center aisle.

Bella was on her feet, clapping and sending him a beautiful smile. He nodded to her, his spirit lifting to match the rousing response from the audience and one very special young lady.

⌐═☙❧═⌐

Bella made her way up the center aisle, following her father and Mark Clifton. She had delayed them at their seats as long as she could, and now she had to think of some other way to make them stay in the auditorium until she could meet James. A quick glance through the crowd gave her the answer.

"Father, isn't that Mr. Helmsworth, the editor of the *Evening Standard*?"

Helmsworth glanced her way and lowered his bushy, silver eyebrows.

"Where?" Her father scanned the crowd.

Bella nodded toward the tall, silver-haired man who stood near the door to the lobby on the far right. She had met the editor when her parents had invited him to dinner at their London home, before they moved to Broadlands. His sour expressions and pointed remarks that evening had left a clear impression in Bella's mind.

"Yes, I'm afraid that is Helmsworth. I'll have to speak to him now that he's seen me." Her father set off through the crowd toward the editor, leaving Bella and Mark by the center door.

Mark leaned toward Bella. "There is a nice little restaurant not too far from here that serves a wonderful pot of tea and the best scones in the city. Why don't we stop in and take tea there?"

Bella's stomach tensed. "Thank you, but I'm not really hungry."

"Well, I certainly am, and we could at least enjoy a cup of tea together."

"I'm not sure what my father has planned this afternoon."

Mark grinned. "We don't have to include him if you'd rather not."

Her cheeks flushed. "That is not what I meant."

"I'm sorry. I didn't mean to embarrass you." But the mischievous glint in his eyes let her know he enjoyed teasing her.

"I'm not embarrassed. I'm just not sure if we can accept your invitation." She shifted her gaze away and searched the crowd once more. Where was James? If he didn't find her soon, her father might agree to go with Mark, and then she would have no choice in the matter.

Her father walked back toward them. "Well, that was unpleasant." He lowered his voice. "I'm certainly glad Randolph Rankin oversees operations at the *Evening Standard,* and I don't have to deal with Helmsworth on a daily basis."

Bella nodded and forced a tight smile.

"I was just telling Bella I plan to stop at Peckworth's for tea. It's only a short walk. I hope you'll join me."

Before her father could answer, James strode up the aisle. "Mr. Grayson." He lifted his hand to catch her father's attention.

Relief rushed through Bella, and she turned toward James.

"Well, Mr. Drake, that was a fine speech." Her father gave James's hand a hearty shake. "I'd say you and Professor Steed made a very favorable impression on everyone here today."

"Thank you, sir." He nodded to Bella. "Miss Grayson."

"Yes, you were truly inspiring." She sent him her brightest smile.

A happy glow filled his face. He shifted his gaze to Mark.

"Good show, Drake." But Mark didn't extend his hand to James. "Do you honestly think you'll be able to live up to your predictions?"

James straightened, and the muscles in his jaw tightened. "I wouldn't make them unless I intended to fulfill them."

A few men had followed James up the aisle and waited nearby, looking as though they hoped to speak to him. Bella glanced from those men to James. Now she not only had to find a way to separate herself from Mark and her father, but she had to steal James away from his admirers.

"So, Mr. Grayson, shall we go?" Mark motioned toward the door.

Bella darted a glance at James, then turned to her father. "Why don't you go ahead, Father? I have an errand I need to attend to."

Father's brow creased. "What kind of errand?"

"It's just something I have to take care of."

"Bella, why the mystery?"

"Please, it's nothing for you to worry about." She smiled, leaned forward, and kissed her father's cheek. "Besides, a woman must have some secrets."

"I'm not sure your mother would approve of you traveling around the city on your own."

"There's no need to mention it to her. I'll be home before she even has time to worry about me." Bella stepped back and sent James a direct glance, hoping he would catch her invitation to follow.

James returned a slight nod. "Which way are you going, Miss Grayson?"

"I'm headed east, toward Saint Paul's."

"So am I. Perhaps I could escort you and alleviate your father's concerns." James shifted his gaze to her father. "Mr. Grayson, with your permission?"

"Very well. You may go." He waved them off. "But, Mr. Drake, be sure you bring Bella home before five, or her mother will scold us both."

"I will, sir." He smiled at Bella and motioned toward the door.

"Thank you, Father." She and James exchanged a slight smile, then turned and walked out of the auditorium together.

"Mr. Drake!" One of the men who had been waiting to speak to James followed them into the lobby. His blond hair was streaked with silver at the temples, and he had a thick moustache. "May I have a moment, please?"

James sent Bella an apologetic glance, then turned toward the man. "Yes sir?"

The man scanned James's face with an intense gaze. "I wanted to tell you how much I enjoyed your speech."

"Thank you." James nodded politely, but his expression seemed wary.

"I'm sure you'll make that flight to France very soon."

James nodded. "That's our goal."

"Very good. I'll be eager to follow your progress as you make your preparations."

"I hope our presentation today will cause the press to take notice, and then you'll see more coverage of our efforts in the news."

"Yes, I wasn't even aware of you or your plans to fly across the Channel until today."

Bella wished she could tell them she was working on another article for the *Daily Mail*. In fact, she had so much material, she planned to ask Mr. Elmwood if she could break it into two articles, one focused on Professor Steed and the other on James.

The man tipped his head, his eyes reflecting his admiration. "Your family must be very proud of all you've accomplished."

James stiffened, and a shadow seemed to cross his face. "Thank you, but you'll have to excuse us. We must be going."

"Of course. I don't want to delay you." But the man didn't step away. "It was good to meet you." He held out his hand.

James shook it and thanked him. Then he placed his hand lightly on Bella's back and guided her away from the man. "I'm sorry about that."

"There's no need to apologize. I'm afraid you've just had your first taste of fame."

James glanced over his shoulder. "Is that what it was?"

"Yes, you'll have to get used to being famous and having a crowd follow you around town."

"I'd hardly call one man a crowd." James stopped at the corner and glanced her way. "It's odd that man never introduced himself."

"I suppose he was just a little awestruck."

James grinned and shook his head. "Well, it doesn't matter. I'll probably never see him again."

Bella nodded, grateful they'd found a way to leave Mark and her father behind. Setting off with James made her feel as though she was embarking on a delightful adventure. They might only have a few hours to spend together, but she intended to make the most of them.

Thirteen

J ames scanned the next page of *Burke's Peerage*, trying to make sense of the information about the Drake family. It was a fairly common name, so there were several pages with the various branches of the family's genealogy listed.

He glanced across the table at Bella. She had taken off her hat and collected several books and old newspapers from the shelves in the research room. They were strewn around her, covering most of her side of the table. Sunlight from the window shone around her, highlighting the glints of gold in her dark-brown hair and the soft-pink blush in her cheeks. Her dark eyelashes fluttered as her eyes skimmed over the page. He swallowed, struck again by her lovely face and form.

She looked up and met his gaze. "Find anything interesting?"

His neck warmed. He looked down at the page. "There's a Sir John Bernard Drake, who was registrar and knight attendant of the Order of Saint Patrick 1853–92, keeper of state papers in Ireland 1867–92, barrister-at-law of Middle Temple, born 5 January 1820, educated in London, married 8 January 1856 to Barbara Frances McFarland."

"He would be from your grandfather's generation. Does it list his sons?"

"Let's see." James looked farther down the page, trying to focus his thoughts on their search. "Their children are Constance Mary Drake, born 18 April 1857. Sir Henry Farnham Drake, born 12 June 1859. Bernard Louis Drake, born 3 March 1863. And Ashworth Peter Drake, Captain 4th Battalion of the Royal Irish Rifles, born 8 September 1864."

"No Daniel Drake?"

James sighed and sat back in his chair. "Not in this family."

"But that's the right time period. I wonder if those could be your father's cousins."

James huffed. "I have no idea."

Bella sent him an understanding smile. "Let's keep looking." She dropped her gaze to the newspaper and continued reading. A few seconds later she looked up. "This article mentions a Daniel Drake."

James straightened. "What does it say?"

"Sir Daniel Arthur Drake and Lady Lucille Marian Drake hosted a debutante ball in honor of their youngest daughter, Lillian Marie, at Harmon House on 7 May."

"What year?"

"Eighteen eighty-three, the year before you were born. But if he had a daughter making her debut that year, that would make him too old to be your father."

"Perhaps he has a son named Daniel?"

Bella scanned down the page. "There's a sister, Alice, but no mention of any brothers."

James suppressed a groan. What did he expect—that he would just waltz in here and find his father during their first hour of research? Still, he had hoped these pages would reveal one Daniel Drake who was the right age. "This is like searching for a diamond in the sand at the seashore."

"Let's not be discouraged—we've only just begun our search."

James glanced at his watch. It was almost four. They would have to leave soon if Bella was going to be home by five o'clock.

The door opened and a tall man with red hair who looked about twenty-five walked in. James recognized him as one of the young reporters they'd met when they'd toured the *Daily Mail* but couldn't remember his name.

"Ah, Miss Grayson, it's nice to see you again." The reporter sent her a friendly smile.

Bella rose. "Mr. Finney. It's good to see you." She motioned toward James. "You remember Mr. James Drake. He was with us the day my father gave us the tour and introduced us to the staff."

"Yes, it's good to see you as well, Mr. Drake."

James rose and shook hands with the reporter. "Mr. Finney."

The reporter turned back to Bella. "So, what brings you to the research room?"

She glanced at James, then looked back at Mr. Finney. "We're looking for the answer to a genealogy question."

Mr. Finney smiled and tucked his hands in his jacket pockets. "Well, perhaps I can help. I'm known for tracking down leads. Whether it's finding an eye witness to a crime or someone to give background information for a story, I'm your man."

Bella glanced at James, waiting for him to decide how to respond.

James shifted his weight to the other foot. If he wanted the reporter's help, he'd have to tell him the rest of the story. Was he ready to reveal his background to a man he hardly knew? The reporter seemed sincere. James hoped he was trustworthy as well. He met Finney's gaze. "I'm searching for a family member."

Finney's brow creased. "Someone's missing?"

"No, I was separated from my parents when I was an infant."

"I'm sorry to hear that." He narrowed his eyes. "So you're looking for your parents?"

"My mother died when I was four months old, and I think my father believes I died then, as well."

"I'm sorry. That sounds like a tragic story." Mr. Finney motioned toward the chairs. "Why don't we sit down, and you can tell me more?"

They settled in around the table, and James spent the next few minutes relaying the facts about his birth, his mother's death, and his search for his father.

When James was finished, Finney crossed his arms and looked across the table at James. "So here's what we know. You were born in 1884 to a wealthy young woman from a titled family in Kent. Your grandparents wanted to hide the fact your mother was pregnant and unmarried. So they planned to send her to Ireland to have the baby and leave you there, but she refused and ran away to have you in secret."

James's throat burned, listening to Finney recite those facts. No matter how many times he heard them, he couldn't help feeling sorrowful for all his mother had endured.

"When you were four months old, she died in a fall from the cliffs above Saint Margaret's Bay. She was holding you when she fell, but somehow you survived." He stopped and tapped his fingers on the table. "The circumstances of your mother's death are quite unusual. There must have been a police investigation. Have you talked to them yet?"

"They said it was an accident. I didn't see the point."

"There might be a file with the names of people they questioned. Surely they would have tried to contact your father in a case like this."

"That's a good idea." Bella sent James a hopeful look. "We could speak to the police in that area and see what we can learn."

Finney looked at James again. "You said the Graysons live on the estate where your mother was raised?"

"Yes, it was quite a revelation to learn her family owned Broadlands before the Graysons."

Finney turned to Bella. "Are there any members of the staff who stayed on and might remember what was happening in the family around the time James was born?"

"I spoke to the housekeeper. She's the one who gave us the information about the young man named Daniel visiting Sir Richard after Laura's death."

Finney rubbed his chin. "Perhaps there are others who could add to the story."

Bella nodded. "I could ask."

"And what about the church where your mother is buried? The rector or someone else there might remember more about her death and who attended the memorial service."

James gave his head a slight shake. "It's been twenty-four years, and the housekeeper said it was a private graveside service."

"Still, there might be someone who remembers something that could be helpful."

James made a mental note to look into it. "Reverend Jackson hasn't been at Saint Matthew's that long, but he might have heard something or know someone who could help us."

Finney clasped his hands in his lap. "My advice would be to follow every path and see where it leads. But it doesn't sound like this will be an easy case to solve on your own. You might want to hire a private detective."

James leaned back in the chair. If only he could. But he and the professor had spent almost all their money building their airplanes. The only way they would recoup those funds was to win that race and claim the prize money.

James glanced at his watch and rose from his chair. If they didn't leave soon, Bella would not be home by five o'clock. "I appreciate your help, Mr. Finney. But it's time for us to go."

The reporter stood. "Of course. I have a story to finish by five as well. But I'll give this some more thought and let you know if I come up with any other ideas."

"Thank you, Mr. Finney." Bella sent him a pleasant smile.

"You're welcome, Miss Grayson. Good day to you both, and good luck." He walked over to the shelf and pulled out a book.

Bella pinned on her hat, and James helped her slip on her jacket. After Mr. Finney left the room, she turned and faced James. "I'm sorry we didn't find any clear answers today. Perhaps Mr. Finney is right, and you should consider hiring a private detective."

James looked away. "I'm not sure about that."

"But you'll be preparing for your flight, and I'm afraid my mother will keep me busy, attending events with Sylvia."

"I've waited twenty-four years. It won't hurt to wait a little while longer." James picked up the copy of *Burke's Peerage* and walked back toward the bookshelf. He couldn't very well admit his lack of funds was the reason he couldn't hire a private detective. What would Bella think if she found out his bank account was nearly empty? And what about her parents? They would never give him permission to call on Bella if they found out he'd spent almost all he had, chasing his dream. He shoved the book back in place.

"James? What's wrong?"

He shook his head and motioned toward the door. "We should go. I don't want to upset your parents by bringing you home late."

She looked up at him, her eyes shadowed with concern and perhaps something more. "I'm grateful that you trusted me enough to tell me about your family. I promise I'll do everything I can to help you find your father and reconnect with him, if that's what you want when the time comes."

Her gentle words washed over him like a calming wave, and affection warmed his heart. "Thank you, Bella. You're very kind. Most people would consider my background a black mark and want to distance themselves as far as possible from me."

"Well, I don't feel that way, not at all. There's nothing you could've done to change your parents' choices. No one should hold them against you."

"But some people do, and my past has a way of not only tarnishing my reputation but all those who are close to me."

"This is 1909. Surely people realize what happened between your parents is not your fault. You are your own man. You'll make your own choices and establish your own reputation."

"I wish that were true."

Her eyes sparked. "It is. And you must believe it!"

He grinned and shook his head. "Woe to anyone who disagrees with Miss Isabella Grayson!"

"That's right. Now we better hurry home, or my mother will send out a search party."

He offered her his arm. She slipped her hand through, and they walked out the door together, with a new wave of hope rising in his heart.

Rain drummed on the roof of Bella's London home, and the wind howled under the eaves. She lifted her pen and glanced toward her bedroom window. Heavy gray clouds filled the stormy sky, and raindrops drizzled down the glass.

She took a sip of tea and looked back at the article on her desk. She skimmed what she'd just written and sighed. For the last half hour she'd been revising the final section of the article, but it still wasn't right.

Professor Steed was a remarkable man with many worthy accomplishments, and she wanted people to understand and appreciate how much he had poured into his quest to achieve powered flight.

Lightning flashed across the sky. She glanced toward the window again, waiting for the clap of thunder. When would this dreadful weather change? It had been raining for more than a week with only a few short breaks. No doubt James had been grounded the entire time, and now Sylvia would have to travel to the palace for her presentation in a downpour.

Bella shook her head and tried to focus on the article again.

Someone knocked on her door. "Come in," she called.

The door opened and their London maid, Ethel, waited there. "Excuse me, miss, but Mrs. Grayson would like you to come to Miss Sylvia's room."

"All right. Thank you, Ethel." Bella set aside her pen and rose from her chair. She was surprised her mother hadn't sent for her earlier. Mother and Mrs. Palmroy, the woman who was Sylvia's sponsor for the presentation, had been helping her sister dress for the last hour.

As she walked down the hall, Bella pondered their relationship with Mrs. Palmroy. Every debutante who wanted to be presented at court had to be sponsored by a woman who had been presented herself. Usually the girl's mother filled that role, but their mother had come from a middle-class family, and she had not had the opportunity to be presented to Queen Victoria.

When that was the case, women like Mrs. Palmroy were hired to take on the role of sponsor. Paid sponsors were usually widows, or those who came from aristocratic families with reduced circumstances. Though they might have diminished fortunes, they could still use their social standing to make proper introductions and sponsor the daughters of those who had new money and wanted to move up in society. Of course, Mrs. Palmroy would be paid discreetly, and the funds would be called a gift, but everyone knew the truth, even if they were too polite to speak of it.

Mrs. Palmroy had been Bella's sponsor two years ago, and now she would see that Sylvia made a successful debut at the palace today.

Bella tapped on Sylvia's door and entered. Ethel followed her in. Her sister stood before the full-length mirror dressed in her flowing white presentation gown. The rows of gathered satin, lace, and beading made her look a bit like a frosted cake. Bella suppressed a smile at that thought.

Sylvia's cheeks glowed pink and lines creased her forehead. "Oh, Bella, I can barely walk. This dress is so heavy. What am I going to do?"

Her mother lifted her finger. "Nonsense! You look lovely, and you'll grow accustomed to the weight of the dress and train in time."

Bella sent Sylvia an encouraging smile. "Mother is right. I'm sure you'll do splendidly."

Mrs. Palmroy touched Sylvia's shoulder. "Turn this way, my dear, and let me help you with your feathers and veil."

Sylvia rotated to face Mrs. Palmroy, and the dress and long train wrapped around Sylvia's feet.

The older woman tucked two large ostrich plumes into the back of Sylvia's elaborate hairstyle and bent them forward. "They should be tilted a bit to the left."

"Be sure you secure them well." Her mother narrowed her eyes at the floppy feathers. "We don't want them to come loose when she curtsies before the royal family."

"I don't know why I have to wear them." Her sister wrinkled her nose and scowled at the feathers in the mirror.

"We're simply following the rules for court dress." Mrs. Palmroy placed another pin in Sylvia's hair. "There, that should keep them secure."

Bella surveyed Sylvia's dress, noting each required feature: short sleeves, low-cut neckline, full-length white evening gown with a train attached at the shoulders, white gloves, and the feathers and veil. As long as a debutante's presentation gown met those requirements, the design could be as unique as they liked.

Her mother handed Sylvia her bouquet of pink-and-ivory roses. "You look beautiful, Sylvia. Now, just be sure to remember everything Mrs. Palmroy taught you, and I'm sure you'll do very well."

Her sister gazed into the full-length mirror, still looking a bit uncertain.

Bella stepped up behind Sylvia and beamed a smile over her shoulder. "You look very much like a beautiful bride. And perhaps in a few months or a year, we'll refashion this gown and you'll wear it on your wedding day."

Sylvia's eyes sparkled and her smile returned. "Oh, Bella, I've waited so long for this day. I can hardly believe it's finally here."

"Well it is, and you must enjoy every moment."

Mrs. Palmroy checked the clock on the fireplace mantel and turned toward Ethel. "Please go down and ask them to bring the carriage around front. We'll be ready to leave in a few minutes."

"Yes ma'am." The maid left the room.

Mrs. Palmroy glanced from their mother to Sylvia. "I know it's a bit early, but I think we should go. There's sure to be a long line of carriages at the palace, and the sooner we arrive, the sooner we'll be able to go inside and dry off."

"I wish I were going with you." Her mother took Sylvia's cape off the bed.

Mrs. Palmroy patted her mother's arm. "You've no need to worry about anything. I'll make sure Sylvia is well taken care of. After the presentation, we'll have her photograph taken. Then I'll take her to the reception and make some introductions. I expect we'll be home by ten o'clock this evening, and then she can tell you all about it."

"Thank you, Mrs. Palmroy." Her mother smiled through misty eyes. "We appreciate your kindness so much. It's a comfort to know Sylvia is in such good hands."

"You're welcome. It's a pleasure to guide such a special young lady as she makes her debut."

They all helped Sylvia gather her dress and train and then walked with her down the stairs. The butler, two footmen, the housekeeper, and three maids waited at the bottom of the stairs to see Sylvia off.

Bella hurried into the library. "Father, Sylvia's ready to leave."

"I'm coming." He rose from his chair at the desk and strode out to the entrance hall. As soon as he saw her, he smiled. "Sylvia, you look splendid! I'm sure even the King will be impressed."

"Thank you, Father." She leaned toward him and kissed his cheek. "I'm truly grateful. I know all of this must have cost a fortune."

"Don't worry about the expenses. You just go to the palace and make us proud."

"I'll try."

"That's the spirit."

Sylvia looked toward the door. "Well, I suppose it's time."

Her mother placed a white velvet cape around Sylvia's shoulders and kissed her cheek. "Have a wonderful time, my dear. We'll be waiting up for you."

Sylvia kissed her mother. "Thank you."

Mrs. Palmroy picked up the long train and draped it over Sylvia's arm. "We must try to keep your dress dry."

Sylvia nodded and lifted her skirt a few inches.

The butler and a footman sprang ahead, opened the door, and then offered umbrellas to shelter Sylvia and Mrs. Palmroy as they hurried to the carriage.

Bella and her parents gathered outside, under the covered front entrance.

Sylvia climbed into the carriage, and the footman tucked her dress hem inside and closed the door. She smiled out the window, then lifted her hand and waved to Bella and their parents as the carriage rolled off down the rainy street.

Bella crossed her arms against the chill and watched the carriage disappear around the corner. Memories of her own presentation flowed through her mind as she walked back into the house.

It had been a thrilling evening, one she would never forget. Unlike today, the sun had been shining as she rode to the palace past waving crowds, who cheered and wished her well. Then she'd followed the procession of debutantes and their sponsors through the beautiful palace and up a broad staircase. She had waited in line for almost an hour in the upper hallway before it was her turn to enter the drawing room. Finally, her name was announced, and she curtsied before the King and Queen. She'd gone in and out in less than two minutes, but all had gone well, and Mrs. Palmroy praised her poise and graceful curtsies.

Bella walked inside the house and sent up a prayer for her sister. *Lord, be with her as she goes to the palace. May she feel Your peace and presence. Help her remember her training and give her confidence. But most of all, help her know she is loved and special to You and to us.*

Her father returned to the library, and Bella was about to follow her mother upstairs when Peter, the second footman, stepped forward with a silver tray.

"A letter arrived for you, miss."

"Thank you, Peter." She took the letter and glanced at the handwriting. The strong masculine script gave her a hint, and a delightful shiver traveled through her. She turned the envelope over and read James's name and London address on the back.

Her heart lifted, and she hurried up the stairs to read her letter in private. She settled into the chair by the fireplace in her bedroom and carefully tore open the envelope.

Dear Bella,

I hope you are enjoying your time in London, though I suspect the rainy weather may have put a damper on some of the events you hoped to attend. The professor and I decided to stay in town since it has been too stormy for me to fly. I'm hoping the weather will clear soon, and we can head back to Kent.

Mr. Robertson, the president of the Aero Club, invited us to dinner last evening, and when we arrived we were pleased to see seven members of the club were joining us. We had a lively discussion, and there were several interesting ideas shared around the table and after dinner in the drawing room.

The most interesting bit of news is that the French are planning to host the first International Air Meet this summer near Reims. The date is set for 22–29 August. A committee has been formed, and aviators from several nations have been invited to attend.

Of course the professor and I want to take part, and we made that known to Mr. Robertson. He promised to send word to the committee. It will be quite a challenge to dismantle one of our airplanes and ship it to France, and then make arrangements for it to be delivered to Reims. The cost of such a trip will be quite high, and we will need to recruit sponsors to help cover those expenses. But if we are the first across the Channel, the prize money would more than meet the need. There will be several different events at Reims, and they will be offering prizes for each one. Winning one or more of those could also help cover the cost of attending.

Please pass on this news to your father. It should be a very exciting event, and I'm sure he'll want to send some reporters and photographers to cover it for the Daily Mail. I'm looking forward to meeting the other aviators and seeing how the Steed IV will perform in a competition. It would be wonderful if you and your family could attend. It would certainly make me happy to know you were there, cheering me on.

Has your father heard if the Navy will be able to provide an escort ship for my flight across the Channel? Mr. Robertson was excited about that possibility, and he praised your father for making that suggestion. We are all eager to hear if it will be possible. Having the escort would be a helpful safety measure, but I am determined to fly soon, with or without the escort. Please let us know when you have any news.

All these rainy days have given me plenty of time to think about our

efforts to locate my father and find out what truly happened to my mother.
I decided to pay a visit to the police station in Dover on Tuesday. They
directed me to a smaller station a few miles away. I'm sorry to say it
was a fruitless journey. All the records there were destroyed in a fire three
years ago. None of the men I spoke to remembered any details about my
mother's death, and they didn't know who conducted the investigation.
I was hopeful when I set out that day, but quite discouraged when I
returned to London.

    I considered stopping at Saint Matthew's and searching the
churchyard for my mother's tombstone on the way back, but it was so
rainy, I decided to put it off and wait for a clear day. It seems every
time I try to learn more, I run into a closed door, and I'm no closer
to knowing the truth than I was before I began looking. But I will keep
knocking on those doors until one of them opens.

    Even though it's only been a week since we were together, I confess
that I miss you, Bella. I know I may not have the right to say something
like that to you, but I do hope and pray one day I will. Until then, know
that you are always in my thoughts and prayers.

    With fond affection,

    James

Bella read the last paragraph once more and lifted her hand to her heart.
What sweet, tender words, and how wonderful that James had written them to
her. A wave of awe washed over her. He missed her, thought of her, and prayed
for her. The same was true for her. James was never far from her thoughts. Each
day she checked the weather, wondering if he would be making another test
flight. When it was clear, she prayed for his safety and asked the Lord to give
him success and guide him across the Channel very soon.

    How she wished she could reply to his letter and encourage him, but what
would her parents say?

    The season was moving into full swing, and her mother had filled their
social calendar. Her parents expected her to keep her promise and encourage
the young men she met when she and Sylvia attended those events, young men
with impeccable backgrounds and wealthy, influential families.

Since she'd met James, she'd realized shared interests as well as shared faith and goals were just as important as breeding and situation, if not more so.

How could she keep her promise to her parents and encourage potential suitors, yet not discourage James? The thought of giving her heart to anyone but him seemed impossible.

She rubbed her forehead and closed her eyes. *Lord, I care for James, so very much. And it seems that he cares for me as well. But there are so many obstacles in the way, not the least of which is his family background. Please clear away those obstacles, and make a way for us to be together!*

She paused, considering her words. What if God's plan for James did not include her? That thought pulled her up short.

If she truly cared for James, then she should want what was best for him, and not just pray that her own hopes and desires would be fulfilled.

She settled her heart and began again. *Lord, please bless and guide James. Watch over him. Fulfill all his hopes and dreams. Show us both Your will and how to fit into Your plans.*

Fourteen

B ella gasped and stared at the final paragraph of her latest article. "Father!" She spun around and strode into the dining room, holding out the newspaper to him. "Look at this! They cut off the last section of my article!"

Father laid aside his copy of the *London Herald* and frowned at Bella. "What is all this about?"

She spread out the second section of the *Daily Mail* on top of his newspaper and pointed to her article. "Look, right here. That's not the end. They chopped off at least a quarter of what I wrote." She leaned closer, read the final paragraph again, and moaned.

Her father scanned the article and focused on the ending. "It is rather abrupt."

"Of course it's abrupt. There are supposed to be three more paragraphs about James Drake with an introduction to the next article in the series where he is the focus." She glared at the page. "How can they do that?"

Father glanced at the other articles and pointed to the next column. "I suppose they had to cut your story to fit in these others. You know the rule in journalism. You begin with the most important information because the editor may need to shorten your story to fit the page."

"But he never did that with my other articles!"

"Then you should consider yourself lucky."

"Oh, what will James think?" She rubbed her forehead. "This is so unfair."

Her father sighed. "There's nothing you can do about it now. But I wouldn't worry. Next Sunday, when the other article comes out, he'll be pleased."

Bella paced across the room. She had to do something. James didn't deserve this kind of treatment, especially not after he already carried the burden of his parents' painful choices. If only she could explain her intentions and why he had been left out of the article.

Her father watched her with lowered eyebrows. "I know what you're thinking, Bella. But you may not say anything to James Drake. You made a promise to your mother and to me, and you must keep it or I'll have to put a stop to you writing for the *Daily Mail*."

"Father, please. If I could only explain what happened and what's coming, I know that would help. I'm sure James wouldn't tell anyone else."

"That is not the point. Your mother and I have kept our part of the bargain. Now you must keep yours. Enjoy the season. Encourage the suitable young men you meet, and keep your journalism private."

"I'm not asking to announce it to the world; I only want to tell James."

He shook his head. "This article was written by I. J. Wilmington. That's all he needs to know."

Bella crossed her arms and stared out the window. She wished she hadn't agreed to write under a pseudonym, but if she hadn't, she never would've seen any of her articles published. She hated keeping her writing a secret from James. It made her feel guilty and dishonest. But what choice did she have?

In one week, the next article would be published. James would be featured in glowing terms, and he would receive the respect and admiration he deserved.

James pushed open the back door of Martha's cottage at Green Meadow and stepped into the warm kitchen. A delicious, savory scent wafted past his nose, making his mouth water. "Martha, we're back."

The professor followed him through the door, carrying a basket with a bouquet of red tulips and a loaf of bread baked by Hannah.

Martha walked into the kitchen wearing a sunny smile. "Ah, you're home at last." She glanced at the basket and then up at the professor. "And what's this?"

His face turned ruddy as he held it out to her. "Just some bread and flowers from town."

She accepted the basket with shining eyes. "That was very thoughtful. Thank you, Thaddeus."

He glanced away, but a smile tugged at his lips. "It was no trouble."

"Come, sit down. I want to hear all about your time in London." She placed the basket on the counter. "I kept the stew warm for you, and we can slice the bread and have that too."

"That's kind of you, Martha." The professor pulled out a chair and took a seat at the table. "How have you been?"

"Just fine, although it's been awfully quiet without you and James here." She sent the professor another smile, then arranged the tulips in a vase and set them on the table. "These are lovely, Thaddeus, and they're my favorite color."

James couldn't help smiling as he watched their interaction. The kindness and affection between them was growing more obvious every time they were together. He only wished the professor would speak up and assure Martha of his feelings for her. What held him back?

Martha walked to the stove and lifted the lid on the stew.

"I wish you could've heard the professor give his lecture." James sat down at the table, across from the professor. "He did a fine job, and he received a standing ovation."

Martha stirred the stew. "I read all about it in the newspaper." She looked over her shoulder at the professor. "I was very proud of you, Thaddeus."

He watched her with a tender smile. "Thank you, Martha."

"In fact, I cut out the article and saved it for you." She set aside the spoon and walked out of the kitchen. A few seconds later, she returned with the newspaper clipping and handed it to the professor.

The professor adjusted his glasses and lowered his gaze to the article.

James stood and walked around the table to take a closer look. He supposed this article was written by one of the reporters who had questioned them after the lecture. He'd almost missed meeting Bella because of the swarm of reporters who had surrounded them.

The next morning they'd found articles about the professor's lecture in three London papers. But this one was from the local newspaper, *The Dover Sentinel,* and it gave a good summary of his remarks.

The professor lifted his head. "It's a fine article."

"It certainly is." Martha shifted her gaze to James. "Will you set the table for us?"

"Of course." He took bowls and plates from the shelf, then grabbed silverware from the drawer.

Martha poured the stew into a large bowl and carried it to the table. "Have you seen the *Daily Mail* article?"

The professor looked up. "Yes, we saw it the day after the lecture."

"No, not that article, the one in today's paper."

The professor cocked his head. "There was another article today?"

"Yes, quite a nice one."

"We didn't take time to pick up a paper this morning."

"Well, you're in for a surprise, then." She glanced at James. "Would you get the paper? It's by my chair." She nodded toward her chair by the fireplace.

He walked over and picked up the folded newspaper, his spirits lifting. He knew they couldn't be ignored forever, especially not after the professor's lecture. The *Daily Mail* had been running a series of articles about the pilots who were preparing to fly across the Channel, and for the last several weeks he'd eagerly awaited seeing his name in print. But his frustration had grown each Sunday when a new article appeared and there was no mention of him or the professor.

It was strange. No one had contacted them for an interview, but he supposed they could've taken the information from the Aero Club lectures and used that as the basis for an article.

"It's on the front page of the second section." Martha patted the professor's hand. "Wait until you read it. I was so proud of you!"

As James walked back to the table, he scanned the headline, "Founder of Aviation Science Leads the Way Across the Channel." A photograph of the professor took up two columns on the right. A wave of unease traveled through him as he passed the newspaper to the professor and sat down.

"Well, will you look at that!" The professor grinned at Martha.

"The whole story is about you." Martha pointed to the photograph. "It's wonderful. Wait until you read what they said."

The professor spread it out on the table. "Read it for us, James."

He nodded and scooted his chair closer. "'Professor Thaddeus Steed, inventor, scientist, and enthusiastic aviation pioneer, is about to accomplish his greatest feat—sending a man across the English Channel in an airplane of his design. After more than thirty years of building models, conducting experiments, and overseeing test flights, Professor Steed believes he has found solutions to the issues that have prevented safe and controlled powered flight.'"

The professor laughed and slapped the table. "My goodness, someone is finally giving us the credit we deserve!" He squinted toward the top of the article, then took his glasses from his pocket and put them on. "*I. J. Wilmington.* I wonder if he was one of those reporters who questioned us after the lecture."

James shook his head. "I don't know, but he's the same one who wrote the last few aviation articles."

The professor nodded, and they silently read the rest.

James searched for any mention of his name, but he didn't find it until the last line. *"Professor Steed is assisted by James Drake, who hopes to pilot the Steed IV on the first flight across the English Channel."*

He stared at the abrupt end of the article. That was it? After all he'd contributed to the research and design . . . After all the risky test flights he'd taken and all the records he'd broken . . . His efforts deserved one line?

He sank back in the chair, fighting the selfish thoughts darting through his mind.

"Surely there must be more to the article?" The professor scanned the rest of the page and then turned and looked at the second and third pages. "I don't understand. They should've written more about you, James. We're a team. We couldn't have done it if we weren't working together."

James rose from the table and turned away. "It's all right."

"No, this is not honest reporting. You deserve as much credit as I do for what we've achieved."

James paced toward the sink and stared out the window. It was strange. The other articles had focused on the pilots with only brief mention of the designers and teams who supported them. This article was totally the opposite, focusing on the professor and practically ignoring James.

He clenched his jaw. He had a choice to make. He could either hold on to his disappointment at having been overlooked, or he could let it go and be grateful his mentor had been honored with a feature article.

He wrestled with it a few more seconds, then walked back to the table. "You've spent your entire life working toward this goal. You deserve to be the focus of that article and a hundred more."

The professor rose and laid a firm hand on James's shoulder. "Thank you, James. But I know this: without our partnership, we would not be where we are today. I'm proud of you, and I'm grateful. I would rather they'd written about us both, but your day will come. Very soon you'll make that flight, and your name will be famous across England and all over Europe."

James nodded, his hopeful feelings returning. The professor was right. When he flew to Calais, he would make his mark and finally have an honorable name and reputation.

"Oh, James, I almost forgot. You received a letter." Martha rose and retrieved an ivory envelope from the fireplace mantel. She smiled as she handed it to him. "It's from the Graysons."

James's heartbeat picked up speed. He tore open the letter and pulled out an invitation and a separate note.

Martha sent him an inquisitive look. "What is it?"

He lowered his gaze and read the engraved type. "The Graysons are inviting me to Sylvia's ball in London on the twenty-fifth."

Martha smiled and nodded to the professor. "Isn't that special?"

"Yes, it's very thoughtful."

James opened the note, read the signature, and his heart lifted. Bella had written to him.

Dear James,

Thank you for your letter. I was so happy to hear from you. I'm sorry the weather has kept you in town and on the ground. Since you're reading this letter, you must be back in Kent. I know you are eager to take to the skies again. I'm praying for calm, sunny days so you can resume your flights soon.

Father just received word today that a Navy ship will be made available to escort you on your flight across the Channel. While he was waiting to hear back from the Navy, he contacted the Masterson Company. They have tugboats based in Dover, and they have agreed to send a tug along as an escort, as well. I hope this news encourages you and Professor Steed as you move ahead.

I know your focus is on that wonderful endeavor, but I hope you will be able to accept our invitation to attend Sylvia's ball on the twenty-fifth. We would very much like to have your company that evening. Please let us know if you can come, and I will be sure to save a dance for you.

Thank you for relaying the news about the International Air Meet at Reims, and for letting us know that you plan to enter. I'm happy to say Father is already making plans to take the family and attend. He'll also be sending reporters and photographers, as you suggested. I'll be ready to cheer you on as you compete for those prizes.

We are eagerly waiting to hear you give your twenty-four-hour notice for your flight. I don't care what my mother has planned or what event I'm scheduled to attend. When that day comes, I will be there to see you off.

Thank you again for writing. I'm looking forward to seeing you soon, at the ball or when you make your flight across the Channel. What a wonderful day that will be!

Until we meet again,
Bella

James read the last few lines again, and his chest expanded.

"Well, is it good news?" Martha glanced from the letter to James.

"Yes, very good news. The Navy has agreed to provide an escort ship for my flight, and another company will send along a tugboat." Bella's response and sweet words meant even more than the assurance of a naval escort, but he decided to keep them to himself.

"Excellent!" The professor nodded to James. "We'll make those final adjustments to the tail rudder that Mr. Robertson suggested and take a few more tests flights. Then all we need to do is wait for the right weather conditions, and we can give notice for our flight."

A surge of energy flowed through James. "It won't be long now."

When that day finally came, it would not only test the design and durability of his airplane, but it would also test his skills and courage as a pilot. And when he completed that flight and won the prize, he would finally receive recognition for his work. He could then make plans for a future with Bella.

Fifteen

I believe I have the next dance." Mark Clifton smiled and held out his hand to Bella.

"Yes, that's right." She returned a smile, but her gaze shifted to the empty doorway. Where was James? Why hadn't he come?

The string quartet struck the first notes of the waltz, and Mark led her across the highly polished wooden floor to the center of the ballroom. With another warm smile, he placed his hand on her waist. She laid her hand on his shoulder, and they stepped off in time to the music. He looked dashing in his black tails and white waistcoat and tie, but she would much rather be dancing with James.

The scent of roses and gardenias from the elaborate floral arrangements floated in the air as they made the first circle around the dance floor. Twenty or more couples swirled around them, the women in beautiful evening gowns with flowers, feathers, and jewels in their upswept hair.

Bella wore a lavender gown with a diamond and amethyst necklace and matching earrings. Lavender silk roses were tucked into her hair along with a jeweled comb. She felt almost like a princess tonight, and she had received many compliments—more than she'd received at any other event so far this season. But this was Sylvia's night to shine, and Bella had done all she could to turn the attention toward her sister.

She spotted her mother seated on the edge of the room with several other mothers and chaperones. They all watched their daughters and charges carefully, evaluating each young man they danced with and comparing what they knew about him, his family, and his prospects in whispered discussions.

Bella glanced over Mark's shoulder toward the door once more. She had been watching for James ever since the first guests arrived. She had already

danced six times, twice with Mark and once with four other men. Still James
had not come.

Her mother was a skilled hostess, and she had introduced Sylvia and Bella
to every eligible young man in the ballroom within the first half hour. Now
Bella's dance card was almost filled. She had been tempted to write in James's
name so she could keep her word and save him at least one dance, but if he
didn't come soon, those last two spaces would be filled.

Where could he be? If he had been injured during a test flight, surely the
professor or Martha would've sent word. Perhaps it was an issue with the train
or an accident on his way across town had delayed him.

"Bella?"

She looked up and met Mark's gaze. "Yes?"

"You seem miles away. I hope I'm not boring you."

"Oh no, not at all." She forced a smile and looked into his eyes.

"So, are you enjoying the evening?"

"Yes, it's wonderful that so many people have come to support Sylvia and
make her debut special."

"Yes, the guest list is quite impressive—a duke, three earls, a baron, and a
good assortment of landed gentry." Mark scanned the dancers. "Your family is
gaining a great deal of respect in society."

That seemed like an odd way to evaluate the guests, but she supposed
coming from a wealthy, aristocratic family, Mark was used to thinking about
rank and titles before anything else.

Movement by the door caught her attention. James walked into the ballroom and looked her way. Their gazes connected, and Bella smiled. But his
brow creased as he watched her circle the floor with Mark. He turned away
without returning her smile and started across the room toward her father and
Sylvia.

Questions flooded her mind as he spoke to her father. Why had he sent her
that cool look? Was he upset because she was dancing with Mark? What did he
expect her to do—wait for him and not dance with anyone else until he
arrived?

A cloud of frustration settled over her. She was dancing with Mark because James was almost an hour late to her sister's ball. If he wanted her special

attention, he should have arrived on time and been the first to ask her to dance.

The waltz ended, and Mark escorted her back to her father and sister. James stood next to her father, engaged in conversation with him and another man, but he didn't look her way as she and Mark approached. She stood beside him for a few seconds, waiting for him to turn and greet her, but he did not. Heat flooded her face.

Her sister sent her a curious look. "Is everything all right?"

Bella lifted her chin and scanned the ballroom, avoiding eye contact with James. "Yes, everything is fine."

Sylvia leaned closer. "Bella, what is it? I can see you're upset."

She gave her head a slight shake. "I'll explain later."

Charles Haversham, the son of the Earl of Rothbury, approached. He was a tall, slim man with curly blond hair and a toothy grin. He gave a slight bow. "May I have the next dance, Miss Grayson?"

Bella glanced at her dance card. No one else had asked for this dance. She sent him a warm smile. "Yes, Mr. Haversham. I would be delighted."

His eyes widened at her warm response, and he offered her his hand. She took it, and they walked out to the dance floor.

Bella told herself not to look at James, but she couldn't seem to make her eyes obey. As she whirled past James, he glanced her way. For a brief second she thought she saw a flash of pain in his eyes, but she couldn't be sure. He averted his gaze and continued his conversation with her father and another man.

"You are an excellent dancer, Miss Grayson."

"Thank you." She knew she should return the compliment, but it wouldn't be true. He was not moving in time with the music, and he had stepped on her foot the first time they had circled the floor. Still, she was glad he had asked her to dance and saved her from the embarrassment of being ignored by James.

Charles leaned closer and lowered his voice. "I must say you are the loveliest woman here tonight."

Surprise rippled through Bella. "Since this is my sister's debut, I think you should save that compliment for her."

He chuckled. "She is pretty, but you outshine her by far. I've never seen such dazzling blue eyes and dark glossy hair."

She looked past his shoulder, her cheeks flaming. His compliments were much too personal, since they had only been introduced that evening.

Just then James looked her way, chilly questions reflected in his eyes.

She swallowed and sent Charles a coy smile. "That's very kind of you to say."

"Kindness is not the feeling I had in mind."

She pulled in a sharp breath, and guilt hit her heart. What was she doing? Did she think flirting with Charles would make James jealous? That was not who she was and not the way she wanted to be known. She would speak to James as soon as this dance was over and straighten out this misunderstanding. She could not let it ruin the evening or their friendship.

❧

James tried not to watch Bella as she danced with her next partner, a tall, thin man with foppish blond curls. His dress and confident manners marked him as a member of the wealthy aristocracy, just the kind of man her parents probably thought would be a good match for Bella.

He stifled a groan and looked away. This evening was not turning out as he had hoped. His train had been delayed by mechanical troubles for almost an hour. When he finally arrived, he'd found Bella waltzing across the room with Mark Clifton, and it had shaken him.

He hadn't expected to see his rival here tonight, let alone dancing with Bella as soon as he walked in the door. He scowled at Clifton. Why didn't the man dance with someone else instead of standing next to him, gazing at Bella as if she were his favorite dessert?

Clifton looked his way and sent him a teasing half smile. "Too bad you arrived late. You missed quite a few dances."

"It couldn't be helped. My train broke down outside Dartford."

"While you were sitting on that stalled train, I danced twice with Isabella, and I enjoyed a very friendly conversation with her father."

James clamped his mouth closed to hold back his curt reply.

Clifton's gaze returned to Bella. "She's quite a vision tonight, isn't she?"

James couldn't deny it. She was breathtaking, with her lovely smile and that silky lavender dress swirling around as she floated across the dance floor.

Clifton's lifted his eyebrows and grinned. "Beautiful and quite skilled."

Heat flashed up his neck and he glared at Clifton. What did he mean by that?

Clifton chuckled. "There's no need to take offense. I was talking about her journalism skills."

"Her what?"

"I'm sure you've seen the series in the *Daily Mail* about those of us preparing to fly across the Channel."

James stared at Clifton. What did he mean?

Clifton leaned toward him. "Isabella is a freelance journalist for the *Daily Mail*. She writes under the name I. J. Wilmington."

A shock wave jolted through James.

Clifton laughed. "You didn't know? She didn't tell you?"

Stunned, he stood there like a stone. How could Bella be the author of those articles? It wasn't possible . . . was it?

"It's always been her goal to write for one of her father's newspapers," Clifton continued in a nonchalant tone, "but her parents don't want it known. That's why she writes under a pseudonym."

A burning sensation climbed up his throat. Was that why she'd come to his workshop at Green Meadow—to secretly gather information for her articles? Was it all just a game to convince him to tell her about his design and test flights so she would have a unique angle for her stories?

A more disturbing thought struck. She hadn't even used what she'd learned to write about him and his accomplishments. Instead, she'd taken that information and included it in her articles about Mark Clifton, his cousin Pierre Levasseur, and all those other French pilots.

Suddenly, it all became clear. That was why she'd gone to France—to personally interview Blériot and de Lambert. They had all been featured in her glowing articles and received praise for their aviation feats, but she'd left him out of every story except for that one measly sentence last Sunday.

Heat flooded his neck and face. She hadn't really believed he would win the race across the Channel. She had one purpose in mind when they'd met: to forward her own career by weaseling her way into his life and taking whatever she could learn from him.

James clenched his jaw, disgust churning his stomach. He'd been a fool to believe her, and a greater fool to think she truly cared about him. He turned away from Clifton and strode toward the door.

The dance ended and Bella applauded the musicians. She nodded to Charles Haversham. "Thank you."

He smiled and gave a slight bow. "You're welcome. I hope you'll favor me with another dance."

Her gaze darted past his shoulder, searching for James. She only had one open space left on her dance card, and she couldn't give it to Charles. "I'm sorry . . . If you'll excuse me. There's someone I must speak to."

Without waiting for his reply, she turned away and started across the room. Her father and Mark Clifton stood together where she'd left them, but James was not with them. She scanned the ballroom, a light-headed, dizzy feeling flooding through her.

She finally spotted him striding toward the door. Her heart leaped. She changed course, hoping to intercept him, but he walked out of the ballroom and headed for the front door.

Why would he leave without even speaking to her? She hurried out of the ballroom and across the empty entrance hall. "James!"

He kept walking.

"Please wait!"

He stopped and slowly turned to face her. His mouth was set in a firm line, his eyes narrow, and his posture rigid.

"Why are you leaving? I . . . I promised I would save you a dance." She lifted her dance card from the ribbon tied around her wrist and held it out for him to see.

He lifted his eyebrows in a mocking slant. "Why would you want to dance with me? Do you have more questions you want to ask?"

"Questions? I don't understand."

"Don't give me that sweet, innocent look. I know what you've been doing and why you've been doing it."

She stared at him, trying to make sense of his words.

"You're the author of those articles."

"Articles?" Her voice cracked.

"Yes, you know, the series in the *Daily Mail,* the series you wrote."

She swallowed. This couldn't be happening. Who had told him?

"How could you do it, Bella? How could you lie to me like that?"

"I didn't lie . . . I couldn't tell you."

He huffed. "Oh, that's right. Your parents don't want anyone to know. But you had no trouble telling Mark Clifton."

"He was in France when we went to de Lambert's camp. He translated the interview, and he guessed what I was doing."

"Stop! I don't want to hear your excuses. I know you came to Green Meadow to gain my trust so you could get information for your articles."

She opened her mouth to deny his words, but they were partially true.

"You used me and our so-called friendship as a stepping-stone to advance your journalism career." He shook his head. "If that's not dishonest, then I don't know what is."

"I wanted to tell you, but my father insisted I keep it a secret. He said if I didn't, he'd put a stop to the series."

"And you couldn't let that happen, could you? So you kept pumping me for information and writing your stories, all the while pretending you cared about me and wanted to help me find my family." He laughed, but there was no humor in it. "I bought that whole story, hook, line, and sinker."

"That wasn't a lie. I truly do want to help you."

He narrowed his eyes again. "You are quite an actress."

Heat flushed her face. This was unfair. He didn't understand. She had gathered some information for her articles during her visits to Green Meadow, but he was much more to her than a source of information. Hadn't she proven that when she'd spoken to the housekeeper and met him in secret in the garden? Didn't those efforts mean anything to him?

He was wrong, and she wasn't going to let him blame her for this mix-up.

She lifted her chin. "The only thing I withheld from you was that I was writing those articles. Everything else I said and did was offered in true friendship, and if you can't see that, then you are very shortsighted."

His eyes widened. "I'm shortsighted?"

"Yes!" She clenched her hands, her thoughts spinning. "And if we're being honest, don't you think it's time you admitted you sought friendship with me and my family so you could gain financial support for your flights?"

He pulled back. "That's not true!"

"Oh, really?" She fired the words at him. "That's probably what you had in mind all along. You thought if we became friends, you could use that connection for your own financial gain, so you have no right to be angry with me."

He squinted at her. "You honestly think I crashed my airplane near your home on purpose? That I plotted and planned our meetings so your father would give me his support?"

She glared at him. "That makes just as much sense as what you're saying about me."

He stared at her, then shook his head. "I'm not listening to any more of this." He spun away and strode toward the door.

Pain sliced through Bella's heart, but she pressed her lips tight. She would not call him back this time. If he wanted to take offense because she had kept her promise to her parents, then that was fine with her.

He grabbed the doorknob and pulled the door open, then stopped and looked over his shoulder. "Since you have such a close connection with the *Daily Mail,* you can pass on a message for me. I'm giving my official twenty-four-hour notice. The next time you see me, I'll be flying across the Channel." He walked out and jerked the door closed with a bang.

Bella looked out the window and watched him hustle down the steps and disappear into the foggy London street. Hot tears stung her eyes. She tried to blink them away, but it was no use. They overflowed and ran down her cheeks. He didn't care about her. If he did, he would have accepted her explanation and understood her predicament, rather than storming off in an angry huff.

Regret rose, swamping her heart. James would take to the sky tomorrow and face unknown dangers. What if something happened and this was the last time she saw him? Would his final memory of her be those angry words and hurtful accusations?

She sank down on the steps and lifted her hand to cover her eyes. "I'm sorry," she choked out past her tears, but it was too late. James was gone, and there was nothing she could do to change what she'd said and done.

Sixteen

James glared out the workshop window at the anemometer spinning on top of the pole. The winds were at least ten miles per hour and coming from the wrong direction, but he wouldn't let that stop him. "I'm going to fly today."

The professor looked out the window with a worried frown and shook his head. "The conditions are not right."

"But I gave my notice to the *Daily Mail.*"

The professor lowered his eyebrows. "And why you did that without consulting me is what I'd like to know."

James turned away and stifled a growl. He couldn't very well admit he'd given notice because he was angry with Bella and feeling like a fool for believing she could ever care for him. He tried to push away the memory of their angry confrontation, but it ran through his mind again.

There might be an ounce of truth in what Bella had said about him, but it didn't outweigh her pound of deception. He clenched his jaw and pushed those punishing thoughts away. He was done fretting about Bella Grayson.

James turned toward the professor. "If I want to be first, I need to stop wasting time and get out there." He strode across the workshop, grabbed his jacket off the hook, and shoved his arm into the sleeve.

"You are not wasting time. You've been conducting research and making test flights. And now you're waiting for the proper conditions to give you the best chance of making a successful flight."

James fished his goggles out of the box by the door. "Well, I'm not waiting any longer."

"But the winds are strong today. It's too dangerous."

"You just don't want me to take any risks."

"That's not true! It's a risk every time you take off, but I've stood by you, spun the propeller, and cheered for you on every flight."

"Then cheer me on today." He pushed open the workshop door and stepped outside. Morning dew sparkled in the bright-green grass, and the breeze rustled the bushes by Martha's garden fence. The winds might be a challenge, but the sky was mostly clear, and he intended to take off from Dover in the next twelve hours, with or without the professor's approval.

"James, listen to me!" The professor followed him out the door, his voice rising. "You've only flown out over the Channel with the help of a mild tailwind. The winds are westerly today and much too strong. You would be fighting headwinds all the way across. You have no experience with that!"

"I'm not worried. I'll be all right." James glanced down the road. Ethan Shelby, Martha's son, and three other men walked up the road toward the workshop. A little farther down the road he spotted John and Andy, the two young boys from the neighboring farm who often came to help. James had sent word to them late last night that he would be flying this morning and asked them to come at eight.

The professor's shoulders sagged, and he lifted his hand to his forehead. "I don't understand. Why does it have to be today? It's not like you to be so stubborn."

"You call it stubbornness. I call it determination. And that's the exact quality I need to take me across the Channel." He turned and faced the professor. "Now, are you coming to Dover with me or not?"

The professor shifted his troubled gaze down the road to the approaching men. His face had gone pale and his hand shook slightly. He reached for James's arm. "Please, son, we've always made these decisions together based on my research and your practical experience . . . Now is not the time to . . ." He gasped, then grimaced and lifted his hand to his chest.

James's heart lurched, and he lunged toward him. "Professor!"

The old man's eyes widened, and he hunched over, clutching both hands over his heart. James grabbed hold of the professor's arm as the old man's legs gave out.

Panic shot through James. "Hold on!"

Ethan ran toward them and reached for the professor's other arm. "Let's take him into the house."

The professor moaned as they lifted him and carried him toward Martha's kitchen door. His eyes slid closed, and he pressed his lips into a tight line.

A dark wave of dread poured over James. He couldn't lose the professor, not now, not when they were so close to seeing the old man's treasured dream become reality. But chasing that dream was what had caused this terrible problem. No, that wasn't true. It was James's headstrong, foolish actions that had pushed the professor past his limits.

"I'm sorry," James whispered in a broken voice. "I didn't mean for this to happen."

"It's all right, my boy. Not your fault." The professor's voice was soft and strained.

Ethan shouldered the door open and backed through, holding the professor's shoulders while James carried his lower half.

Martha spun around, gasped, and dropped her dish towel. "Take him into the sitting room."

The three men who'd come with Ethan looked in the back door.

"One of you take our horse and ride to the village for the doctor." Martha's voice rang with authority as she motioned them away.

James and Ethan settled the professor on the sofa. James loosened his tie and the button at his neck, then pulled an afghan from the back of the sofa and spread it over him. "Just rest. You'll be all right." *Please, God, have mercy,* he prayed, as he knelt beside the sofa.

The professor opened his eyes. "Whatever happens, you're my son. Remember that."

James gripped the professor's hand. "I will. I'm sorry for arguing with you. I won't fly today."

He sighed. "You'll know when the time is right."

James nodded, but his throat was so thick he couldn't answer.

Martha bustled in with a washcloth and glass of water. She motioned for James to move out of the way, and then she hovered over the professor. With a tender hand, she wiped his face and offered him the water. He lifted his head and took a sip. "There now, just lie back and rest. We've sent for the doctor. I'll stay with you."

"Thank you, Martha," he whispered and closed his eyes. "You know I've always loved you."

"Oh, Thaddeus." Tears misted Martha's eyes. "I've wanted to hear you say that for so many years. I know what's in your heart, and you know what's in mine."

He took her hand. "I do, and I'm sorry I haven't spoken about it before."

"There's no need to worry about that now. Just rest."

James swallowed and stepped away, his own eyes burning from watching the tender scene play out between Martha and the professor.

Why did it take a tragedy to make them all see the truth and speak plainly? The bonds of love that connected him and Professor Steed were stronger than any ties he would ever have with Daniel Drake, if he ever found him. It was time he put an end to his pointless search and appreciated what God had given him and what the professor had always offered—unconditional love that ran deep and was proven from years of care and kindness.

❦

Bella lifted the binoculars and scanned the cloudless sky above Saint Margaret's Bay for the hundredth time, but there was no sign of the Steed IV. The breeze teased the hair beneath her straw hat, tugging a strand loose. She brushed it off her cheek and lowered the binoculars with a weary sigh.

Closing her eyes, she tried to swallow the sick feeling rising in her throat. If the smelly old tugboat would just stop rocking, she would be fine. She braced herself against the railing and slowly opened her eyes. Glancing up at the white cliffs, the truth washed over her in a convicting wave.

Even if the water were as smooth as glass, she would still feel terrible. The painful memory of her heated exchange with James was the real reason for her swirling stomach and dull headache—that, and having only three hours of sleep last night.

Much of what he'd said about her was true. She had put her own desires ahead of everything else, and she'd hurt James and destroyed his trust in her. She regretted it now, but there was no way to go back and undo what she had done. The die was cast. She had made her choice, and now she would have to live with it.

"How much longer are we going to wait?" Martin Johnson, the photographer from the *Daily Mail,* adjusted the camera strap around his neck and lifted his eyes to the cliffs.

"As long as it takes." Her father glared toward the shore, then raised his eyes to the blue sky.

"But surely if Drake was going to fly today, he would've taken off by now."

Bella turned to catch the breeze, trying to judge the speed and direction. "He might be waiting for the wind to change."

Johnson squinted. "What's the wind have to do with it?"

Bella gave her head a slight shake. They had been aboard this tugboat for seven hours, and she did not have the patience to explain the importance of wind currents to the photographer.

Her father pulled his gold watch from his pocket and checked the time. "Let's wait until six. If he doesn't take off by that time, then we can assume he has decided not to fly today. I'll speak to the captain." He set off down the deck.

Bella rested her arms on the railing and stared out across the water toward the rocky beach. They were about a half mile from shore, and she could see a few people strolling along the pathway below the cliffs.

One of the sailors approached Mr. Johnson. "Can I take a look?" He pointed to the camera.

"Sure, just step back from the railing. I wouldn't want you to lose your balance and drop the camera in the water."

The sailor grinned. "You can trust me. I've got my sea legs."

"Is that right?"

"Yes sir, I've been walking the deck of a boat since I was a boy." The sailor lifted the camera and looked through the lens toward the shore. "That's my home, right up there on the cliffs."

Bella glanced at the small houses lining the top of the cliff on the left, and a question formed in her mind. "How long have you lived above Saint Margaret's Bay?"

"Thirty-six years. I was born there, and I've lived in that same house all this time."

She turned and fixed her gaze on him. "Do you remember hearing about a woman who fell from the cliffs? It was a long time ago. You would've been just a boy."

He lowered the camera and looked her way. "Yes, I do. My brother Steven and I were down at the beach that day. I didn't see her fall, but Steven did."

Bella stared at him. "You were there that day?"

The sailor nodded. "It was a terrible accident. We ran over to her, but another man and woman were closer. They got there first." He held out the camera to Johnson.

The photographer slipped the camera strap around his neck again. "That must have been a dreadful sight, especially for a boy."

"It was shocking, but she didn't look too bad, just like she was sleeping, though her neck was turned at an odd angle." He focused on Bella again. "The strangest thing was . . . she was holding a baby."

The photographer's mouth dropped open. "A baby?"

"Yes, she had a baby in her arms when she fell. She must have held on tight to him all the way down and then taken the blow herself to shield him. He survived, but she didn't."

Bella crossed her arms over her chest and suppressed a shiver. "What happened to the baby?"

"Steven and I ran over, and a few other people gathered around. The baby was crying loud and strong. The woman who got there first picked him up and tried to calm him, while the man tried to help the lady." He stopped and rubbed his chin. "But she was already gone."

Though James had told Bella the story, it still made her queasy stomach surge to hear the sailor describe being there and seeing it all. "What happened then?"

"A crowd gathered. The police came and questioned us, but there wasn't much we could say."

"They questioned the others as well?"

"Yes, but no one knew who she was. Though I did hear a rumor later that she was the daughter of the Earl of Canningford."

"And the baby? What did you hear about him?"

He shook his head. "Nothing that I recall. The earl's estate is a good ten miles away. We don't hear much about folks like that, not in our village."

She bit her lip, sorting through what he'd told her.

He started to turn away, but then he stopped. "One more thing." He glanced toward the cliffs again. "We saw a man up top, looking over after she fell."

Bella's breath caught. "A man? What did he look like?"

He shook his head. "I couldn't say. He was only there for a second or two. Then he was gone."

"Did you tell the police?"

"Yes, but I suppose he had disappeared by the time the police talked to us."

"Was there anything about the accident in the newspaper?"

He lifted one shoulder. "I wouldn't know. I was only twelve at the time and not in the habit of reading the newspaper."

Bella nodded. "Of course."

"Well, I best get back to work. The captain likes us to look busy even if we have nothing to do." He touched his hat. "Good day to you, miss. Sir." He strolled off down the deck.

Martin Johnson looked her way. "You sure had a lot of questions for him. Are you thinking of writing a series about unsolved murder mysteries?"

"What makes you think that woman's death was murder?"

He shrugged. "It might have been an accident, but it does sound suspicious, especially with that man looking over from the top. She could've been pushed, or maybe she jumped."

Bella didn't like to consider either of those possibilities. "Perhaps she just slipped and fell over the edge."

"With a baby in her arms?" He shook his head. "That doesn't seem very likely."

"Well, I think we can eliminate the idea that she jumped. Why would she do that, holding her son, and then try to protect him when she fell? That doesn't make sense."

"You're right. It's more likely she fell or was pushed."

Bella looked toward the top of the cliff as she considered those painful possibilities. Had someone pushed Laura Markingham over the edge? Who would do such a dreadful thing . . . especially knowing she was holding James in her arms?

"It's strange. You wouldn't think a woman from a wealthy, titled family like that would end up falling off a cliff and dying on a rocky beach."

"Being wealthy doesn't guarantee a pain-free, happy life." Her thoughts shifted from Laura Markingham to her own struggles and those of her family.

Gaining wealth had given them a beautiful estate, but it had strained her parents' health and marriage. Striving to move up in society and grasp a position that matched their income had put pressure on all of them.

If she and Sylvia received proposals from wealthy, titled young men this season, it would help their parents gain greater acceptance in the eyes of those with influence in society. That was how the game was played, and it made her parents judge potential suitors in a very different light than they would have, even a few years ago.

Bella closed her eyes, her heart sinking. Becoming wealthy might have opened some doors for her, but she wasn't sure she wanted to walk through them, especially if they would separate her from James forever.

What was she thinking? Right now there was no possibility of a future with James. And she couldn't blame her parents for the rift that separated her from him. It was her fault. She had put her quest to become a journalist ahead of everything else and ignored the gentle voice, warning her that she was not being honest or treating James as she wanted to be treated.

What had happened to her common sense and loyalty?

She had traded their friendship for a chance to see her articles published, and too late she realized it was not worth the price.

❦

James followed the doctor and Martha into her kitchen. He glanced toward the sitting room where they'd left the professor, then faced the doctor. "How is he doing today?"

"He seems stronger. That's a good sign, but we mustn't rush things. His attack was a mild one. Still, he needs to take it easy for quite a while."

Martha clasped her hands and nodded. "I'll make sure he rests."

"Good. He can get up a bit, but he needs to avoid all strenuous activity, eat a light diet, take two naps a day, and most of all, he needs to stay calm. You must avoid discussing anything with him that would make him feel anxious or upset."

James grimaced and shifted his gaze away. If he hadn't argued with the professor yesterday, this might not have happened. He couldn't go back and change that now, but he could make sure it never happened again. He would slow down, listen well, and be reasonable. Flying across the Channel was important, but he wouldn't want to win that prize at the expense of the professor's life or health.

"I'll check back with you in two days." The doctor placed his hat on his head. "Keep a good eye on him, and let me know if there is any unexpected change."

James and Martha thanked the doctor, and Martha showed him out the back door.

James walked into the sitting room, determination coursing through him. He would make sure the professor followed the doctor's orders. It wouldn't be easy, but it was his responsibility, and he would see to it.

The professor lay on the sofa, a frown creasing his forehead as he stared at the ceiling. "What did he say?"

James settled in a chair across from the sofa. "He said you're improving, but you need to rest and not exert yourself."

He puffed out his cheeks and blew out a breath. "I feel fine."

"I'm glad to hear it, but you're assigned to the sofa for now."

"I'll become an invalid if I have to lie here much longer."

"He said you can get up, but you have to take it easy and nap twice a day."

"That's poppycock! I'll do no such thing." The professor sat up and glared toward the fireplace.

"You have to do what the doctor says, or you'll find yourself in a worse predicament. And you don't want to worry Martha."

The professor's stern expression softened, and he glanced toward the kitchen. "She's been very kind."

"Yes, she has." A smile tugged up the corner of James's mouth. "She's quite fond of you, though I don't know why."

The professor sent him a sheepish look and settled back. "Yes, I suppose you're right. I don't deserve her kindness."

The professor's response to Martha the past two days confirmed the wall between them was finally coming down, and James was glad to see it.

Martha walked in carrying a tray. "I thought you might like some tea, and I made some egg sandwiches."

"That sounds perfect." The professor looked up at her with a light in his eyes. "Thank you, Martha."

She set the tray on the table in front of the sofa and poured him a cup of tea. "I'll warm up some chicken soup later. That's light and nourishing."

"I love your chicken soup." He took a sandwich from the plate.

"It's my mother's recipe." She sat beside him on the sofa, closer than usual, and poured herself a cup of tea.

The professor looked toward the window. "So, what's the weather forecast for tomorrow?"

James knew where he was headed with that question. "About the same." He took a sandwich and avoided making eye contact.

"What does that mean?"

"It means I'm not flying for a few days, so you can stop asking and enjoy your tea."

The professor's frown returned. "You're not grounded just because I have to stay off my feet."

James shifted in the chair. He didn't want to argue with the professor, but he was not flying until they could both be out there to do their part.

"James, look at me." The professor waited until James met his gaze. "I want you to check the wind and weather every day. If the conditions are right, I want you to give your notice and fly."

"There's no need to worry about that right now."

"Yes, there is a need. We have a race to win, and I'm counting on you to keep working toward that goal for both of us."

James gave his head a slight shake. He didn't want to fly without his friend and mentor to see him off.

"I mean it. I won't have you tied down in the house with me." The professor's firm, steady gaze made his message clear. "We've worked too hard and too long to let anyone else take that prize when it's well within our reach."

He had better agree before the professor became any more agitated. "I'll check the weather in the morning."

"And at least three more times tomorrow. If everything looks good, send notice to the *Daily Mail* and prepare for your flight the next day."

"All right. I will, as long as you promise to listen to Martha and the doctor."

The professor grinned and stretched out his hand. "Let's shake hands on that."

James grabbed hold, held on tight, and looked into the old man's eyes. Warmth and understanding flowed between them. Where would he be without the love and guidance he had received from Professor Steed?

He might never find his father or know the truth about what had happened to his mother, and he might have been disappointed in love, but he had a strong anchor in his devoted mentor and in God's goodness and provision. That was more than enough for him.

Seventeen

B ella stared out Sylvia's bedroom window, her heart sinking as the sun dropped behind the trees in the park across the street from their London home. Another day had almost passed, and still, she hadn't heard anything from James. She shouldn't be surprised. In the heat of her anger, she'd used her sharp words to pierce him through and accused him of using their friendship for his own gain.

Doubt flooded her heart as she recalled his shocked reaction. She'd only said it because she wanted to strike back at him for his accusations against her. Now she regretted it all so very much. If only she could take back what she'd said. But she had learned a painful lesson—there was no way to recall hurtful words once they were spoken.

"Do you think I should wear the coral dress or the blue?" Sylvia held up both dresses and stepped in front of the full-length mirror.

"What?" Bella turned, only half hearing what her sister had said.

"Which dress would be best for the garden party tomorrow?"

"They're both lovely, but I suppose the blue brings out the color of your eyes."

Sylvia smiled. "Then blue it is." But her smile faded as she searched Bella's reflection in the mirror. "What's wrong?"

Bella hadn't told Sylvia about her heated exchange with James. Her sister had been floating on a cloud after the ball. As they prepared for bed that night, Sylvia had told Bella about her favorite dancing partners and recounted several conversations. Bella hadn't wanted to spoil the evening, so she'd kept the painful encounter with James to herself.

Sylvia laid the dresses on her bed, concern filling her eyes. "Tell me what it is, Bella."

Hot tears pricked Bella's eyes at her sister's tender words. "I'm afraid I've ruined my friendship with James. I don't think he'll ever speak to me again."

Sylvia reached for her hand. "Oh, that can't be true. Sit down and tell me what happened."

Bella sat on the bed. "He learned about my articles, and he thinks I used him to get the information I wanted without telling him the truth about being the author."

Sylvia settled on the bed beside her. "But you couldn't tell him. Father and Mother forbade it."

"I explained that, but he heard about it from Mark Clifton."

Sylvia's eyes widened. "How did he know?"

"He was in France when we went to interview Count de Lambert, and he acted as our translator. Even though Father and I were together, it was obvious I was asking all the questions. After the interview, he kept quizzing me, even though I told him I couldn't explain. Finally, he guessed I was writing a story for the *Daily Mail,* and I couldn't deny it."

"But why did he tell James?"

"I don't know." Bella released a heavy sigh.

What had motivated Mark to mention her articles to James? Was he trying to goad James with that confidential information and imply he had a closer relationship with her? She had sensed a subtle rivalry between them, but she thought it was based on their race to be the first across the Channel. Was there another reason? Could Mark be trying to discourage James from pursuing her?

Sylvia narrowed her eyes. "Well, if Mark Clifton were a gentleman, he would keep that kind of information to himself."

"I wish he would've. You should've heard James. He was so angry. But underneath I think he was hurt and disappointed in me."

"I'm sorry, Bella. But I'm sure you can make things right if you just speak to James."

"I tried, but he wouldn't listen. He stormed out the door, and I haven't heard a word from him since."

"Give him some time, and I'm sure everything will be as it was before."

A small seed of hope sprang to life in Bella's heart. Would James eventually forgive her and want to renew their friendship? If only he would, she would be so grateful and never keep a secret from him again.

A knock sounded at Sylvia's door, and her sister called, "Come in."

Their father stepped into the room. "Ah, Bella, here you are. I was looking for you." He lifted a telegram. "We're heading back to Dover early tomorrow morning. Mark Clifton has given his notice."

Stunned, Bella rose. "Mark Clifton?"

"Yes. I've sent word to the Navy and to Captain Rockland. But this time I want to start up on the cliffs and watch the takeoff, rather than go out with the captain and spend the day on the water, waiting for the airplane to appear."

Bella stared at her father, trying to process the news. "But what about James Drake? Has he given notice?"

"Nothing more since he spoke to you at Sylvia's ball."

Bella's mind spun. She had no idea Mark was so close to making his flight, and neither did James or the professor. They would be devastated if Mark beat them across the Channel. "We have to send word to James and Professor Steed."

"We can't do that." Her father shook his head. "It wouldn't be fair."

"But James gave notice first."

"True, but he never took off."

"He must've had a good reason."

"I'm sure he did."

"Then can't we tell him Mark Clifton is ready to fly tomorrow?"

"No, Bella, we can't! Every pilot has had the same amount of time to prepare. Whoever is ready first and completes the crossing wins the prize."

She crossed her arms. There must be some way around her father's edict.

"Bella." Father's voice carried a stern warning. "You may not send word to James Drake. Do you understand?"

"Please, Father!"

He lifted his hand. "As the owner of the *Daily Mail* and the one offering the prize money, I must be totally aboveboard about this. We can't give James Drake an unfair advantage by telling him about Clifton's plans."

Heat surged into Bella's face. She wanted to beg her father to change his mind and let her send a message to James. But her father was right. She must set aside her own hopes and cover this story no matter who was flying.

"Be ready to leave tomorrow morning at five. We'll drive out to the cliffs above Dover to watch the takeoff. Then we'll head down to the dock and board the tugboat to follow Clifton across." Her father narrowed his eyes. "Agreed?"

Bella straightened her shoulders. She was a journalist, and she'd given her word to Mr. Elmwood that she would cover the Channel crossing. "I'll be ready."

Her father turned and walked out of the bedroom.

Bella sank down on the bed and stared across the room. She had never seen Mark Clifton fly, but if he was giving notice, then he must believe he was actually ready to make the crossing.

If he was successful, what would happen to James? All his hopes were pinned on winning that prize. But crossing the Channel meant more than that to him. It would validate his work and give him the possibility of a promising future.

All of that would be lost if Mark flew first.

Sylvia sat down beside her and laid her hand on Bella's shoulder. "Everything will be all right, Bella."

She shook her head. How could that be true?

The bedroom door opened again, and their father looked in. "I forgot to tell you. There's one more thing. Horace Elmwood is holding off on publishing your article about James Drake."

Bella pulled in a sharp breath. "Why?"

"When Drake gave notice, Elmwood decided he wanted to use your article with the coverage of Drake's crossing."

"But he didn't fly."

"I know, and now we don't know if he ever will."

"What will happen to my article?"

"If Mark Clifton makes it across tomorrow, that will be the top story, and I doubt Elmwood or anyone else will want to read about James Drake."

"Are you saying he won't publish it at all?"

"If Clifton wins that prize, he'll be a hero here and in France. And I'm sorry to say it, but James Drake will simply be the man who dreamed of crossing but never did."

A dizzy wave washed over Bella, and she lifted her hand to her forehead. She'd held on to a slim hope that James would be pleased when he read her article and that he'd be willing to forgive her. But this news snuffed out that tiny flame of hope and, with it, the possibility of regaining James's trust.

James pulled a wire cutter from the toolbox and leaned over the airplane's tail rudder. It was a good thing he'd put off his flight. Several wires in the tail section had come loose during his last test flight from Dover. He had to rewire and tighten those before he would be ready to fly again.

The workshop door slid to the side and Ethan rushed in. "James!"

"Over here." James stood.

"That other pilot, Mark Clifton, is headed out to the cliffs with his airplane. There's a crowd following him."

Alarm shot through James, and he strode over to the window. The sky was cloud covered, and the winds were still gusty from the southeast. "Are you sure he intends to fly today?"

Ethan lifted his hands. "That's what everyone is saying."

Was Clifton crazy? James tossed the wire cutters on the workbench and grabbed his jacket off the hook. "Would you saddle a horse for me? I'm going in to let Martha know what's happening."

Ethan nodded and sprinted toward the barn.

James took the path to the back door of Martha's cottage. He couldn't tell the professor that Clifton intended to fly; the news would be too upsetting. But he had to let Martha know he was leaving or she'd worry about him if she came out to the workshop and found him gone.

He slipped quietly in through the back door, but he didn't see Martha. He hustled across the kitchen and looked into the sitting room. The professor dozed on the sofa, and Martha sat in the chair across from him with her knitting in her lap. She looked up, and James motioned her to join him in the kitchen.

She laid aside her knitting and tiptoed toward him. "What is it?" she whispered.

He leaned down. "Mark Clifton is taking his airplane out to the cliffs. It looks like he's going to fly today."

"Oh no." She sent a worried glance toward the sitting room.

"I'm going out there, but don't say anything to the professor."

"I won't." She took his hand. "I'll pray."

"Clifton will need those prayers if he tries to take off in this weather."

She nodded, then tightened her hold. "I'll be praying you'll have the right response whatever happens."

James gave a grim nod, then walked out the back door and jogged toward the barn. Ethan led Martha's saddled bay out to meet him.

"Thanks, Ethan." James placed his foot into the stirrup and swung into the saddle.

"I'll follow you out in the wagon."

James nodded and urged the horse to a canter. It was about nine miles to the cliffs. Would he make it before Clifton took off? He leaned down and spurred the horse to a gallop.

Twenty minutes later, he crested the hill and quickly scanned the scene. Clifton's airplane sat in the middle of the meadow with its nose pointed toward France. A group of about thirty people gathered around. Two motorcars were parked nearby. One looked like the sleek black model owned by Charles Grayson.

James's stomach sank like a rock. So it was true. Today he would see his dream snatched away by another. He dismounted and tethered the horse to a tree at the edge of the meadow before setting off toward the crowd.

Help me, Lord. I need direction.

"Please move aside." A photographer waved his hand to part the crowd and then positioned himself to take a photograph of Mark Clifton and his cousin Pierre Levasseur standing beside their biplane. "Very nice. Now, let's have one with Mr. Grayson."

Bella's father stepped out from the crowd and joined Clifton and his cousin.

"Shake hands." The photographer leaned down and looked through the camera again.

James shook his head. Clifton hadn't even taken off. There was no guarantee he would make it across. Yet, there they were, congratulating him like he had already won the prize.

He looked through the crowd and spotted Bella. She held a small notebook and pen as she recorded information for another one of her newspaper articles. He clenched his jaw and looked away.

A gust of wind blew past and the sky darkened. A shiver raced down James's back. What was Clifton thinking, trying to fly in weather like this? Didn't he realize these winds would pick him up and send him straight into the choppy sea?

He had to stop him. He pushed his way through the crowd toward Clifton.

The pilot looked up as James approached, his eyebrows taking on a haughty slant. "Well, if it isn't my *friend* James Drake. Glad you could be here for this momentous occasion."

James stepped closer and lowered his voice so that only Clifton could hear. "You realize the winds are too strong. They're going to drive you off course."

Mark sent James a smug smile as he tugged on his gloves. "It sounds like you're afraid I'm going to beat you across."

"I want to win this race, but I don't want to collect that prize because you crashed into the ocean and destroyed your airplane." He leaned toward Clifton, his voice intense. "These winds are going to kill you. Call it off. No one will criticize you if you wait for better conditions."

A muscle in Clifton's jaw jumped, and he narrowed his eyes. "You're just trying to make me lose my nerve."

"I'm trying to save your neck, though I don't know why."

"Step aside, Drake."

"Don't do it, Clifton."

The pilot gave a mocking huff, turned away, and climbed into his airplane.

The crowd surged closer again, cheering and waving. Levasseur and his team motioned everyone to stand back.

Charles Grayson approached James. "What did you say to him?"

James's throat burned as he watched Clifton wave to the crowd. "I warned him the conditions are dangerous, but he wouldn't listen."

Grayson's eyes flashed. "You believe the risks are greater than the reward?"

"Yes! Taking any airplane up in good weather is a risk enough, but trying to cross the Channel when the winds are like this is a fool's errand."

⌒⌒⌒⌒

Bella longed to hear what James and her father were saying, but she couldn't walk over and join them. Everything she'd said to James at the ball rushed through her mind, and her throat burned. How could she explain? What could she say to him, right here in front of her father and everyone else?

Bella's father walked over to rejoin her, but his serious gaze remained on Mark's airplane.

"James Drake seemed quite animated. What did he say?"

"He's concerned about the winds. He urged Clifton to cancel the flight."

"He thinks it's that dangerous?"

"Drake doubts Clifton will make it across in these conditions."

Bella shifted her gaze to James. He stood back with his arms crossed and lines creasing his face.

A cold tremor passed through Bella. What if he was right? Was Mark's flight doomed? She reached for her father's arm. "Please, talk to Mark. Tell him to wait until the winds calm down."

Her father lowered his dark eyebrows. "If he won't take advice from Drake, I doubt I could convince him to change his plans."

Bella turned and scanned the scene once more. A gust of wind rushed past, nearly blowing off her hat. Why wouldn't Mark listen? Was it foolish pride or a stubborn spirit that made him ignore the warning? Maybe it was a terrible combination of both.

"Friends, please stand back." Pierre Levasseur waved his arms. "We are preparing to start the engine. Everyone must stay a safe distance away."

The crowd moved out, forming a larger circle around the airplane.

Levasseur spoke to Mark, then stepped up to the propeller and spun the blade. The engine sputtered and roared to life. Those standing in front moved to the side, opening up the pathway toward the cliffs.

Bella's heartbeat pounded in her temples. She glanced at James. Their gazes connected and held for only a second, but it was long enough to read the deep concern in his eyes. He'd tried to warn his competitor of the danger, but Mark hadn't listened. Now all James could do was stand back and wait to see what would happen.

Mark's team released the airplane, and it raced across the meadow and rose into the sky. The crowd cheered. One man waved a British flag and another waved the flag of France.

"Let's go!" Her father took her arm, and they hustled toward their motorcar. Martin Johnson, the photographer, hurried after them, toting his camera, and then jumped into the front seat. The driver had already started the engine. He held the rear passenger door for Bella and her father. Then he hustled into the driver's seat, and they raced across the meadow toward the road.

Bella held on to her hat and leaned to the left, trying to keep the airplane in view. It dipped and swayed on a frightening, unsteady path. The difference between his lack of control and James's steady flight pattern was startling.

Their motorcar rounded the curve, and she lost sight of the airplane. She gripped the side of the car and leaned forward as they rolled downhill. They passed the next curve and she looked up.

The biplane came back into view, and it followed a dizzying path through the sky, swerving, dipping, and then plunging toward the water. Bella's hands flew up to cover her mouth.

The photographer and the driver both gasped.

"He's going to crash!" her father shouted.

But at the last moment the airplane leveled out, skimming over the surface of the water with only a few feet to spare. Slowly, he rose higher and turned slightly south. But the winds continued to batter him, sending the airplane on a wild ride. Finally, he circled north and headed back toward the cliffs.

"What's he doing?" The photographer rose up on his knees, trying for a better view. "Why is he headed back this way?"

Bella gripped the edge of her seat. "He's giving up."

"Turn around!" her father shouted. "Take us back up to the top!"

The driver made a quick turn and then drove up the hill at top speed. Bella hadn't written a word in her notebook, but she was certain she would never forget the way Mark had narrowly escaped crashing into the ocean at a terrible speed that would have surely killed him.

Their motorcar crested the hill, then rumbled across the meadow. They came to a stop just as Mark touched down about one hundred yards away. His airplane rolled across the meadow toward Levasseur and those who had stayed behind to watch.

Her father climbed out of the car. "Come on. Let's hear what he has to say." He turned to the photographer. "Johnson, take a photograph as he climbs down."

"Yes sir." Martin Johnson ran ahead with his camera.

Bella followed her father across the grass and joined the crowd waiting for Mark. The airplane slowed and rolled to a stop. Levasseur rushed forward. Mark took hold of Levasseur's hand and climbed down. His face looked pale and he appeared to be a bit unsteady on his feet as he walked toward them.

"What happened?" someone shouted. "Why did you come back?"

Mark lifted his goggles and looked around the group. "The airplane was not responding well. We need to make some adjustments to our equipment. I nearly had to ditch the airplane in the ocean, but I was able to bring it up and around."

A murmur of approval moved through the crowd. "Good work!" "Well done, Clifton." "You'll make it across next time." The group clapped, and Levasseur slung his arm around Mark's shoulder.

Clifton lifted his hand, smiled, and waved to the crowd, but his smile looked forced and he still appeared shaken. Martin Johnson took another photograph. Then Mark walked away from the airplane with Levasseur. When they were a good distance from the crowd, they stopped and bent their heads together in an intense conversation.

The crowd began to disperse. Bella turned and searched for James. Had he gone back to Green Meadow? Did he know Mark had given up the flight and returned to Dover?

She spotted him on the far side of the field. He stood with Martha's son,

Ethan, near a farm wagon. James reached to untie the reins of a pretty brown and black bay, while talking to Ethan. They were too far away for Bella to hear their conversation, but she could see James's calm expression and relaxed posture.

A wave of relief rolled through her as well. Even though Mark hadn't listened to James, he'd made it back safely. Now James would have another opportunity to try for the prize. And from what she'd seen today, he had stronger skills and a much better chance of completing the flight than Mark Clifton.

Her father shook his head. "Well, that flight was a flop."

"At least Clifton didn't end up in the Channel." Martin Johnson tapped his camera. "And I got some great shots."

"That will make Elmwood happy." Father took his watch from his pocket, then looked at Bella. "I'm sure he'll want to run this story in tomorrow's paper. Can you compose your article while we drive back to London?"

Bella nodded. "I'll do my best." It would be a challenge to focus her thoughts and write the article while they drove to town. But the events were fresh in her mind, and she was eager to report what had happened today above the White Cliffs of Dover.

Bella followed her father and Martin Johnson toward the motorcar. Before she climbed in, she turned and searched for James once more. She watched as he mounted his horse and looked in her direction. Her heartbeat picked up speed, but she couldn't look away and pretend she didn't care.

His gaze was sure and direct. He touched his cap and gave a slight nod, then rode off following Ethan toward Green Meadow.

Eighteen

James adjusted his hat, trying to keep the cold, drizzling rain from running down his neck. It might not be the best morning to search Saint Matthew's churchyard for his mother's gravestone, but he couldn't fly in this weather, so he might as well use this time to see what he could learn about his family.

Rain dripped from the evergreens just past the stone wall to his left. A robin darted through the trees, then landed a few feet away and pulled a long worm from the soggy grass.

He bent and wiped his hand down the face of an old gravestone. Brushing away the mud and bits of moss, he read the names engraved there: *Harold Dickenson and his beloved wife Alice Dickenson, their daughters Henrietta and Abigail.* Below their names the dates of their births and deaths were listed. The girls had only lived a short time. Henrietta had died when she was three and Abigail when she was one.

He sighed, stood up, and looked across the churchyard, his spirit feeling as somber as the rain-soaked scene.

What was he doing here? He thought, after the professor's heart attack, he would let go of his search. But he couldn't put the questions out of his mind. As the professor recovered, the urge to find his father and learn the truth about his mother's death had returned. He wouldn't be able to put it to rest until he did all he could to follow each lead to the end.

He crossed the spongy ground to the next gravestone, scanned the name, and froze. *Laura Markingham, beloved daughter and sister, 1866–1885. Infant son, 1884–1885.*

He stared at the words, and a sudden coldness filled his core. They hadn't even known his name. But that wasn't true. They had known—they just hadn't cared enough to carve it there with his mother's. He squeezed his eyes tight and tried to quiet his churning thoughts.

This was his mother's grave, not his own. Why did he care if they thought of him as a nameless child, unworthy of any family connection? The whole thing was a lie, a disgusting attempt by his grandfather to blot out any memory of James and hide the fact that he had survived the fall.

"Mr. Drake?" Reverend Jackson walked up the gravel path toward him. He wore a tan raincoat and carried a large black umbrella.

James nodded to him. "Good morning, Reverend."

"I don't mean to disturb you." He glanced at the gravestone, and a question lit his eyes.

"It's all right. I was just . . ." James swallowed hard, surprised and a bit embarrassed by the emotion clogging his throat.

"Would you like to come in and dry off? I could offer you a hot cup of tea and a listening ear." Compassion shone from the reverend's dark-brown eyes.

James considered the reverend's offer. He liked this man. His sermons were insightful and practical, and they always gave him something to consider between Sundays. Perhaps he could ask his advice and find out what he knew about his mother's family.

"Thank you." At least he wouldn't have to stand there in the rain and face the repercussions of his discovery alone. They walked into the church, and Reverend Jackson led him to the office behind the sanctuary. The reverend shook out his umbrella, then leaned it against the windowsill to dry. He took off his coat and hung it on a hook by the door. James shed his coat and hat and hung them next to the reverend's.

"So what brings you to Saint Matthew's on a wet day like this?" He pointed to a chair and invited James to sit down. Reverend Jackson filled the teakettle and set it on the coal stove in the corner.

"I was looking for my mother's grave."

Reverend Jackson looked over his shoulder. "Your mother?"

"Yes. Her name was Laura Markingham."

The reverend's eyebrows arched. "The same Markinghams who were formerly at Broadlands?"

"Yes. Did you know the family well?"

The reverend took a seat behind his desk, facing James. "I've only been at this parish for seven years, and the Markinghams were not regular in their church attendance."

That didn't surprise James.

"We saw them on Christmas and Easter, and perhaps once or twice a year for another service. So no, I wouldn't say I knew them well." He folded his hands and sat back, waiting for James to continue.

"I only recently learned my mother's identity. She died when I was four months old, and I was raised by others who . . . are not connected with my mother's family."

A slight frown creased Reverend Jackson's forehead. "So you were adopted and your name changed to Drake?"

"Not exactly." He told the reverend the rest of what he'd learned about his mother and father and the events that had changed all their lives. The reverend listened patiently, nodding and asking a few questions for clarification.

"I thought my mother's grave might be here, since Saint Matthew's is the closest church to her family's estate." He looked toward the window. "What I didn't expect was to see myself listed there as her deceased, nameless son." The words tasted bitter on his tongue. "How could my grandfather do that?"

Reverend Jackson tipped his head. "And you believe he knew you survived the fall?"

"Yes, he knew the truth. Anna Steed wrote to him and told him everything. But he didn't answer her letter. He didn't want to have anything to do with me."

Reverend Jackson gazed across the room for a few seconds, then looked at James again. "What if there was another reason?"

"What do you mean?"

"We don't know why your grandfather acted as he did, or why God allowed it. Perhaps he was trying to protect you."

"Do you mean God or my grandfather?"

Reverend Jackson smiled. "Certainly God has always been watching over you and offering His love and protection, and that could have been your grandfather's motivation as well."

"Then why would he ignore Anna's letter and spread the lie that I died with my mother? I don't see how you can ascribe any noble motive to someone who would do something like that."

"I've always found it's better to give people the benefit of the doubt rather than assume they have evil intentions."

James turned that thought over in his mind. Could there be some other explanation for his grandfather's actions?

"Have you considered contacting Sir Richard and asking him for an explanation?"

James's gut clenched. He had no desire to meet the man who had set into motion the events that had destroyed his mother's hopes and changed James's life forever. "I can't imagine speaking to my grandfather."

Reverend Jackson studied him for a few seconds, his gaze penetrating. "It's difficult to move into the future with freedom and joy if we are carrying a load of pain from the past, especially if we are holding on to a lack of forgiveness in our hearts."

The reverend's convicting words stirred James's conscience. Did God honestly expect him to forgive his grandfather for what he had done to him and his mother? If he met the man, would he have to express his forgiveness in person? How could he do that when all he felt toward his grandfather was bitterness and resentment?

"My advice would be to seek peace and pursue it with your grandfather and anyone else you feel has wronged you. Then stand back and see what the Lord will do." Confidence filled Reverend Jackson's voice, and kindness radiated from his eyes.

A storm of emotion swirled through James. How could he reach out and make peace with the man who had done so much harm? Sir Richard should have supported his daughter in her time of need and made sure James was well cared for, but he hadn't. Instead, he had manufactured a story to earn sympathy from friends and family, and preserve his reputation.

And what about his father? Was he equally at fault, or had he believed Sir Richard's lie and been fooled into believing James had died with his mother? But before that, he should've helped Laura and done what he could to make sure she and James had what they needed.

He clenched his jaw. It was too hard. He couldn't forgive them. Not now, not ever. He rose from his chair. "I should be going. Thank you for . . . listening to my story."

"I'll do more than that." Reverend Jackson rose. "I'll pray God guides you and gives you His grace and peace in the days ahead." He extended his hand.

James took hold. Warmth flowed from his hand into James's, but it only made the reverend's convicting words cut deeper. James let go and turned away. He took his coat and hat from the peg and walked out of the church.

He trudged back toward Green Meadow through the last of the misty rain. As he climbed the hill and passed the farm gate, the sun broke through the clouds, turning a strip of the sky a brilliant blue. Rays of gold and coral brushed across the clouds, and raindrops sparkled in the grass and dripped from the trees. The birds called to each other, exchanging peaceful songs.

The scene soothed his troubled thoughts. Perhaps the reverend's prayers were already being answered.

Dodging the puddles, he made his way past the barn. He looked up and spotted the professor standing in front of the open workshop doorway. James lifted his hand and waved. "What are you doing out here?"

The professor scanned the sky and looked up at the anemometer atop the pole. "I think you should send your notice to the *Daily Mail.*"

James looked across the open fields toward the eastern sky. "But the weather has been stormy all week. You think it's going to change tomorrow?"

He nodded toward the west. "Look, it's already changing."

"But what about the winds?"

The professor pointed to the weather vane. "They've shifted. I have a feeling this is the change that we've been waiting for."

James's heart pounded. Was it really time? Would he actually take off tomorrow and set a new record that would astound the world? Energy thrummed through him as he turned and searched the professor's face. "You're sure? You want me to send a telegram to the *Daily Mail?*"

The old man grinned and nodded. "This time tomorrow, you'll be headed across the Channel and preparing to touch down near Calais."

James whooped, then hugged the professor. The old man held on tight, laughing and slapping him on the back.

Bella dashed across the front hall of their London home. There was no time to waste! She had to hurry upstairs, pack her suitcase, and be ready to leave in fifteen minutes, or her father would go without her. Grabbing up her skirt, she started up the stairs.

Her mother followed her across the hall. "Bella, where are you going in such a rush?"

Bella stopped on the lower landing. "James Drake sent his notice. He intends to fly across the Channel tomorrow. Father and I are driving back to Broadlands so we can watch him take off and I can cover the story."

Her brow creased. "But what about the dinner party at the Hendersons' tonight? We accepted their invitation. They're expecting you."

"I'm sorry, Mother. I hope you and Sylvia have a lovely time. Please give them my apologies."

Her mother's mouth drew down at the corners. "You know the guest list for a party like this is planned to have an equal number of men and women. What am I supposed to say? How will I explain your absence?"

"I don't know." Bella lifted her hands. "Tell them I was called away with Father to cover a story for the newspaper."

Mother's eyes flashed. "You know very well I can do no such thing!"

Bella pressed her lips together, barely holding back a grin. "I'm sorry, but I really need to go up and get ready. I only have a few minutes to pack."

Her mother lifted her hand to her forehead. "Honestly, Bella, how many times are you going to ignore your commitments and race off for some silly newspaper story?"

"It's not silly, Mother. This flight is going to change the world, and I have to be there to see it."

"We'll only be in London for a few more weeks, and you're missing all the best parties!" Her mother followed her up the stairs.

"I've only missed a few."

"The purpose of the season is to meet prospective suitors. But they come to call and you're not here. They invite you to the theater, and you decline. They ask you to ride with them in Hyde Park, but you're too busy writing your stories! It's no wonder you haven't received a proposal!"

Bella spun around at the top of the stairs. "I can't help it if the men in this town are not interested in me."

"Oh, Bella, why do you have to be so difficult?"

"Please, Mother, I don't want to argue with you."

Her mother moaned and leaned against the banister.

Her father walked into the front hall and looked up the stairs. "Bella, why are you standing there? We need to leave right away."

"I know, Father. Can you please explain to Mother?" Bella turned and started across the upper hall.

"Charles, how can you let her go chasing off after all those aviators?"

"Calm down, Madelyn. She is not chasing anyone. Horace Elmwood is impressed with her writing skills. He wants her to cover the story, and she accepted the assignment. We can't very well go back on that now."

Her parents' voices faded as she entered her room and shut the door. The editor was impressed with her writing skills? He hadn't said a word to her, but he had continued publishing her articles, and he'd given her the wonderful opportunity to cover the crossing.

Perhaps writing this article about James would smooth out the issues between them. Her heart lifted as she took her suitcase from the wardrobe and laid it on the bed.

Please, Lord, watch over James and give him a successful flight tomorrow. Help me write the very best article possible, and then use it to show James how much I admire and respect him. Restore our friendship and bring us together again.

"Bella!" Her father's voice rang out from the front hall.

"Coming, Father!" She grabbed a few items from the drawers and tossed them in her suitcase. She placed her notes and papers inside and closed the latches.

Tomorrow would be a red-letter day as she'd watch James take off from Dover and then follow him across the Channel to France.

<hr/>

The sun was just peeking over the hillside when James and Ethan rolled the Steed IV out of the workshop and onto the dewy grass.

James looked up and scanned the clear sky. A few tiny stars blinked and then faded as the sun's rays brightened in the east. A smile broke across his face, and his spirits soared with the rising sun. Today he would chart a new course for himself and for the advancement of aviation.

"It looks like a fine day for flying." Ethan sent him a broad grin.

James glanced up at the weather vane and anemometer, checking the winds. "The conditions are good. I just hope they stay that way."

The back door to Martha's cottage opened, and she and the professor stepped outside.

"Good morning." The professor lifted his hand to them.

Ever since his heart attack, Martha had insisted he spend the night in her guest room, rather than the cold, drafty workshop. She kept a close eye on him during the day and encouraged him to spend most of his time resting and reading. She prepared simple, healthy meals the professor enjoyed. And every day he seemed a bit stronger and eager to do a little more—a walk to the barn, a stop at the chicken coop to collect the eggs, and then he would look in on James at the workshop.

It was a huge relief to see his strength and enthusiasm returning. James was grateful for God's healing touch and Martha's kindness and care.

Martha held out a basket to James and Ethan. "I made a fried-egg sandwich for each of you, and there's coffee in the thermos."

James wasn't sure he could eat anything. Not only was it early, but he was feeling a little uneasy about what lay ahead. "Thank you, Martha, but I'm not hungry yet."

"You'll need your strength for the journey. You don't want to get halfway across and feel light-headed and woozy." She continued holding out the basket.

The professor nodded and sent him a look that seemed to say he had better listen to Martha and not ruffle her feathers.

"All right. Thank you." James took a sandwich and passed the basket to Ethan. Martha poured him a cup of coffee. James bit into the sandwich and forced down a bite. It tasted fine. He was just too excited to enjoy it.

The professor gazed at the Steed IV. "She's a fine machine. I think we can trust her to take you all the way to Calais."

James took another bite and nodded. "I'm counting on it."

"Do you have everything you need?"

James checked the pocket of his jacket for his compass and map. He nodded and finished off the last bite. The flight should take about forty-five minutes. All he had to do was fly twenty-two miles southeast across the Strait of Dover, then make a safe landing at the site they had selected on the map.

"The naval ship will escort you and then bring you and the Steed IV back, but I want you to take this money in case you need it." The professor handed James a folded five-pound note.

James thanked him, then tucked the money into his pocket, touched by the fatherly gesture.

"You've got the map?"

"Yes, I've got it." James patted his pocket again. They'd gone over all these details several times. All the arrangements had been made. All the test flights had been completed. Every part of the airplane had been checked and double-checked. Now all he needed to do was take off from Dover and accomplish the impossible.

James downed the last of his coffee and passed the cup back to Martha. He thanked her, then turned to the professor. "I'm ready."

His mentor's eyes glowed. "Yes, I believe you are." He laid his hand on James's shoulder. "I'd like to pray for you before you set off."

James nodded, his throat tightening. "Thank you. I'd appreciate that."

Martha and Ethan came closer and they gathered in a circle, their arms reaching around each other. James could feel the professor's warm hand on his shoulder, and Martha's smaller hand on his back. Their touches sent a reassuring wave through him.

"Father, we come to You this morning, asking You to give James Your strength and wisdom for this flight. Guide him across the ocean. Make his path smooth and straight. Send Your angels ahead of him to protect him and lead him. Give him a safe landing in France, and then bring him home to us. We trust You with great hope and expectation for what will be accomplished today. Thank You. In Jesus's name we pray, amen."

"Amen," James replied, while Martha and Ethan added the same.

John and Andy, the two neighbor boys, hiked up the road toward the workshop with John's father and Andy's two older brothers. James lifted a hand, thankful for their good timing. With their help, he wouldn't have any trouble towing the Steed IV out to the meadow above the cliffs.

James turned back to the professor. "Thank you. This will be your victory as much as mine. I'll ask Ethan to come back to let you know when I actually take off."

"I appreciate that, but you're not getting rid of me yet." He smiled and nodded toward Martha. "This dear lady has consented to ride out in the wagon with me so we can see you head out."

James shot a questioning glance at Martha. "Are you sure that's a good idea? I thought he was supposed to avoid excitement."

"He'll feel more anxious waiting here at home, wondering if you made it off safely, and we can't have that."

The professor smiled at Martha. "We understand each other well."

James debated it a moment more, then nodded. "All right, I'll see you there." He strode off to greet the men who'd come to help him, then sent John and Andy to bring out the horses and hitch them to the wagon, while the others helped attach the towline to the front axle of the Steed IV.

He glanced down the road toward Broadlands, and thoughts of Bella flooded his mind. Had she heard he would be flying today? Would she come to watch him, or would she stay in London to attend another round of balls and parties with Mark Clifton and her other upper-class friends?

He pulled in a deep breath, trying to relieve the tight band around his chest. He was just anxious about the flight. It had nothing to do with Bella. He shook his head, silently scoffing at himself. Who was he trying to fool?

He was about to set off on the most important journey of his life, and he wished with everything in him that Bella cared enough to be there to see him off.

He didn't like it that she'd hidden the truth about those articles, but his anger had cooled, and now he regretted the way he'd spoken to her. Looking back, he could see why she might think he'd sought out her friendship in the hope of securing her father's support. But that was not his primary motivation and he wished she would believe him.

Would his flight today help bridge the gap between them? Could it somehow make up for the hurtful things he'd said and the way he'd walked out and slammed the door? Doubts swirled through his mind.

Making a successful crossing would not be enough. He needed to talk to her and have an honest exchange if he wanted to put those issues to rest.

And that's what he would do. As soon as he returned home from France, he'd go to London or Broadlands or wherever she was, apologize, and tell her how much she meant to him. Surely with the prize money in his pocket and the acclaim that would follow, she would forgive him, and her parents might even welcome him into their circle of friends.

Nineteen

B ella leaned forward, silently urging their motorcar up the winding road toward the White Cliffs of Dover. Couldn't their driver go any faster? She closed her eyes, willing herself to be calm. It was only a few minutes after six. Surely James had not taken off yet.

She glanced across at her father. "Do you think we'll be in time?"

"We'd better be, or you'll have to interview the onlookers to get the details for your story."

She nodded, hoping Martin Johnson, the photographer from the *Daily Mail*, would already be there, capturing images to go with her article. The weather looked perfect for the flight, with calm winds and only a few high, scattered clouds.

A thrill raced through her. James's flight would be banner news, and she was going to write the story and make sure the world knew about his fantastic feat.

They reached the top of the hill, turned off the road, and started across the grassy meadow. Relief rushed through Bella. She was not too late!

The Steed IV was parked in the center of the meadow with about a dozen people gathered around. A farm wagon stood nearby, and Professor Steed and Martha were seated on the front bench.

She scanned the crowd around the airplane, searching for James, and spotted him near the left wing, checking some of the wires. A rush of joy flooded through her. He looked wonderfully handsome in his navy-blue jacket and gray cap. His goggles hung around his neck, swaying as he walked toward the tail of the Steed IV.

The motorcar rolled to a stop, and Bella and her father climbed out. Clutching her small notebook, she hurried across the meadow toward the crowd. A low hum of conversation floated on the morning air as she approached. Martin

Johnson stood up front, taking photographs of the airplane and those who had come to watch James take off on this historic flight.

Another motorcar drove across the field and parked a short distance away. The passenger door opened, and Mark Clifton and his cousin Pierre climbed out. Mark looked across the field, taking in the scene, but he didn't come any closer. His cousin leaned toward him, waving his hand toward the crowd as he spoke to Mark.

"Look, it's Mark Clifton," one of the men called.

Several people turned toward the aviator who had tried and failed on his first attempt across the Channel.

What was Pierre saying to Mark? He shook his head and crossed his arms, his stern gaze fixed on James and the Steed IV.

Mark was obviously not happy to see James preparing to take off. He glanced her way, and his frown eased. He nodded to her.

She sent him a brief smile, but then she looked away quickly and jotted down a sentence in her notebook, trying to look busy and unable to break away to speak to him.

Her father walked through the crowd toward the farm wagon. She followed him and said hello to Martha, while her father greeted the professor.

"This is the day we've all been waiting for." Martha's eyes glowed as she watched James circle the airplane once more.

The professor tipped his hat and smiled. "Miss Grayson, it's a pleasure to see you again."

"Thank you. It's good to see you as well." It seemed odd that the professor wasn't bustling around the airplane with James as he had for each test flight. He looked a little pale. Perhaps he had not been well. She considered asking about his health, but this didn't seem like the time or place for that question.

Her father looked past Bella's shoulder. "Ah, Mr. Drake."

Bella's heart leaped, and she turned.

James walked toward them, his intent gaze focused on her father. "You received my official notice?"

"We did. That's why we're here." Father looked toward the Steed IV and then back at James. "Are you ready to fly?"

"I am, sir."

"Would you like to make a statement for the *Daily Mail* before you take off?"

"I would." James shifted his gaze to Bella. "I'm grateful for those who believed in the dream of powered flight and supported me in this endeavor. I would not be here today without the partnership of Professor Thaddeus Steed. And if I am successful, I intend to share the recognition and award with him."

Bella quickly jotted down what he'd said in her notebook.

James reached out and shook hands with her father. "Thank you, Mr. Grayson." Martin Johnson took a photograph of the two men and then asked them to wait while he took another. The photographer stepped back, and James looked up at the professor once more.

The old man laid his hand on James's shoulder. "Godspeed, my boy."

James nodded and looked at Martha.

"We'll see you soon." Martha's eyes grew misty, and she slipped her arm through the professor's.

James turned toward Bella. He stood tall and gazed down at her with a serious, determined look. A muscle flickered in his jaw, and a touch of some unnamed emotion shone in his eyes.

Her hands suddenly felt clammy, and she almost dropped her pen. There was no guarantee James would make it all the way to Calais, but she didn't want him to see her fear. Keeping her gaze steady, she looked into his eyes. "I'll be praying for you."

He worked his throat, then nodded to her and strode toward his airplane.

The crowd clapped and called out to him. "You can do it, Drake!" "On to Calais!" "Have a good flight!" "We're behind you!"

James climbed aboard and settled into his seat. Martha's son, Ethan, stepped up to the propeller, and after a short exchange with James, he gave it a spin. The roar of the engine vibrated the airplane and the ground around them. The crowd moved back to clear a path for the airplane.

James looked her way once more and lifted his hand. Then the Steed IV rushed across the grass, picking up speed for several yards, before it lifted smoothly into the air. The crowd cheered. Johnson ran down the meadow after the airplane, taking more photographs.

Bella clasped her hand to her heart. The airplane rose higher and zoomed out over the edge of the cliff.

"Come on, Bella!" Her father hustled across the field to their car, and once again they raced down the winding road to the bay where the tugboat waited.

James's heart surged forward as he pulled back on the stick, and the Steed IV rose up into the air, leaving the grassy meadow and cheering crowd behind.

He shot out over the cliffs, and an exhilarating thrill rushed through him. The winds lifted the airplane, sending him higher. He held on tight, making slow, careful adjustments to stay level. The air rushed past, chilling his face in spite of the temperature being in the mid-sixties. The salty sea breeze filled his nose and lungs.

He could hardly believe this was really happening. He pulled in a few deep breaths to steady his nerves, then set his course southeast toward France.

Straight ahead, he spotted the British naval destroyer HMS *Tartar* that would act as his escort. A minute later, he zoomed over the long ship, and several sailors waved from the deck. He grinned and lifted his hand, thankful to know they would follow him across the Channel and provide a free trip home for him and his airplane when he completed this flight.

He glanced over his shoulder. In the distance, a small tugboat followed the destroyer. It seemed he would have two escorts today. That was fine with him. It would soon be time to celebrate, and as the professor always said, the more the merrier.

He shifted in his seat and checked the oil pressure gauge and tachometer. Everything seemed to be working well, but he stayed alert and made careful corrections to the wings and rudders as the wind currents changed.

He checked his watch and was glad to see he'd already been flying for about nine minutes. The coastline of France and hills rising beyond Calais looked clearer now. He and the professor estimated the flight would take forty to forty-five minutes, but it depended on the winds and his ability to stay on course.

The memory of Bella watching him prepare for his flight flashed through his mind. He'd been so glad to see her that he didn't know what to say. Had she come as a reporter for the *Daily Mail* or as his friend? She had carried a small notebook and recorded his brief statement, but her smile and the look in her eyes seemed to say she wanted to be both friend and reporter. And he was beginning to think that might not be such a bad idea after all.

A blast of wind hit him from the west. He gripped the wheel on top of the stick and made careful adjustments to the rudder with the foot pedals. He considered flying higher to try to avoid those winds, but he wasn't sure that would help. The professor had advised him to keep his airplane two hundred to three hundred feet above the choppy water of the Channel. They both believed that was the safest altitude, and he was doing his best to stay in that range.

Thoughts of the professor made him swallow hard, and he fixed his gaze straight ahead. The professor would be so proud and happy if James was successful today, and he would gladly share the spotlight with the professor when the time came to receive the prize.

He flew on at a steady pace for a few minutes, then checked his watch again. It was two minutes after seven. He'd been in the air about twenty-three minutes. A wave of excitement coursed through him. He was more than halfway.

Looking over his shoulder, he strained to see the coast of England, but it was only a gray-green line above the intermittent white cliffs. Turning, he gazed ahead to the coastline and rising hills of France. Below, the deep-blue water swayed and danced with whitecaps, rising and disappearing again. Overhead, the clear blue sky stretched out like a bright canopy with soft mounds of cotton-white clouds to the northeast.

What an amazing sight. As long as he lived, he would never forget this day. Nothing could compare to this amazing feeling!

❧

A stiff breeze ruffled Bella's skirt and tugged on her ivory straw hat. She leaned against the tugboat railing and looked through the binoculars, training her gaze on James. His takeoff had been perfect, and his flight pattern surprisingly smooth even with the wind picking up. Watching him soar across the blue was one of the most thrilling sights she'd ever seen.

This day was a turning point in her life. She was covering the most extraordinary story of the year, maybe the decade, but even more important, she was watching the man she loved achieve his greatest dream.

Joy pulsed through her as that thought settled in her heart. It was true. She loved James Drake. Since the first day they'd met, she'd thought he was someone special. And now, after all the experiences they'd shared, she knew he was the man she admired above all others.

His bravery and intelligence set him apart, and his devotion to the professor showed his caring heart. He could be reserved and a tad quick to take offense, but knowing his background, she understood why he struggled to trust her and believe she truly cared about him. Some people might say his parents' choices cast a shadow over his reputation, but she didn't agree. He was building his own reputation, and she was so very proud of him.

If they could just have a few moments alone together, she was sure they could talk through their differences and work things out. She straightened her shoulders and made her decision. As soon as they reached France, she would speak to him, and if that wasn't possible, she would seek him out when they returned to England.

<hr>

James checked his instruments again, then strained to search the French coastline, looking for the lighthouse that would mark his path toward the landing area.

A thin stream of pale-gray smoke flew back from the engine, carrying the smell of burning oil. He squinted and leaned to the right, scanning the electrical wires leading to the engine. Nothing seemed out of order there.

The stream of smoke increased and fluttered past his shoulder. What was going on? Could the cast-iron pistons be overheating? He'd had that problem once before, but not with this engine. He thought the new design would prevent that problem from reoccurring.

His thoughts darted through his options. France was closer now than

England, but he was probably fifteen or twenty minutes from his landing site south of Calais. Could he make it that far?

The acrid smell of burning oil stung his nose and made his eyes water. A strange keening cry came from the engine. The airplane jerked, and he tightened his hold on the stick.

He needed a plan, and he needed it now. *Lord, help me!*

He shot another glance over his shoulder. The HMS *Tartar* was at least a mile behind him with the tugboat chugging along beside. How long would it take the ship to reach him if he had to land in the Channel? Would his airplane stay afloat, or would it sink to the bottom and take him with it? Would he even survive a crash landing in these rough waters?

⟡

Bella lowered her binoculars and turned to her father. "How much longer until we reach France?"

"I'd say we're at least halfway." Her father kept his binoculars trained on James. "Drake's doing a superb job. I can't believe how much control he has compared to Mark Clifton. It must be the design of his airplane."

She smiled. "I'd say it's more the skill of the pilot."

"I suppose you're right."

Martin Johnson stood a few feet away, making adjustments to his camera lens.

The tug took an unexpected dip, and cold water splashed Bella and Father. She gasped and stepped back.

"Good heavens, what a wild ride." Her father wiped his hand down his face, but he looked as though he was enjoying this adventure as much as Bella was.

She wiped the lenses of the binoculars on her dress, then raised them and scanned the sky again. She spotted the airplane, and the hairs prickled on the back of her neck. A plume of smoke drifted behind James. She blinked and twisted the binocular settings. The view cleared, but the plume grew larger. "Father, something's wrong!"

"What?" Her father shook off his dripping binoculars.

"Look! There's smoke coming from his airplane." Bella stared through the

lenses, her heart sinking as the trail turned darker and fanned out into a wide
stream.

Lord, help him!

"He's losing altitude!" her father shouted.

Bella's heart leaped to her throat. The nose of the airplane dipped toward
the ocean. He seemed to still be in control and on a steady path, but he was
headed for the Channel.

"Captain!" Her father's voice rose. "Our man's going down!"

Bella stared, unblinking, as the Steed IV dove toward the water, skimmed
across the waves, then hit with a huge splash. Water shot up into the air at least
twenty feet. Could James stay afloat until help arrived? Or would he have to
swim, while his plane sank out from under him?

She gulped in a breath. "Is he all right?"

"I can't tell." Her father's grim tone sent a fearful shiver through her.

Martin walked back toward them, an anxious look on his face. "What do
we do now?"

"Hold on!" her father shouted.

The tugboat picked up speed and passed the destroyer. Bella shifted a few
feet down the railing to try to get a better view, but now that James was in the
water, it was more difficult to see him. The waves surged and the boat rose and
fell, as she scanned the water.

"I can't see him!" Fear almost choked off her words.

"Let's run up to the bridge. We'll have a better view from there." Her father
and Martin hustled inside and jogged up the metal stairs.

Bella followed close behind, her mind darting ahead from one scenario to
the next. *Please, Lord, keep him safe until we arrive.*

Several of the crew had gathered on the bridge and were looking out the
windows. The captain motioned them inside.

Her father stepped up beside the captain. "Did you see him go down?"

The captain nodded. "We're headed straight for him."

One of the men pointed out across the water. "There he is!"

Bella raced to the front window. The sailors stepped aside, making room
for her. She raised her binoculars, scanning the sea. The motion of the speeding

tug made it difficult to steady herself, but James finally came into view, or at least she could see his airplane.

She swallowed, scanning back and forth, searching for him. Panic twisted through her, blurring her view. Why couldn't she see him? Had he fallen out and drowned? No! He had to be there!

"I see him!" Her father's voice rose with hope. "He's sitting up top!"

Bella blinked, looked again, and finally saw his head above the waves. Relief flooded through her. They were still so far away he was barely visible, but he seemed to be upright and the airplane was floating, at least for the moment.

Bella turned to the captain. "How long until we can reach him?"

The captain narrowed his eyes. "I'd say five to seven minutes, but the *Tartar* may get there first. A big ship like that might be slow to pick up speed, but once they do, they can cut through the water faster than a tug."

Bella nodded and lifted her binoculars again. As if the destroyer had heard the captain's words, the huge ship surged past, rocking the tug and almost knocking Bella off her feet.

Her father grabbed hold of her arm to keep her from falling. "He's not wasting any time."

The wake from the destroyer jostled the tugboat. Bella widened her stance and gripped the ledge. The waves finally settled, and she looked through her binoculars again.

The destroyer was closing in on James. He lifted his hand and waved.

That was a good sign, a very good sign.

It took another five minutes for the tug to reach the downed airplane. Bella, her father, and Martin returned to the deck as the tug slowed and swung around beside the destroyer.

A lifeboat from the *Tartar* rocked on the waves next to the partially submerged airplane. One crewman stood on top between the wings, connecting a towline. The nose and engine had sunk below the surface, but the wings and tail still floated on the sea.

While the crew worked to secure the airplane, Bella scanned the lifeboat for James. She saw him near the bow, watching the salvage efforts with a concerned frown. His clothes and hair were soaked, and his face was pale. "There's James." Bella pointed him out to her father.

"Drake, are you all right?" her father shouted.

James looked up. "Yes." His voice was strong, but Bella could see the pain and disappointment in his expression. Her heart ached for him. He'd made a gallant effort and flown farther across the Channel than any other pilot, but his machine had let him down and failed the test.

He held his left arm against his body and winced when one of the crewmen draped a blanket around his shoulders.

Bella clenched her hands. Was he injured? She gave her head a slight shake. He was alive, on his feet, and talking. His injury couldn't be too serious. *Thank You for protecting him, Lord. It could've been so much worse.*

Father turned to her. "I'm going aboard the lifeboat to speak to Drake."

Bella nodded. "I'll go with you."

"No, Bella. You can't."

"But, Father—"

"I mean it!" His intense expression brooked no argument. "This time you must listen and do as I say. I'll get a statement from Drake, and you can use that in your story."

She wanted to speak to James herself, more to be assured he was all right than to get a quote for her article. But she understood why her father refused to let her go. There was no ladylike way to climb aboard the lifeboat dressed as she was in a long skirt with not much width.

Her father called out to the lifeboat and asked for permission to come aboard. The crew conferred and gave permission. He hustled up to the bridge and asked Captain Rockland to move closer. A few minutes later, with some careful maneuvering, the tug slid into place next to the lifeboat. Her father climbed over the side of the tug and jumped down into the boat.

He approached James and shook his hand. Martin lifted his camera and took several photographs from the tug. Bella watched, wishing she could hear James's account, but she was grateful her father would pass on what James had said. He nodded several times as he listened to James, and then he slapped him on the back. James grimaced, but her father didn't seem to notice.

The lifeboat crew tossed the towline to one of the sailors on the tugboat. They attached it to a wench and slowly raised the airplane from the water. Shouts filled the air as one of the men gave orders to the others. Water poured from the airplane in a gushing stream. They slowly swung it around and then lowered it onto the deck of the tug.

The landing gear was bent, and there were several tears in the fabric of the wings and tail. The cross wires along the body were twisted and broken. Bella had no idea how long it would take to repair that kind of damage, or if it was even possible.

James had a second partially built airplane, but she didn't think it had an engine. Could they salvage the engine from the Steed IV? She suspected being submerged in salt water, even for a short time, would cause some damage. Perhaps they wouldn't even want to use it since it had been so unreliable.

Bella glanced at the lifeboat again. James stood with her father, his gaze trained on his damaged airplane, his shoulders sagging and his lips pressed in a grim line.

Tears pricked her eyes and she blinked hard. This day had dawned with so much promise. Now they were facing a great setback, and it threatened to make them all lose heart. But she would not let that happen. She would write her story in a way that gave hope. The world needed to know that even though James had not made it all the way to Calais, he was not defeated. And that was front-page news!

Twenty

James crossed Martha's kitchen and poured himself a cup of hot black coffee. Maybe that would give him a shot of energy so he could face the day, because right now all he wanted to do was trudge to the workshop and crawl back in bed.

"Sit down, James, and eat some breakfast." Martha set a plate of sausages on the table and motioned toward the empty chair.

He leaned against the counter. "I'm not hungry."

Martha shifted her worried glance from the professor to James. "Is your wrist bothering you? Maybe you should take that medication."

James shook his head without answering. His wrist was throbbing, but he didn't want to take the medication the ship's doctor had sent home with him. It would be a killer on an empty stomach, and right now he couldn't tolerate the thought of breakfast.

He turned his head, trying to stretch his neck and ease the uncomfortable knot at the back of his sling. He frowned into his coffee cup, while the chorus of condemning thoughts marched through his mind again. A tight sling and a sprained wrist were the least of his problems.

The professor looked up from the newspaper. "This is a good article. Why don't you sit down and take a look?"

"Why would I want to read about ditching my airplane in the Channel? I was there, and it was bad enough going through it the first time."

The professor smoothed his hand over the front page. "I think you'd be pleased to read what this fellow"—he leaned down and squinted at the by-line—"I. J. Wilmington has to say."

What would the professor think if James told him I. J. Wilmington was really Bella Grayson? He grimaced and silently dismissed the idea. It wasn't his secret to tell. "Not interested."

"There is no need to be curt."

Guilt pricked his conscience. He was exhausted from a short night and his aching wrist, but that was no excuse for being rude to Martha or the professor. "Sorry." He slid into the chair and glanced at the headline: "Pilot's Brave Attempt Falls Short."

His gut clenched, and defeat burned in his throat. *Falling short* was just another way of saying he'd failed, and that was exactly what had happened. He'd failed to reach France, destroyed his airplane, wasted their savings, and thrown away his chance to be first across the Channel. He rubbed his forehead and released a weary sigh.

The professor turned the newspaper around toward him. "Holding on to a negative attitude is not going to solve the problem."

James shifted in his chair. Of course the professor had a point. It was natural to be disappointed after such a defeat, but he should not take out his frustration on his friends.

"Just because you were not successful on your first attempt, that doesn't mean you're finished. What do I always say? If you fall down, you get back up and try again."

Martha nodded. "That's an important lesson we all need to take to heart."

The professor patted the newspaper. "Chin up, my boy. Read the article. Then we'll discuss what to do next."

James gave a slow nod, then dropped his gaze to the opening paragraph.

Aviator James Drake made his mark in history yesterday when he attempted his first flight across the English Channel. With single-minded focus and outstanding skill, he set off from Harmsford Meadow above Saint Margaret's Bay near Dover at 6:48 a.m. A small crowd gathered to watch his departure, and they were amazed by his smooth takeoff and his expert control of the Steed IV airplane, which he designed in partnership with Professor Thaddeus Steed of London.

The tension in his neck eased as he read on. Bella had reported the facts clearly, but the tone of her article surprised him. She'd praised his efforts and made him sound more like a hero than a failure. Was that what she really believed, or had her father or the editor asked her to slant the article that way? Whatever her reason, he should be grateful.

James looked up and met the professor's gaze. "You're right. It's a good article. She was very generous."

The professor's eyebrows rose. "She?"

He stifled a groan, debating his reply. Martha and the professor were trustworthy, and if he told them the truth, they might be able to give him advice about what to do next.

"Bella wrote this, but please don't say anything to her or anyone else. It's supposed to be a secret."

The professor's eyebrows rose. "Why wouldn't she want anyone to know?"

"Her parents are the ones who want it kept quiet."

The professor nodded, but he still looked a bit puzzled.

"Good for her." Martha smiled. "She told me she wanted to be a journalist."

The professor turned to Martha. "She did?"

"Yes. When she and Sylvia came for tea that day you cut your hand, she said she hoped to write for her father's newspaper one day. It's been her dream since she was a little girl."

James let that thought settle in his mind. He dreamed of breaking records with the Steed IV and establishing himself as a skillful pilot and airplane designer. But he'd held on to another dream even longer. Ever since he was a boy he'd longed to know more about his family. Somehow, he thought if he could understand who they were, then he would know who he was and where he belonged. Pieces of those dreams were finally coming together, but he hadn't done it on his own.

Bella had gone out of her way to be supportive of his dreams and help him in his search. But what had he done for her? Regret draped over his shoulders like a heavy blanket, and he shook his head. He had not been understanding or supportive of her dreams. Instead, he'd argued with her and broken off their friendship because she'd kept a secret from him and wounded his pride.

That wasn't right.

If he'd only given her the benefit of the doubt and a chance to explain, they probably could've settled matters in a few minutes rather than letting the argument separate them for far too long. He had assumed the worst about her rather than believing the best, and that was selfish and unjust.

What a fool he'd been!

He rose from his chair. "I have to go see Bella."

"Now?" The professor glanced at the clock. "It's only five minutes after eight."

"I know it's early, but this can't wait." He grabbed a piece of toast off the plate and drained his coffee cup.

A tremor traveled through Bella as she approached Martha's back door. She had stopped at the workshop first, but neither James nor the professor had answered when she knocked. It was early for a visit, but her father wanted to return to London in a few hours, and she was not leaving Kent until she delivered this newspaper and talked to James.

She stepped up to Martha's back door and straightened her jacket. Summoning her courage, she lifted her hand and knocked three times.

Please help me, Lord. I'm not even sure what I'm going to say.

The door opened and Martha looked out. Her eyes widened, and a smile spread across her face. "Bella, we were just talking about you."

"You were?" Bella swallowed. What had they been saying?

"Yes, come in. Have you had breakfast?"

"No, I haven't, but I'm not hungry." She followed Martha into the kitchen. "I brought you a copy of the *Daily Mail* and some lemon scones."

"That was thoughtful." Martha placed the basket on the table.

James stood by the professor with his arm resting in a sling tied around his neck. "Good morning, Bella."

She sent him a tentative smile. "Morning." She couldn't quite read the emotion in his eyes, but he didn't seem upset that she'd come. That was a relief. She held out the newspaper. "I thought you might like to read this, but it looks like you already have a copy."

"We do, but thank you for bringing it." James's hands were full, so the professor took the newspaper and laid it on the table.

The professor looked from James to Bella. "Not eating breakfast seems to be a problem with too many young people these days."

"Nothing to worry about. They can eat later." Martha sent the professor a pointed glance, then looked at Bella. "You'll have to excuse us. We have some things we need to do."

The professor's eyebrows rose. "We do?"

"Yes. Remember, you said you would help me fix that broken arm on my rocking chair." Martha tilted her head toward the sitting room.

"Oh." His eyes widened. "That's right. The arm on the rocker is broken, and I'm going to fix it." He grinned at James and Bella, then followed Martha out of the kitchen.

Bella darted a glance at James, barely able to hide her smile.

"They're not too subtle, but they have good intentions." He motioned to the table. "Are you sure you wouldn't like something to eat? Those scones smell great."

"No, thank you. Not right now." She pressed her lips together, searching for a way to start.

James turned toward the window. "It looks like a nice morning. Would you like to take a walk?"

Relief rushed through her. "Yes, I'd like that very much."

He opened the back door and motioned for her to go first.

She stepped outside, a sense of hope building in her heart. The morning air was fresh and cool, and sunlight glittered in the trees. Rain had fallen overnight, but most of the clouds had blown away. Puddles dotted the gravel path, and birds sang from Martha's garden. "It looks like it's going to be a beautiful day."

"Yes, almost as nice as yesterday." He started down the path that led toward the fields and stream, and she fell in step beside him.

After a few seconds he said, "Thank you for bringing the newspaper. It will be good to have an extra copy."

"So . . . you read the article?"

"Yes."

She tensed and looked his way. "What did you think?"

He hesitated a moment. "You're an excellent writer."

"And . . ."

He squinted, looking as though he was searching for the right words. "You gave the story quite a positive spin."

She slowed. "You think I was biased in my reporting?"

"No, that's not what I meant. It was just so . . . glowing. You made me sound like a hero."

She smiled. "Exactly. That's how people think of you."

He sent her a doubtful glance.

"It's true. I interviewed several people before and after, and they were all very impressed."

He shook his head. "I only made it halfway. Then I ditched in the Channel and destroyed my airplane. That's not exactly what I'd call a successful flight."

"You passed the halfway mark, and up to that point your flight was flaw- less. When your engine failed, you could've panicked, but you kept control of your airplane and saved your own life by landing the way you did. I'd say that's not only heroic; it's amazing."

He frowned toward the trees, still looking unconvinced.

She stopped and turned toward him. "I wrote the story in an honest, straightforward manner. My father and the editor, Mr. Elmwood, agreed, or it never would've been printed."

He lifted his hand. "All right. I understand, and I certainly don't want to argue with you about your articles."

She pulled in a calming breath. "Sorry. I guess I tend to take criticism of my writing a little too personally."

"I'm not criticizing you, Bella, not at all. I'm just trying to get a clear pic- ture of what really happened yesterday and straighten out my own thoughts." He reached for her hand, and his touch was warm and comforting. "Thank you for being there, and for writing the story the way you did."

"You're welcome."

"There's something else I need to say." He tightened his hold on her hand and slowed his steps. "I'm sorry for what I said at Sylvia's ball. I should've taken things in stride and given you a chance to explain instead of blowing up and running off."

Her heart swelled. She'd longed to hear those words, and now she was so touched by them she could hardly speak. "I'm sorry too. I wanted to tell you everything, but I felt like my hands were tied." She shook her head, determined not to make any more excuses. "I never should've agreed to keep my writing a secret, especially from you."

"It's too bad your parents put you in that position."

"It wasn't entirely their fault. I so wanted a chance to write for Father's newspaper, I would've agreed to just about anything."

He sent her a tender smile. "It's all right. I understand."

His kindness pierced her heart. She had to tell him the rest. "There's more to the promise I made to my parents."

"What do you mean?"

She slipped her hand from his. "This is my third season, and Mother and Father are not happy that I haven't made more of an effort to encourage the men I've been introduced to in London."

"What does that have to do with your writing?"

"The only way they would give their permission for me to write those articles was if I promised to be more encouraging to suitors."

He stopped and turned toward her. "So, it was sort of an exchange?"

"Yes." She swallowed hard. "I not only promised to encourage them, I said I would accept a marriage proposal from one of them by the end of the year."

His eyes widened and he stepped back.

Regret swamped her heart. "I know it was foolish and impulsive. I never should've made that promise."

His brow furrowed. "When did you agree to this?"

"It was months ago."

"Before we met?"

A sinking feeling hit her stomach, but she couldn't lie to him. "No, it was after."

His jaw tensed and he looked away.

She'd hurt him again, and she hated that. "I'm sorry, James. If they asked me to make that promise today, I'd never agree to it."

He met her gaze. "Not even if they offered you a full-time position writing for the *Daily Mail*?"

"No, not even then." She clasped her hands tight. There was so much more she wanted to tell him, but he hadn't said anything about his feelings or intentions. Still, she had to try to make him understand. "I've wanted to write for my father's newspaper since I was a little girl, and seeing those articles published was like a dream come true. But if I'd known writing them would hurt you and separate us, then I never would've started down this path." She lifted her gaze to meet his. "Please forgive me."

Emotion flickered in his eyes as he studied her. "I understand, and I forgive you. I'm just not sure what this means for us."

Bella blinked. *Us?*

He reached for her hand again. "Bella, I knew the moment we met you were someone very special. If I could, I'd go to your father today and ask him to release you from that promise and give me permission to call on you as a suitor."

Warmth and joy flooded Bella's chest. James wanted to speak to her father?

"But I don't think he would agree. All I have to offer right now is a depleted bank account, a questionable family background, and a botched flight across the Channel."

"But you're a respected aviator and airplane designer. Your wrist will heal, and you'll fly again."

He shook his head. "Not for a few weeks. And who knows what will happen by that time. I have no idea if I'll still have a chance to win that prize."

Bella held tight to his hand, wishing there was some way to change those facts. But he had a point. Given the way things stood right now, her parents, especially her mother, would not welcome James to call on Bella.

"Even if my wrist were healed, we need a new engine, one that will keep running when there's a lot of moisture in the air."

"Is that what caused the problem yesterday?"

"That's the professor's theory, and it makes sense. The engine worked well on our test flights at Green Meadow, but it failed over the water. Still, we won't know for sure until we install a new one and try another test flight over the Channel." He shook his head. "But we don't have the funds to buy a new engine at the moment, so I'm not sure what we're going to do."

She gave a slow nod, pondering the problem. "I think we should talk to my father."

He turned toward her, his face brightening. "Do you really think he'd consider me as a potential suitor?"

Her heart flip-flopped. "I think the first step is to persuade him to pay for the new engine. That would show him you're determined to complete that flight. The more he invests in you and your airplane, the greater commitment he'll feel, and the happier he'll be when you succeed. That will be the time to talk to him about calling on me properly."

James gave a slow nod. "Yes, that sounds like a good plan."

"We're leaving for London in a few hours. Why don't you come with me to Broadlands and talk to him now?"

"All right. I'll just tell the professor, and then we can go."

Bella watched him jog back toward Martha's cottage and a prayer rose from her heart. *Thank You, Lord, for protecting James and for helping us work through these problems. Please soften my father's heart and help him see James as I do. Guide their conversation, and please provide what's needed for James to fly again. Thank You!*

Twenty-One

J ames straightened his shoulders as he walked through the central hall at
Broadlands with Bella. His wrist was throbbing again, and his eyes still felt
gritty from his short night, but if he was going to fly again, he needed a new
engine.

Bella looked up at him. "Don't worry. Everything will be fine."

He nodded, but the knot in his stomach cinched tighter. If Charles Grayson offered his support, he'd have another chance to win the race, but if he
refused, James's hopes would be dashed—not only for capturing that one-
thousand-pound prize, but also for winning Bella's hand.

Bella stopped at the library door. "Would you like me to come with you,
or would you rather speak to him alone?" she whispered.

"Come with me."

She smiled, confidence glowing in her eyes, and they walked into the library together.

Mr. Grayson stood by his desk, sorting through papers. He placed a file in
his open briefcase and looked up. "Ah, Mr. Drake, good morning." His gaze
dropped to the sling. "How is the arm?"

James crossed toward Mr. Grayson. "It's just a sprained wrist. I'll be fine in
a week or two." At least he hoped he'd be able to use it that soon.

"Good." He glanced at Bella, then looked back at James. "So, what brings
you to Broadlands this morning?"

"I thought you'd like to hear an explanation for what happened yesterday."

A flash of surprise lit Mr. Grayson's eyes. "I would. Why don't you have a
seat?"

They all sat down, and James explained the professor's theory. "We believe
we know how to alter the pistons to keep the engine from overheating. That
should make it more reliable for flights over water." He met Mr. Grayson's gaze.

"And we wanted to ask if you might be willing to lend your support and cover the expense of a new engine."

Mr. Grayson's brow creased. "It seems like I just paid for the last one."

"Yes sir, you did, and we're very grateful." James waited, giving Mr. Grayson time to consider his request.

Mr. Grayson drummed his fingers on the arm of the chair, then looked at James. "I was impressed with your performance yesterday. You displayed great control of your airplane from takeoff until that unexpected water landing. Even then, you managed to bring your airplane down in a way that kept you afloat. That was quite an achievement."

James looked Mr. Grayson in the eye. "Thank you, sir."

"I believe you would've made it all the way to France if your engine hadn't failed you."

"I agree, sir. That's why I want to order that new engine as soon as possible and prepare for my next flight."

Mr. Grayson studied James with a serious look for several seconds. "All right, Mr. Drake. I'll do it. I'll cover the cost of the new engine with the hope of seeing you back in the sky very soon."

Relief rushed through James. "Thank you, sir!"

Mr. Grayson rose, crossed to his desk, and pulled open the center drawer.

Bella sent James a triumphant smile, and he returned the same.

The butler walked into the library, carrying a silver tray. "Excuse me, sir. A telegram has arrived for you."

Mr. Grayson took the telegram from the tray. "Thank you."

The butler turned and left the room. Bella glanced at James, questions flickering in her eyes. James focused on Mr. Grayson as he opened the telegram and scanned the message.

"My stars!" Mr. Grayson looked up. "Louis Blériot and Count de Lambert have both given notice. They intend to fly tomorrow if the conditions are favorable."

Those words hit James like a blow to the chest, knocking the wind out of him.

"Father, are you sure?" Bella rose and crossed to look over his shoulder.

Her face paled and her eyes clouded. She looked up and shot a painful glance at James.

Mr. Grayson shook his head. "It seems your flight has challenged them to step up and make an attempt."

James pulled in a shaky breath and glanced at Bella. What could he do? Was there any point in ordering a new engine? That would take a few days, and even then, his wrist had to heal before he could fly.

Mr. Grayson looked toward his desk. "I'm not certain I should still write that check."

"Father, of course you should! We have no idea if Blériot or de Lambert will be successful. James still has a chance, and now we know time is of the essence."

Mr. Grayson glanced at the telegram. "I suppose you're right. It's a risk, but it's a risk I'm willing to take." He took out his pen and filled out the bank draft.

James rose and crossed to stand beside Bella. What would he do without her?

Mr. Grayson turned and handed the check to James. "They've not beaten us yet. Go order that new engine."

"I will, sir. Thank you." But his somber tone betrayed his concern. With Blériot and de Lambert ready to fly from Calais, victory for James seemed less likely than ever before. He swallowed hard and nodded to Bella. Then he turned and walked out of the library.

Bella's heart ached for James as she watched him leave. What a terrible blow this must be for him, especially after his failed flight the day before. But he'd maintained his composure in spite of the news in that telegram. She stepped away from the desk, intending to follow him.

"Bella, this changes our plans. We'll be staying in Kent for the time being."

She stopped and turned toward her father.

"If one of those French pilots does make it across, I want to be at Dover to see it. And I'm sure Mr. Elmwood will want you to cover the story." He sent her a pointed glance.

"Yes, I suppose he will." But she didn't relish the idea of reporting that one of the French pilots had taken the prize. She pushed that disappointing thought away. It hadn't happened yet, and there was no need to borrow trouble from tomorrow.

She walked out of the library and into the central hall, but James had already disappeared. She quickened her pace, pulled open the front door, and scanned the grounds. She spotted him at the bottom of the circular drive.

"James, wait!" Bella grabbed up her skirt and hurried down the steps.

He turned and looked her way, squinting against the sunlight. The tired slope of his shoulders and the lines creasing his forehead tore at her heart.

She caught up with him. "We'll be staying in Kent."

He gave a slow nod. "Of course, you wouldn't want to miss that story."

She closed her eyes, fighting her own wave of frustration. "What I mean is, I'll be here at Broadlands. If there's anything I can do to help you or the professor, please let me know."

His expression eased, and he glanced back at the house. "You've already done more than I could've hoped for."

But it wasn't enough. His spirits still needed a boost. An idea came to mind, and she reached for his hand. "Come with me."

He hesitated a moment, then tightened his hold on her fingers. She led him around the side of the house and across the west lawn.

"I suppose I should ask where you're taking me."

She sent him a soft smile. "There's something I want to show you."

He gave a slight nod, and his mouth tugged up at the corner.

The sound of splashing water and birds' songs greeted them as they entered the fountain garden. Pink and white peonies and a few early roses filled the flower beds around the fountain and sent their sweet fragrance into the air.

James's gaze traveled over the scene, his expression easing. "This garden looks totally different in the daylight."

Memories of their moonlight meeting stirred her heart. They followed the path around the fountain, and her steps slowed. Ahead of them stood a broad archway covered with vines. Clusters of brilliant yellow flowers hung down from the branches, filling the ceiling of the archway with a golden cloud and shadowing the path below.

James stepped under and looked up. "Wow, this is amazing. I've never seen flowers like this."

"The gardener told me they're called laburnum, but some people call them golden chain flowers. They only bloom this time of year." She gazed up at the showy blossoms. The flowers swayed in the gentle breeze, and their subtle fragrance drifted past.

He lifted their clasped hands to his chest, drawing her closer. "It's beautiful. Thank you for showing me."

She nodded, sending him an encouraging smile.

"I don't know what's going to happen tomorrow, Bella. If one of those French pilots makes his crossing . . ." His words trailed off, and he looked away.

"I'm not worried. You'll make that flight and win the prize, or you'll win the next race."

He looked down at her. "How can you be so sure?"

"Because of all the men I've met in London or anywhere else, not one of them can compare to you."

"Not even Mark Clifton?"

She shook her head. "No comparison."

He smiled, but as his gaze traveled over her face, his expression softened and tenderness filled his eyes. "I love you, Bella."

Her heartbeat raced, and a sense of wonder flooded through her. "I love you, too."

He leaned closer and rested his forehead against hers. Her eyes drifted closed and she released a soft sigh, treasuring their closeness and the words they had just shared. They had opened their hearts to each other, and it bound them together in a new and deeper way.

He lifted his head and looked into her eyes. "I promise I'll do everything I can to win this race and find a way for us to be together." With his eyes reflecting the sincerity of his words, he lifted her hand and kissed her fingers.

Amazement tingled through her. James loved her. It was almost too wonderful to believe.

"I should go. I need to tell the professor about your father's generosity in paying for the new engine. He'll be relieved."

"Will he go to London with you to order the new one?"

"He's not up to traveling right now."

"He's not?"

James's forehead creased. "He had a heart attack the day after Sylvia's ball."

Bella gasped. "Oh no. I'm so sorry. I didn't know."

"It was a mild one, but the doctor wants him to take things at a much slower pace, and I'm sure Martha would not approve of him traveling to London anytime soon. I'll go Monday when the shop opens again."

Bella pondered that for a moment. "I hope I'll see you at church tomorrow, but I'm not sure I'll be able to come."

He caught her meaning and sobered. "I understand. I'll wait for you and hope for the best." Tenderness returned to his gaze.

"Thank you." She stood on tiptoe and kissed his cheek.

His eyes widened and he grinned. "Wow, I'll have to promise to wait for you more often."

She laughed, then tucked her arm through his, and they walked out from under the golden archway and into the bright sunlit garden.

Conflicting thoughts tumbled through James's mind as he passed the workshop and walked toward Martha's cottage. This should be one of the happiest days of his life. He'd told Bella he loved her, and she had repeated those same words to him with sweetness and conviction. But the shocking news that Blériot and de Lambert were ready to fly cast a shadow over everything.

Bella seemed to think he still had a chance to beat them, but he wasn't so sure, and that worrisome thought gnawed at him.

"Hello, James."

He looked up and spotted Martha and the professor seated together in Martha's side garden.

The professor rose, his expression eager. "How did the meeting go with Mr. Grayson?"

James took the check from his pocket and held it up. "He gave us the funds for the new engine."

"Oh, that's wonderful!" Martha beamed a smile at the professor. "What an answer to prayer!"

"I knew he wouldn't disappoint us, especially not with Bella standing by your side." As the professor studied James's face, his smile faded. "What's wrong?"

James shook his head. "It's nothing for you to worry about."

The professor lowered his bushy white eyebrows. "Did you have another disagreement with Bella?"

"No. We're fine."

"Well, then, what is it?" He narrowed his gaze. "I'm not an invalid, and I don't want you to feel you have to hide things from me."

James looked away, debating what to say. It might be better to give the professor a warning of what could happen. At least then he'd be prepared rather than shocked if Blériot or de Lambert completed his flight.

James focused on the professor. "While we were talking to Mr. Grayson, he received a telegram. Both Louis Blériot and Count de Lambert have given notice. They plan to fly tomorrow."

The color drained from the professor's face, and he sank down in his chair. "I didn't expect that. I knew it could happen, but I didn't think they were ready to attempt a crossing."

Martha leaned closer and laid her hand on the professor's arm. "It will be all right, Thaddeus."

The professor stared across the garden and shook his head. "After all our work."

James squatted in front of the professor. "I don't want you to worry. I'll go into town first thing Monday morning and order the new engine. If it will only take a day or two, I'll wait there. If it's going to be longer, I'll come back and keep working on the airplane. Then as soon as we have that new engine installed, we'll be ready to fly."

The professor shook his head. "You can't fly with your wrist the way it is."

James set his jaw. "I'll have to try."

"No! You need two strong arms to battle those winds and keep control of your machine. You're not going up again until your wrist has healed."

James was about to argue, but Martha gave her head a slight shake.

"There's no need to worry about that right now," she said.

James rose. "I agree with Martha. Let's focus on what we can do today."

"Yes, we must not let these challenges discourage us." The professor shifted his gaze to James. "Let's go out to the workshop and make a list of what needs to be done."

James tensed, and he shot a questioning glance at Martha. The professor had rarely visited the workshop since his heart attack. Was he strong enough to get back to work without damaging his health?

Martha picked up her shawl from the back of the chair. "I'll go in and fix lunch while you two make your list. But don't stay out there too long. You don't want to let your lunch get cold."

Affection lit the professor's eyes as he gently touched Martha's arm. "We'll just take a look, then come back for lunch in a few minutes."

Martha glanced at James, and he could read her silent request to make sure the professor didn't stay in the workshop too long.

James nodded to her, then crossed the garden and opened the gate.

The professor passed through and set off at a brisk pace. "Well, my boy, we have our work cut out for us."

"That we do." James fell into step beside the professor, and a renewed sense of optimism spread through him. They might be facing their greatest challenge, but they would tackle it together, as friends and partners, and so much more.

Twenty-Two

B ella! Bella, wake up!"

Someone pounded on her bedroom door. Bella rolled over and squinted at the clock. It was only five fifteen. "Father, is that you?"

"Yes, it's me! Get up and get dressed! Louis Blériot took off from France this morning. He's on his way to Dover. He might've already landed! We have to get out there right away."

Bella blinked to clear her vision, then threw back the blankets and climbed out of bed.

"I'll give you ten minutes. If you're not ready, I'll go write that story myself!"

"I'm coming!" She hurried to her wardrobe and flung open the doors, her thoughts in a dizzy whirl. Could it be true? Had Blériot really flown across the Channel while they all slept in their beds? Did James know? Her heart plummeted at that thought.

What if Blériot had engine trouble, as James had, or some other problem? Had he landed in the rough water somewhere between France and England? She pushed away that thought. There was no way to know unless she went out to the cliffs to see for herself.

She grabbed a skirt and blouse she could put on without the help of her maid and dressed as quickly as she could. Her fingers fumbled as she buttoned her blouse and pulled on her stockings. She glanced at the clock and grabbed her hairbrush from the dressing table. With quick strokes, she ran a brush through her hair and twisted it up in a knot. Thank goodness her hat would cover that mess.

She snatched the yellow straw hat with the blue-and-yellow-striped ribbon and plopped it on her head. Then she plucked a hatpin from the drawer, stuck it through the back of the crown, and hurried out of her room. Was she in time? She looked over the banister at the top of the stairs.

Her father stood in the central hall, looking up with his watch in his hand. "Hurry, Bella! We need to get out there!"

Bella trotted down the steps, and they strode out the front door.

Bella slid into the waiting motorcar, and her father climbed in after.

"Take us to Dover Castle." Father's face was ruddy and his expression intent. He was a newspaperman, and this was an important story he did not want to miss.

A shiver traveled down Bella's arms. She was a journalist, and she wanted to cover this story, but she dreaded the thought of seeing Blériot or anyone else take this victory from James.

Ten minutes later they reached the top of the hill and rounded the curve. Dover Castle came into view, and about two hundred yards away, in a hilly field, a crowd gathered around an airplane parked at an odd angle.

"There he is!" her father's voice rang out.

Bella shifted in her seat, searching across the meadow.

Her father leaned forward. "Cross the field and park as close as you can."

"Yes sir." The driver turned off the road and drove across the grass.

"You'll need these." Her father passed Bella a small leather-bound notebook and fountain pen.

"Thank you." In her rush, she'd completely forgotten to bring her notebook.

They parked near two other motorcars and a few wagons and horses. Father climbed out and strode across the field. Bella hurried to keep up. About twenty people surrounded the airplane, including four policemen. Their faces were animated as they talked among themselves and examined the French flying machine. Blériot stood near the left wing, speaking to one of the policemen.

Bella's father stepped forward. "Monsieur Blériot, congratulations!"

"Ah, Monsieur Grayson!" The pilot reached out and shook her father's hand. He reeled off a few sentences in French, then laughed and switched to English. He was obviously excited and relieved to be safely on the ground in England.

"Monsieur Blériot, it's good to see you again." Bella stepped up next to her father. "Would you be willing to make a statement for the *Daily Mail*?"

"*Oui, merci.*" His dark eyes danced. "I am most happy to speak to the *Daily Mail*."

Her father nodded. "Tell us how the day began."

Bella took rapid notes while Blériot recounted the events of the morning. He'd taken off from a farm near the beach at Les Baraques, then followed the French destroyer *Escopette* for a few miles. He soon passed the ship, and conditions became hazy. For about ten minutes he lost his bearings and wasn't sure if he was going in the right direction. Finally, the English coast came into view, but he'd drifted north of Dover. So he turned south and looked for a good landing spot. The cliffs and the castle came into view, and then he saw a man waving a French flag. He circled the field twice before landing.

Another motorcar pulled to a stop nearby, and everyone turned to see who had arrived. The door opened and a woman in a long checked coat climbed out followed by two other men.

Blériot strode across the field and welcomed the woman with a kiss on both cheeks. He took her hand and led her back toward Bella and her father. "This is my wife, Alice. She came on the *Escopette*."

Alice nodded and smiled and greeted them in French. But she didn't speak English, so they continued the interview with her husband.

Bella's mind spun as she took more notes about the airplane, the crowd of onlookers, and the French pilot with dark eyes, a full moustache, and a slight limp.

The men who'd come with Madame Blériot congratulated him in French, and then they turned toward the airplane and seemed to be discussing the landing and minor damage to the aircraft.

Bella turned to her father. "Do you think we have everything we need for the story?"

He nodded. "Let me speak to Monsieur Blériot about coming to London to receive his prize."

Bella's thoughts shifted to James, and her excitement faded. Most people would see Blériot's flight as a great victory, but it would be a discouraging defeat for James and Professor Steed. She couldn't bear the thought of telling James, but if she didn't, would he think she'd kept another secret from him? Closing her eyes, she stifled a groan.

Lord, what shall I do? You know how much this is going to hurt James.

James yawned as he stepped out of the chicken coop and pulled the door closed behind him. He glanced down at the basket with a satisfied nod. Nine eggs were more than enough for a fine Sunday morning breakfast. Martha would be pleased.

A horse and rider galloped up the road toward the cottage. As they came closer James lifted his hand and waved.

Ethan pulled back on the reins, and his horse skidded to a stop, stirring up a cloud of dust. "Have you heard the news?"

"What news?"

"Tom Rushford was fishing this morning, and he saw a flying machine circle Dover Castle and then land."

James tensed and scanned the sky to the east. Could it be Mark Clifton making an early morning test flight, or was it de Lambert or Blériot? "Did he say if it was a biplane or monoplane?"

"He said it looked like yours, so it must have been a monoplane. But I knew you weren't flying. Do you think it could be one of those French pilots?"

"I'm not sure, but it doesn't sound good."

Ethan climbed down. "What are you going to do?"

"Can I take your horse?"

"Sure." Ethan passed him the reins in exchange for the basket of eggs. He glanced toward the cottage. "What should I say to Mother and Professor Steed?"

James climbed into the saddle, which was no easy trick with one arm in a sling. "Tell them what you heard, and then say I went to check it out. But try not to upset the professor."

"How am I supposed to do that?"

"I don't know. Just try to be calm yourself." James wheeled the horse around. "I'll be back as soon as I find out what's going on."

He set off at a trot but soon urged the horse to a gallop. His thoughts raced ahead as he sped along, jumping fences and cutting across fields. Fifteen minutes later the castle came into view. Everything looked peaceful, with no one about this early in the morning.

Where was the airplane? Was he too late? He rode on and took the path that led around the castle.

When he reached the top of the hill, the view of fields to the north opened up. His mouth fell open and he pulled in a sharp breath. People were gathered around a monoplane parked on a gentle slope. The nose of the airplane pointed toward the castle and the tail, toward France. Four motorcars, and several wagons and horses waited nearby.

Before he could process what he was seeing, a young lad ran up the hill toward him. "Come see the flying machine!"

"Who's the pilot?" James forced out the question.

The boy scrunched up his face. "I think his name is . . . Belly-row?"

James stared across the field, and a cold wave washed over him. So it was true. This morning, while he fed the horses, gathered eggs, and dreamed of winning Bella's hand, Louis Blériot had flown across the English Channel and captured the coveted prize.

He'd lost the race. There would be no thousand-pound prize, no government contract to design and build airplanes, and no hope of a future with Bella.

Dazed, he rode closer until he spotted Blériot. The French pilot with the thick moustache waved toward his broken propeller, looking as though he was explaining to the men who were gathered nearby what had happened when he landed. But he spoke in French, so James only caught a few words.

"Ladies and Gentlemen, may I have your attention?"

James's gaze darted to the man speaking, and another shock jolted through him. Charles Grayson stood near the wing of the airplane. He lifted his hand, waiting for the crowd to settle down and turn his way.

Bella stood next to him, her notebook and pen in her hands. She scanned the crowd, and her gaze connected with James's. Her eyes flashed, and she bit her bottom lip. Sympathy flooded her eyes. She glanced at her father and then back at James, looking as though she wanted to speak to him, but the crowd stood between them.

He clenched his jaw and looked away, trying to douse the pain. His defeat was complete. He'd failed the most important test of his life, and he'd earned her pity. Tugging on the reins, he turned his horse away, but Charles Grayson's words stopped him.

"As I'm sure you all know, the *Daily Mail* offered a prize of one thousand pounds to the first aviator who successfully completed a flight across the English Channel, and today that amazing exploit has been accomplished by Monsieur Louis Blériot."

The crowd clapped and a few men cheered.

"This record-breaking flight will no doubt be recorded in history, and Monsieur Blériot will be known as the courageous and triumphant pilot who did what many said could never be done. We want to offer our hearty congratulations and invite Monsieur and Madame Blériot to London for the award ceremony, which will take place tomorrow."

The crowd burst into applause again, and several people stepped forward to shake hands with Blériot and offer their congratulations.

James wheeled the horse around and set off at a trot, but rather than taking the road back to Green Meadow, he headed toward the cliffs.

"James!"

Was that Bella calling? He didn't look back. He couldn't face her, not right now. He didn't want to speak to anyone.

He galloped away, following the path along the cliffs. The wind rushed past, numbing his thoughts and blowing away some of the sting of defeat. Finally, he reached the road above Saint Margaret's Bay and slowed his horse.

Riding closer, he looked out over the edge. The sea swirled and crashed on the rocky beach below, and the salty wind stung his eyes. He stared down into the foaming tidewaters, his thoughts swirling.

For the last two years he'd focused his time and energy on reaching one goal. He'd pinned his hopes on what he would accomplish and what that would mean for his future.

What would he do now?

How would he make a name for himself or even find a purpose for his life? And what about the professor? How would he handle this defeat, especially with his heart issues?

James swung his leg over the saddle and slid to the ground. He grabbed the reins and walked down the path toward the point. Lifting his gaze, he stared across the Channel. In the distance, the blue-gray line of the French coast was clearly visible today. So close, and yet so impossibly far away.

Memories of his last flight rushed through his mind—the thrilling takeoff over the cliffs, the smooth and steady flight above the choppy water. Everything had gone so well until the engine overheated and failed. He shook his head. What was the use of thinking about that now? It was over.

What am I supposed to do, Lord? I gave it my best effort, but it was not enough. I let the professor down, I let Bella down, and I've lost the prize money.

He waited, searching the sky, longing for some kind of answer, but the only sound was the cry of the seagulls and the wind whistling around his ears.

It was time to go home, back to Green Meadow and the professor and Martha. Somehow he'd have to find a way to comfort his friend and mentor. But at least he would not have to do it alone. Martha would be there, and she would help the professor face this defeat.

That thought eased some of his burden. Even if they hadn't won the race, their time in Kent had reunited Martha and the professor, and at this stage in his life, that might be a better prize than seeing James make the crossing. Finding that one special person you want to share your life with was a prize in itself.

That bittersweet thought made his throat tighten, and the truth dawned in his heart. He'd met Bella because he'd come to Green Meadow. He would always be grateful for that. Even though he'd lost the race, he'd found the woman he loved. She was a treasure, much more valuable than any prize offered by the *Daily Mail*.

He climbed back into the saddle and urged the horse toward the road.

Yes, Blériot had beaten him today, but he must not lose Bella. There had to be some way he could still prove his worth and win her hand.

Twenty-Three

The clock stuck eleven as Bella and her father walked into their London home on Monday night. They'd spent the day escorting Louis and Alice Blériot around London, from one event to the next. Bella had put on a brave face and dutifully taken pages of notes, recording what happened at each event and capturing quotes from the speeches, but the joyful response of the cheering crowd was a stark contrast to her mood.

She couldn't erase the memory of seeing James's face fall as he listened to her father praise Blériot yesterday morning at Dover. As soon as her father finished his short speech, she'd tried to speak to James, but he'd ridden away without looking back. Ever since, she'd felt like a heavy weight was pressing down on her heart.

How could she be happy and celebrate when he was discouraged and suffering from his defeat? With a weary sigh, she crossed the entry hall toward the stairs. "I'm going up to bed. Good night, Father."

"You'll need to get that article written and turned in first thing tomorrow morning."

Bella looked over her shoulder. "I'm exhausted. I'll have to get up early and work on it tomorrow."

"You made a commitment, Bella. Horace Elmwood is counting on you."

"It won't take long to write the article. I have everything I need in my notebook."

He lowered his eyebrows. "Don't embarrass me by turning in a haphazard story or missing your deadline."

Her face flushed. "I have turned in every article on time, and I'll deliver this one by eleven, as promised."

"I should hope so. An opportunity like this doesn't come along every day, especially for a young woman." Her father's sharp tone grated across her tired nerves.

Would he ever be pleased with her efforts? Would they ever be enough?

Horace Elmwood had praised her series, remarking on her concise writing and the perfect timing of her articles leading up to James's flight and then Blériot's crossing. He said they had stirred the entire city of London and driven the *Daily Mail*'s circulation to new heights . . . but receiving a positive comment from her father seemed nearly impossible.

The front door opened, and Sylvia and Mother walked in. Bella stopped on the lower landing.

"Oh, Bella! I'm so glad you're here." Sylvia hurried across the entrance hall and started up the stairs to meet her. "I have so much to tell you, but first, I want to hear all about your day. Mrs. Lampson told us there was a great crowd to greet Blériot when he arrived on the train this morning."

"Yes, people were lined up ten deep from the station all the way to the Savoy Hotel. The police had to clear the road for Father's car. It was like a wild parade. I've never seen anything like it."

"Oh, that must have been so exciting!" Sylvia led the way through the upper hall. "What was the event like at the hotel?"

Bella pushed open her bedroom door and Sylvia followed her in.

"There was a luncheon with several important guests—Lieutenant Ernest Shackleton, the explorer, was there, as well as Mr. Harry Gordon Selfridge."

"How many people attended?"

"At least one hundred and fifty and scores more outside. Father gave a speech and presented Monsieur Blériot with a large silver rose bowl from the British representatives of Blériot's firm, and then a silver cup and the one-thousand-pound prize. After that, there was another reception, and then a dinner at the Ritz." Bella stifled a yawn. "Tomorrow the Aero Club will award him the gold medal before he returns to France."

"Oh, I wish Mother would've let me go with you today. The luncheon was so boring. Half the guests were missing. Mother thinks they stayed away to try to see Monsieur Blériot. It must have been so thrilling to meet the man who set such an amazing record."

Bella's thoughts turned to James, and an ache filled her chest. She slipped off her jacket and laid it over the back of the chair.

Sylvia followed her across the room. "Bella? Are you all right?"

She slowly turned and faced Sylvia, then shook her head. "I saw James yesterday at Dover when Father and I drove out to meet Blériot at his landing site. Oh, Sylvia, he looked so discouraged, like his last hope had been destroyed." A lump lodged in Bella's throat, and she blinked her stinging eyes.

"Oh, Bella, I'm sorry. Here I am asking you about Monsieur Blériot when I should've known it would be hard for you to see James lose that prize."

Bella sank down on her bed. "It's not just the prize."

Sylvia sat beside her. "It's not?"

"We hoped winning that race would give James a chance to impress Father so he could call on me properly."

Sylvia's eyes widened. "He told you he wants to call on you?"

Bella sniffed and nodded. "He said he loves me. And I love him, so very much. But I don't think Mother and Father will allow James to call."

Sylvia sent Bella a sympathetic look. "If you love each other, surely that has to count for something."

If only that were true, but her parents' list of qualifications for suitors had been drilled into them, and James didn't have those credentials.

She lifted her hand and rubbed her eyes. "Oh, if only James's engine hadn't failed, he would've been the one we ushered around London today. Then he could've easily gained the backing he needs to start his company and show Mother and Father he could support a wife and family."

"That might've won Father's approval, but I'm not sure it would be enough to please Mother. You know how particular she can be."

"Yes, she's particular all right."

"There has to be some way you can win them over."

"I wish I knew how."

Sylvia reached over and squeezed Bella's hand. "Don't give up hope. We'll find a way."

Bella turned toward her sister. "You are such a dear. I'd be miserable without you. You must promise never to marry until we both have our futures settled."

Emotion flickered in Sylvia's eyes, and she slipped her hand from Bella's.
"Sylvia?"

"A lot has happened while you were in Kent."

Bella focused on her sister. "What do you mean?"

"I've met someone, and he's paid a great deal of attention to me at the last few parties. He called here at the house on Friday."

"Really? Who is it?"

"His name is Stephen Russell." Sylvia's smile returned. "He's wonderfully kind and courteous, twenty-one, and ever so handsome. His father is the Earl of Wessex, and his family estate is Haverly Hall in Berkshire. Mother is pleased, but of course Father hasn't met him yet because he's been in Kent with you."

Questions whirled through Bella's mind. "So, you're saying you care for him?"

"I think so. He's very attentive, and he has a wonderful sense of humor. We can talk about anything, and it feels like we've known each other for a long time, though we've only spent a few hours together."

Bella didn't want to put a damper on Sylvia's hopes, but some of the men who had pursued Bella had only done so because they hoped to use her future inheritance to shore up their family's troubled financial situation. "What do you know about his family?"

"I've only met his mother. She's very nice. And as I said, his father is an earl with an estate in Berkshire."

"But what about their financial situation? Has Mother looked into that?"

Sylvia lifted one shoulder. "She checked *Burke's Peerage* and spoke to a few of her friends. Everything we've learned so far makes him sound like an ideal match."

Bella's apprehension eased. "Then I'm sure he's just as wonderful as he seems, and I'm happy for you."

"Thank you, Bella." Sylvia's smile faded, and concern lit her eyes. "What are you going to do about James?"

"I don't know. If only Mother and Father would get to know him as I do, then they'd see that he's a wonderful man with a fine character and great potential. In my opinion, those qualities are much more important than a title or inheritance."

"Their hearts would have to soften a great deal to agree with that."

Bella lay back across the bed. Her sister was right. It would take more than getting to know James or seeing him win an aviation prize to convince her parents he was the man she should marry.

She closed her eyes. *Lord, You know how much I love James, but I love my parents too. I don't want to hurt them or marry against their wishes. Please, soften their hearts and help them accept and appreciate James. Let them see we're a perfect match. And help me trust You while I wait for You to work out all these things in Your time and according to Your will.*

<hr />

Bella walked into the lobby of the *Daily Mail* and headed for the lift. She had only five minutes to make it to Mr. Elmwood's office and turn in her latest article, or she would miss her deadline.

"Good morning, Miss Grayson." The uniformed man at the reception desk nodded to her as she passed.

She gave him a brief smile, then hurried on and pressed the button to call the lift.

"Miss Grayson." Mr. Finney, the reporter she and James had spoken to in the research library in late April, stepped up beside her. "This is a nice surprise. I was going to write to you today."

"You were?"

"Yes." He grinned. "I have a lead for you."

Her face warmed. How had he found out she was writing for the *Daily Mail*? "What kind of lead?" The lift doors slid open, and they stepped inside.

"I believe I found the Daniel Drake you're looking for."

Bella's startled gaze riveted on him. "How did you do it?"

"Last week I was covering the trial of Joseph Ellington. He is accused of murdering Doctor Arthur Lowell, and Daniel Drake was called as a character witness for Ellington."

"Goodness, a character witness for a murderer?"

"An accused murderer. The trial isn't over yet."

"Yes, of course. What did you learn about him?"

"I did a little investigating, and I found out he owns a large paper company.

He and Ellington have been friends since they attended Cambridge together, and they're in the same club."

"And you think he could be James's father?"

"It's possible. He's forty-five, a widower with two daughters." Mr. Finney cocked his eyebrows. "His address is number fourteen, Grosvenor Square."

Surprise rippled through Bella. "That's a very elite area."

The lift door slid open, and Mr. Finney stepped out. "He's quite wealthy. It seems most of his money came through his wife's family."

Bella nodded as she followed him into the newsroom. "Did you learn anything else about him?"

Mr. Finney's mouth tipped up in a grin. "He's a member of the British Aero Club."

Bella's steps stalled. "Really?"

Mr. Finney nodded. "Fascinating, isn't it—father and son, both drawn to aviation?"

"Yes, it is." Bella glanced at the clock on the wall and gasped. "I'm sorry. I have to go. Thank you so much. I really appreciate your help!" She hurried toward the stairs. Grabbing up her skirt, she dashed up to the top floor and ran down the hall to Mr. Elmwood's office. She stopped outside the door and straightened her jacket, then walked in. His young assistant greeted her and showed her into Elmwood's private office.

The editor glanced at his pocket watch as she stepped up to his desk. "I'd say you're cutting it quite close, Miss Grayson."

She pulled the article from her portfolio and handed it to him. "You said eleven o'clock, sir."

He glanced at the opening lines and motioned to the chair in front of his desk. "Have a seat."

"Thank you." She settled in the chair and tried not to fidget. Even though he'd published every article she'd submitted, each time she turned one in she worried he'd finally realize she wasn't a real journalist, just a hack with unrealistic dreams.

He finished reading and lifted his gaze to meet hers. "Something's missing."

She sat up straighter. "What do you mean?"

"Where's the zip?" He lifted his fist in the air.

"The zip? I'm sorry, sir. I don't understand."

He tossed the papers onto his desk. "Your stories are usually exciting and full of life, but this one reads like a dull list of events."

A dizzy wave washed over Bella. This was it—the day she'd been dreading. He was going to toss her story in the trash and send her home.

"Everyone in this city is going crazy, trying to catch a glimpse of Blériot," Mr. Elmwood continued. "They're excited, and they want to read a story that reflects that excitement."

Bella swallowed. "Yes sir. I understand."

He sat back and clasped his hands across his stomach. "So, what's going on? Why doesn't this read like a thrilling recount of an amazing celebration?"

Bella sank lower in her chair, the truth of the situation pressing down on her. "I'm afraid I let my personal feelings influence my writing."

"You have personal feelings *against* Blériot?"

"No sir. It's just . . . I was hoping James Drake would be the first across, and it's been disheartening to see someone else receive the accolades that should've gone to him."

"Hmm, I see." Mr. Elmwood rubbed his chin. "Well, we all would've liked an Englishman to claim the prize, but that's not the way it played out."

"No sir. It's not."

"So, can you fix this article, or am I going to have to run it as is?"

Bella straightened. "Is there time?"

He lifted his watch from his pocket. "I'll give you thirty minutes, but that's all. If we don't get this downstairs to the typesetter by eleven forty-five, it won't make the next edition, and we've got to run this story." He passed her the papers and rose from his chair. "Sit here. There's more paper in the top left-hand drawer. I've got to check on something downstairs. Rewrite the article and leave it here when you're finished."

"Yes sir."

He stepped out from behind his desk. "Your father told me you'll be going to the International Air Meet at Reims next month."

Bella looked up. "Yes, our whole family is planning to attend."

"I'd like you to send me some stories with a human interest angle, like you did with those first few articles in your series."

Bella's eyes widened. "You would?"

"Yes. Will you take that assignment?"

"Yes sir! I'd be happy to."

"Good. Maybe three or four articles, featuring the pilots we haven't covered yet and some of the most exciting events." He started to turn, then lifted his finger. "Oh, I almost forgot." He reached into his drawer, pulled out a long white envelope, and handed it to her.

"What's this?"

"Your paycheck."

Bella blinked and stared at him.

He grinned. "Did you think you were working for free?"

"No sir. I mean . . . we didn't discuss payment."

"Well, your check is in the envelope, and I hope you'll be satisfied."

"I'm sure I will be. Thank you."

"All right. The clock is ticking! Get to work, and make the words sing like you did before!"

Bella nodded. "I'll do my best."

"I'm counting on it." The editor strode out the door.

Relief poured through Bella as she watched him go. Mr. Elmwood had not only given her a chance to redeem herself and her article, but he'd offered her a new assignment and handed her an unexpected paycheck. What a wonder!

⁕

James looked in the mirror, lifted his chin, and adjusted his tie. He wished the professor had come to London with him, but Martha and the doctor had encouraged him to stay at Green Meadow, and the professor had reluctantly agreed.

That meant James was on his own to take care of their business in town, but at least Professor Steed didn't have to deal with seeing Blériot's celebration and pretending it didn't cut him to the heart.

When James had arrived in town late Monday morning, he'd gone directly to the machine shop and ordered the new engine. Then he'd almost missed his afternoon meeting with Mr. Robertson, president of the Aero Club, because the huge crowd following Blériot was blocking the streets.

That afternoon, he and Mr. Robertson would meet with Mr. Sparks and Mr. Knowles, two respected businessmen who were members of the Aero Club and hopefully future supporters.

He adjusted the collar of his white dress shirt. Why did they make it so tight? Well, it didn't matter. If wearing this uncomfortable collar was what it took to make a good impression on those men and secure the funds he needed to get to Reims, then that was what he would do.

He'd just have to pray he didn't pop a collar button during the meeting and embarrass himself.

The doorbell rang downstairs. "Hannah, can you get that?" He turned and listened, but he didn't hear her footsteps in the lower hall. She might not have heard the bell or his call, so he grabbed his suit jacket and headed downstairs.

When he reached the landing, he scanned the entrance hall, but he didn't see Hannah. The bell rang again, and he hustled the rest of the way downstairs. "I'm coming," he called, then crossed the hall and pulled open the door.

Bella stood on the doorstep. She looked up and sent him an apprehensive smile. "Hello, James."

He blinked, his thoughts so scrambled he couldn't put a sentence together. "Bella."

"I hope it's all right that I came. I would've sent you a message, but I have such important news—it couldn't wait."

"Please, come in."

As she stepped inside, Hannah walked into the entrance hall, carrying a stack of clean towels. "Oh, I'm sorry. I didn't hear the door."

"It's all right, Hannah. This is Miss Bella Grayson." James turned to Bella. "This is Hannah Hamlin. She takes care of our home and has been keeping an eye on everything while we're away."

Bella nodded. "I'm pleased to meet you."

Hannah dipped a slight curtsy. "Thank you, my lady."

Bella smiled and sent a glance his way, but she didn't correct Hannah.

"Shall I put on the teakettle?"

"Yes, thank you, Hannah. We'll be in the sitting room."

Hannah nodded, then bustled off toward the kitchen.

Still feeling a bit dazed by Bella's unexpected arrival, he motioned to the left. "It's this way."

She walked ahead of him into the sitting room and took a seat by the fireplace. "I'm so glad you're still in town. I thought you might have already returned to Green Meadow."

"No, I won't be going back until Thursday. The new engine should be ready by then." He sat across from her, debating if he should say something about Blériot, but decided against it. They both knew his successful flight threw a wrench in their plans, and he wasn't ready to tell her what he hoped to do about it. "So, you said you had some news?"

Her eyes lit up. "Yes. Do you remember Mr. Finney, the reporter we met at the *Daily Mail*?"

"Yes, I remember him."

"He was covering a trial last week, and one of the witnesses was named Daniel Drake."

James's heart lurched. "Does Finney think he's my father?"

"He's in his midforties, so he seems to be the right age. He owns a paper company and is quite wealthy." She leaned forward. "And listen to this. He's a member of the Aero Club."

James's jaw dropped. "Are you sure?"

"That's what Mr. Finney said." She tipped her head. "Isn't it amazing that he has an interest in aviation, just like you?"

"Yes, it's stunning and a bit unsettling." What other similarities were there between him and his father . . . if this Daniel Drake was his father?

"Mr. Finney gave me his address. It's number fourteen, Grosvenor Square."

James considered that for a moment. Homes in Grosvenor Square were worth a fortune. Only aristocratic families could afford property there.

Bella leaned forward slightly. "Will you go see him?"

"I'm not sure I should just show up at his door."

"I suppose you could write, but you're leaving town on Thursday, so you might want to call on him while you're here."

James looked toward the window. For years he'd wished he could find his father and hear answers to the questions he'd had for so long. But how would his father feel about James arriving unannounced at his home? What about his father's family? Would a surprise visit be awkward and painful for them?

He met Bella's gaze again. "What about his family?"

"Mr. Finney said Mr. Drake's wife passed away, but he has two daughters."

James's eyebrows rose. "I have two sisters?"

"Yes, though they're your half sisters."

"Still, I've never had any siblings. Even knowing I have half sisters seems pretty amazing."

Hannah walked in with a tray. "Here's your tea. And I baked some nice lemon biscuits this morning. I hope you'll enjoy those." She set the tray on the table in front of Bella and looked up at James. "Shall I pour for you?"

"No, thank you, Hannah. That's all we need."

The light in Hannah's eyes dimmed. "All right, then." She nodded to James and left the room, looking a bit disappointed.

"I'll pour." Bella reached for the teapot.

"Thank you." James took a biscuit from the plate. "I suppose I should go and speak to him. We won't really know if he's my father unless he confirms the facts himself."

Bella passed him a cup of tea. "I'm free this afternoon. I could go with you if you like."

Touched by her offer, he nodded. "I'm not sure what will happen, but I'd be happy to have your company."

"I'm glad to go along." She took a sip of her tea and looked at him over the rim of her teacup. The sweet message in her eyes sent a wave of gratefulness through him. With Bella at his side, he could face whatever the future might hold.

⁂

Bella walked with James across Grosvenor Square. The day was warm, the air damp and a bit uncomfortable. They stopped at the corner, waited for traffic to clear, and then crossed the street.

She lifted her gaze and scanned the red-brick-and-white-stone homes lining the far side of the street. The impressive facades seemed to announce the owners' wealth and prestige.

"There it is, number fourteen." James nodded toward the third house on right.

Her stomach tensed. *Lord, please prepare James and Daniel Drake.*

They stepped up to the door. James lifted the brass knocker and rapped three times. He lowered his hand and stood back, his posture and face tense.

"Whatever happens, we'll see it through together," she said softly.

His gaze connected with hers, but before he could respond, the door opened, and a tall butler looked out at them. "May I help you?"

"Good afternoon. I'd like to speak to Mr. Daniel Drake."

"And your name, please?"

"This is Miss Isabella Grayson, and I'm Mr. James Drake."

The butler's eyebrow arched for a split second, but then he resumed a neutral expression. "I'm sorry, sir. Mr. Drake is not at home."

"When will he return? It's important that I speak to him about a personal matter."

"Mr. Drake is out of town. I'm not certain when he will return."

James glanced at Bella, disappointment shadowing his eyes.

"You're welcome to leave your card if you like."

James looked at the butler again. "I'd like to write a message, if I may."

"Very well, sir." The butler opened the door wider and invited them to step inside. "Please, follow me." He led them into the first room on the left.

Bookshelves filled with leather-bound volumes lined two walls in the spacious room. Comfortable furniture was grouped around the fireplace. A large desk and chair sat in one corner. It was a masculine room, with heavy golden-brown drapes at the windows and the scent of pipe smoke in the air.

The butler crossed to the desk, took out paper and pen, and laid them on the blotter. He turned to James. "You may sit here to write your message." He stepped back, but he did not leave the room.

"Thank you." James lowered himself into the chair and picked up the pen. His hand hovered over the paper for a few seconds before he began to write.

Bella glanced around, searching for anything that might connect Daniel

Drake to James. There were no family portraits on the walls, only several paintings of horses and hunting parties and a few country landscapes.

Her gaze moved back to the desk. To the left of the blotter sat a framed
photograph of a middle-aged man with two young women. Bella studied the
man and tried not to show her surprise. The resemblance between him and
James was obvious in the shape of his face, especially his square chin and high
forehead.

James set the pen aside, blew on the ink, then folded the note in half. He
rose and turned to the butler. "Would you please give this message to Mr.
Drake as soon as he returns?"

The butler stepped forward and accepted the folded note. "Yes sir."

"Can you give us any idea when he might return to London?"

"I'm sorry, sir. I cannot."

James exhaled and gave a slow nod. Bella touched his arm with her elbow.
He glanced at her, and she looked toward the photograph on the desk. He followed her gaze, and his eyes widened for a split second.

The butler studied them. "Is there anything else I can do for you, sir?"

"No, thank you. You've been very helpful."

"If you'll follow me, please." The butler led them into the entrance hall,
then opened the front door. They thanked him and stepped outside.

When the door closed Bella turned to James and whispered, "You saw the
photograph on the desk?"

"Yes." He guided her away from the door. "That was probably Daniel
Drake and his daughters."

"He looks a lot like you."

James's brow creased. "I suppose we should say I look a lot like him."

"I'm sorry he wasn't home, but at least you were able to leave a note."

"Perhaps it's better this way. At least now he'll have a bit of warning."

Bella pressed her lips together, but she couldn't hold back her question any
longer. "Did you tell him who you are?"

James's mouth tugged up at the corner. "You want to know what I wrote?"

"Yes, please. I was tempted to look over your shoulder while you were writing, but I didn't want to be rude."

He grinned, looking amused by her honesty. "I said, 'I believe we may have a family connection, and I'd like to meet and discuss it with you.' Then I gave him my address in town and at Green Meadow and asked him to contact me."

"That's perfect—just enough to pique his interest and make him curious to know who you are."

"I hope so, but we'll have to wait and see what happens." He stopped at the corner and turned toward her. "My meeting doesn't start until three. What do you say to a stroll in the park?"

She smiled. "That sounds lovely."

He reached for her hand, and she wove her fingers through his. They crossed the street and started down the curved path around the edge of the shady park.

"I have some news," he said. "I was going to tell you right away, but then this business with Daniel Drake came up and overshadowed everything."

"What's the news?"

"In spite of Blériot beating me across the Channel, or perhaps because of it, Mr. Robertson from the Aero Club wants to help me find sponsors to pay for our expenses to attend the Air Meet at Reims."

Bella gasped. "That's wonderful!"

"We don't have all our sponsors yet, and it's an expensive trip, but Robertson is determined the British should be represented by at least three pilots, and he thinks the men we're meeting today might provide the rest of the funds."

"Oh, James, I'm so happy for you."

"Let's hope it all comes together in time."

"Yes, I'll pray it does."

"Robertson also gave me more information about the events. There will be several competitions each day, and they're offering prizes for those who win first, second, and third." His enthusiasm grew with each statement. "They already have entries from three countries and hope for a few more."

"It sounds like a wonderful opportunity." She glanced at his sling. "Will your wrist be healed in time?"

"The doctor said I should be able to fly by mid-August, if I'm careful until then."

"Then you must do as the doctor says and make sure you give it time to heal properly."

He gave a mock salute. "Yes ma'am."

"Sorry, I don't mean to be bossy."

"I don't mind. It's rather nice to have someone care enough to order me around."

She softened her tone and looked up at him. "I do care, very much."

He returned a tender smile, and she slipped her arm through his. "I have some news as well."

He lifted his eyebrows. "What's your news?"

"I told you Father made reservations for our family to go to Reims."

He nodded. "I'm glad you're coming."

Bella swallowed and looked up at him. "This morning the editor of the *Daily Mail* asked me to write some articles while we're there."

A smile broke across James's face. "Congratulations, Bella! That shows he appreciates you and your writing."

"You don't mind?"

"No, of course not. You've been more than supportive of me and my dreams, and it's past time I did the same for you."

Bella's throat tightened. "Oh, James . . . I don't know what to say."

He grinned, a teasing light in his eyes. "Bella Grayson, without words. Now that is something new."

She laughed, and they strolled on around the park. Treasuring the moment, she leaned on his arm and wished this walk never had to end. But she couldn't stop time or change the courses their lives were on, no matter how much she wished she could. She would have to stay in London and finish out the season, and he would have to return to Green Meadow and prepare for Reims. Hot tears pricked her eyes.

"Bella, what is it?"

"I was just thinking we might not see each other until we go to Reims."

His steps slowed. "Won't you be coming back to Broadlands before then?"

"I'm afraid not. Mother has plans for me and Sylvia almost every day until early August."

He took her hand and guided her off the path to a secluded spot. "May I write to you?" The sincerity of his gaze melted her heart.

"Yes, please do."

"And will you write to me?"

"Yes, as often as I can."

He stepped toward her and traced his fingers down her cheek, then gently pulled her closer. "I'll miss you, Bella."

She leaned her head against his chest and listened to the steady beat of his heart. How comforting it was to be in his arms. How much she would miss him.

He rested his chin on top of her head and slipped his good arm around her. "I know things are complicated with your parents and the promise you made, but I hope you'll wait for me, Bella, just a little longer."

She looked up at him, searching for the right words.

He took her hand again. "I don't have much to offer right now, but if I win some of those prizes at Reims, that should give me the finances and recognition I need to launch our business. Then I can go and speak to your father."

Her heart fluttered and felt like it would take flight.

"So . . . will you wait?"

"Yes, I'll wait, and I'll pray for your success at Reims."

His gaze softened, and he leaned down and kissed her forehead.

She rested against his chest once more, praying their time apart would pass quickly.

Twenty-Four

B ella rose to her feet and lifted her hands in front of her mouth as James
swooped down in his Steed V and flew past the grandstand at Reims. The
crowd rose and cheered, waving their hats and handkerchiefs. Music from the
marching band filled the air, and colorful flags fluttered from the edge of the
grandstand.

"That's my boy!" Professor Steed yelled, lifting his hat off his head.

"Calm yourself, Thaddeus." Martha laid her hand on the professor's arm.
"Remember what the doctor said."

"Oh, I'll be fine." The professor looked down at Martha, his eyes glowing
with a happy light. "Seeing James fly like this is the best medicine in the world!"

Bella had to agree. After two months apart, seeing James again had made
her weary heart feel renewed. And watching him fly with such amazing precision made her even more determined to see him receive the recognition he
deserved.

It was the fifth of eight days at the *Grande Semaine d'Aviation de la
Champagne,* the first International Air Meet. The six-mile rectangular course
was laid out on the Plain of Bétheny, only three miles north of Reims.

Rainy, windy weather had limited the number of flights earlier in the
week, but today the winds were calm and the sun was shining. Almost every
seat in the grandstand was filled, and an overflow crowd had spread out across
the fields around the course. Earlier that day, one official had told her father
more than one hundred thousand people were in attendance.

Bella and her family, along with the professor and Martha, were seated in
the second row of the covered grandstand, prime seats her father had secured
for them at a hefty price. She glanced down the row as her father, mother, and
Sylvia rose to their feet, applauding the next passing airplane.

Sylvia looked her way. "Isn't it thrilling? Watching Wilbur Wright fly last summer was exciting, but seeing all these airplanes fly at one time is even more amazing!"

Bella nodded and scanned the sky. Seven airplanes buzzed around the course at varying heights and speeds. Most of the pilots were French, but Britain, Austria, and the United States of America were also represented.

A movement near the scoreboard caught Bella's attention, and she gasped. "Look! James's first lap was faster than Mark Clifton's!"

Sylvia grinned and clapped. "Well done!"

James was competing in his second event of the day, the *Grand Prix de la Vitesse*. He had to fly three timed laps around the circuit, and the fastest pilot would win ten thousand francs. But even if he didn't place first, there were prizes for those who placed second or third. Surely James would win one of those and be well on his way to having the funds he needed for their future plans.

Bella's father turned to her. "Bella, did you see who just entered the dignitaries' box?"

Bella leaned forward and tried to look through the crowd, but there were too many people blocking her view. "Who is it?"

"The British delegation with David Lloyd George, chancellor of the exchequer, and General Sir John French. You'll want to make note of that for your article."

Bella pulled out her notebook and jotted down their names. "I'm glad the general is here. That must mean they're discussing using airplanes for the British military."

"It's about time!" Her father lifted his binoculars and looked toward the dignitaries' box. "Those British officials had better pay attention. The French government has already given out contracts for their military."

Sylvia grabbed her arm. "Here comes James!"

Bella turned and fastened her gaze on the Steed V as James made his turn and flew toward the grandstand. Her heart felt like it would burst with joy as he raced past, with the loud roar of his engine vibrating through the air. The crowd erupted again, their cheering so loud it made Bella's head throb.

She watched him complete that leg of the circuit, then make his next turn around the tall pylon at the corner. She kept her gaze trained on his airplane as it grew smaller and flew two miles south, toward the next turn.

Bella's mother fanned her flushed face with a program. "Charles, can we go to lunch soon? We've been out here for hours."

Father checked his watch. "It's only eleven fifteen."

"But all this heat and noise is giving me a headache." Mother continued her furious fanning and sent a pained glance down the row.

Father shifted his gaze back to the field. "I don't want to leave until I see the scores for this event."

"But, Charles—"

Sylvia rose. "I'll go with you, Mother."

Bella sent her sister a grateful glance, then stood so her mother and Sylvia could pass in front of her. She sat down, lifted her binoculars, and searched across the sky again. Mark Clifton's airplane was circling out past the third pylon. Was he having trouble with his engine again?

The Steed V came into view, and James flew toward the grandstand once more. This would be his final lap. Bella rose to her feet. "I'm going down to the maneuvering area. I want to interview James as soon as he lands."

The professor grabbed Bella's hand and looked up at her. "Tell James how pleased and proud we are." Professor Steed had promised Martha he would spend most of the day in the stands rather than down on the field with James, and he was making a valiant effort to keep his word.

Bella's throat tightened, and she squeezed the professor's fingers. "I will. I promise."

She slipped her hand from his, scooted past him and Martha, and started down the steps. It took at least three minutes to make her way through the crowd to the gate leading to the maneuvering area and aircraft sheds.

When she finally reached the gate, a man stepped forward, blocking her path. *"C'est une zone restreinte."* His glare made it clear he did not want to let her go through.

Bella pulled her press card from her pocket and held it up. "I'm with the *Daily Mail*."

The man narrowed his eyes, then shook his head. *"Non, où avez-vous obtenu ce passé de presse?"*

Bella's face flushed. She might not understand every word he'd said, but she knew he'd questioned where she had obtained the card. "I am a journalist for the *Daily Mail*. That's my name, right there, Isabella Grayson." She pointed to the card. "Please, let me pass."

He scoffed and shook his head. But he opened the gate while he grumbled something else in French.

Bella rolled her eyes and strode past. Just because she was a woman, that didn't mean she couldn't be a reporter. She thought the French were more progressive.

The crowd roared behind her. She turned just in time to see James touch down, roll past the judges' box, and turn into the maneuvering area.

Bella lifted her hand to her hat and hurried across the open field toward the aircraft shed assigned to James.

⚜

Energy surged through James as he rolled the Steed V to a stop at the edge of the maneuvering area. He pulled off his goggles and lifted his hand to the small crowd of mechanics and officials waiting for him near the sheds. Some of the men clapped and others shouted congratulations in French and English.

Ethan ran forward. "Great flight, James!"

"How was my time?" James climbed out and jumped to the ground.

"They didn't post the total yet, but you looked good."

"Thanks." James grinned and slapped Ethan on the shoulder.

"Someone's waiting for you." Ethan nodded toward the shed.

James looked up. Bella stood by the open doorway. She met his gaze and sent him a radiant smile.

His chest swelled, and warmth flowed through him. He stepped around the wing and walked toward Bella. Some of the mechanics slapped him on the shoulders as he passed by, but he didn't slow down to speak to any of them. At that moment, the only person he wanted to see was Bella.

He opened his arms, and she stepped into his embrace. He pulled her close and closed his eyes. A few of the men hooted behind him, but he didn't care.

"I am so proud of you." Her voice was hushed and full of emotion.

"Thank you." He hated to let her go, but he lowered his arms and stepped back.

She looked up at him with shining eyes. "That was an amazing flight! The professor was so excited—Martha could barely keep him in his seat. He said to tell you how pleased and proud he is."

James nodded and lifted his hand to rub his eyes. "I'll go up and see him in a few minutes."

"They're posting your time!" Ethan called.

James turned toward the scoreboard and grabbed Bella's hand.

"Twenty-five minutes, forty-one seconds." She looked up at him, uncertainty in her eyes.

He blew out a breath, his spirits deflating a bit. "Glenn Curtiss is still in first by twelve seconds, but I beat Clifton's time by almost two minutes."

"How many more pilots have to fly in the event?"

"Hubert Latham and Paul Tissandier signed up. They have to get their flights in soon if they want them to count. We might not hear the final results until this evening."

Bella nodded, her smile warm and encouraging. "The crowd loved you, and a delegation of British officials arrived just as you started your second lap. Father said General Sir John French is with them."

James glanced toward the grandstand. "Do you think your father could introduce me to him?"

Bella gave an eager nod. "That's a wonderful idea. Do you want to go up there now?"

"Not yet." He tipped his head toward the shed. "Come with me." He led her inside to a cool, shady spot near the corner.

"Is everything all right?" she asked softly.

"I just need a minute alone with you before we go back out in the crowd." He stepped closer and wrapped his arms around her again. She slipped her hands around his back and leaned her cheek against his flight jacket.

"I'm so glad you're here," he said. "I've missed you so much."

"I wrote to you every day."

"And I loved your letters, but it's not the same as being together."

She looked up at him with an endearing smile, and it made his heart feel like mush. He leaned down and kissed her cheek, breathing in the sweet scent of flowers in her hair. Two months apart had been torture. If he hadn't had his preparations for Reims to keep him busy, he would've gone crazy from missing her.

"I should've known there was something going on between you two." Mark Clifton's harsh voice cut through the air.

Bella jerked back, and James turned toward the doorway of the shed.

Clifton glared at James as he walked inside, and then he shifted his gaze to Bella. "Do your parents know about this?"

Heat surged into James's face. "I don't think that's any of your business."

"I'm a friend of the family, and I consider it my business to protect Isabella."

Bella lifted her chin. "I'm perfectly safe. There's no need for you to be concerned."

Clifton huffed. "I just found you locked in the arms of a man with a dubious reputation."

Bella's eyes flashed. "There's nothing wrong with James's reputation."

Clifton pointed at James. "Ask him who he really is and about his family. Then tell me what you think of him."

"I know everything I need to know about James. He's a man of honor and integrity, and nothing you say will change my mind."

"What if I told you Drake is just a name he pulled out of the sky. His mother wasn't married when he was born, so you know what that makes him."

James clenched his fist and stepped forward. "Why you—"

Bella grabbed his arm. "James, don't listen to him."

"He has no father," Clifton said, with a haughty lift of his chin. "At least none who will claim him."

Bella shook her head. "You don't know what you're talking about."

"I would have to agree." Another man stepped into the open doorway. The bright sunlight behind him made it difficult to see his face.

Clifton turned around. "Who are you?"

"My name is Daniel Drake. I'm James's father."

The air whooshed out of James's lungs, and he stared at the man.

Daniel Drake walked into the shed and faced Clifton. "Now, if you'll excuse us, I'd like to speak to my son in private."

Clifton sputtered a curse and strode out of the shed.

Daniel Drake shifted his gaze to James. "I'm sorry. That wasn't how I'd hoped to begin this conversation." He walked forward slowly. "I just returned to London a few days ago from a business trip to Canada. I received your note, and I did a bit of checking. I believe you're right. We do have a family connection." He stopped in front of James. "I believe you are my son."

James held his gaze steady. "How do you know that's true?"

Drake's mouth tipped up at the corners. "I suspected it when I saw you with Professor Steed at the Aero Club's spring lecture. I spoke to you that day, outside the auditorium."

The memory of meeting him in the lobby of the auditorium flashed through James's mind.

"I wasn't sure at the time, but when you attempted your flight across the Channel, your name and photograph were in the newspaper. And the more I studied that photo, the more I began to believe it was true."

A sense of wonder flooded through James, and he glanced at Bella. Her article had helped him connect with Daniel Drake.

"I went to your London address, and your housekeeper told me you were flying at Reims this week. I considered writing to you, but I decided it might be better if I came and spoke to you in person."

Bella stepped back. "I should go."

James reached for her hand. "No, I'd like you to stay."

"Are you sure?"

James turned toward Drake. "Do you mind?"

"Not if you'll introduce me."

"This is Bella Grayson." He wanted to explain how special she was to him, but he was feeling so dazed he could barely speak her name.

Drake looked back and forth between James and Bella. "Do you have time to talk now, or should we arrange a meeting later?"

"I have time now." He couldn't imagine waiting any longer when the man claiming to be his father stood right in front of him. He motioned to the three wooden folding chairs at the back of the shed. "Let's sit down."

James settled in his chair and looked across at Drake. "I'd like to know what happened between you and my mother."

Drake nodded. "That's a good place to start." He clasped his hands between his knees. "Your mother and I met in London when she was seventeen and I was nineteen. We fell in love that spring, and when she returned to Kent, we exchanged letters secretly through her sister Judith and Judith's friend, Nancy.

"I loved Laura, and I wanted to marry her, but my parents had already arranged my marriage to Diana Hargrove. Her family was quite wealthy, and my parents thought that was the best way to solve their financial problems.

"Soon after I became engaged to Diana, Laura wrote and told me she was expecting a child. I explained things to my parents and told them I wanted to marry Laura, but they said they would disown me if I broke my engagement to Diana. I struggled with the decision for some time, but I finally gave in to their threats and went ahead with the marriage." He shook his head. "That decision has caused me a great deal of pain and regret."

James clenched his jaw. What about his mother? Had Drake even thought of how his decision hurt her? "I don't understand why you couldn't have at least helped Laura."

Sorrow lined Drake's face. "I tried, but I didn't try hard enough."

"From what I've heard, you never sent her any money." James's tone made his feelings about the matter clear.

"At first I couldn't. I had no funds of my own. But after you were born, she wrote to me again, asking for my help. I answered her letter, and I arranged to see her . . . and to see you."

James stared at him. He had no idea his father had seen him when he was an infant.

"I had access to money after I married Diana, and I could do what I wanted with it. So I traveled to Kent to visit Laura." He pressed his lips together and looked down for a few seconds. "We went for a walk out near the cliffs. She brought you along and carried you in her arms, and for a few minutes we pretended all was well, and we were a loving, happy family."

James's throat burned, pierced by the man's words.

"I asked her to come with me to London and let me look after you both. I said I'd give her a flat there, and we could see each other often." He stopped and lowered his head. "To her credit, she wouldn't agree to be my mistress. I pleaded with her, but she backed away, shaking her head and telling me it was impossible. I reached for her, begging her to reconsider."

James clenched his jaw, bracing himself for what was coming.

"She stepped back once more, and the wet ground crumbled under her feet. I lunged forward and tried to grab her, but it was too late." He raised his hand and covered his eyes. Sagging against the chair, he wept.

A cold tremor shook James to the core.

Bella glanced his way, tears glistening in her eyes.

"I'm sorry, so very sorry." Drake pulled a handkerchief from his pocket and wiped his eyes. "I loved your mother very much. I never meant to put her in danger or harm her in any way, and I've lived with that guilt and grief for twenty-four years."

James stared at him, his mind numb. What could he say? There was no way he could change any of those terrible events or absolve Drake's guilt.

Drake cleared his throat and took a few moments to recover his composure. "I went to your grandfather and tried to speak to him, but he was so angry, the conversation lasted less than two minutes. He told me you died with your mother, and I believed it was true. I never imagined you could survive a fall like that."

James shook his head, still trying to understand that twist in the story. "Why would Sir Richard make up such a lie?"

"He was hurt, and I suppose he thought keeping you from me was a way to punish me for what happened to Laura."

"But it didn't seem like he really cared about Laura before or after she died."

Drake sighed. "He's a hard man, and he was bitter about everything that happened to his family."

James considered that for a moment and shook his head. He might never understand Sir Richard's decision, but in the end it hadn't stopped him and Daniel Drake from finding each other.

Drake straightened and looked into James's eyes. "So I've come here today to meet you and tell you this story, but there's more to be said."

James stilled, his heartbeat pounding at his temples.

"What I did to you and your mother was disloyal and unloving. My selfish choices took your mother from you and left you without a father all these years. Those are deep and painful losses. I don't deserve it, but I'm asking you to forgive me for all the pain I've caused."

A powerful ache throbbed in James's chest, and he could barely force out his words. "I don't know what to say."

"That's all right." Drake lifted his hand. "This is a lot to take in, and I'm sure you need time to think it through." He rose from his chair.

James stood and faced Drake. "I do need some time."

Drake nodded, sadness clouding his eyes. "I understand."

James couldn't help feeling he'd let the man down. But it was too much to sort through in a short conversation. They were talking about matters of life and death and years of questions and pain.

Ethan ran into the shed. "Latham is getting ready to fly his three laps."

Drake turned to James. "I'll go. You have important matters to see to."

James knew he should say something to ease his father's mind, but no words came.

Drake turned and walked out of the shed without looking back.

⌒≈≋≋≋⌒

Bella glanced at James as they walked out of the shed, her heart aching for him. She'd been surprised and grieved by Daniel Drake's story, but James seemed even more shaken, and she couldn't blame him. Those were the tragic events that had shaped his life, and he was hearing the story from his father, whom he'd just met for the first time.

What an earthshaking series of events.

She wished she could take James's hand and guide him away to a quiet place where he could sit down and have a few minutes to think in peace. But they were in the middle of a race day, and he would have to put aside these issues and deal with them later. At least she was here with him, even if all she could do was stand by his side and offer her silent support.

"Bella!" Her father's voice rose above the buzz of an airplane engine and conversations around the sheds. He strode toward them, his face flushed and his eyes shooting daggers.

Her steps stalled. Something was terribly wrong. James sent her a questioning glance, but she had no idea why her father was so upset.

He glared at Bella as he drew closer. "What were you thinking? Don't you realize your foolish behavior is going to tarnish your reputation and mine?"

"What are you talking about?" Her words rushed out.

"Don't pretend to be innocent. You know very well what I'm talking about! I just spoke to Mark Clifton, and he told me he caught you . . . kissing this man in public!"

Bella gasped. "That's not true!"

"Don't lie to me, Bella. It won't erase what you've done."

"I'm not lying!"

Perspiration beaded on her father's forehead beneath the brim of his hat. "I knew you were becoming too attached to Drake. I should've put a stop to it, but I trusted you to behave properly. Now I see how you used the excuse of writing your articles so you could spend time with him."

"No, Father, please."

James stepped forward. "Bella is telling the truth. I hugged her after that last race, and I kissed her cheek, in the shed, in private, but that's all. The only person who saw us was Mark Clifton." The muscles in James's cheek rippled.

Her father pointed at him. "You should not be touching my daughter. You're not engaged. You haven't even asked my permission to call on her."

"You're right. I'm sorry, sir. I should've asked your permission. The truth is, I love Bella very much. I was planning to speak to you about our future plans as soon as I won some of the events here this week. That should give me enough money to start our design company and—"

"That's enough!" Her father raised his hand. "I don't want to hear any more. It's out of the question, especially after what I've just learned about you. I won't have my daughter involved with someone whose family and reputation is tainted like yours."

"That's not fair!" Bella's voice rose. "A man should not be judged by the choices his parents made, but by the way he lives his life. James is an honorable man, and I love him."

"Well, I certainly wouldn't call it honorable to be sneaking around behind my back, trying to woo my daughter without my permission!" He glared at James. "I want you to keep your hands off Bella, and you can put any idea of future plans with her out of your mind."

Hot tears flooded Bella's eyes, and she shook her head. This couldn't be happening. How could her father listen to Mark Clifton and make such a terrible decision?

Stone-faced, James turned and walked away, taking a piece of Bella's heart with him.

❧

Friday morning dawned clear with light winds; a perfect day for flying. James rose early and met Ethan at the shed to add the extra seat to the Steed V. The *Prix de Passagers* was scheduled that day, and Ethan would be riding along with James. All they had to do was fly once around the course with the fastest speed and they would take home ten thousand francs.

But he'd never taken up a passenger before.

James sighed and rubbed his gritty eyes. He'd tossed and turned half the night, his mind filled with painful questions he couldn't answer. Was there any way he could convince Mr. Grayson to change his mind and allow him to see Bella? And what should he do about Daniel Drake? How could he say he forgave him, when what he'd done was selfish and wrong and caused such terrible consequences for everyone concerned?

He pushed away those thoughts. He had to focus on today and prepare for the race. Gripping the wrench, he tightened the last bolt on the new seat. "Ethan, can you hand me that cup of coffee?" When his friend didn't answer, he looked up.

Ethan sat slumped in the chair with his head down.

James tossed aside the wrench. "Ethan, are you all right?"

His friend moaned. "No, I feel terrible."

James crossed the shed and squatted down in front of him. "What's wrong?"

Ethan looked up, his face pale with a slightly gray-green tinge. "I'm sorry, James. I'm sick. I can't fly with you today."

James put his hand on Ethan's knee. "It'll pass. You'll be all right."

"I don't think so." Ethan lifted a shaky hand to his forehead. "I better walk over to the hospital tent. Maybe they can give me something for my stomach."

"All right." James nodded. "I'll go with you."

"No, it's not far. There's no need for you to come." Ethan rose with a grimace, then shuffled out of the shed, clutching his stomach.

James stared after his friend as a whole new series of problems flooded his mind.

"Good morning, James." The professor walked into the shed, then glanced over his shoulder. "What's wrong with Ethan? He looks miserable."

James shook his head. "I'm afraid he's ill and on his way to the hospital tent."

The professor's white eyebrows rose. "Isn't he supposed to fly with you today?"

"That's right." What was he going to do now? Who could take Ethan's place?

"We can work on that problem in a minute." The professor shifted his gaze to the Steed V and rubbed his chin. "I've been thinking about the issues you'll face when you carry a passenger." He walked past the wing and looked at the second seat James had just installed. "The added weight will increase your drag, and balancing the machine with two people on board will be quite different."

James glanced toward the field. "I suppose I'll have to withdraw now."

"Don't withdraw. I'll fly with you."

A smile tugged at his lips. He wished he could say yes, but there was no way. "You know there is nothing I'd like more than taking you up for a flight, but I think Martha would kill us both if I agreed to that."

"Oh, she coddles me like I'm a china teacup. I feel fine."

"I'm glad to hear it, but I don't think you should push yourself."

"Why not? You always say flying is exhilarating. It would probably be good for my heart."

"That's not a theory I want to test today."

Martha and Bella walked into the shed.

He hadn't seen Bella since the explosive confrontation with her father the day before. She looked his way, her eyes reflecting what looked like a plea for understanding.

"We saw Ethan walking into the hospital tent." Martha strode toward them. "I spoke to the nurse. She said there are more than twenty people who have come down with food poisoning since last night. Ethan's symptoms seem to be the same."

Concern lit the professor's eyes. "I'm sorry to hear that. Food poisoning can be very painful."

James's thoughts flashed back to the previous evening. He'd been so upset after Daniel Drake's visit and Mr. Grayson's rebuke that he'd gone straight back to the hotel and skipped dinner. Maybe that was a blessing that saved him from a visit to the hospital tent.

Martha looked his way. "Now that Ethan's ill, who's going to fly with you?"

The professor rose up on his toes. "I was just trying to convince James that I should go in Ethan's place."

Martha's eyes widened. "Thaddeus, please tell me you're joking."

"No, I'm quite serious. James needs a passenger in order to compete, and I'm ready to go with him."

Martha shook her head. "I'm sure the doctor would not want you to take that kind of risk."

"If I don't go, he'll have to withdraw."

Bella stepped forward. "I'll fly with James."

Alarm shot through James. "No! It's too dangerous!"

"Why do you say that? Is it because I'm a woman?"

He sent the professor a quick glance, hoping for some help. But the professor looked toward the roof, apparently unwilling to take sides.

"You're a skilled pilot, and the Steed V has performed perfectly every day this week. I don't see any reason why I shouldn't go with you."

"It would cause quite a sensation," Martha added with a smile.

James turned toward Martha. "You're in favor of it?"

"I think it's a reasonable suggestion. Bella's a healthy, sensible young woman, and you're a fine pilot. I'd say you two make a good team."

"She is lightweight," the professor added. "That would help with the issues of drag and balance."

James lifted his hand to his forehead. "I can't believe this. You all think Bella should fly with me?"

"Yes." All three of them answered, and Bella beamed him a hopeful smile.

"What about your father? He's already angry with me. If anything happens, he'll never let me come within a mile of you."

"But if we're successful, it might make him soften his stance."

James wasn't sure about that.

Bella stepped closer and looked up at him. "I trust you, James. I know I'll be safe with you. Please let me be your passenger today."

How could he say no when she asked in such a sweet, persuasive way? He struggled with it a moment more, then sighed. "All right. I'll take you, but you have to do exactly as I say."

"I will. I promise."

James and the professor spent the next twenty minutes checking over the airplane and discussing the situations James might encounter and how to deal with them.

James ran out to the officials' box and told them he was ready to take his next flight. Then he gave them Bella's name as his passenger. The official's eyebrows rose, but he assigned him a takeoff time in fifteen minutes. James turned to go just as Mark Clifton sauntered up behind him.

"I heard you lost your passenger this morning. That's too bad."

James clenched his jaw and stepped to the left, intending to walk around him. But Clifton shadowed his move and blocked his path. "I also heard you had quite an interesting conversation with Charles Grayson yesterday."

"Thanks to you," James ground out.

Clifton sent him a smug smile. "Just protecting what's mine."

Fire flashed through James. "Bella Grayson is not yours."

"Maybe not yet, but she's certainly not going to be yours."

"Get out of my way."

Clifton held up both hands. "My, you're certainly touchy today."

James glared at Clifton and stepped around him.

Clifton chuckled. "I'll see you in the sky, and wait until you see who's riding along with me."

James kept walking, but he had to grin at that comment. He didn't care who was flying with Clifton in this race. They would all be in for a surprise when they saw Bella seated next to James in the Steed V.

Twenty-Five

B ella climbed into the seat beside James and smoothed out her skirt. It did little to calm the wild fluttering in her stomach. She'd watched James fly for months and often imagined how exciting it would be to take off and soar into the sky. Now she was going to experience it for herself, and it seemed almost too amazing to believe.

Martha walked forward and held up a pair of goggles and a length of rope. "You'll need these."

Bella took off her hat and slipped on the goggles. "What's the rope for?"

"I'm going to tie it around your skirt to keep everything covered and proper."

Bella's cheeks warmed. "Oh, thank you, Martha." She lifted her feet so Martha could capture all the fabric of her skirt and petticoats and then re-pinned her hat, while her friend tied a neat knot.

"That should do it." Martha grinned. "Take care now."

"I will." Bella squeezed Martha's hand. "Thank you."

James lowered his goggles, adjusted his gray cap, and looked her way. "Are you ready?"

Tingles raced down her arms, and she pulled in a deep breath. "Yes, I'm ready."

The professor stepped back and lifted his hand. "Godspeed, my boy! May the Lord give you a safe and speedy flight."

"Thank you." James returned the professor's smile and touched his cap.

One of the French mechanics spun the propeller and stepped back. James adjusted the throttle. The airplane rolled forward, and they taxied to the end of the maneuvering area.

Another airplane waited for takeoff in front of them.

James shifted toward Bella, and his arm touched hers. "That's Clifton." He nodded to the waiting airplane, then stilled. "Is that your father with him?"

Bella leaned forward, trying to get a better view. The man wore a dark suit and flat cap, but she could only see part of his back and not his face.

The guard at the starting post waved his flag, and Clifton's airplane roared toward the starting line. As it rose into the air, the man seated next to Clifton turned and waved toward the grandstand.

Bella gasped. "It is Father! I can't believe it. He never said a word about flying with Clifton."

"He probably didn't want your mother to worry." James grinned. "That's a stroke of good luck. Maybe he'll be so wrapped up in his flight he won't even see you're flying with me."

"If we can see him, he'll probably see us."

James flashed a smile. "I hope he sees the back of us by the time we pass that second pylon."

"You're racing the clock, not Mark Clifton or my father."

"True, but wouldn't it be grand to wave at them as we pass by?"

Bella laughed and shook her head. "You're terrible."

He returned a cheeky grin. "I know."

"Are you ready, Mr. Drake?" The guard holding the starting flag lifted it in the air.

James sobered and looked straight ahead. "Ready!"

The flag dropped. James adjusted the throttle again, then took hold of the wheel on top of the stick. The airplane raced forward and rose into the air just before they passed the starting line and judges' box.

The wind rushed past, and Bella lifted her hand to her hat. "This is marvelous!" She raised her voice to be heard above the roar of the engine.

They flew on for one mile and rounded the first pylon. Bella leaned to the right to try to see her father and Mark. The airplane dipped in response to her movement.

"Whoa! Hold still," James called, as he made a quick adjustment to his controls.

"Sorry." Bella leaned back, determined not to make that mistake again.

"We have to stay balanced."

Bella nodded. "I understand."

Mark and her father were about a half mile ahead of them. Mark's path was rather erratic compared to James's smooth flight. Bella remembered watching the day Mark had taken off from Dover and had a similar problem. He couldn't blame the winds today. The conditions were perfect. The fault must lay with his airplane's design and his lack of skill.

Clifton's airplane jerked and pitched to the right. Bella gasped and clutched one of the guide wires. James leaned forward, his intense gaze trained on Clifton.

"What's wrong with his plane? What's happening?"

"It looks like he has engine trouble."

Mark's airplane sputtered and weaved as he rounded the second pylon. They were almost three miles from the grandstand, the farthest point away on the six-mile circuit. Below them were open fields dotted with haystacks drying in the sun. There was no clear place to land.

James's eyes widened. "He's going down!"

"Father!" Bella's heart thundered as Mark's airplane dove toward the field. She lifted her hand to cover her mouth and stifle her scream. The plane clipped the top of a haystack, flipped over, and crashed to the ground.

Too stunned to speak, Bella stared at the downed airplane.

"We've got to help them!" James clenched his jaw, pushed the stick forward, and circled around, descending toward the crash. "Hold on!" He maneuvered past two haystacks, and they landed with a hard jolt that nearly knocked Bella out of her seat. Thick piles of grain wrapped around the wheels as they rolled forward, coming to a stop only a few yards from the crumpled wreckage. James jumped down and ran toward Clifton's airplane.

A strange dizzy buzzing filled Bella's head, but she yanked off the rope from around her skirt, jumped to the ground, and ran after James.

Lord, help us!

Both men were trapped under the toppled airplane, but she could see her father's feet and legs and hear someone moaning. The strong smell of petrol hung in the air.

"I'll lift the wing. You pull him out!" James reached down and heaved the wing up about three feet.

Bella scrambled underneath. "I've got you, Father." Gripping his jacket, she dragged him out and across the field a few feet away.

"Bella? Is that you?" Her father's voice was shaky as he blinked up at her.

"Yes, Father. It's me." His glasses had disappeared, and he had a small cut on his nose, but at least he was talking to her. She shot a glance at James. He held up the wing, waiting for her. She turned to her father. "We have to get Mark out." She ran toward the airplane again.

"Clifton looks unconscious." James gritted his teeth and adjusted his hold on the wing. "His injuries may be more serious than your father's. Pull him out as gently as you can."

Bella gave a quick nod, then climbed under the airplane again.

James was right. Mark had a big gash on his forehead, and blood dripped down the side of his face. She pulled in a shuddering breath and took hold of his shoulders.

A whooshing sound filled the air, and flames erupted from the engine. Bella gasped and pulled back, covering her face.

"Bella! Get out of there!"

Heat singed her hands, but she had to help Mark. Gripping underneath his arms, she held her breath and slowly dragged him out.

As soon as Mark's feet were clear, James dropped the wing and took her place, pulling Mark away from the burning airplane.

James searched her face. "Are you hurt?"

"No." Her hands stung, but she wasn't worried about that. Her father lay in the field where she'd left him. She rushed to him and knelt at his side. "Father, talk to me. Tell me where you're injured."

"We've got to move them farther away!" Urgency filled James's voice.

She looked over her shoulder at the flaming airplane. The fire had spread to the grain lying in the field. She turned back and took hold of her father's arm. "Can you stand?"

"If you'll help me." He lifted his hand, and she pulled him to a sitting position and then to his feet. She slipped her arm around his waist and guided him across the field, away from the flames.

James took hold of Mark and pulled him across the field, following Bella and her father.

The wind picked up, fanning the flames. The fire crackled and roared, spreading across the fabric on the wings and scorching the wooden frame of Clifton's airplane. Smoke blew toward them and stung Bella's eyes. She coughed and tried to wave it away from her face and her father's as she helped him sit down in the field.

He looked up at Bella. "How did you get here so quickly?"

"I was flying with James. We were only a short distance behind you." Bella's throat tightened as she watched James take off his jacket, fold it, and place it under Mark's head.

A dazed look filled her father's face. "You were flying with James Drake?"

"Yes, Father. I'm sorry." Bella bit her lip and took hold of her father's hand, trying to hold back her tears.

Her father watched James pull off his dress shirt and use it to staunch the blood on Mark's forehead, and his eyes flooded. "No, I'm sorry." He shook his head. "I misjudged him. We would've died in that fire if he hadn't landed and come to help us."

Bella tightened her hold on her father's hand and glanced toward the blazing airplane. Flames leaped across the piles of grain, creeping toward the Steed V. She dropped her father's hand and swung around. "James!"

He looked up.

"Your plane!"

He jumped up as the wingtip of the Steed V burst into flames. Pain rippled across his face, and he clenched his hands.

Bella's throat ached. He'd made a brave and honorable choice, giving up the race to stop and help Father and Mark. But he hadn't expected it to cost him his only airplane and steal his chance to compete in the rest of the events.

Mark moaned and tossed his head.

James knelt beside him and laid his hand on Mark's shoulder. "Easy, Clifton. You're going to be all right."

Horses' hooves sounded in the distance. Bella turned and looked across the field. A fire wagon and a motorized ambulance drove toward them, followed by three motorcars and another horse-drawn wagon. Bella released a shuddering breath. The medical team would care for her father and Mark, and she hoped the fire could be controlled before it did any more damage.

But what about the Steed V? Flames licked across the right wing, eating up the fabric at a terrible rate.

The ambulance rolled to a stop nearby and five men rushed out.

James lifted his hand. "This man needs your attention first."

Three members of the medical team surrounded Mark, and two others hustled toward her father. Bella stepped back to give them room to work.

James crossed to stand at her side. "Are you sure you're all right?"

"Yes, I'm fine." She glanced at Clifton. "What about Mark? Do you think—" Her words choked off, and she couldn't finish her sentence.

James slipped his arm around her shoulder, drawing her closer. "From what I've seen, Clifton is a pretty tough character. I expect he'll live to fly again."

Bella leaned her head against his shoulder, drawing comfort and strength from his touch.

The firemen unrolled two hoses and quickly connected them to the tank on the wagon. Some men manned the pump, while the others held the hoses and sprayed the flames.

"I'm so sorry about your airplane," she said softly.

James shook his head. "I shouldn't have parked so close."

"You didn't know Mark's plane would catch fire."

"The fuel tank must have broken open and splashed on the hot engine. The professor and I talked about that possibility." James straightened and looked down at her. "It's a blow to lose the Steed V, but there's no price too high to pay for a man's life, or two men in this case."

Bella stood on tiptoe and kissed his cheek. "You're a wise man, and I love you very much."

<hr />

The next two days passed in a blur as James finished out the week at Reims. Though he couldn't compete in the rest of the events, he salvaged the engine from the Steed V, and he and the professor spent a few hours discussing design modifications for their next airplane. He'd also been kept busy meeting with military officials and businessmen from England and France. He and the professor had made several promising contacts, and they planned to follow up on them as soon as they returned to England.

The fact that he'd taken Bella up as a passenger and then landed to rescue Mr. Grayson and Mark Clifton had made him a bit of a celebrity. Several newspapers had run front-page articles about the rescue, including the *Daily Mail,* with a firsthand account written by Bella.

Amazed by what had happened, he shook his head. What seemed like a terrible disaster had turned into an unexpected blessing. Wasn't that just like the Lord—taking the painful and broken experiences of their lives and making them into something beautiful.

Monday night arrived, and James was proud to escort Bella to the award dinner held in the large dining hall next to the grandstand at Reims. Flickering lanterns hung around the room, and candles glowed in the center of each table. The dining hall could hold six hundred people, and it looked like almost every seat was filled that evening. The sound of conversation rose around them as the dinner concluded and the waiters cleared away the plates.

They were seated at a round table in the front of the large hall near the speaker's platform. James looked around the table and a sense of gratitude flowed through him. Bella sat on his left, and the professor, Martha, and Ethan were on his right. Bella's parents and her sister, Sylvia, filled the other seats at their table.

Mark Clifton was unable to attend the dinner because he was still recovering in the hospital at Reims. They had visited him that afternoon, and he'd apologized to James and Bella and thanked them for everything they'd done for him. It had eased the sting of Clifton's earlier hurtful words, and James was satisfied with that.

He glanced around the room, looking for Daniel Drake. He hadn't seen him since their conversation at the shed. Had he stayed to see the rest of the events, or had he returned to London?

James had pondered Drake's request for forgiveness, and though James was now more open to the idea, he still wasn't sure what he would say the next time he saw Drake, but he was certain of one thing: he wanted there to be a next time.

A bald, rotund man wearing a black dinner jacket with a white vest and tie stepped up to the podium. He greeted them in French and then in English. "Good evening. My name is Claude DuPont. On behalf of the international committee, I want to welcome you to our award ceremony." The audience clapped and Monsieur DuPont continued. "We come together tonight to celebrate the wonderful achievements of the brave aviators who took part in *Le Grande Semaine d'Aviation de la Champagne*—the first International Air Meet at Reims!"

The crowd applauded again, and James and Bella exchanged a smile. It was wonderful, having her here by his side, sharing this moment together. He might have only placed in one event, but he was still proud to be among those who had flown at Reims.

Three members of the committee were introduced, and they came up to the podium to award the prizes. James clapped as each aviator was named and walked forward to receive his award.

Hubert Latham was the first-place winner of the altitude prize for flying at a height of 510 feet. Louis Blériot walked forward to accept the prize for the fastest single lap, with a time of seven minutes, forty-seven seconds. Henri Farman flew 112 miles to win the prize for the greatest distance, and he would've flown farther if the sun hadn't set and the officials called him in for a landing.

They announced Farman was also the winner of the passenger event. He had completed his lap while carrying two passengers and astounded the crowd with that amazing feat.

Bella reached under the table and took James's hand. Comforting warmth flowed from her fingers into his. She smiled, and he could see she was proud of him, even if he hadn't won. That meant more to him than any award. He squeezed her hand, then let go and clapped for Farman as he accepted his prize.

When the applause died down, the committeeman spoke again. "Now, we want to announce the winner of the Gordon Bennett Aviation Trophy, the most prestigious event of the meeting. Three teams representing France, Britain, and America competed in flying two laps of the circuit in a timed trial. With a time of fifteen minutes, fifty point four seconds, the winner is Mr. Glenn Curtiss of the United States of America."

James applauded as Glenn Curtiss rose from the table next to theirs and strode up the steps to the platform. He shook hands with the committee members and accepted the bronze sculptured trophy featuring a winged seraph with a biplane on top. Curtiss thanked the committee, his wife, his assistants, and Mr. Gordon Bennett Jr., the publisher of the *New York Herald*. Finally, he nodded to the audience and returned to his seat amid loud applause.

Bella leaned toward James. "That means the second International Air Meet will be held in the United States next summer. Do you think we should make our reservations?"

He grinned. "That sounds like a wonderful idea."

"And now I would like to call to the platform Mr. Charles Grayson, owner of the *Daily Mail* of London."

James leaned toward Bella. "What's this about?"

She gave her head a slight shake. "I don't know."

Bella's father walked up the steps to the podium. He shook hands with the man who had introduced him, then turned toward the audience. "Ladies and Gentlemen, it has been a remarkable week, with many new records set and amazing demonstrations of skill and courage. We have seen outstanding aerial performances that we would never have imagined possible only a few months ago.

"But I would not be here today if it were not for the bravery and sacrifice of one man." Bella's father focused on James.

James stilled, but energy buzzed through him.

"Mr. James Drake flew to my rescue when Mr. Mark Clifton's engine failed and we crashed in the field between the second and third pylons on Friday. He and my daughter, Isabella, who was bravely riding along as his passenger, risked their lives to land near us and pull Mr. Clifton and myself from the flaming wreckage." He stopped and looked down, taking a moment to compose himself.

After a few seconds he looked up again. "So it gives me great pleasure to award this special life-saving prize of one thousand pounds to Mr. James Drake." He took a white envelope from his suit pocket.

James blinked and stared at Mr. Grayson.

"Go on, James." The professor tapped his arm.

Applause filled the air around him. He stood and walked forward, still trying to grasp what was happening. The crowd rose to their feet, giving him a standing ovation. He stepped up and met Mr. Grayson at the podium.

Bella's father placed his hand on James's shoulder. "Why don't you say a few words?"

James nodded and turned toward the audience while the applause continued for several seconds. "Thank you. Thank you very much." The audience sat down, and a hush fell across the room.

James shot off a quick prayer, then glanced at Bella. Her eyes glowed, and she sent him an encouraging smile.

He scanned the room. "This has been an amazing week. I feel blessed and grateful to be here, among so many fellow aviators whom I admire. Flying with you all is a great honor, and I look forward to seeing you again at the next meet."

The crowd clapped, and a few whistles rose from the aviators' tables.

"And though I wish I were taking home one of the first-place aviation prizes, this prize means even more to me." His throat tightened, and he had to swallow and blow out a breath before he could continue. "I'm grateful to my mentor, Professor Thaddeus Steed, who has always taught me to value what is most important in life—my faith, my family, and my friends.

"When I flew down to help Mr. Grayson and Mr. Clifton, I didn't do it alone. Miss Isabella Grayson was my passenger and partner in that rescue, and she deserves recognition as well." He smiled at her. "Bella, will you please stand?"

James applauded with the crowd. Bella rose, her cheeks flushed as she nodded to the crowd and then sat down.

"You don't have a chance to save someone's life every day. And I'm grateful the Lord allowed me to do that for Mr. Grayson and Mr. Clifton. It is certainly a day I will never forget."

James turned to Bella's father. "Thank you, Mr. Grayson. I promise to put this prize money to very good use."

"I'm sure you will." Charles Grayson offered a rare smile. The crowd applauded again as they both returned to their seats.

James sank into his chair, his knees feeling a little shaky.

Bella leaned toward him. "That was a wonderful speech. How did you do that without any preparation?"

He shook his head. "I have no idea." But then he recalled his prayer. "I take that back. I had help." He lifted his eyes toward the ceiling, and they both grinned.

The ceremony concluded, and people flocked forward to shake hands with James and congratulate him and Bella.

When the crowd finally thinned and drifted away, the professor stepped forward with Martha at his side. She tucked her arm through the professor's and smiled up at James. "That was very kind of you to mention Thaddeus in your speech."

The professor glanced away, looking a bit embarrassed. "You certainly didn't have to do that."

James grasped the professor's hand. "You deserved that recognition and much more. I never would've learned to fly or come to Reims without everything you've taught me—about aviation and about life. Thank you."

Tears glimmered in the old man's eyes. "You're welcome. It's been a joy and a privilege. I couldn't be more proud of you." He opened his arms, and James stepped into his embrace. The professor patted him on the back a few times before letting him go.

"Well, it's getting late." Martha looked up at the professor. "We should get back to the hotel so you can rest."

The professor glanced toward the windows. "It looks like there's a nice moon out tonight. I think we should take a short walk before we return to the hotel." There was a gleam in his eye as he smiled at Martha.

Her cheeks turned pink as she returned his smile. "That sounds like a lovely idea, Thaddeus."

Bella watched them stroll across the dining hall with a dreamy smile. "They are so sweet together. I'm glad they have each other."

"So am I." He reached for Bella's hand and wove his fingers through hers. "It *is* a nice night, and a walk in the moonlight sounds inviting. Do you think we can slip away?"

"I'd love that." She glanced toward the doorway. "But my parents are waiting for me."

"If you tell them I'll escort you back to your hotel, they might agree."

"I'll ask." She squeezed his hand, then walked across the dining hall toward the doorway where her parents stood together.

James turned back to the table and picked up one of the programs. Perhaps someday he'd show it to his children and tell them about flying at the first International Air Meet, and what a thrill it had been to take part.

"James?"

He turned and pulled in a quick breath.

Daniel Drake stood a few feet away. "I was hoping there'd be a moment when I could speak to you alone."

James shifted his weight to the other foot. "I didn't know if you were still here or if you'd gone back to London."

"I stayed." Drake walked a few steps closer. "I wanted to see you fly."

"Sorry about that."

"No, Son, don't apologize. I saw you on Friday, and you were amazing. I'm very proud of all you've done this week."

James's throat tightened, and he looked away. "Thank you."

"I mean it, James. You're a fine young man, and you've grown up wise and strong without any help or interference from me." A shadow seemed to pass across his face. "Maybe that was the way things were supposed to be all along."

James wasn't sure about that. For years he'd longed to know his father and sense his love and affirmation. And now, even with the painful mistakes Drake had made in the past, James still wanted a relationship with him.

Drake held out his hand. "Thank you, James. I'm glad we had a chance to meet."

James gripped his father's hand and held on tight. "I have something I want to say."

A touch of wariness flickered in his father's eyes. "All right."

James swallowed. "I've thought about what you said, and I want you to know I forgive you."

Surprise flashed across his face, and moisture glittered in his father's eyes. "That's a gift I don't deserve."

They came together and embraced for a few seconds.

James blinked hard as he stepped back. "The professor and I are starting a company to build airplanes. We have a few investors who are interested, but I wondered if we might pay you a visit and tell you about our plans."

His father nodded. "I'd like that. I'm inspired by what I've seen this week.

I think investing in aviation would be a wise business move. And knowing it would give me an opportunity to help my son makes it an ever better idea."

James's chest swelled. He reached out, and they shook hands again. "I'll be in touch, and we'll talk again soon."

"I'll look forward to it, James. Thank you." He turned to go.

James clenched and unclenched his hands. "Goodbye, Father."

Daniel Drake's steps stalled. He turned, his eyes shining. "Goodbye, Son."

Bella walked into the dining hall, but her steps slowed when she saw James's father walking toward the door. She smiled at him as he passed, and then she hurried over to James. "You spoke to your father?"

James nodded. "We had a good exchange. I told him I forgive him."

"Oh, I'm so glad." She slipped her hand into his. "I know that wasn't easy."

"No, it wasn't. But it was the right thing to do. It's time to let go of the past and look toward the future."

"I couldn't agree more."

He tightened his hold on her hand, and they walked out of the dining hall and stepped onto the moonlit path.

⌑

Crickets chirped along the pathway, and a light breeze drifted past, carrying the scent of the sun-warmed grain drying in the fields around them. In the distance, a train whistle blew as it carried passengers back to the hotels in Reims.

Bella gazed across the fields. Silver moonlight shimmered on the grass and treetops. A sense of peace flowed through her, and she released a sigh. "It's such a lovely night."

"I'm glad we can enjoy it together." He slowed, lifted their clasped hands, and kissed her fingers.

A delightful thrill traveled through Bella. "Tonight was perfect, wasn't it?"

"And it's not over yet."

She smiled, anticipation making her heart flutter.

They strolled on, enjoying the soft serenade of the insects and soaking up the beauty of the evening. She looked up at him. "This has been such a special week. So much has happened. I'm sure I'll remember it forever."

He nodded. "It's been life changing for me."

She tipped her head. "In what way?"

"Meeting my father and hearing the rest of the story has helped me understand who I am." There was a special warmth in his voice when he called Daniel Drake his father. "It's like the missing pieces of the puzzle about my family and my past have finally fallen into place. And I've learned something important."

"What's that?"

"It's not easy to forgive someone when what they've done has caused a deep wound, but when you do, it benefits you as much, or maybe more, than the person you forgive. It's like a burden is lifted off your shoulders, and it opens the path for healing and restoration."

"That's profound."

James kicked at a small stone and grinned. "I don't know about that. But I do know I'm thankful you helped me find my father and he and I have a chance to start down that path together."

Her heart lifted and gratefulness flooded in. She had helped James in that search, but it was the Lord who had arranged the events that finally brought them together. He was the One who had opened the door for the possibility of healing and restoration, and James had taken the courageous step to walk through it.

"Meeting him and hearing everything he said makes me think about the bigger picture."

"What do you mean?"

"Looking back now, I see how God has been watching over me all my life, protecting me, placing me with people who cared for me. Even though I wasn't related to them, they chose to love me and treat me like a member of the family. That's a great example of God's grace and kindness."

Bella leaned closer to James. "It is amazing to think how God had His hand on you ever since you were born, and not just you. I see it in my life too."

James sent her a questioning glance. "Your life seems perfect."

She smiled and shook her head. "Maybe I haven't faced the same struggles you have, but I've often wished for a closer relationship with my parents, especially my father. I thought becoming a journalist and writing for the *Daily*

Mail would help me win his approval. But now I know that's not the answer.

"He's an imperfect person just like I am. And I need to find my worth in my relationship with the Lord and who I am in Him. He loves me just as I am, whether I write a million articles or none at all."

James tipped his head. "So, you don't want to be journalist?"

She laughed softly. "No, I do want to write for the *Daily Mail,* but I don't want to tie my worth to that, or to any career. I want to love my father and mother and have a good relationship with them. But I don't want to be striving to gain their approval and lose sight of who I am."

James's gaze softened. "You're right, Bella. You're special and loved just the way you are. You don't have to strive for that."

At that moment, looking into his eyes, she believed it. His love was a wonderful reflection of the Lord's love for her. He made her feel cherished, and that was a gift she'd longed for all her life.

He stopped and turned to face her, taking both her hands in his. "I love you, Bella, so very much. I love your strength and courage. I love your sweet, caring spirit. I love the way we challenge each other to reach our goals. I think we're made for each other, and we can accomplish more together than we ever could on our own." He pulled in a deep breath. "I know we've talked about the future, but there's an important question I've been waiting to ask."

A shiver of delight raced down her arms, and she looked into his eyes.

"Bella Grayson, will you marry me, be my wife, and share this crazy adventure with me?"

Her heart felt like it would take wing. "Yes! Oh yes!" She threw her arms around his neck and held on tight. This was the man she loved with all her heart.

He picked her up and swung her around in the air, and their laughter rose like a song into the starry sky. When she finally came back to earth, he lowered his head, his lips met hers, and he kissed her tenderly, giving her a sweet promise of all the love they would share in the days to come.

Epilogue

Two Years Later, August 1911

Bella picked up a tray with a platter of scones, and bowls of lemon curd, strawberry jam, and clotted cream. She crossed the kitchen and stepped out onto the terrace at the back of their home. Bright summer sunshine warmed her face. A light breeze lifted the hair off the back of her neck, and she released a soft sigh. What a perfect day!

Glancing around the terrace, she checked to see what else she might need to bring out, but everything was ready. She consulted her watch, and excitement tingled through her. She could hardly wait for everyone to arrive and to see their faces when she and James shared their happy news.

"Let me get that for you." James reached for the tray.

"I'm all right." Bella lifted her chin, but she couldn't hold back her smile.

"Of course you are. You're perfect." He grinned, then leaned down and placed a kiss on her forehead. "But I'd still like to help."

"Very well." She released the tray, her heart light as she watched him carry it to the long table in the center of the terrace. He looked as handsome as he had the day she'd married him a little over a year ago. How blessed they were—how happy. And now their future looked even brighter.

Drake Aviation was up and running, turning out several new airplanes every month. She and James spent part of their time in London, living in the professor's old house so James could be close to the aviation workshop and she could be near the offices of the *Daily Mail*. But they also spent a good amount of time at the house on the Broadlands Estate that her parents had given them as a wedding gift. It was much smaller than her parents' lavish manor house, but it was just right for her and James.

"Hello there!" Professor Steed and Martha passed under the rose archway and stepped onto the terrace.

"Where shall I put these biscuits?" Martha held out the cloth-covered basket.

Bella kissed Martha's cheek. "Thank you, Martha. They smell delicious. Let's put them right here." Bella returned to the table, moved the bowl of fruit salad to the side, and placed the biscuits next to a tiered plate of sandwiches.

Martha scanned the table and gave an approving nod. "My, everything looks lovely. You must have been working all afternoon."

"It didn't really take too long. I enjoyed it, and James helped."

Humor lit Martha's eyes. "You'll have to ask him to give Thaddeus husband lessons."

Bella grinned. "Good idea." Martha and Professor Steed had wed a month after their return from the International Air Meet at Reims, and they now spent most of their time at Green Meadow. They came into London once a month so he could meet with James, Daniel Drake, and the other members of the board at Drake Aviation, but they seemed quite content with the peaceful country life they shared in Kent.

"Bella, are you out here?" Sylvia and her husband, Stephen Russell, came around the side of the house and joined them on the terrace. They had recently returned from their wedding trip, and Sylvia's face glowed as she reached out and embraced Bella.

"Welcome home." Bella wrapped her arms around her sister.

"Thank you. It's so good to see you."

Bella stepped back. "How was your time in Italy?"

"Wonderful." Sylvia's admiring gaze followed her husband as he walked over to speak to James.

"Tell me what you liked best."

"Rome was interesting, with all the historical sites, but it was terribly hot. Tuscany was cooler and very beautiful. We happened to be in Siena during the Palio. That's a huge festival with a thrilling horse race in the central piazza. And we visited museums and churches and strolled beside the river." Sylvia sighed, and a dreamy look filled her eyes. "We had such a lovely time."

"I'm so glad." Bella squeezed her sister's hand, and they exchanged smiles.

"I thought you might be back here." Bella's father stepped out the door and onto the terrace, followed by her mother. Her father carried some folded newspapers under his arm.

"We knocked on the front door, but no one answered." Bella's mother set a dish of small fruit tarts on the table.

Bella hurried over to greet her parents, giving them each a kiss on the cheek. "I'm glad you're here. Sylvia and Stephen just arrived."

Her mother smiled and nodded, looking more relaxed than usual as she greeted her daughter and son-in-law. Perhaps she was relieved Bella's father had finally sold the *Evening Standard* and the *London Herald* and had spent more time at Broadlands the last few months.

He held out the newspapers to Bella. "I thought you might like a few extra copies of your latest article in the *Daily Mail*."

"Thank you, Father. That was very thoughtful." She hesitated a second, then asked, "What did you think of it?"

He rubbed his chin. "Well, I don't approve of the suffragettes' tactics, but you presented the facts in a fair and logical manner. That's not easy to do when the subject stirs up such strong emotion on all sides." He nodded to her. "Good work, Bella."

Her smile bloomed. "Thank you, Father."

Bella had continued writing articles for the *Daily Mail* as a freelance journalist and had covered many interesting stories and events in the last two years. Since her wedding, she'd written them under her married name, Isabella Drake. Her parents had been surprised to see that, but as time passed, they came to accept her decision. Her father even seemed a bit proud of his journalist-daughter, and her mother was so pleased that Bella was finally married and settled in her own home, she seemed content to ignore it.

James stepped up next to her and slipped his arm around her shoulder. "Everyone's here. Shall we go ahead and have our tea?"

Bella smiled and nodded. "Yes, I think we're ready."

"Let's all gather around." James waited until everyone moved closer, then turned to the professor. "Would you say a prayer?"

"Of course." He removed his hat, and Stephen and Bella's father did the same. "Heavenly Father, we are thankful for this beautiful day and for time together with all these special friends and family. We're grateful for the many blessings You have bestowed on us. We thank You for Your goodness and faithfulness toward us. We're also thankful for the food we can enjoy and for the hands that have prepared it. With grateful hearts we pray these things in the name of Jesus, amen."

James lifted his head and reached for Bella's hand. "Before we sit down, Bella and I have some news we'd like to share."

Everyone turned toward James and Bella. Her stomach fluttered, and she looked up at James.

"We just received word this morning that the contract is approved, and Drake Aviation will be supplying the British military with a new fleet of airplanes over the next nine months!"

Martha gasped and clasped her hands. "Oh, that's wonderful!"

Sylvia beamed a smile at Bella.

"Congratulations!" Her father stepped forward and shook James's hand. "It's about time they came to their senses and awarded you that contract."

The professor laid his hand on James's shoulder. "Excellent news! We'll make them the finest airplanes they could ever want, and I suspect that will be the first of many contracts to come."

James nodded. "It took quite a bit of negotiation, but overall I'm pleased with the terms. We'll have to hire more men, but we'll have the finances to do that now."

When everyone settled down, James glanced at Bella again. She smiled and nodded, then pulled in a slow, deep breath.

James looked around the group. "We have some other important news to share." He grasped her hand. "Bella and I are expecting our first child, and he or she will be born in February."

Her mother's eyes widened, and her hand flew up to her mouth. "Oh, that's wonderful!" She rushed forward and embraced Bella.

Tears sprang to Bella's eyes, and she patted her mother on the back. "You're going to be a grandmother." Bella laughed and stepped back, then turned to her father. "And you're going to be a grandfather."

He grinned. "That's even better news than the new contract." He turned to her mother. "What do you say, Madelyn?"

She smiled and blinked back her tears. "I don't know what to say, except I couldn't be happier."

James slipped his arm around Bella's waist and smiled at the group. "Thank you. We still can't quite believe it, but we're very excited."

"What a wonderful surprise!" Sylvia hugged Bella. "I'm thrilled for you and James."

"Thank you, Sylvia."

Martha took Bella's hand. "What a blessing! You're going to be a wonderful mother, and James will be such a fine father. I promise Thaddeus and I will do everything we can to help."

"We'll definitely need your help." Bella wiped a happy tear from her cheek. They were blessed, so very blessed—with the love of family and friends and the faithful provision of the Lord. He had seen them through so many challenges and trials, and He would be faithful to carry them through the days ahead. Gratefulness flooded her heart, and along with it, an extra measure of His comfort and peace.

James smiled down at her, his eyes reflecting the same joy that filled her heart. Then he took her hand, and they led their family to the table to enjoy stories and laughter, along with sweet biscuits and a good cup of tea.

Author's Note

The idea for this story first came to me when I visited the National Air and Space Museum in Washington, DC, and saw a model of the Wright brothers' 1903 airplane and a poster about the First International Air Meet at Reims, France. The time period is my favorite, and I thought it would be a great idea to explore. I loved researching early aviation and learning about the brave men who first took to the air in Europe and America. Their courage, ingenuity, and determination are inspiring!

My main characters in this story are fictional, but I included several real people as secondary characters, including Louis Blériot, who was the first to fly across the English Channel and won that thousand-pound prize offered by the *Daily Mail.* The characters Pierre Levasseur and Mark Clifton are inspired by French cousins and airplane designers Léon Levavasseur and Hubert Latham. I tried to stay true to the historical events as they occurred in 1908–9, but I adjusted some of the dates of flights to fit the flow of the story. I also condensed some of the events at the First International Air Meet at Reims into fewer days to keep things moving forward and give the reader the best story possible.

Readers Guide

1. Bella's path to becoming a journalist was challenging. What were some of the obstacles she faced? What did you think of the way she overcame them?

2. How would you describe Bella's relationship with her parents? What were their goals for her, and how did Bella feel about those goals?

3. What prompted James's desire to be the first to fly across the English Channel? What obstacles did he need to overcome to reach that goal?

4. Why do you think Professor Steed did not want to discuss the events surrounding James's birth or early life? Do you agree or disagree with his choice to hold back that information until James asked for the truth?

5. What did you think about James and Professor Steed's relationship? What qualities do you think James learned from the professor?

6. It took a lot of courage for James to attempt to fly across the Channel. What made that flight unique and dangerous?

7. Bella hid the truth about her articles from James, and that ended up causing conflict in their relationship. Do you think James was justified in being angry with Bella for withholding the truth about her authorship?

8. When James crashed into the Channel, his dreams took a nosedive with him. What did you think of the way he handled that disappointment?

9. Why do you think the professor was slow to acknowledge his romantic feelings for Martha? What did you think of their relationship?

10. James believed winning the race across the Channel would give him a respectable reputation, one that would make him feel proud instead of ashamed and one that would help him win Bella's heart. Was James right? Was that the way to Bella's heart?

11. What did you think of Bella's decision to fly with James as his passenger at the air show? Would you have liked to fly with James?

12. When James saw Mark Clifton's airplane crash, he chose to abandon his hope of winning that event so he could land and help them. What did you think of his decision? How did his decision to forfeit the race end up helping him achieve his goals?

Acknowledgments

I am very grateful for all those who have given their support and encouragement and who have provided information in the process of writing this book. Without your help, it would never have been possible!

I'd like to say thank you to the following people:

My husband, Scott, who always provides great feedback and constant encouragement when I talk about my characters, plot, and what's happening next. Your love and support have allowed me to follow my dreams and write the books of my heart. I will be forever grateful for you!

Steve Laube, my literary agent, for his patience, guidance, and wise counsel. You have been a great advocate who has represented me well. I feel very blessed to be your client, and I appreciate you!

Shannon Marchese, Kendall Davis, Rachel Lulich, and Laura Wright, my gifted editors, who helped me shape the story and then polish it so readers are able to truly enjoy it.

David McCullough, for the information in his book *The Wright Brothers;* Ron Dick and Dan Patterson for the information in their book *Aviation Century: The Early Years;* and Joshua Stoff for his wonderful book *Picture History of Early Aviation, 1903–1913.* I also learned much from Peter Jakab, curator for the *Early Flight* exhibit at the National Air and Space Museum, Smithsonian Institute. I appreciate your input!

Kristopher Orr, the multitalented designer at Multnomah, for the lovely cover design! They just keep getting better and better!

Jamie Lapeyrolerie, Chelsea Woodward, Lori Addicott, Laura Barker, and the entire Multnomah team for their great work with marketing, publicity, production, and sales. This book would stay hidden on my computer if not for your creative ideas and hard work. You all are the best!

Darna Michie, owner of East Angel Harbor Hats, who created the lovely hat for our cover model to wear for the photo shoot and who did it in record-breaking time. I love your beautiful hats!

Cathy Gohlke, fellow author and friend, who constantly encourages me to trust the Lord for grace to write stories that will transform hearts. You have blessed my life in so many ways! Let's both keep pressing on to serve the Lord with this gift of writing.

Judy Conroy, dear friend, who patiently listens to my story ideas and lets me talk them through. Your enthusiasm and friendship is a wonderful blessing. I miss you so much now that you're in Tennessee, but I trust we'll be visiting each other soon and have more stories to share.

My children, Josh, Melinda, Melissa, Peter, Ben, Galan, Megan, and Lizzy, and my mother-in-law, Shirley, for the way you cheer me on. It's a blessing to have a family that is so supportive!

Most of all, I thank my Lord and Savior, Jesus Christ, for His love, wonderful grace, and faithful provision. I am grateful for the gifts and talents You have given me, and I hope to always use them in ways that bless You and bring You glory.

About the Author

CARRIE TURANSKY has loved reading since she first visited the library as a young child and checked out a tall stack of picture books. Her love for writing began when she penned her first novel at age twelve. She is now the award-winning author of nineteen inspirational romance novels and novellas.

Carrie and her husband, Scott, who is a pastor, author, and speaker, have been married for more than thirty years and make their home in New Jersey. They often travel together on ministry trips and to visit their five adult children and five grandchildren. Carrie also leads the women's ministry at her church, and when she's not writing, she enjoys spending time working in her flower gardens and cooking healthy meals for friends and family.

She loves to connect with reading friends through her website, http://carrieturansky.com, and through Facebook, Pinterest, and Twitter.

Don't miss any of Carrie Turansky's previous novels!

Do you love WaterBrook & Multnomah Fiction?

Be the first to know about upcoming releases, insider news and all kinds of fiction fun!

Sign up for our Fiction Reads newsletter at
wmbooks.com/WaterBrookMultnomahFiction

Join our Fiction Only Facebook Page!
www.facebook.com/waterbrookmultnomahfiction

WATERBROOK   MULTNOMAH

waterbrookmultnomah.com

31901062672458